VALLEY OF DEATH

Slowly, Joe rode down the gentle slope, into the valley of death. The bodies were white, so terribly white. At first he didn't understand why; then he realized it was because most of them were naked, stripped of the last trappings of mortal life.

A few were still in uniform. Joe dismounted, and, leading his horse, began walking through the grisly area. Already buzzards were feasting on the remains. A soldier was lying with his back to Joe, and Joe didn't want to look into his face because he didn't want to recognize him. The bodies were more spread out than he would have thought, as if there had been several defensive positions, rather than one. But given the fluidity of battle, and the fact that there had been no cover, Joe knew the soldiers had done the best they could . . . .

YESTERDAY'S REVEILLE

Robert Vaughan

St. Martin's Paperbacks

YESTERDAY'S REVEILLE

ISBN: 0-312-95694-0

Printed in the United States of America

St. Martin's Paperbacks edition / February 1996

10 9 8 7 6 5 4 3 2 1

A LETTER FROM THE AUTHOR

I am a retired U.S. Army warrant officer. While a member of the Seventh Cavalry (1963–1966) I was given a collateral duty that ignited a passion that has burned in me for over thirty years. I was historical officer for the Seventh Cavalry and therefore custodian of all regimental memorabilia, including Custer's hat, gauntlets, and saber, as well as several of his morning reports and officers' field diaries.

As my interest in the subject grew, I studied history books, memoirs, and archives. I even exchanged letters with a fascinating ninety-six-year-old gentleman who, as a boy, had known Custer and could remember vividly the day Custer left Fort Lincoln on his last scout because his own father had ridden into eternity with him.

I was on active duty in the twentieth century cavalry, but my soul was answering muster roll call with troopers who had served a century before. For me, the post-Civil War, nineteenth century army was no longer a silent trumpet gathering dust in some long-abandoned western post. It was a bugle's call, as immediate as the one I heard playing reveille every morning.

Over the past three decades it has become politically correct for historians writing of the nineteenth century to beatify the Indian and demonize the soldier. The common soldier is depicted as an illiterate ne'er-do-well, fleeing from the law or a failed life back East. The cavalry officer is held up to be an alcoholic misfit or a pompous martinet seeking glory. While some soldiers and officers might have fallen into such categories, the majority of the army was just as it is today: professionals following a calling. They were neither saints nor sinners, but servants of their government.

Though they never fielded forces of more than 15,000 men, the army surveyed railroad lines, guarded construction crews, defended trails west, provided protection for settlers, miners, ranchers, and farmers, and engaged the Indians in over 250 battles, not counting small skirmishes of platoon size or less. *They were nearly always outnumbered,* and often the Indians were better armed, due to the greed of white traders. The Indians were better horsemen, fought as a way of life, knew their home territory, and could move as silently as the dust. But in the end, the West was opened and peace was won by the United States Army.

Yesterday's Reveille is the story of that army. The literal historian will find some factual anomalies in my account. For story continuity I have made a few changes in dates, locales, and events. I have taken some liberties with the Battle of the Washita, and my depiction of Fort Hays is more generic than authentic. Also, those who have speculated about Custer's interest in the presidential nominating conventions that year speculated about the Democratic Convention in St. Louis. But because the earlier date of the Republican Convention fit my story, I used it. However the most important question to ask is, not did I write the story *factually,* but did I write it *truthfully*? I believe I did.

> Robert Vaughan
> Chief Warrant Officer–3 (Ret)
> Sikeston, Missouri

★★★

One

Oh, the drums would roll, upon my soul
this is the style we'd go
forty miles a day on beans and hay
In the regular Army O.
—Barracks ballad, circa 1870

The deer raised its mouth from the water and looked around, its ears twitching nervously. Suddenly it darted away, startling the animals who had heard nothing. Then the other creatures heard the sound as well—a low rumbling that began to swell, growing louder and louder until it was like thunder. It filled the trees with its pounding until, finally, bursting over the crest of the embankment came its source: a troop of cavalry at the gallop.

Captain Joe Murchison was riding at the head of the troop, bent low over his mount's neck. The horse's mane and tail were streaming out behind, and its nostrils flared wide as it worked the powerful muscles in its shoulders and haunches. Following Joe was a guidon bearer, his red, white, and blue ensign snapping in the wind. Then came the entire body of men, all urging their animals to the fastest possible pace.

The cavalry column hit the shallow river in full stride, and sand and silver bubbles flew up in a sheet of spray, sustained by the churning action of the horses' hooves until huge drops began falling back like rain. Joe led the column of men toward an island in the middle of the river.

"Bugler! Sound the dismount!" Joe shouted as they reached the island.

Raising the instrument to his lips, the bugler played his call, and the troopers of M Troop, Seventh Cavalry, brought their steeds to a halt. In a few cases the halting action was so abrupt that the horses slipped down onto their hindquarter haunches in response to the desperate demands their riders made of them.

"Cap'n! Let's don't stay here to be shot down like dogs!" one of the soldiers called. "We can't fight 'em off! There are too many of them!"

"We'll make our stand here," Joe said.

"Cap'n, we got to skedaddle!"

"First Sergeant!" Joe shouted.

"Yes, sir!"

"Shoot any man who tries to run."

"Yes, sir!" the first sergeant replied.

"Quinlin, who are the best marksmen in the troop?"

"That'd be me and Corporals McDonald and O'Braugh, sir," Sergeant Quinlin answered.

Joe pointed to the neck of the island, which faced the western bank of the river, the direction from which they had just come.

"See if the three of you can squirm down through the tall grass. Take a position as near to the point as you can get, and do as much damage as you can when the Indians start across the water."

"Don't you be worryin' none, Cap'n. We'll have the heathens floatin' facedown in the river like so many logs. Mickey, Galen, come on!" Quinlin shouted.

"The rest of you men," Joe ordered, "dig yourselves in."

"We were ridin' light for the scout, Cap'n! We left our spades behind," one of the men answered.

"Then use your mess kits, your knives, your fingernails," Joe replied. "I don't care how you do it, just *do* it! We've got about two minutes to get ready for them!"

As the men got on their knees and began digging desperately, Joe remained erect, calmly walking back and forth, holding his pistol by his side.

"Now, men, Quinlin, McDonald, and O'Braugh will engage first!" Joe shouted his instructions. "But don't be spooked into shooting when you hear them. I want you to hold your fire until I give the word. Hold it until the last possible moment. Then make your shots count!"

There were one hundred sabers in Troop M, consisting of ninety-eight men and two officers. It was a part of the Seventh Cavalry's expedition for the summer of 1875. Captain Murchison and Lieutenant Agee, his executive officer, had separated the troop from the Seventh shortly after reveille this morning. Their mission was to scout ahead of the main body, to locate the Sioux who had left the reservation. Ten minutes ago they found many more Sioux than they had bargained for when the point man crested a little hill and rode right into an encampment of Hunkpapas that numbered from eight hundred to one thousand warriors.

The Indians, who rarely posted lookouts, did not realize how close the soldiers were and were caught by surprise. The warriors were unmounted, their ponies gathered in a great herd on the far side of the camp. However, most of the warriors *did* have their weapons with them, and when they saw a lone soldier suddenly appear in their village, they began firing with the righteous fury of a people whose sanctuary had been violated. Yelling in frustration and rage, the warriors bolted for their horses.

The trooper who was riding point came galloping back to warn Joe of what was ahead. If the horses had been on the eastern side of the village, Joe would have been able to scatter them. But the ponies were on the western side, protected by a natural draw and watched over by young Indian boys, so that when the warriors needed them, the horses could be retrieved.

Joe figured it would take the Indians at least three minutes to get to their ponies and get mounted in sufficient numbers to give chase. That three minutes was his only advantage, and he used it to withdraw to the island in the river where he would make his stand.

"Trooper Flynn!"

"Yo, sir!"

"Are you riding Prince Barney?"

"Aye, sir, I am," Flynn replied. Flynn, atop Prince

Barney, had won the regimental horse race held at Fort Lincoln the previous month.

"Well, you've another race to ride, Trooper. The race of your life. Get back to Custer. Tell him where we are. Tell him to send help immediately. We'll hold them off as long as we can. If he comes up fast enough, some of us may still be alive."

"Aye, sir," Flynn replied. "Horse holder! Bring up Prince Barney!"

With the cavalry dismounted, every fourth trooper became a horse holder, and one of them now brought Flynn's horse to him. Quickly, Flynn put his foot into the stirrup, then swung into the saddle.

"Go with God, lad!" one of the sergeants shouted, slapping Prince Barney on the rump. The other troopers cheered and called encouragements to Flynn as he hit the water on the east side of the island, heading back for where they had left the regiment. Joe watched horse and rider gallop away until they crested the embankment; then he turned back to await the Indians.

"I hear them!" one of the soldiers said nervously. His announcement wasn't necessary, however, for by then everyone could hear them. Above the drumming of the hoofbeats came the cries of the warriors themselves, yipping and barking and screaming at the top of their lungs as they rode in pursuit of the soldiers.

The Indians crested the bluff just before the river; then, without a pause, they rushed down the hill toward the water, their horses sounding like a thundering herd of buffalo.

"Remember, men! Hold your fire!" Joe shouted. "Hold your fire until I give you the word!"

The Indians stopped just at water's edge, then, holding their rifles over their heads, began shouting gutteral challenges to the soldiers who were dug in on the island.

"Hu ihpeya wicayapo!"

"Huka!"

"Huka hey!"

"Get ready, men," Joe said calmly.

With no recognizable leader, the Indians suddenly

rushed into the water, riding hard across the fifty-yard-wide shallows, whooping, hollering, and gesturing with rifles and lances. There were three warriors who pulled ahead of the others, and when they were halfway across the water, Joe heard three distinct shots from the point of the island. The three warriors in front went down.

"Steady," Joe said, speaking to his men as calmly as he could. "Steady, now."

The remaining Indians crossed the river, then started up the sandy point.

"Fire!" Joe shouted.

The troop fired a volley that took out a significant part of the middle of the attacking Indians. The devastating volley was effective, for the warriors who survived swerved to the right and left, riding by rather than over the soldiers' positions.

The Indians regrouped on the east bank of the river; then they turned and rode back in a second charge. The soldiers had managed to reload their breech-loading Springfields, and as the Indians reached the island for their second attack, they were met with another volley as devastating as the first had been. Again, a significant number of those in the middle of the charge went down.

The Sioux pulled back to the west bank of the river to regroup, watched anxiously by the men on the island. By now the river was strewn with dead Indians. There were at least fifty or sixty of them, lying facedown in the shallow water as the current parted around them.

"First Sergeant!" Joe called. "Get a count of our casualties!"

Joe reloaded his revolver while the first sergeant moved from squad to squad, taking a count.

"None dead, seven wounded, sir," the first sergeant reported a moment later. "Lieutenant Agee is the worst."

"Lieutenant Agee? Will he pull through?"

"I don't know, sir. Maybe, if we can get him to a surgeon in time."

"Yes, well, the thing is, I can't guarantee that," Joe said. "But, do what you can to make them comfortable."

"Yes, sir."

"Cap'n, it looks like someone's gettin' 'em stirred up to come again!" one of the men called out.

Joe was wearing a pair of binoculars on a strap around his neck, and he used them now to look at the Indian who had moved out in front of the others to assume a role of leadership. It was often like this with the Indians, Joe had learned. They had no structure of command, merely leaders who could lead only if the others chose to follow. It appeared that such a leader was now emerging from the band across the river.

Joe did not recognize the warrior leader, but at well over six feet he was considerably taller than most Indians Joe had ever seen. The tall Indian was riding a big gray as he moved back and forth among the other warriors, shouting encouragement at them.

"Cap'n Murchison, Lieutenant Agee wants to talk to you, sir," someone said, passing the word up the line.

Joe moved over to where his lieutenant lay, badly wounded. Lieutenant Agee was holding his hand across a tunic that was already soaked through with blood.

"How are you doing, Charley?" Joe asked.

"I'm afraid I have my death wound, Captain."

"No, we're going to get you out of here."

Agee shook his head. "The only way you're going to get out of here is if you can hold off the Indians until the regiment arrives."

"If that's what it takes, that's what we'll do," Joe replied.

"Yes, sir, well, I've got an idea that might help," Agee said, grunting through his pain.

"Let me hear it. I'm always open to suggestions."

Agee raised his hand to point, and it was covered with blood. "Have someone take me down to the neck of the island, just across from Quinlin and the others," he suggested. "I'm a pretty good shot. I'll pick off one or two when they come back."

"Across from Quinlin? There's no cover or conceal-ment there. The Indians will see you."

"So what if they do? It'll draw their attention away from the others."

Joe shook his head. "Use a live decoy? Never."

"Joe, I don't figure on being alive for more than an-other hour or so. If I'm going to die, let it count for something. Please!"

Joe met Agee's intense gaze. He remembered meet-ing the young lieutenant's parents last year when they came out for a visit. He thought of them now and of how proud they had been of their son—a recent gradu-ate of the military academy. Joe could visualize the pain they would feel when they learned of his death. Perhaps some pride in the way he died would assuage the hurt.

"All right, Charley, if that's the way you want it," Joe finally said. He turned to two troopers who were near by. "Wheeler, McComb, get Lieutenant Agee down to the point, just across from where Quinlin and the oth-ers are. Stay low. I don't want the Indians to see that you have to carry him out there."

"Yes, sir," McComb answered for both of them.

"Thanks, Joe," Lieutenant Agee said.

The two troopers got on their stomachs on either side of the lieutenant. Then they began wriggling down through the tall grass until they were invisible even to Joe, who knew where to look. A short time later, he saw Lieutenant Agee only partially concealed behind a clump of weeds. A few minutes after that, Wheeler and McComb returned.

"Lieutenant Agee is in position, sir," McComb said.

"Is he still alive?"

"Just barely."

"Cap'n! They're comin' ag'in!" one of the troopers in the line shouted.

"All right, get ready men, here they come!" Joe called.

With the big Indian in the lead, the Hunkpapas started their attack.

"Hold your fire, men! Hold your fire!" Joe called.

The thundering horses came across the open expanse of water, then up onto the sandy beach.

"Now!" Joe shouted.

The volley boomed with the report of cannon fire, felling Indians and their mounts. Again the charging Indians swerved right and left, like rushing water parting around a rock. They swept by on both sides of the soldiers, firing down into them as they passed, then riding across the river to regroup on the other side.

"Quinlin!" the first sergeant shouted, cupping his hands around his mouth as he yelled. "Quinlin, if you hear me, don't answer! Don't give your position away! But if you can, when they come back, take out the big bastard on the gray!"

The Indians managed a fourth charge, their horses leaping over the bodies of the Indians and horses who had fallen before. As before, Joe withheld fire until the last possible moment. The big Indian avoided the volley by leaning down to be shielded by one side of his horse. Joe fired at him but missed. He watched as the Indians reached the west side of the island. Then, in what must have been an extraordinary effort for him, Lieutenant Agee rose up. The big Indian, catching Agee's movement out of the corner of his eye, turned toward him. When he did, that gave Quinlin the opening he was looking for. Joe couldn't pick out the sound of the sergeant's shot from among the many who were shooting, but he did see a puff of smoke emerge from the grass where he knew Quinlin was hiding. The Indian leader lurched once, then pitched forward off his horse with the back of his head shot away.

When they saw their leader go down, the other Indians turned their fury on to Lieutenant Agee, the only soldier in plain view. A dozen or more Indians shot Agee, while an equal number managed to pierce his now-lifeless body with their lances. The soldiers were now firing at will, and Joe had the satisfaction of seeing that at least three of the warriors who had visited desecration upon Agee's body wound up paying for it with their own lives.

By now more than a hundred Indians lay dead on

both banks of the river, in the water, and on the sandy beaches of the island. But the Indians had extracted their toll, as well, for the number of wounded troopers had increased to thirteen—and there were now three dead, including Lieutenant Agee.

The Indians did not make another charge against the island. Instead, they crossed over in considerable numbers, both upstream and down, so they could occupy positions in the surrounding bluffs on both sides of the river. In this way they were able to keep Joe and his troop effectively trapped on the island.

Joe knew now that their survival depended upon whether or not Trooper Flynn managed to get through to carry word of their plight back to Custer. If Flynn made it, Custer would no doubt be able to effect a rescue by nightfall. But if Flynn didn't make it, if he had been caught and killed by the Indians, it would be only a matter of time until Joe and every man on the island with him would suffer the same fate.

There was sporadic firing throughout the rest of the day as the soldiers on the island and the Indians on the bluffs continued to exchange shots. After sunset that evening, Joe counted more than two dozen campfires scattered about on both sides of the river. He and the men of M Troop listened as the warriors banged their drums and shook their rattles and bells. They could also hear the Indians singing their death songs and war chants.

As the soldiers looked anxiously out into the night, the thought on everyone's mind was the same:

"Did Flynn get through?"

"Sure, he got through. He was on the fastest horse in the regiment, and in the entire U.S. Cavalry, too, I'm thinkin'."

"But he had a long way to go, and Prince Barney was tired. And there were a lot of Indians out today."

"Don't you be worryin' none about Flynn. He made it. You can bet your boots on it."

"Yeah? Well, where's Custer? He should'a been here by now."

"He'll be here."

"When?"

"Soon."

But when midnight came and there was still no Custer, even the most optimistic began to lose hope.

Joe moved around, checking with each trooper as they improved their defensive positions, digging deeper and more effective rifle pits. He congratulated them on the job they did during the day just past and built up their confidence for the day to come.

"Listen to the heathens singin' over there," one of the sergeants said, squirting out a stream of tobacco juice. "They'll be back tomorrow, thick as they was today."

Joe smiled. "I expect so," he agreed. "But when they do come, we'll trade them thirty Indians for one trooper, just like we did today."

"Damn right we will!" someone shouted.

Joe visited the wounded. There was still a lot of fight in the lightly injured, though some of the more grievously wounded were barely clinging to life.

"First Sergeant," Joe said when he returned to his own position, "pair the men off: one man to sleep, one to keep guard. They can alternate every two hours. If the Indians can't effect dislodgement by any other means, they will surely try to wait us out."

From both sides of the river the incessant drumming and singing continued until after two in the morning. Finally the fearsome cacophony stopped, the last fire winked out, and for the last few hours before dawn, all was quiet save for the gentle lapping of the river and the soft sigh of wind in the trees.

Joe slept from three until five. When he awoke, he sat with his back against a tree, watching the eastern horizon as it gradually grew lighter. Suddenly and unexpectedly, the still dawn was interrupted by music . . . not Indian singing, but martial music. It was the regimental band playing "Garryowen"!

"Listen, men! Listen!" Joe shouted joyfully. "Wake up! The regiment is here!"

Almost immediately after the opening bars of the music came the crash of gunfire; then, bursting out of dawn's blue shadows came the Seventh Cavalry Regiment, more than six hundred strong, yelling at the top of their voices and firing carbines and revolvers. The Indians were caught sleeping, and those who weren't killed in the initial engagement made a mad dash— many without their horses—into the surrounding hills.

Joe saw the buckskin-clad Custer crossing the river then, his big horse, Vic, kicking up spray as it came toward him. Smiling, Custer took off his hat and waved at Joe. Joe waved back.

"Benteen!" Custer shouted to one of his officers. "Chase them down! Kill as many as you can, deny horses to the rest."

As the Seventh swept on by, led by Captain Benteen, Custer dismounted in front of Joe. Joe hurried over to report to him.

"Sir, Troop M reporting. Thirteen wounded and five dead. All present and accounted for!"

"Very good, Captain. Surgeon!" Custer shouted after he returned Joe's salute. "See to the wounded here!"

"Yes, sir!" one of the doctors answered.

"Did Trooper Flynn get through to you?" Joe asked.

"Yes, he did. Good man, your Flynn," Custer replied.

"I'm glad. When you didn't show up last night, we were worried the Indians may have caught up with him."

Custer smiled. "Oh, but we *were* here last night."

"I beg your pardon?"

"We were here," Custer said again. "But if nine years of Indian fighting has taught me anything, it is that the best time to attack Lo is early in the morning. Hit him after one of his nighttime orgies of beating the drum, dancing, and caterwauling, and you get him when he is most vulnerable. Don't you agree?"

"Yes, sir, I suppose so," Joe said.

Left unspoken was his thought that perhaps if Custer had come to the island the moment he arrived, the surgeon might have been able to save the two men who died during the night.

"Where is young Agee?" Custer asked, looking around.

"It pains me to report that Lieutenant Agee was killed." Briefly, Joe explained the circumstances of Agee's death.

"I am saddened that such a young man would have to die, but what more glorious way for a soldier to give his life?" Custer replied. "Captain, your stand here was magnificent. Your defense of this island is the type of action from which generals are made."

"Generals, sir?"

"Yes, why not? I made general at the age of twenty-three." Custer reached out to take Joe's hand in his. "It may take you a little longer, but I've no doubt that one day they will be calling you General Murchison."

"General Murchison? General Murchison, sir?"

Joe was startled by the voice, and he looked around to see the young West Point cadet who had been assigned to him. Had he been asleep or just remembering? Whatever it was, it took him a moment to return to the present . . . and he had to remind himself that this wasn't Dakota Territory in the summer of 1875; this was West Point, New York, and it was June of 1941. Yet so vivid was Joe's recollection that it was almost as if he had actually been back on Agee's Island physically, rather than just in his memories. He held up his palm and looked at it. Even now, he could feel the pressure of Custer's handshake. Was that really sixty-six years ago? Or was it just the previous moment?

"General Murchison?" the cadet said again.

"Yes, Mr. Throckmorton, what is it?" Joe finally replied, putting his hand back in his lap.

"I'm sorry to disturb you, General, but they want us in the chapel now."

Throckmorton walked over to the concrete bench where Joe had been sitting, warming himself in the sun, then reached out to put his hand on Joe's arm. Joe waved him off.

"I'm old, son, I'm not a cripple," Joe said. "I can get into the chapel under my own power, if you please."

"Yes, General," the cadet replied, duly chastised.

Joe chuckled. "Oh, don't take it personally, Mr. Throckmorton. It's just that when you are my age, every step you take under your own power is a victory of sorts."

Throckmorton stood at attention while Joe raised himself, then started toward the Cadet Chapel, which rose majestically before them.

"Beautiful, isn't it?" Joe said, pointing to the building.

"None more beautiful, sir," Throckmorton agreed.

Built of native granite, the Cadet Chapel's battlements and towers were standing high on a hill, commanding a magnificent view of the academy. Inside, the polished-stone floors, arches, and vaulting of the Gothic church suggested a sense of knighthood, a feeling enhanced by a representation of King Arthur's sword, Excalibur, which was hanging over the entrance.

Battle flags carried in the Civil War, the Spanish American War, and the Philippine Insurrection, were suspended from the triforium. Stained glass windows, dedicated to those classes already graduated, diffused the outside light into vibrant reds, blues, and greens. The sanctuary window above the altar depicted biblical heroes and carried the motto of the United States Military Academy: Duty, Honor, Country. The motto was repeated in stone below and was also stitched on the red kneelers at the altar rail. Joe knew it was impossible for cadets to attend chapel and not be aware of the great traditions of the corps, and of their own position in the long, unbroken gray line.

And on this fine, June day, the members of the Class of '41 were feeling an even greater sense of their legacy, for this was their graduation day and they were about to become commissioned officers in the U.S. Army.

The importance of the day was further underscored by the inclusion of special guests, with particular attention being paid to the alumni of classes from the distant past. Many of these gentlemen, even though no longer on active duty, were, as was Joe, wearing the

army blue that had been such an important part of
their lives. The array of medals and ribbons spread
across their chests indicated service in World War I, the
Philippine Insurrection, the Spanish American War,
the border incursion against Pancho Villa, and even the
Indian campaigns.

Joe joined these ancient and ennobled warriors to sit
with bowed gray heads in a pew reserved just for them.
Like the young cadets of today, these same men had
once been awed by the venerated traditions of this in-
stitution. Now they were a part of it.

Ironically, the most distinguished guest on this auspi-
cious occasion was not a graduate of West Point. He
was, however, part of the tradition of duty, honor and
country, for, as president of the United States, Franklin
Delano Roosevelt was the commander in chief of them
all.

After the service was concluded, Joe watched President
Roosevelt swing his brace-encased legs out of the pew,
then get to his feet. Sitting so long in the cramped
space had made the act of trying to walk with canes
and braces even more difficult than normal.

"Let me send someone for the wheelchair," Eleanor
suggested when she saw an expression of pain flicker
across her husband's face.

"No," the president insisted. "The American people
do not want to see their president as a cripple . . .
especially in these troubled times."

"Franklin, do you think there is one man, woman, or
child in America who does not know that you are af-
flicted?" Eleanor asked.

"Don't nag him, dear; Franklin is right," Sara, the
president's mother, said. "With the world enveloped in
war, America must remain strong—and our people
must know that we have a strong leader at the helm."

"Yes, Mrs. Roosevelt," Eleanor demurred. "Of
course you are right."

As the presidential party made its way laboriously
out of the chapel, Joe stood erect just inside the nar-
thex. Joe was tall, white-haired, and dignified-looking

in the uniform of a major general. When the president saw him, he stopped, smiled, and extended his hand.

"General Murchison," the president said. "How good to see you."

"Good morning, Mr. President," the General replied, shaking Roosevelt's hand. He nodded at the president's wife and mother. "Ladies," he added.

"Good morning, General," Eleanor replied.

"You're looking dapper this morning, Joseph," the president's mother said. "And as handsome as ever, I must say."

General Murchison smiled. "It's easy to see where your son gets his political charm, Mrs. Roosevelt."

"Oh, for heaven's sake, Joseph. I may be Mrs. Roosevelt to everyone else, but I always have been, and always will be, Sally to you. I thought we had that settled long ago."

Roosevelt laughed out loud. "Look at Mama, will you, Eleanor?" he said, putting the emphasis on the second syllable—*mamá*—in the way of the Europeans. "Why, I do believe there is a budding romance going on right under our very eyes."

"Franklin, don't be brash," the president's mother scolded. "The general and I are old friends of long standing, as you well know."

"Indeed, I do know," the president said. He smiled. "But Mama is right, General. You look as if you could come out of retirement today."

"I may be ninety-four years old, Mr. President, but I stand ready to serve at your discretion."

Roosevelt laughed again. "What is it with you old war horses? General Pershing stopped by my office last week to tell me the same thing."

The general smiled. "Jack is a good soldier. He was a good soldier when I knew him as a young lieutenant."

"I do seem to recall General Pershing telling me that he once served with you," Roosevelt said. "I've no doubt but that he owes his brilliant military career to the tutelage you gave him."

"General Pershing served with a great many officers while he was coming up, Mr. President. I would not want to be presumptuous enough to suggest that I had anything to do with the success of his career."

"Yes, well, our nation has always been blessed with good military leaders. Let us hope that the trend continues. Lord knows we may have need for them in the days ahead, what with the evil ambitions of such men as Hitler and Mussolini. Terrible fellows, they."

"Do you feel we will become involved in the war in Europe?" Joe Murchison asked.

"I can't honestly answer that question. As you know, General, I campaigned on the promise not to send any American boys to fight on foreign soil, and I intend to try to keep that promise. But I am more and more convinced that we are going to become embroiled in this thing, despite our best efforts to avoid it. Winston Churchill certainly wants us involved, and I must confess that he makes a good case for his cause. Whether or not England survives may well determine whether democracy is to survive."

A young, serious-looking aide leaned into the group. "Mr. President, don't forget, you have a luncheon with the superintendent and the secretary of war," he reminded, a gentle way of helping the president get away from the conversation.

"Yes, yes, I'm on my way," Roosevelt replied. He smiled at Joe. "Well, I must be off. Do take care of yourself, General, and drop by the White House to see me sometime."

"It would be an honor, Mr. President," Joe replied.

The president, accompanied by his wife and mother, resumed his laborious walk out to the waiting limousine. General Murchison followed them onto the front steps of the chapel, then stood there and watched as the big Packard drove away.

"General Murchison?" a voice said quietly.

When Joe turned, he saw Cadet Throckmorton standing just behind him.

"Ah, yes, the ubiquitous Mr. Throckmorton. Tell me, my dedicated young friend, what is next on the agenda?"

"Whatever you want, General. The next hour is your time, and I am at your disposal."

Joe nodded. "I want to visit the cemetery. I would like to say hello to some old friends."

"Very good, sir," Throckmorton replied. "This way, sir."

General Murchison started toward the cemetery with Cadet Throckmorton walking to his left and two paces behind.

"The building at the entrance of the cemetery is the old chapel, sir," Throckmorton pointed out, as if he were conducting a tour of the campus.

"It may be the old chapel to you, Mr. Throckmorton, but for me it is as immediate as this morning. It was there that I received my commission. Though it wasn't located at the entrance to the cemetery then."

"No, sir. When the new chapel was begun, the plan was to destroy the old. But the corps rose up in protest, and the old chapel was disassembled brick by brick and plank by plank, then reassembled in this location."

"There could be no finer location for it," General Murchison said.

"You were class of '66, General?" Throckmorton asked.

"Yes."

"How many of your class are left, sir?"

"Only one," General Murchison replied. "I have the unenviable position of being the sole surviving member of that class."

"I know your background, sir," Throckmorton said. "May I say that your class could not be more nobly represented."

General Murchison chuckled. "Young man, you are going to make some general an excellent aide-de-camp."

"Thank you, sir. Is there any grave you particularly want to visit? Custer's perhaps? I know you served with him. He is right over—"

"Thank you, son, I know where he is," General Murchison interrupted, holding up his hand. He found another stone bench, similar to the one he had been sitting on earlier, and took a seat. Looking out over the tombstones, obelisks, and columns of the cemetery, he spoke again to Cadet Throckmorton. "If you don't mind, Mr. Throckmorton, I'd like to just stay here for a while."

"Yes, sir. I'll be right over here, sir."

Cadet Throckmorton moved to a spot on the walkway where he could be in position to turn away unwanted intruders and allow the old general to have his memories.

THE U.S. MILITARY ACADEMY
WEST POINT, NEW YORK
JUNE 1866

The tall, blue-eyed, sandy-haired young man walked over to the window of his third-floor room, pulling at his cadet-gray trousers to keep the uniform seams straight. He put his hands on the window ledge and stood looking across the quadrangle at the granite facades of the barracks buildings fronting the Central Area from the opposite side of the square.

Muted, familiar sounds drifted up to him from the quadrangle below: the measured footfalls of errant cadets walking their punishment tours, the ringing of steel-rimmed caisson wheels on cobblestones, the rattle of a dozen leather slingstraps being slapped as one, and the barked commands of a drill sergeant.

There were also the smells: floor wax and shoe polish, a hint of kerosene from the lamp, and the aroma of roast pork from the cadet mess.

In the past four years the sights, sounds, and smells of West Point had become a part of Cadet Joseph Thomas Murchison's heritage. The cumulative effect of those things were as visceral a part of him as his heart and lungs. And though he was about to leave this place, he knew this place would never leave him.

Behind Joe, in the two-man room that had been his home for four years, he heard his roommate, William

Preston Dixon, packing. Graduation was the next day, and the graduation ball was tonight.

"What are you going to do with your tar bucket?" Bill Dixon asked. The tar bucket was the tall plumed hat worn by cadets when they were in their full dress uniform.

Joe turned around to look at his roommate. Bill was considerably shorter, with red hair and a ruddy complexion. "I'm going to wear it tomorrow, for graduation," Joe answered.

"I know that. I mean afterward. How are you going to pack it without squashing it?"

"I packed two trunks," Joe explained. "That way there's enough room without having everything mashed."

"Yeah, that's a good idea," Bill agreed. "I should have thought of that. But then, maybe that's why you're graduating number one in the class and I'm number thirty-four. By the way, did you get your dance card filled?"

"Yes. I left it with the dance committee, and it was returned to me this afternoon with all the blanks filled in."

"So was mine. I wonder what they'll be like."

"Who?"

"Why, the girls whose names are on our dance cards, of course. I wonder what they're like."

"Why does it matter?" Joe asked. "In one more week we'll be at Jefferson Barracks."

"What if I told you that every girl on your dance card was exactly like Miss Philbin?" Bill teased. Miss Philbin was a rather horse-faced woman who worked in the cadet mess. Her unattractiveness was exceeded only by her unpleasant disposition.

"Heavens, no!" Joe replied with a gasp.

Bill laughed. "Well, then, it does matter, doesn't it?"

"I suppose so."

"Actually, only the first girl's name is important, for you will be her official escort for the night. Whom did you get?"

Joe looked at his card. "Delano," he answered.

"That's odd. So did I. Mary Delano."

"The name I have is Sara Delano."

Bill smiled. "Great. They must be sisters! We'll have a fine time!"

The ballroom was gaily decorated with bunting and flags and brightly glowing chandeliers. It was literally bursting with life, full of young women who floated about wrapped in yards of butterfly-bright silk dresses and wearing dangling earbobs that sparkled and flashed from beneath saucily curled black, brown, and yellow hair. The graduating cadets were all in their dress-gray uniforms, gold-trimmed. In addition to the cadets, there were several men in dress blue. These were the active army officers present, ranging from the commandant of cadets on down to the lieutenant who was the instructor of mathematics.

There were flowers in abundance, too, tucked behind a delicate ear or demurely placed in the cleavage that showed above the bodices of the dresses. Some of the flowers had already found their way into the button-holes of some of the cadets as they whirled the ladies about on the dance floor, the unauthorized uniform ac-coutrements being overlooked on this gala occasion. Beyond everything else, there was dancing, laughter, conversation, gaiety, and the tinkling of glasses as the young men celebrated what would be their last social event as West Point cadets.

Joe wandered over to the hors d'oeuvre table, where he examined a beautiful swan-shaped ice sculpture. Then he looked back at the ballroom floor and squinted his eyes slightly to allow the movement and color of the dancers to swirl about like a rapidly turning kaleidoscope.

"I believe you are Mr. Murchison?" a voice asked.

Joe turned around to see a young girl with light-blue eyes and long auburn hair. She was tall and stately and, in her emerging pubescence, already showing signs of the beautiful woman she was surely to become. But she was young . . . so young that Joe wondered what she was doing here.

"Yes," Joe replied.

The young girl stuck out her hand. "I am Sally Delano. It is actually 'Sara,' but I prefer 'Sally.'" Despite her tender years, there was a maturity about her—not only in her looks but in her poised demeanor—that intrigued Joe.

"How old are you?" Joe asked as he shook her hand.

The girl smiled. "My grandmother says one should never ask a woman her age, for she is surely to be older or younger than she wants to be."

"I . . . I'm sorry," Joe replied, chastised by this cool young lady. "It's just that you're not what I expected."

"I'm sorry if I disappoint you."

"No, no, it isn't that," Joe said. They stood looking at each other for a long, awkward moment. Once again the girl extended her hand and smiled. "Where are your manners, Joseph? My name is on your dance card, yet I am practically having to beg you to dance with me."

"Excuse me. Would you honor me with this dance, Miss Delano?"

"I would be delighted," she answered. "But I told you, my name is Sally."

They moved out onto the dance floor, and Joe was pleasantly surprised to find she was a very good dancer.

"Sally Delano. If you don't mind a personal question . . . how did you manage to get your name on the graduation dance committee's list? I thought that all the girls selected had to be at least eighteen."

"Warren Delano is my father. He is not without some influence in official circles, and being his daughter has some advantages."

"So he got your name on the dance list?"

Sally smiled. "Yes, but he doesn't know it. He thinks he signed for my sister only, but before the letter left the house, I added my name, too."

Joe laughed. "I must confess, Miss Delano—"

"Uh–uh. Sally, remember?"

"All right, Sally. I must confess that I do admire your resourcefulness, if not your honesty. But that leaves me in the awkward position of being escort to a young girl who can't be a day over seventeen."

Sally smiled. "I'm fourteen."

Joe gasped. "Fourteen? My God! What can I do with someone who is only fourteen?"

"Why, Mr. Murchison, what did you *want* to do?" Sally asked innocently.

"Nothing," Joe blustered. "It's just that . . . fourteen is so young."

"If you had been the escort for a nineteen-year-old girl tonight, would you have married her?" Sally asked.

"No, of course not."

"Would you have become friends?"

"Perhaps."

Sally smiled up at Joe, and he had to admit that she was a delightful young lady, for all her tender years.

"Well, then there is nothing lost," she said. "I think you and I could become very good friends. In fact, when you go to your first assignment, if you will write to me, I promise to be a most faithful correspondent."

"I'm sure you would be," Joe said. "But I'm afraid I'm going to be much too busy to write—especially . . ." Joe let the sentence hang.

"Especially to a fourteen-year-old?"

Joe laughed sheepishly. "Yeah."

"That's all right, I understand," Sally replied. "Though, you might find that writing to someone to whom you have no more commitment than mere friendship could be a liberating experience." The music stopped. "Thank you for the dance, Mr. Murchison."

Joe watched the girl walk away; then he let out a long breath of relief. "Miss Delano, I'm glad you are only fourteen. If you were nineteen or twenty, I don't know that I could resist you. You are going to be some charmer when you are of age."

★★★

Two

It took three months for Joe to receive his orders. In the meantime he was required to cool his heels as a supernumerary in the Department of New York. It was difficult, having a job with no real duties, so when word came for him to report to the office of the adjutant, he did so with an eagerness he couldn't hide.

The adjutant for the Department of New York was a man named Captain Elias Thurman. Thurman was in his late forties, bald, and overweight to the point of obesity. Having advanced as far as he could go in the army, he was bitter about his dead-end assignment, and his bitterness had left a permanent scowl on his face.

"You are being posted to Fort Berthold, Dakota Territory," Captain Thurman said, looking up at Joe through his thin wire-rimmed glasses.

"Yes, sir!" Joe replied, smiling.

Thurman leaned back in his chair, causing it to squeak under his weight. He stroked his multiple chins. "You are happy about going to the frontier, are you?"

"Yes, sir."

Thurman waved at a fly.

"Well, I suppose there is something to be said for duty in such a remote area. Lord knows, I could use a less demanding assignment. Here I am, the adjutant of the entire military district of New York, in the biggest city in America, and I am having to do it as a captain, with no staff to help me."

He waved at the fly again.

"It is a terribly demanding job with awesome responsibilities," Thurman groused.

He picked up a fly swatter and killed the fly.

"But someone has to do it. We can't all be running around out West, having sport with a few ragged Indians. Some of us must remain here, making the decisions that keep the army going."

"Yes, sir, I'm sure that is so," Joe said.

"I have a job to do. It's an important job and I wouldn't have it any other way," Thurman continued. He reached for a large brown envelope. "By the way," he added, "I am shipping thirty new recruits to Jefferson Barracks, Missouri, for further reassignment. I was going to hold them until Jefferson Barracks could send an officer after them, but that won't be necessary now that you are going that way. You will have to report to Jefferson Barracks to make transportation arrangements for the rest of your journey, so I am sending the recruits in your charge."

"You are sending the recruits with me, sir?"

"You can handle them, can't you?"

"Yes, sir, of course," Joe said. "I just didn't know anything about it, that's all."

"How could you know? I just made the decision. You will forgive General Sherman and me, I am sure, if we don't consult with our junior officers before we make decisions concerning the disposition of our troops?" Thurman asked sarcastically.

"I'm sorry, sir," Joe said. "I didn't mean to imply anything."

"Never mind," Thurman said, handing Joe the envelope containing the orders and travel vouchers for the new recruits. "Just see to it that these men get to Jefferson Barracks."

"Yes, sir."

Thurman jerked his thumb at a door in the back of the room. "They are in there now, waiting for you, just beyond that door."

"Thank you, sir," Joe said.

The room where the men were waiting hung heavy with a combination of tobacco smoke and the rank odor of unwashed bodies. The men were dressed in military uniforms, but that was the only military thing about them. Some were lying down, some were sitting, and some were standing, but none, not even those standing, bore any semblance of military posture.

Joe waited for someone to recognize him and call attention, but though several glanced his way, he didn't warrant a second look. Those who were engaged in their own private conversations continued to speak, as if oblivious of his presence.

"Attention!" Joe shouted.

There was a momentary pause in the buzz of conversation, but it was momentary only. The men went right back to what they were doing, totally ignoring Joe.

Joe pulled his saber, then, using the flat of his blade, struck the man nearest him.

"I said, come to attention!" Joe shouted again, this time putting everything he had into his voice. His command filled the room, overpowering all conversation and this time catching everyone's attention.

"You!" he barked, pointing his saber at one of the men sitting on the floor, leaning against the wall. "Get up and stand at attention, or so help me, God, I'll run you through. All of you!" he shouted to the others. "I want all of you at attention!"

Joe began making motions with his sword until gradually, one by one, the men stood up.

"Who the hell are you?" one of the men asked.

"I am Lieutenant Murchison. All you need to know is that I am an officer in the United States Army, and from now on when you address me or any other officer, you will say 'sir.' And when I, or any other officer, come into a room, the first one of you to see me or that officer will call attention, and you will all comply. Is that understood?"

Some nodded. Most just stared morosely.

"I said, *is that understood?*" Joe bellowed, booming out the last three words.

"Yes, sir!" the men yelled back in one voice.

Joe smiled. "Well, now, that's more like it. You," he said, pointing to one of the soldiers, who though not

quite at attention was closer to it than the others.
"Come here. We are going to demonstrate the position
of attention. The rest of you, watch."

Joe started from the bottom and worked his way up:
heels together; feet spread at a forty-five-degree angle;
legs, hips, back and arms straight; head and eyes
straight ahead.

"There, that's pretty good," Joe said when he had
the soldier all lined up. "Now, let me see the rest of
you do it."

With a lot of banter, the others began to approxi-
mate the position of attention.

"One more thing!" Joe shouted. "When you are at
the position of attention you do not talk. You must
remain silent."

The babbling ceased as the men worked hard to respond to their new officer's command.

"Lieutenant," Captain Thurman called, sticking his
head through the door at that moment.

"Yes, sir?"

"I've got one more for you. In there, Todd."

The man called Todd mumbled a "yes, sir," then
came into the room. Stopping, he saluted Joe sharply.

"Trooper Seth Todd reporting for duty, sir."

Joe was surprised not only by Todd's military bearing
but by his age. He was at least forty, whereas every
other recruit in the room was between eighteen and
twenty-five.

"Trooper Todd, do you have any military experience?" Joe asked.

"Some, sir," Todd replied without elaboration.

"I see. Well, the rest of you men, watch Trooper
Todd. He seems to know what he is doing."

By the time Joe and his men reached the train station four hours later, the other passengers in the depot
were treated to a body of soldiers marching in parade.
Many thought they were witnessing the transfer of a
seasoned company of men.

Three Days Later

Joe looked through the window as the train pulled into the station in Hillsboro, Illinois. It was from here, a little over four years ago, that he had left to go to West Point. This would be his first time back.

Hillsboro looked the same. It was dominated by a large brick courthouse that occupied the center of the square and was surrounded by the brick-paved streets of the downtown area. Joe smiled when he saw Charley Roberts, the station agent, hurrying out of the depot. Charley Roberts was the only station agent Hillsboro had ever had, and he was as much a landmark of the town as the courthouse itself.

Yesterday Joe had detrained in Indianapolis to telegraph his parents that he would be passing through Hillsboro today. He hoped they had received the message, for he would have no time to go out to the farm to see them. According to the conductor, the train would stand in the depot for twenty minutes only, which meant that if he was going see his parents, they would have to come into town to meet him.

A cluster of people were standing on the platform as the train pulled into the station, but Joe didn't see his parents among them.

Had they not received his telegram?

Joe felt a profound sense of sadness. To pass through his own hometown and not get to see them was worse than not passing through at all. Then he felt a surge of joy. Over by the depot building itself, standing in front of a familiar and well-worn farm wagon, were his mother and father.

Joe's father was a big man, well over six feet tall and weighing over two hundred pounds. He was wearing a suit—he stood there in his unaccustomed clothes, his big farmer's hands looking out of place as they protruded from jacket sleeves that were too short—and Joe's mother was wearing her best dress. Seeing them like that, realizing they had gone out of their way to look their best for him, brought a lump to his throat. He looked away quickly, lest tears come to his eyes, and he had to take several deep breaths until he got himself composed.

"Trooper Todd," he called.

"Yes, sir?"

"I'm going to step off the train for a few minutes. You're in charge until I get back."

"Yes, sir. You have a good visit, sir. Your folks look like fine people."

Joe looked at Todd in surprise. "How do you know who my folks are?"

"I figure they must be the nice-looking gentleman and the pretty lady standing over there by the wagon."

"Yes, that's them," Joe said.

"Don't worry about the men, sir. They'll be just fine."

It did not escape Joe's notice that Todd had said, "*They'll* be just fine," as if he were separated from them. Joe was impressed with Todd's knowledge of military procedure and by his ease with it. He had appointed Todd to the rank of acting corporal to help him manage the troops during the trip, and Todd had accepted the added responsibility as if he had been doing it all his life.

Joe stepped down from the train, then looked over toward his mother and father. He saw a wide smile spread across his mother's face and a controlled look of pride on the face of his father. His mother started toward him.

"Martha, wait," Joe heard his father say, and she stopped, then waited until Joe reached her.

"Hello, Ma," he said. He opened his arms in invitation, and, with a little shout of joy, she moved into them. He hugged her tightly, breathing in the smells of her that he could remember: lye soap, a hint of lilac, and cinnamon.

"Oh, my, how you have grown," she said.

Joe laughed. "Ma, I haven't grown but one inch since I left for the Point."

"But it seems more, don't you think, Ed?"

"Your problem, Martha, is that you still see a little boy. You forget that he's a man," Joe's father, Ed, replied. He stuck out a massive paw and Joe took it. "It's good to see you, boy. How long can you stay?"

"Oh, Pa, I thought you understood. I can't stay at all." Joe pointed to the train. "There are thirty-one men on that train who are under my command. I'm taking them to Jefferson Barracks, and when the train pulls out, I have to be on it."

"Joe, there'll another train going in the same direction tomorrow," Martha said. "Your pa and I thought we might see Mr. Roberts and get you on that one. That way you would be able to spend an entire day with us."

"I wish I could, Ma," Joe said. "But I have these men to look after."

"Oh," Martha said. Tears welled in her eyes, then spilled down her cheeks. "I had so hoped."

"Ma, I'll get a furlough soon, I promise. Then I can come home for several days."

"But can't you just stay for one day, Joe?"

"Martha, leave the boy be," Ed said gruffly—more gruffly than he intended, for he was fighting back his own disappointment, as well. "He's a soldier now, and he's got a soldier's duty to do."

"I must say that the two of you look very nice," Joe said.

Ed put his finger to his shirt collar and pulled it away from his neck.

"Yes, well, this-here collar was your ma's idea," he said. "I got better things to do than get dressed up in the middle of the week like some drawin'-room dandy."

"But you look so handsome, Ed," Martha said. "And what have you got to do that's more important than comin' down to see your son?"

"Well, nothin', I reckon, if you put it that way," Ed agreed.

The train whistle blew one long and three short toots, the signal to the brakeman to release the brakes.

"All aboard!" the conductor called.

"I have to go, Ma," Joe said.

"Oh, son, write to us. You didn't hardly write none

when you was in West Point. Won't you write more
often?" Martha pleaded.

"I will, Ma, I promise," Joe answered.

"Lieutenant, you'd best be gettin' on board!" the
conductor called as the train began to move.

Joe hugged his mother, who held him tightly, as if by
her efforts she could keep him there.

"For heaven's sake, Martha, let the boy go," Ed said.
"Didn't you hear what he said? He has thirty-one men
under his command."

Reluctantly, Martha dropped her arms by her side.
Joe reached out to shake his father's hand.

"Be gone with you, now," his father said taking his
hand, then dropping it quickly. "The train is leavin',
and you got men to look after."

Joe looked at both of them, trying desperately to
come up with some final word that would amuse them
and make the parting easier. But try as he might, he
could think of nothing except the obvious.

"Good-bye," he said. "I love you both."

Martha found a handkerchief in her reticule and began dabbing at her eyes, for she was crying openly now.

"Go," Ed said. "I don't want you missing the train
on our account."

Joe turned and saw that the train was already at the
end of the platform. He started running toward it.

"Hurry, soldier boy!" someone on the platform
shouted, and Joe's cheeks began to burn. He hoped he
wasn't making a spectacle of himself in front of his
men. Finally he caught up with the last car, then
hopped easily onto the trailing step. He swung up onto
the observation platform, then turned to look back at
the Hillsboro depot as it seemed to move off behind
him. He saw his mother and father embracing each
other, and he gave one final broad wave. His father
raised his hand slightly, then lowered it to hold his
mother again. She was crying into the chest of his Sunday suit.

Though there was talk of building a bridge, as yet no
such structure spanned the Mississippi River at St.

Louis. As a result, passengers bound for St. Louis and points west had to detrain on the Illinois side of the river, then take ferry boats across to the Missouri side.

"You fellas will be wantin' to land at Jefferson Barracks, I expect," the ferry captain said when Joe approached him to make the arrangements to transport himself and his men across the river.

"Yes," Joe said.

The ferry captain pulled out a preprinted form and handed it to Joe. "Fill out the number of fellas you're responsible for; then sign it," he said. "That's all you got to do. I'll turn it in to the army paymaster myself."

Joe filled out the form, glad that getting them across the river was so easy.

The ferry put in at LaClede's Landing in St. Louis to off-load its passengers and wagons, then went downstream for approximately two miles to land at the foot of a series of wooded hills. Set back in the trees and hills and clearly visible from the river were the redbrick and white limestone buildings of Jefferson Barracks.

"Here you are, Lieutenant," the ferry operator said. "This is Jefferson Barracks."

"Thank you," Joe said. He squared the hat on his head, then walked down the boat gangplank where he was met almost immediately by a sergeant who came along a wooden pathway toward him.

The sergeant saluted. "Beggin' the lieutenant's pardon, sir, but would you be newly reportin' in now?" he asked in a thick Irish brogue.

"Who are you?" Joe replied.

"The name is Reagan, sir. Sergeant Timothy Reagan at your service. 'Tis detailed, I am, to meet any new recruits as might arrive an' take 'em to their appointed place or to provide newly arrivin' officers with such information as they may need."

"Very good, Sergeant Reagan." Joe handed the sergeant the brown envelope containing the papers of the recruits he had brought with him. "These men are recruits from the Department of New York. And I am to report to officer postings for further orders. Would you happen to know where that would be?"

"Aye, that I do, sir. If the lieutenant would be for checkin' inside that wee buildin' over there, there's them that will take care of you," Reagan said. He pointed to a well-shaded redbrick building set deep in a neatly tended lawn.

"Thank you, Sergeant."

"And you, lads, foin-lookin' bunch that you be. Would you be for standin' at attention now so's I can get a proper count?" the sergeant asked the recruits in his rolling brogue.

Joe turned the recruits over to Sergeant Reagan and walked across the well-tended lawn toward the building for officers' postings. Halfway there, he heard a loud cracking sound, then cheering voices. Looking toward the corner of the field, he saw two teams of men playing baseball, their efforts being urged on by several spectators.

"Run, Mike, run!"

Joe saw the batter running around the bases while, in the field, another man was chasing the ball the batter had just hit.

"Throw it in, George! Throw it in!"

Joe had played quite a bit of baseball while at West Point, proving to be very adept at it. The West Point nine had taken the measure of baseball teams from Columbia, Cornell, and Penn State, and Joe was acknowledged by all as the best player on the team. Then while visiting New York once, he watched the New York professional team in contests with other members of the Association of Professional Base Ball Players. He had even played in a practice game with the professionals, and the manager, seeing him play, asked if he would like to join the team.

"You can make more money as a baseball player than you can in the army," he had been told.

Joe had been very flattered by the invitation, but he turned the offer down.

"Joe! Joe Murchison!" someone called, and Joe turned to see who had hailed him. A smiling young second lieutenant with a sweeping mustache and a Van-dyke beard was hurrying toward him. The mustache and beard were recent affectations, but it didn't keep Joe from recognizing his roommate from the academy. "I might have known if there was a baseball match being contested that you would be somewhere nearby," Bill Dixon teased.

"Well, I see you made it here," Joe said happily. "I wasn't sure but what you wouldn't get lost en route."

"How can one get lost coming to Jefferson Barracks?" Bill asked. "You just go to the middle of the country, and there it is."

Joe laughed. "Do you have further orders yet? Do you know where you're going?"

"Why, to the same place you are, old roommate of mine," Bill answered. "We are both going to Fort Berthold, Dakota Territory. And we're leaving tomorrow."

"Tomorrow?"

"By riverboat," Bill said. "Come on, I'll show you where to go. I've been here for a week now, and I know this place like the back of my hand. Tonight we can go into the city. I've found some wonderful places for dining. We'll have a fine going-away dinner."

The next day, as directed by orders, Lieutenants Joseph Thomas Murchison and William Preston Dixon presented themselves to Captain Lee Martin of the Missouri River steamer *Western Angel*. One other soldier was there, also going to Fort Berthold. He smiled and saluted when he saw Joe.

"Good morning, sir. I'll bet you thought you had seen the last of me," the soldier said.

"Trooper Todd. Shouldn't you be at drill?"

"No, sir. The army offered to suspend drill and training to anyone with previous military experience if that person would volunteer for an immediate posting to Fort Berthold. I volunteered, sir."

Bill was just coming back from talking to the boat's purser at that moment, so Joe introduced Seth Todd to him.

"Trooper Todd was with me on the train," Joe explained, "and he was of great service to me. He will be traveling with us."

"Yes, well, he'll be the only one," Bill said.

"The only soldier?"

"The only passenger, other than us," Bill said. "I just spoke with the purser. This boat is carrying nothing but military supplies, including a large quantity of gunpowder. Because of that, no civilian passengers can be carried. I'm afraid it's going to be a long, lonesome trip with just us and the men of the boat crew."

Joe chuckled. "Did you have something else in mind?"

Bill smiled. "What would have been the harm in having a beautiful young woman on board?"

Joe laughed. "A great deal of harm, if there be only one. As long as you're making believe, why not two?"

Todd cleared his throat loudly, then added, "Sirs?"

Joe and Bill laughed.

"All right, three, then," Joe amended. "As long as they're in our imagination."

"On the other hand, there is a positive side to our lonely trip," Bill suggested. "There are twelve staterooms on the steamer and, according to the captain, we can take our pick. Even you, Private. I'll bet you've never traveled in a stateroom before."

"No, sir, not as a private," Todd agreed.

"Not as a private?" Bill asked.

"No, sir," Todd said, without further elaboration. "If the lieutenants would care to go aboard now, I'll take care of the gear."

"Thank you, Todd," Joe said.

Bill and Joe went aboard then to look over the *Western Angel* while, behind them, Trooper Todd took care of transferring their baggage.

Sometime later, with the boat fully loaded, Captain Martin climbed into the towering wheelhouse and pulled on the chain that blew the boat whistle. His action caused a deep-throated tone audible on both sides of the river. The paddle wheel began spinning backward, and the boat pulled away from the dock, then turned with the stern wheel pointing downriver and the bow presenting itself upstream. The engine telegraph was slipped to full forward, and the wheel began spinning in the other direction, until finally it caught hold, overcame the force of the current, and started propelling the boat upstream.

For the first part of the journey they were on the Mississippi, and they beat their way against the strong, six-mile-per-hour current around a wide, sweeping bend, with the steam relief pipe booming as loudly as if the city of St. Louis were under a cannonading. Finally they reached the mouth of the Missouri, turned into it, and the trip was begun.

For the rest of the day the *Western Angel* worked its way up the Missouri River, its two engines clattering, the paddle wheel slapping, and the boat itself enveloped in a thick smoke that belched forth from the high, twin chimneys. Joe had learned quickly that they were called chimneys and not stacks.

By nightfall they were near the town of Washington, Missouri. As the crow flies, Washington was a distance of no more than forty-five miles from St. Louis, though they had already come ninety miles through the twisting river. A railroad track ran alongside the shore at that point, and the train they saw heading for St. Louis would be there in not much over an hour. An hour and a half by rail to cover the same distance that had taken the riverboat ten hours.

Looking at the train, Joe mused that it was too bad the railroad did not yet reach Fort Berthold; if it did, the trip could be made in a matter of days rather than weeks. Then, in almost the same thought, he was glad he wasn't going by train, for surely he would be able to see more of this magnificent country from the deck of a boat than he would through the confining window of a rapidly moving railway car.

TWENTY-ONE DAYS LATER

Joe took his writing materials to a capstan in the bow of the boat so he could write a couple of letters. Captain Lee had assured him that if they met no more

boats coming downriver, he would personally post the
letters when he returned to St. Louis.

"Aren't we likely to meet any more boats?" Joe
asked.

"I couldn't say," Captain Lee replied. "Once you get
this far up the river, the boats start comin' fewer and
farther between. We might see one in the next few
hours, or there might not be another boat come by for
three or four weeks. But you may as well go ahead and
write your letters, Lieutenant, so that your correspon-
dents get used to the long space between mail runs."

"I guess you're right," Joe agreed.

Joe wasn't sure why he wanted to write to someone
as young as Sally Delano, other than the fact that at
the graduation ball he had found her charming, despite
her tender years. But he felt a need to correspond with
someone—other than family—and, by her very age,
there was little chance of this situation ever going beyond friendship.

He began to write:

Aboard the steamboat *Western Angel*
Upper Missouri River
October 5, 1866

Dear Miss Delano:
    How surprised you must be to receive this let-
ter from me. I beg of you to forgive my presump-
tion, but I am currently experiencing so many
marvelous sights and adventures that I feel I must
share my observations with someone.
    I am, as of this moment, sitting upon the bow
capstan of a steamboat, making my way up the
Missouri River. Though the captain has told us
how dangerous the river is, one cannot help but
be awed by its beauty. I wish you could see it,
Miss Delano. Under the early morning and late
afternoon suns, it is a shimmering sheet of gold.
By day it is a stream of molten silver, filled with
hundreds of uprooted trees. The trees, massive
things, hang up on sand bars and are periodically

released to charge down the river like giant torpedoes, bent upon destroying our gallant little boat.

The name of our steamer is the *Western Angel,* but to hear the crew talk it is more a devil than an angel. It seems to consume a prodigious amount of wood, which we replace at periodic stops along the way. Although the roustabouts (that is how the crewmen refer to themselves) don't like the stops, for it means backbreaking labor for them, I must say that we passengers enjoy the stops very much, for it gives us a chance to explore firsthand this new land we are passing through.

One of the passengers making the trip with me is Lieutenant William Preston Dixon. You may remember him from the Cadet Graduation Ball. As your sister's name was first on his dance card, Bill was her official host for the evening. He was also my roommate at the academy, and I am particularly happy that he will be sharing the adventure of a frontier post with me.

Mr. Dixon has confided something to me that I will share with you. It is his ambition to be the president of the United States. Can you imagine anyone actually holding to such a lofty ambition? I have known him for four years, and should Lieutenant Dixon actually attain his goal, I cannot but feel that he would be a wonderful president. He has all the attributes that make men noble. He is honest, trustworthy, and imbued with a keen sense of duty.

I do not know what to expect of my assignment to Fort Berthold. The purpose of the fort, I am told, is to keep peace with the Indians and to punish those who would visit mischief upon the white miners and settlers in the area. Whatever my duty shall be, I will endeavor to perform it to the best of my ability.

Dear Miss Delano, I hope you have not found this letter an unwanted intrusion. Should you care

to write me, you may address your letters to me
thusly:

Lieutenant Joseph T. Murchison
U.S. Army,
Fort Berthold, DT.

I will endeavor to answer as promptly as my
duties allow.

Sincerely,
Joseph T. Murchison

After finishing the letter to Sally Delano, Joe wrote
another to his parents. He had just completed it when
he heard the first officer, Mr. Plimpton, call up to the
wheelhouse.

"Cap'n Martin! Smoke comin' up!"

Joe stood up and walked forward to join the first
officer.

"Is it a boat, Mr. Plimpton?" Joe asked.

"Aye, sir. Looks like you're goin' to get that letter
mailed quicker'n you thought," Plimpton replied.

In the wheelhouse above, Captain Martin pulled on
the whistle cord, and the deep dual tone of the *Western
Angel* rolled out across the river, then came back from
the nearby bluffs.

The distant boat answered with its own call.

"That'll be the *Queen Bee*," Plimpton said. "I recognize her whistle. We'll hail 'em and pass over your letters and see if they have any news from upriver."

Martin blew the whistle again, and again the heavy
bleat of the *Western Angel* rolled out from the boat.

The *Queen Bee* answered a second time. It was still
not visible, but its smoke hung just over a bluff that
blocked the view around the bend. In addition to its
whistle, Joe could hear the booming of the approaching boat's steam relief valves, echoing back from the
bluffs in counterpoint to the *Western Angel*'s own cannonading. As they came up on a wide bend in the river,
Joe could see the *Queen Bee*, working its way downriver. Once in sight, the two boats closed on each other
rather quickly; then they maneuvered to come side by
side. Finally, with the skillful application of power and

a deft adjustment of rudders, the boats were together. A mailbag was passed across to the *Queen Bee*.

"You're riding awfully low in the water, Captain!" the captain of the *Queen Bee* shouted through his megaphone.

"I'm carrying supplies for the army at Fort Berthold," Captain Martin called back. "Cannonballs and such."

"Well, then, ye'd best be watchin' out for the Chambers bar," the captain of the other boat warned. "It's some higher than it has been."

"Much obliged," Martin called back. "Have you seen any Injuns?"

"None as was makin' trouble," the captain of the *Queen Bee* answered. "But it's best you keep your eyes open just the same."

"Thanks, I'll do that," Captain Martin replied.

With a final salute, the boats parted, then went their own ways.

"What is the Chambers bar?" Joe asked.

"The steamboat *A. B. Chambers* went down there several years ago," Plimpton explained. "The wreckage caused eddies and swirls that eventually built up a large sandbar around it. I remember before the *Chambers* sank, it was easy passage through this stretch of the river."

"How long have you been going up the Missouri?"

"I took my first trip up the river in '51," Plimpton answered. "I run it for eight years, then I got caught up in the war, drivin' gunboats up 'n down the Mississippi for Admiral Porter. Ah, there's the bar, just ahead. We're goin' to have to spar over her for sure."

"I don't see anything," Joe said.

Plimpton pointed. "Don't you see the way the water is swirling there?"

Joe looked ahead, but, in truth, he couldn't tell the difference between the spot Plimpton was pointing to and any other spot on the river.

"Nothing," Joe admitted.

"Well, you can count on the captain seein' it."

As if to underscore Plimpton's assertion, Captain

Martin called down from the wheelhouse at that moment. "Mr. Plimpton, bar ahead! Make ready to spar!"

"Aye, aye, captain," Plimpton replied.

"Anything I can do, Mr. Plimpton?" Joe asked.

"Aye, Lieutenant, there is. You and the other two passengers can take up arms and keep a watch on the banks on both sides of the river for Injuns. I reckon Wind in His Hair would like nothin' better than to get a crack at us, especially if he sees us hung up on a sandbar."

"Who is Wind in His Hair?"

"You mean you ain't heard of him?"

"No."

"Well, he's a Yankton Sioux war chief, the son of Chief Fool Dog. I reckon you'll be hearin' of him soon enough. Fool Dog and Wind in His Hair are the ones who keep the soldier boys busy up at Fort Berthold. Just keep your eyes open, Lieutenant. I don't want to be worryin' about him whilst we're tryin' to negotiate this sandbar."

Joe went to the arms chest and pulled out three Spencer rifles, keeping one and passing the others out to Lieutenant Dixon and Trooper Todd. Dixon took the right side and Todd took the left, while Joe went to the bow, ready to provide assistance to whichever side might be required.

As the three cavalrymen were getting into position, Plimpton and the boat crew began fitting the spars. These were grasshopperlike appendages on each side of the boat, designed to lift it up over whatever obstacle it might encounter. With the spars fitted, Plimpton put one man on each pole; then he went to the steam capstan, the same capstan that Joe had earlier used to write his letters.

Captain Martin slowed the engine until the boat was just creeping. It came up onto the bar; then, gently, the bow slid forward until they were grounded.

"All yours, Mr. Plimpton!" the captain called down.

"All right, laddies, here we go now!" Plimpton shouted to the roustabouts.

The men at the spars on each side of the boat put

their poles into the water, then signaled Plimpton, who opened the throttle on the engine that operated the capstan. The capstan began winding up, pulling on the cable, which put tension on the spars. Poles bent, chains clanked, and cables creaked as the front of the boat lifted slightly. Astern, the paddle wheel churned mightily, whipping up a muddy froth at the rear of the boat.

"Put your shoulders to it, boys! Heave!" Plimpton called.

Gradually the boat began to slide forward.

"Yeah, you've got it! Keep it up!"

Finally enough of the boat was over the bar that it could move under its own power. But after only a hundred feet or so, they had to spar again.

They had to repeat the operation four more times, once getting the boat so badly stuck that several of the roustabouts had to get out of the boat and pass a rope under the hull to loosen the grip of the sand. By the time they were in clear water again it was dark, and rather than risk running aground, Captain Martin put in to shore to spend the night.

ON THE UPPER MISSOURI
3 A.M., October 6, 1866

Joe was sound asleep when the explosion occurred. He was in his bed one moment and tumbling through the night air the next. It all seemed so surreal to him that he couldn't be sure he wasn't dreaming. He was hanging in space, feeling the air against his skin, looking down and back at the boat.

The boat was a great concussive blossom of fire, steam, bales, boxes, splinters, and tumbling human bodies. Joe landed in the river, falling into a deep pool. When he popped back up to the surface a few seconds later, he could hear the crackling roar of the fire and the hiss of escaping steam. The steam was so brilliantly white against the black sky that it appeared luminescent.

Some of the items that had been blown from the boat were still coming back down. He watched as the boat's bell landed high on a nearby bluff, then tumbled downhill, clanging loudly all the way until it rolled into the river.

"Bill! Todd!" Joe shouted.

"I'm here, sir!" Todd replied.

Joe saw Todd about fifty yards away, treading water in the river. Like Joe, he had been thrown clear. "Are you all right?" Joe called.

"Yes, sir, I think so," the trooper replied.

"The magazine must have exploded," Joe said.

"No, sir, I believe it was the boiler," Todd replied. "If it had been the powder, there wouldn't be anything at all left of the boat."

"Where's Lieutenant Dixon? Bill! Bill!" Joe shouted.

"Lieutenant, there he is!" Todd yelled, pointing to the listing deck of the fiercely burning boat. "He's still on board! And so's the gunpowder! Mr. Dixon better get the hell off there in a hurry!"

Joe saw Bill Dixon coming through the smoke and fire, carrying someone over his shoulder.

Todd cupped his hands around his mouth. "Lieutenant Dixon! Jump! Jump *now*!" he shouted.

"Bill, get off there!" Joe yelled, waving his arms fiercely.

Unable to hear them because of the roaring fire and hissing steam, Bill assumed the two in the water were just signaling to him that they were all right. He raised one arm to wave back at them, then pointed to the man he was carrying, indicating that he was trying to get him safely off the boat.

"Get off!" Joe screamed.

As Joe was calling, the gunpowder exploded. This time the entire boat disappeared in a blinding flash. A wall of intense heat flashed across the surface of the river, driving Joe and Todd once again underwater. Even submerged, Joe could hear the explosion and feel the concussion of the shock wave. When he came back up, gasping for breath, there was nothing left of the *Western Angel* except a scattering of steaming, smoking splinters and frothy water. Even the fire that had been burning so fiercely as a result of the first explosion was now gone, for there was nothing left to burn.

An eerie silence fell across the night.

"Bill! Bill!" Joe shouted. When he didn't get an answer, he called to Todd.

"Todd, are you all right?"

"Yes, sir, I'm fine," Todd shouted back.

"We'd better get out of the river and look for survivors," Joe ordered, though he had no real hope of finding any.

THREE DAYS LATER

Joe and Todd had walked for three days without shoes and with no clothes other than the longjohn underwear they had been sleeping in when the boiler exploded. Having only longjohns to wear was bad enough, but having no shoes made their progress painfully slow.

"I wish I had my boots," Joe said as he examined the bottoms of his feet.

Todd threw a couple more branches of dead wood onto the campfire. "Me, too," he said. "If I had them, I'd cook them. We have nothing to throw onto that fire but wood."

"Yes, well, at least we've *got* a fire, thanks to you," Joe said. "I remember taking a class in woodsmanship back at West Point. We had to make a fire by rubbing sticks together. I wasn't very good at it, but you seem to do it quite well."

"During the war we didn't always have matches," Todd explained. "There were times when we didn't have much food, either, but I can't recall ever being this hungry for this long. There was always something to eat . . . a rabbit, some field corn, a mule, something."

"Maybe we'll catch a fish tomorrow," Joe suggested.

"It's almost funny, isn't it, Lieutenant?" Todd said. "I mean, here we were, riding upriver on a boat filled with enough rifles, balls, powder, hardtack, and beans to equip and feed an army, yet we don't have one bean or a knife between us. We can't hunt, we can't even defend ourselves if we're attacked by Indians."

"That's true, but then why would any self-respecting Indian want to attack us?" Joe asked. "We don't have anything they'd want, and we certainly aren't much of a threat to them."

"You're right about that, sir. Right now I don't think we could fight off a ladies' literary tea society."

They didn't catch a fish the next day or the next or the next. For six days they followed the river. Joe knew it would eventually lead them to Fort Berthold, but he had no idea of how much farther they would have to go —or even how much farther they *could* go. Both men were now very weak from hunger.

That evening, after a fire was built, Joe and Todd lay on their sides, staring into the flames, each lost in his own thoughts. Finally Joe broke the silence.

"Who are you, Todd?" Joe asked.

"Beg your pardon, sir?"

"Who are you, really? I mean, if I'm going to die out here with you, I'd like to know who the hell it is I'm dying with. Is Seth Todd actually your name? You said you have some military experience, but you didn't elaborate."

Todd sighed. "Todd is actually my middle name, sir. I am Seth Todd Hamby of the King William County Hambys. That may not mean anything to you, but in Virginia it does. My father owned the largest tobacco plantation in the county. I took no interest in the farm because I knew it would one day go to my older brother. I wasn't bitter about it; that's the way it has been in my family for generations.

"I became the black sheep, always in trouble . . . nothing serious, but enough to cause my family grief. I drank too much, I gambled recklessly, I got into fights." Todd was quiet for a long moment. "And, the worst thing of all, I got a girl—a very wonderful girl— into trouble." He cleared his throat. "I wanted to do the right thing by her, but she wouldn't marry me. She said her child would be better off without a father than to have a father who wound up getting himself shot over a game of cards or in a drunken fight.

"I got angry and left. I was in New Orleans when my daughter was born. There was some difficulty during the birth, and the mother died. I returned home as soon as I heard, but by the time I got back, the child had already been given up for adoption."

"Couldn't you have gone to court and stopped that?"

"No court in its right mind would have given me that child. Besides, the child was better off . . . much better off. You see, it wasn't just anyone who adopted her. It was my brother and his wife."

"Did your brother allow you to see her?"

"Oh, yes, I got to see her. I even got to know her—as long as I promised never to tell her who I really was. She called me 'Uncle Seth.' But after a while I left. I bounced from one job to another. I was a brakeman on a railroad, worked in a sawmill in Alabama, as a bouncer in a New Orleans whorehouse." Todd chuckled. "Once I even drove a wagon for a professional theater group. Met the actor John Wilkes Booth. He was a strange bastard, even then.

"Then came the war, and I went off to fight." Todd was quiet for a moment. "Hell, I didn't even have a clear idea of what the war was about, nor did I care. I just figured it was something else to try.

"I was at Bull Run, Fredericksburg, Antietam, and Gettysburg. After that the war sort of blurs for me. I fought in a score of other battles, big and small. And then, in the last days of the war, I was at Sayler's Creek. No doubt you've heard of the Battle of Sayler's Creek?"

"Yes, I have," Joe said. "It was a classic confrontation between cavalry units: the Federals under Generals Merrit and Custer, and the Confederates under General Thomas Rosser."

"It may have been classic, but it was also bloody. Bloody and absolutely useless. It was a vain battle in a lost war for a failed cause. The South lost more than eighteen hundred men in that battle. Did I say men? They weren't men; they were boys, most of them. Some as young as fourteen.

"Then came Appomattox. I watched Robert E. Lee go into that courthouse to surrender his sword, and I saw the wet eyes of the men I had fought with for so long. All I could think of was what a terrible price both North and South had paid for arrogance and pride.

"I remember, also, that I had a letter in my pocket from my brother, explaining that the end of the war would mean instant prosperity for us, as the northern market for tobacco would be higher than it had ever been. He asked me to come back to work with him. He said he figured I'd gotten all the sand out of my system by now. There were hundreds of thousands dead, and I was supposed to go back and grow tobacco.

"Well, I couldn't do it. I didn't even answer his letter. I just looked for some means to get as far away from everything as I could, and the best way for that seemed to be to go to sea. You ever been to sea, Lieutenant?"

"No."

"Well, if you ever do, don't go before the mast. I swear, the lowest slave on the meanest plantation I ever knew has it better than the men in the fo'c'sle. I stayed with it for about a year; then when our ship put into New York, I decided there had to be something better, so I didn't sign on for another voyage. Instead, I went down to the recruiting station and joined the army. That brings me to here."

"Have you seen your daughter since the war?" Joe asked.

"No, sir," Todd replied. "She was nine years old when I last saw her. She was a beautiful child, and I know she is going to be a beautiful woman. I also know that she is a thousand times better off without me."

"Todd, I know I'm not qualified to speak of the war," Joe said. "I came into active service too late to participate. But I do understand the elements of command structure and military discipline. And no matter what your background may have been before the war, you became a good soldier. As a matter of fact, you are perhaps the best soldier I have yet encountered in my admittedly brief military career. I'm sure you feel the battle at Sayler's Creek was a waste of young lives, but being the soldier you are, you followed your orders as you should have. Perhaps you can take some comfort in having done your duty."

"You don't understand, Lieutenant," Todd said almost laconically.

"What is it I don't understand?"

"I didn't *follow* orders at Sayler's Creek. I *gave* them. I was a colonel in command of the Third Virginia Cavalry."

"You were a colonel?"

"Yes, sir. Sounds strange, I guess, given my background. But you might say I inherited the rank. You see, nearly everyone who joined the regiment with me was dead. I was the most experienced one left; so General Rosser gave me the job."

"It must be difficult for you. I mean, once you were a colonel and now you're—"

"I am exactly what I want to be, sir," Todd said, before Joe could finish his comment. After a moment he chuckled dryly. "Although I must confess that I am somewhat *hungrier* than I would choose to be."

Despite himself, Joe laughed as well.

When Joe opened his eyes the next morning, he had to blink several times to make certain he was seeing what he thought he was seeing. Two forked sticks had been set into the ground to either side of the dead, blackened coals of the previous night's fire. A rabbit—already skinned, cleaned, and skewered—was staked across the two forked sticks.

"Todd!" Joe shouted.

Todd opened his eyes and sat up with a start.

"Sir?"

"When did you get him?" Joe asked. "Never mind that! *How* did you get him?"

"I beg your pardon, sir. Get who? Get what?"

"The rabbit!" Joe said, pointing at the carcass.

Todd looked at the fire, then gasped in surprise. "What the hell? Where did that come from?"

Joe looked at Todd in confusion. "What do you mean? You mean you didn't put it there?"

"No, sir. I never saw it before this very moment," Todd said.

"Then where . . . ?" Joe started, then interrupted that question for another. "What the hell is going on here?" With difficulty, he pulled himself to his feet and began looking around. He saw nothing.

"Mr. Murchison, I don't know where that rabbit came from," Todd said. "But as we are both seeing it, I do not believe it to be an illusion. Therefore, with the lieutenant's permission, sir, I intend to cook it."

"My permission? Yes, yes, by all means, yes!" Joe said, practically shouting his answer.

The rabbit was barely cooked before the two men took it off the skewer and divided it. They ate ravenously, pulling the animal apart with their hands and teeth, not even waiting for it to cool. When all the meat was gone, they broke open the bones and sucked out the marrow.

"That is absolutely the best-tasting thing I have ever eaten in my entire life," Todd declared when they were finished.

"I have to agree with you," Joe said. "And at the risk of hurting my mother's feelings, not even her chicken and dumplings ever tasted better."

They heard a sound behind them and, turning quickly, saw an Indian standing there.

"Jesus!" Todd gasped. "Look at that, sir!"

"Don't make any sudden moves," Joe ordered.

The three men stood staring at each other for a long, silent moment; then the Indian bent down, picked something up from the ground beside him, and tossed it toward the two cavalrymen.

"Oh, damn! It's a scalp!" Todd yelped.

"No! No, wait!" Joe said, looking at the object more closely. "Todd, it's another rabbit!"

The Indian made a motion toward his mouth with his hands. Then he moved his jaws as if he were eating.

"You are giving this to us?" Joe asked.

The Indian just stared.

"I . . . we . . . have nothing to trade," Joe said.

The Indian understood the word *trade*.

"No trade," he grunted. "I give."

"Thank you," Joe said. "I don't know how to thank you."

"Let's eat it now, sir, before he changes his mind," Todd suggested.

"Good idea."

When the two men began trying to skin the rabbit with their bare hands, the Indian came over and made a cut in the skin with his knife. Then, in one deft motion, he jerked the skin off. Another cut opened the rabbit's abdomen, and a moment later the rabbit, like the one before it, was roasting over the open fire.

The Indian sat quietly leaning against a rock until the men had eaten the rabbit. Then he stood and motioned for them to come with him.

"We're going to Fort Berthold," Joe said. "Fort Berthold. Do you know the fort?"

The Indian motioned again for the men to come with him.

"We must stay by the river," Joe said, pointing toward the river they had been following.

The Indian shook his head and motioned yet again for them to come with him.

"He really wants us to go with him," Joe said.

"Lieutenant, do you think we ought to trust him?" Todd asked.

"I don't see that we have any choice," Joe replied. "Besides, if he wanted to kill us, he could have done so by now. And he wouldn't have fed us."

"I guess you're right, sir."

"All right, Indian," Joe said. "Lead on, we'll follow."

With a grunt, the Indian turned and began walking.

Although they had been somewhat reenergized by their meal, they were still barefoot and thus unable to keep up with the Indian. As a result, their guide had to stop several times to wait for them. Finally they came over a low ridge and saw in the valley below a small

Indian village. The men and women of the village looked up curiously; then the children and several dogs ran out to meet them. The children laughed and shouted back and forth to each other in excitement. One young boy, braver than the others, picked up a stick and ran up to Joe and Trooper Todd. Joe thought the boy was going to hit them. Instead, he just touched each of them, then, with a loud whoop, ran back to boast of his accomplishment to the others.

A very pretty young Indian woman, wearing an elaborately worked and beautifully decorated doeskin dress, came out of the crowd of Indians, laughing.

"The boy has claimed coups on you," she said.

"You speak English!" Joe exclaimed.

"Yes, I speak English. I am called Quiet Stream."

Joe pointed to the Indian who had guided them. "I would like you to thank him for us. He saved our lives."

She spoke to the Indian, who replied in several guttural grunts and tones. Quiet Stream laughed.

"What did he say?"

"He asks how white man can die of—" She made a circular motion on her stomach. "How do you say *no food*?"

"Starvation?"

"Yes. How can white man die of starvation in the midst of plenty?"

"We have no weapons," Joe explained. "We had no way of hunting."

Their guide spoke again, and Quiet Stream interpreted.

"Why do you walk to fort? Why do you not ride on boat?"

"Our boat blew up and sank."

"Ahh!" Quiet Stream replied. By now the others had gathered around, and she spoke to several of them. They erupted in excited, animated conversation for several moments; then Quiet Stream returned to English.

"We heard a big bang on river," she said. "We

thought it was a boat, but we did not know if anyone still lived."

"We are the only survivors," Joe answered. "I am Lieutenant Murchison. This is Trooper Todd. We were heading for Fort Berthold. Do you know where it is?"

"Yes," Quiet Stream answered without offering any additional information.

"Is it far from here?"

"Two days."

"Two days? Only two days? Thank God. With the generous gift of food from the one who guided us, I believe we are strong enough to make it. Again, you have our thanks. We will go now." Joe started back in the direction from which he and Todd had come.

"If you walk beside river, it will take you seven days," Quiet Stream called to him. "It is two days this way." She pointed to a series of high hills.

"That way?" Joe said.

"Yes. That is the way you must go."

"Sir, if we don't have a compass or the river to keep our bearings, we could miss the fort completely," Todd suggested.

"I know."

"You will not get lost. I will take you," Quiet Stream offered.

"You will take us to the fort?"

"Yes," she said easily.

"Why would you do that? Why would you want to help us?"

"My brother has told me to do this."

"Do you always do what your brother tells you to do?"

"Everyone does what my brother tells them to do," Quiet Stream replied.

"Everyone?"

"Yes. He is a great shaman."

"Who is he?"

"He is called Wind in His Hair."

"Wind in His Hair?" Joe gasped, looking again at their guide. The Indian stared at him impassively.

"Who is Wind in His Hair, sir? Have you heard of him?" Todd asked.

"Yes. Plimpton told me about him. He is a Sioux war chief. He may be one of the reasons we were sent here."

"Then I don't understand," Todd said. "Why did he help us?"

"That's a good question," Joe replied. He looked at Quiet Stream. "Why would Wind in His Hair help us? We are soldiers. We are his enemy."

Quiet Stream smiled. "You have lost much of your medicine . . . your strength . . . since the boat exploded."

"I can't argue with that," Joe agreed.

"There is no honor to kill you when you have no strength. To kill you now would make my brother weaker. But to save you will make him stronger. The medicine that you have lost belongs now to my brother."

"I see. Well, for whatever reason he saved us, I want to thank him." Joe extended his hand, but Wind in His Hair looked away, refusing to take it.

"He will not shake hands with you," Quiet Stream said. "If he does so, some of the medicine he took from you would return to you."

"I meant nothing by it," Joe said. "It was just a friendly gesture."

"The two of you cannot be friends," Quiet Stream said. "You are enemies."

"But, can we not be enemies with honor?" Joe asked.

Quiet Stream translated. Wind in His Hair thought for a moment, then nodded his head. He said something, and then he took Joe's extended hand.

"My brother says that friend and enemy are opposite sides of a reflection in a pool. An enemy who has honor is to be as valued as a friend. My brother will be pleased to regard you as an enemy who has honor."

"All right," Joe said, smiling and shaking Wind in His Hair's hand. "I'll accept that."

Quiet Stream disappeared for a moment, and when

she returned she was carrying two pair of moccasins. She handed a pair to each of the soldiers. "Wear these," she said. "It will be easier for you to walk, and we must walk quickly if we are to reach the fort before dark tomorrow."

That evening they stopped on the banks of a cool, swiftly flowing white-water creek. The water bubbled and broke and frothed noisily over smoothly polished rocks. Thirsty after their long walk, Joe and Todd ran to the edge of the stream, fell onto their stomachs, then stuck their heads under. Each of them sucked in great draughts of water. Finally, their thirst slaked, they pulled their heads out of the creek and sat up.

"Oh, that was good," Todd said, brushing his dripping hair back from his face.

"Yes, it was," Joe agreed. "It's flowing in that direction. It has to be going toward the river."

"Yes," Quiet Stream answered. "This water and the river will meet at the fort."

Quiet Stream walked out into the creek until it was knee deep. She stood there for a long moment, braced against the swiftly flowing current that lapped and swirled around her legs. She was perfectly still as she stared down in front of her.

"What's she doing, sir?" Todd asked.

Joe shook his head. "I don't have the slightest idea," he confessed.

Suddenly Quiet Stream's hand darted down, into the water. When it came out, her fingers were wrapped around a large trout. She threw it up onto the bank.

"Damn, sir! Look at that!" Todd said.

"The fish!" Joe yelled. "Get it before it flops its way back into the water!"

Todd started toward the first fish just as a second came flying toward them. Joe was taking care of the second when a third and final fish wound up on the bank. Smiling, Quiet Stream waded back out of the water.

"Now we eat," she said.

* * *

It was midafternoon of the next day. They had followed
the sun-bejeweled stream for most of the day, though
they continued to maintain a southwesterly direction
even when the stream veered off on its own twisting
course. They always managed to reconnect with the
creek, however, when it came back from its latest me-
andering. Suddenly Quiet Stream held up her hand as
a signal to stop.

"What is it?" Joe asked.

Looking around, Quiet Stream saw a fallen tree and
pointed. "Hide behind tree!" she hissed.

"What is it? What is wrong?"

"Someone is coming."

"That shouldn't pose any threat," Joe said. "If it is
our people, I'll talk to them. If it is your people, you
can talk."

"They are Indian, but they are not my people,"
Quiet Stream said. "You must hide behind tree!"

Joe nodded. "We'd better do what she says."

"Yes, sir," Todd replied as he leapfrogged over the
large, fallen tree. Quickly, Quiet Stream moved a couple of branches over them. Then, evidently satisfied
that the two men were out of sight, she walked down to
the edge of the stream. What she did next nearly made
Joe gasp out loud.

As nonchalantly as if she were all alone, Quiet
Stream pulled her dress over her head, tossed it onto
the bank, then walked out into the water. At first Joe
was puzzled as to why she would do such a thing. Then
he realized what she must be doing. Whoever was coming would have no trouble believing her if she told
them she was alone, for they would not expect her to
be naked if anyone else was around.

And naked she was. Joe believed the picture she was
presenting at this moment was as lovely as Aphrodite's
child. Her hair, as black as a raven's wing, shone
brightly in the afternoon sun. She had a fine, slender
form, with high-lifted breasts and long, smooth legs.
She began splashing herself with water even as Joe
heard the approaching horses.

Three men, all Indians, crested a hill, then rode

down to the water's edge. They stopped on the opposite side of the creek and stared with unabashed appreciation at the show Quiet Stream was giving them. In the meantime, Quiet Stream, as if she had been surprised by the arriving riders, hurried out of the water to pick up her dress. She didn't put it on, but held it in front of her. While this shielded her from the view of the three Indians, it presented her beautifully curved back, still uncovered, to Joe and Trooper Todd.

One of the Indians said something in a guttural tone, and the other two laughed. Quiet Stream answered them, and Joe wished he could understand their language:

"Yankton woman. What are you doing here?" the warrior who dismounted asked.

"Are the Arikara so blind that they cannot see when a woman is bathing?" Quiet Stream replied.

The warrior laughed. *"We can see,"* he said. He looked at the other two riders. *"All can see."*

The other two laughed as well.

"By your nakedness, I believe you are inviting Arikara warriors to lie with you." He smiled broadly, then pulled aside his breech clout to grab himself as he began to walk toward her.

"And what are you going to do with that pathetic little cock? Tickle a mouse, perhaps?" Quiet Stream replied.

The smile left the warrior's face.

"Whore. Soon you will feel enough Arikara cock in you. And when we have finished, we will let our horses mount you as they do their mares."

"Stop!" Quiet Stream warned, holding her hand forward. A knife was in her hand.

The warrior stopped, then laughed derisively. *"Does one Yankton woman think she can stop three Arikara warriors?"*

"I am the daughter of Fool Dog and the sister of Wind in His Hair," Quiet Stream said. *"If you try to do this thing, my father and my brother will hunt you down, and they will make you die many times before you are dead."*

"They will not know how to find me," the Arikara

warrior said. *"After we have finished with you, we will kill you and there will be no one alive to tell the story."*

"You may force yourself on me," Quiet Stream replied. *"And you may kill me."* She moved her knife back and forth like the head of a snake coiled to strike. *"But before you do I will put my mark on you, and all who see it will know it is my mark. By that mark my father and my brother will know you, and they will come for you."*

The Arikara warrior stopped in the middle of the stream. He let go of himself and the breech clout fell back into place.

"Whore," he said. *"You are not worth having Arikara seed planted in your belly."* He shrugged, then went back to his horse and remounted.

"What are you doing so near the white man's fort?" he asked. *"You know the white soldiers do not welcome the Yankton Sioux."*

"The Yankton Sioux do not fear the white soldiers, nor do we let them tell us where we may put our lodges. My brother and several warriors have a hunting camp very near here," Quiet Stream said. *"I came to bathe, but I have been gone for a long time. I think that soon my brother will come to look for me. If the Arikara are as brave as they are loud, you will wait here until he comes."*

The warrior glared at Quiet Stream. *"We will not waste our time, waiting for the brother of a whore."*

Jerking his horse's head sideways with a pull on the rawhide bridle, the Arikara warrior kicked his heels hard against the pony's side. Then, as quickly as they had appeared, the Indians were gone.

Quiet Stream put her dress on again. She stood in silence for a long moment, listening. Then she returned to the fallen tree.

"You may come out now," she said. "They are gone, and we must conclude our journey."

"There," Quiet Stream said a couple of hours later. Joe looked in the direction she pointed. Perched on the end of a high bluff that protruded over the water was a fort constructed of palisade logs. There were two projecting blockhouses on corners opposite each other from which, Joe realized, the guards not only had a view of the river approach and the surrounding countryside, but could also cover, by rifle fire, the outside walls of the fort itself. An American flag fluttered from a pole atop the nearer blockhouse.

Just beyond the fort, and covering an area many times larger than the fort itself, was a large Indian village.

"Who are the Indians who live there, so near the fort?" Joe asked, turning to Quiet Stream.

To his surprise, the young Indian woman was gone.

"Quiet Stream?" he called. "Todd, did you see where she went?"

"No, sir," Todd answered.

"I guess she's afraid of the soldiers. Well, it doesn't matter. We're here, that's the important thing."

"Yes, sir," Todd replied.

The two soldiers turned back around and started off on the final leg of their journey. A short time later Joe and Todd reached the fort itself. Their hair was unruly, and they had a week's growth of beard. There were cuts, scratches, and bruises on their bodies, and the longjohns they were wearing were dirty, torn, and ragged. So unusual was their appearance that a score or more of the Indians from the village outside the fort followed them up to the front gate.

"Haw! Lookee here! Come here, ever'one, an' look at this!" the guard at the gate shouted when Joe and Todd approached the sally port of Fort Berthold.

Several others, seeing the unceremonious arrival, also began to laugh.

"Soldier, summon your superior," Joe said.

"Mister, there ain't no damn civilian gonna come in here an' start tellin' me what to do," the guard replied. "Most especial someone that's paradin' aroun' in his longjohns."

"I am not a civilian. I am Lieutenant Joseph Murchison, and this man is Private Seth Todd. We are the sole survivors of a boat explosion."

"I'm sorry, sir," the guard said, sobering quickly. "Mayhaps I'd better call the corporal of the guard."

"Yes, thank you," Joe replied wearily.

"Corporal of the guard, post number one!" the guard called over his shoulder, and the call was repeated until, working his way through the gathering crowd, the corporal of the guard arrived.

"Corporal, I am Lieutenant Murchison, this is Trooper Todd," Joe said to the corporal. "We are the only survivors of the wreck of the steamer *Western Angel*. Take me to the officer of the day."

"That won't be necessary, Lieutenant, I'm here," a captain said, arriving at that moment, also drawn by the crowd. "We got word yesterday that the *Western Angel* blew up, but we were told there were no survivors. I'm Captain Amos Barber." The captain was wearing a gold sash that looped over his left shoulder and cut across his chest at a diagonal, fastening at his right hip. This was the badge of office for the officer of the day.

Joe and Todd saluted as Joe reported, "Sir, I have the sad duty to report that Lieutenant William Dixon, also en route to Fort Berthold, died bravely while trying to save the life of another."

"Let's get the two of you fed and clothed," Amos Barber said. "Then you can render your entire report to Colonel Moreland, our post commander. Trooper Todd?"

"Yes, sir," Todd replied.

"Report to the commissary, Todd. Tell the quartermaster sergeant I said to feed you and to issue you new uniforms."

"Thank you, sir," Todd replied.

"Mr. Murchison, if you would come with me, I have some uniforms I think you can wear. They won't be a good fit, but I promise you, they will be better than what you have on."

Joe laughed. "That's a promise that shouldn't be all that hard to keep."

★★★

Three

MORNING REPORT:

Officers present for duty:	9
Doctors present for duty:	1
Veterinarians present for duty:	2
Enlisted men present for duty:	96
Officers on sick call:	1
Enlisted men on sick call:	11
Horses present for duty:	56
Horses presently unfit:	6
Horses unfit, or nearly so:	10
Horses serviceable:	40

GENERAL ORDERS, NO. 19:
Until further orders, mounted drill in the fore-
noon will be discontinued. Dismounted drill will
be substituted therefor. The horses of the command will be taken out to graze at 7 A.M. Recall
from grazing will be sounded at 10 A.M. One noncommissioned officer will be in charge of the
grazing detail.

SPECIAL ORDERS NO. 96:
By recommendation of Sec. Lieut. J. T. Murchison, endorsed by Capt. Amos R. Barber, Cmdng.

Off. D Troop, Third U.S. Cavalry, Private S. H.
Todd is hereby promoted to corporal.

By order of Col. A. B. Moreland,
Post Commandant
    For the Commander,   J. S. Canfield,
    Lieutenant and Assistant Adjutant General

When he finished his entries, Corporal Bobbins put his
pen back in the quill and blew on the pages to dry the
ink. Then, lifting the book carefully, he took it over to
the adjutant's desk.

"Here is the morning report, sir," he said.

Canfield took the ledger book without comment.

"Lieutenant Canfield, you reckon we'll be gettin' another cavalry troop here at Fort Berthold?"

"No."

"What's wrong with them people, Lieutenant? I
mean we only got us three line companies in this entire
fort. One of infantry, one of artillery, and one of cavalry. Why, if Lo was to decide he wanted to attack us,
we could scarce fight 'im off."

Corporal Bobbins used the word *Lo* to refer to the
Indians because that was what the line troops called
them. *Lo* was a sarcastic reference to "Lo, the poor
Indian!"—the opening line in English poet Alexander
Pope's poem, *An Essay on Man.*

"You do your job, Bobbins, and General Sully will
do his," Canfield said.

"Yes, sir, I meant no disrespect, sir," Bobbins replied, stung by Canfield's sarcasm.

Canfield took the morning report into Colonel
Moreland's office and showed it to him.

"Ah, good, we've made Trooper Todd a corporal, I
see," Moreland said.

"Yes, sir," Canfield said, "I hope we haven't made a
mistake in doing so, sir."

Moreland looked up. "What makes you think we
may have made a mistake? Do you think Todd doesn't
merit the rating?"

"Todd is very new to the post, Colonel. He and Lieutenant Murchison have only been here a little over a month. Others on post have been around a lot longer."

"Yes, and if any of them were fit to be promoted, they would already be corporals," Moreland replied. "Both of Todd's officers recommended him for promotion. That speaks very highly of him."

"Actually, sir, it was just Lieutenant Murchison who recommended him. Captain Barber did no more than endorse the recommendation. And Mr. Murchison . . ." Canfield let the sentence hang.

"What is it, John?" Moreland asked. "Is there something wrong?"

"Perhaps not, sir. But Lieutenant Murchison and Trooper Todd did go through a most trying ordeal together. Is it not possible that Mr. Murchison's judgment may be swayed by some sort of misplaced loyalty toward Todd?"

"Nonsense. I spoke with Sergeants Muldoon and Carney, and they heartily concurred with Lieutenant Murchison's recommendation. He has impressed his NCOs and the men with whom he works. I see no reason to withhold the stripes if the man clearly deserves them."

"I suppose not, sir," Canfield said. "I just hope he appreciates the rapidity with which he has been promoted."

"By the way," Colonel Moreland said, "I have asked Mr. Murchison to be Mrs. Moreland's and my guest for dinner this Friday evening. I would like for you to come, as well."

"I would be pleased to, sir."

"And, of course, do bring Mrs. Canfield," Colonel Moreland added. "She is an uncommonly handsome woman whose presence would enhance any dinner table." Moreland's eyes took on a glint that Lieutenant Canfield recognized only too well.

"I shall bring her, sir. Mrs. Canfield will be delighted. She so enjoys your dinners."

* * *

Over in the stables at that very moment, Sergeant Muldoon was sitting on an empty barrel, reading an old copy of *Harper's Weekly*.

"Here, now, listen to this," Sergeant Muldoon said to Sergeant Carney. Muldoon and Carney were supervising stable detail. Muldoon cleared his throat before he read aloud. "This here is from *Humors of the Day*. 'My notion of a wife at forty,' says this-here fella, 'is that a man should be able to change her, like a banknote, for two twenties.'" Sergeant Muldoon laughed aloud. "Do you get it?" he asked. "Change one forty-year-old woman for two twenty-year-old women? Ain't that a ripsnorter?"

"I get it," Carney said. He was looking through the door of the stable, across the quadrangle toward the low-lying line of officers' quarters on the opposite side. Like all other buildings of the fort, the officers' quarters were of the blockhouse design, with their back walls forming a part of the exterior walls of the fort. What was holding Sergeant Carney's attention, however, wasn't the architecture of the building, but Mrs. Canfield, who at that moment was sweeping the porch in front of officers' quarters number four.

There were only seven women on the post, and Lieutenant Canfield's wife, Dolly, was clearly the prettiest. She was of medium height, very slender, with light-blue eyes and hair as tawny as a mountain lion's coat in the spring.

"Well, what do you think about it?" Sergeant Muldoon asked. "Don't you think it would be a good idea to change one forty-year-old woman for two twenty-year-olds?"

"I'd give me a forty-year-old *and* two twenty-year-olds for that one right there," Carney said, nodding across the quadrangle.

Muldoon squirted out a stream of tobacco juice, then got up from his barrel and walked over to look across his friend's shoulder. "She's a fine-looking filly, all right," he agreed. "Lieutenant Canfield sure is a lucky man."

"She deserves better'n what she's got," Carney said, rubbing himself. "Hell, *I'm* better'n what she's got."

"You'd better watch that kind of talk, Carney," Muldoon cautioned. "You could wind up in the guardhouse."

As Dolly Canfield swept her front porch, unaware that she was being scrutinized, she thought about the new young lieutenant who had arrived last month. Ever since his arrival, Dolly had gone out of her way to be friendly with him, but Lieutenant Murchison didn't talk much. She didn't know if he was naturally that way, or if his shyness was a result of the ordeal he had gone through when his boat blew up and he nearly starved.

Mr. Murchison lived in the quarters next door to the Canfields', and one morning last week, while sweeping her porch, Dolly happened to look through the young lieutenant's window. He was standing at his wash basin without a shirt. She could see the thick mat of dark hair on his broad chest, which dwindled to a single line of hair on his flat stomach, dipping beneath the waistband of his trousers. Such an intimate view of him caused her to feel a sudden flash of heat, and she was forced to turn away to regain control of herself. Even now, the thought of that scene made her feel a twinge of sexual excitement.

Her conscience told her she should feel guilty about such thoughts, but she didn't feel guilty at all. In fact, after years of husbandly neglect on the part of Mr. Canfield, she was pleasantly surprised to learn she could still even feel a sense of excitement.

Six years ago Dolly was a schoolteacher back in Ohio. Her hometown of Dayton had just raised a new company of volunteers, and the city threw a parade and military ball in their honor. The ball was the most exciting event Dolly had ever attended, and it was there that she met First Lieutenant John S. Canfield.

John Canfield was being particularly honored in Dayton, for unlike the volunteers, he had already been bloodied in battle. An artillery officer, Lieutenant Canfield was at Fort Sumter when the very opening shots

of the war were fired. He was also there when Major
Anderson was forced to capitulate to General Beaure-
gard of the Confederate army.

Although there had been no casualties during the
actual bombardment of Fort Sumter, one of Lieutenant
Canfield's privates was killed when a cannon burst during a final salute to the flag. Those who were honoring
him in Dayton didn't know this, nor did they know that
Major Anderson had written a letter to the War Department in which he censured Canfield for "failing to
respond to the Confederate bombardment with effective cannonading, thus contributing to the early surrender of the stronghold." Lieutenant Canfield was also
cited for "improper maintenance of his artillery pieces,
causing one to burst while paying honors to the National Ensign, the resultant explosion killing Private
Daniel Hough and wounding five others."

The patriotic citizens of Dayton, Ohio, knew none of
that, so Lieutenant Canfield basked in their accolades
for an entire week, during which time he was Miss
Dolly Stewart's constant companion. When he asked
her to marry him, Dolly's senses were so befuddled by
the wartime excitement she accepted.

Dolly was fully prepared to be the loving wife at
home, rolling bandages and going to quiltings with
other war wives while exchanging beautiful letters with
a husband who was "in the field against the Rebels."
But Lieutenant Canfield didn't go back to the war. Instead, he was sent to Fort Berthold in the Dakota Territory, and he insisted that Dolly go with him.

Canfield sat out the war at Fort Berthold. Here,
there had been no glory, no sense of history, nor even
an opportunity to participate in the final victory cele-
brations when the war was won. Fort Berthold was
nothing but day after measured day of drudgery and
boredom, of freezing in the winter and blistering in the
summer. Their only connection with civilization was
through the mail and newspapers that the infrequent
riverboats brought them.

The marriage began to go sour almost from the very
beginning. When the excitement wore off, Lieutenant

Canfield found himself with a wife he really didn't need or want. He considered her excess baggage, and he began to treat her as such.

Dolly, not realizing she was fighting a battle that was already lost, tried hard to preserve the marriage. She really believed she was in love with her husband and at night she eagerly went to him. That was when she discovered that she had a healthy appetite for lovemaking. But even that proved to have an adverse effect because Dolly's enthusiastic response to John Canfield only antagonized him.

"No decent woman really enjoys this," he said in disgust one night when he perceived that she really *was* enjoying it. From that time on, Canfield was always a little wary of his wife, and he watched her as if she suffered from some terrible social disease that could, at any moment, drive her to an act of insanity.

Despite her sour marriage, Dolly Canfield was not a bitter woman. She could have easily succumbed to the travails of an unhappy marriage, but she did not. Instead, she was a vivacious woman who genuinely enjoyed life and liked people. She was quick to smile and slow to complain, and Lieutenant Canfield, of all who knew her, was the only one who did not recognize what a true gem Dolly was.

Corporal Todd, his new stripes sewn to his sleeves, sat at a table in a room at the rear of the sutler's store, writing a letter to his brother back in Virginia.

Dear Tom,

I'm sure you are surprised to hear from your long-lost brother, thinking, perhaps, that I must be dead. As you can tell by this letter, I am not dead. But neither am I ready to return to Virginia, since there is nothing for me there. I know you have offered to let me come home and work with you, and I am sure you would be most generous. But as I have no rightful claim to any of the land, neither do you have any obligation for my support. Please believe me when I say it is better this way.

Sometimes I think it would have been better had I had the good graces to have been killed at Antietam or Gettysburg or Sayler's Creek. Then I could be one of our fallen heroes, bringing honor to the family name instead of shame. But then, shame and I are no strangers, are we?

I now find myself a member of the same army that I once tried so desperately to destroy. Obviously there was no chance for me to get a commission based upon my background, so I enlisted in the ranks. I have just been promoted to corporal and as such am making a little more money than my bare needs. I will be sending some money to you each month. I know that you have no need for it—and that it is but a small percentage of the expenses you have incurred by adopting my daughter, Tamara, as your own child. But it is something I want to do, and I beg you to allow me to do it.

Tamara was only nine when I last saw her, still just a girl. She is fifteen now, a young woman. She must be beautiful in spirit as well as form.

My brother, you are daily in my prayers of thanksgiving that God provided me with someone who would, so freely, take on the burden of raising the daughter I so carelessly brought into this world. Should you care to answer this letter, I am known here as Corporal Seth Todd.

> Your loving brother,
> Todd Hamby.

There was some excitement just after lunch, when a riverboat arrived. The arrival of a riverboat was always an important event, for they brought tinned foodstuffs, military supplies, news, and mail.

The arrival of this boat was particularly fortuitous for Joe, because it took care of a problem he had been having with uniforms ever since his arrival at Fort Berthold. He was pleased to learn that the trunk he had

had shipped after him was on this afternoon's boat. And as the trunk had a full complement of uniforms, including his dress uniform, he would no longer have to borrow ill-fitting ones from Captain Barber.

The boat also brought him two letters. One of them was from his mother, the other from Sally Delano. This was his first letter from her, although he had written her two, the second one dispatched as soon as he had arrived at Fort Berthold to tell her of his ordeal. Choosing her letter to read first, he sat down on an upturned barrel and opened the envelope:

Dear Joseph:

There! I am bold enough to address you by your first name. And, since we are now long-distance friends (two letters from you! I can hardly believe my good fortune!), I think it is high time you call me Sally. If it makes you uncomfortable to address me so, then think of me as your "little sister," for surely you would not hesitate to call your own sister by her Christian name.

How exciting your second letter to me was! And yet what a terrible ordeal it must have been for you to survive a steamboat explosion and then nearly starve to death, finally to be rescued by a savage Indian! I went to church the moment I received your letter and offered up prayers of thanksgiving for your safe delivery.

Joseph, I cannot help but think of your friend and classmate, poor Mr. Dixon. How tragic that he should die while attempting to save the life of another. But what laud and honor shall attend to his name forever. It says in the Bible, "No greater love hath man than this. That he give up his life for a friend." It would appear that Lieutenant Dixon was just such a man—a man to be compared with the saints and martyrs of old.

You said in your first letter that Lieutenant Dixon wanted to be president of the United States some day. You also said that you thought he would have been a good one. Because of the noble way in which he died, I believe that as well. But now we will never know, because he has been taken from us.

How different would this world be if Abraham Lincoln had been killed when he was a young man? Or Thomas Jefferson? Or George Washington? Have you considered that the death of Mr. Dixon may have brought about just as profound a change in the direction our country is to go? Unfortunately, we will never know. For such contemplations are like looking at the machinations of God.

I can't tell you how pleased I am you are writing to me, and I promise to keep up my end of the correspondence.

Your friend,
Sally Delano

Joe put Sally's letter in his tunic pocket, then opened the letter from his mother:

Dere Son,

Thank you for ritin to us to tell us we shud not worry none about the stemebote that blode up and sanked on the river. We wasnt none worried because we didnt know you was on that stemebote. Then, after you told us, Mr. Turner said he remembered reedin in the Montgomery County News about a stemebote that blode up, and when he went back to look it up it was the same one you was on.

God was merceyfull and for that you should offer Him yore prayers as me and yore pa do and also for yore safety which is our big worry what with the Indins and all.

Me and yore pa are doin well but our hearts ache for the day when we can see you agin. The wheat give us a good crop this yere but the corn was spotty.

With much love
Yore ma and pa

FRIDAY MORNING

When Dolly went back into the house after her morning ritual of sweeping the front porch, she found her husband standing over the chest of drawers pouring water into a wash basin. His tunic was off and his yellow galluses hung down to either side of his blue trousers, forming a yellow loop with the broad red stripe that ran down the sides of his legs.

"You were out there long enough," Canfield said. He set the pitcher down and began stropping his razor. "What kept you?"

"I swept the porch in front of Mr. Murchison's quarters, too."

"He can get a private to do that," Canfield said. He soaped his face, then reached around with one hand to draw his skin taut, while with the other he pulled the razor through the lather. "It's not seemly for the wife of the adjutant to do manual labor."

"For heaven's sake, John, sweeping a porch is hardly manual labor. Wives have been doing it for years," Dolly replied. She opened the door to the little potbellied stove and tossed in some more wood, then held her hands over it to take away some of the chill of being outside.

"Yes, for their own household," Canfield said. He dipped his razor in the water, then raised it back to his face. "Not for every stray officer on the post."

"I was merely fulfilling a Christian obligation," Dolly said.

"If you were less concerned with Christian obligation and more concerned with your social responsibility, we would be better off," Canfield said. He studied his face in the mirror. He had a square jawline, with a beard so heavy that it required him to shave twice a day. His hair was dark and curly, and he had thick eyebrows over brown eyes. "And speaking of social responsibility, you have not forgotten, have you, that we are to dine with Colonel and Mrs. Moreland tonight?"

"No, I haven't forgotten. I'll be ready."

"See that you are." Canfield slipped his razor in the

water, then raised it back to his face. "I have heard rumors that someone in General Sully's command is to be promoted to captain next month."

"Do you think it will be you?" Dolly asked innocently.

"Why *shouldn't* it be me?" Canfield replied, snapping the question at her as if she had challenged him. "After all, there are those from my same class at West Point who are now majors and lieutenant colonels, while I remain a first lieutenant. All because I was forced to sit out the war in this godforsaken place. The War Department is punishing me because we surrendered at Fort Sumter. Well, it wasn't I who surrendered. It was Major Anderson. I am an artillery officer, for Christ's sake. Good Lord, the use they made of artillery during the war. I could have made general."

Dolly checked the impulse to remind him that three times during the late war, the War Department had published circulars that would allow artillery officers, at their own request, to transfer back East. Canfield had never taken advantage of the opportunity, saying that his job out here was too important to abandon on a whim.

Canfield pulled his galluses up over his shoulders, then put on his jacket with the red epaulets and the single silver bar, denoting first lieutenant.

"What will you wear tonight?" Canfield asked as he buttoned up his single-breasted tunic.

Smiling, Dolly opened the armoire and pulled out a blue dress. "I thought I would wear this," she said excitedly. "I just finished making it, and I have been looking forward to an occasion when I could wear it."

"I want you to wear the red dress."

"No," Dolly said. "I wore that to the sutler's dance last month, don't you remember? Besides, Colonel Moreland stared at me all night."

"He liked the dress," Canfield said. "He told me so."

"He didn't like the dress," Dolly replied. "He liked where the dress left off. I felt as if his eyes were burning my bosom. I was never so uncomfortable in my life.

That dress is too low-cut. I don't care whether the colonel likes it or not, I won't wear it again."

"Being nice to the colonel might make all the difference in the world as to who gets promoted now," Canfield said.

"John, I will not play the jezebel with Colonel Moreland just so you can be promoted."

"I'm not asking you to play the jezebel," Canfield said. "All I'm asking you to do is to make a good impression on him. Be nice to him, that's all."

"You can't be nice to a lecherous old reprobate like Colonel Moreland. I feel sorry for his wife. Why she stays with him, I'll never know. And you, John. I can't believe I am hearing you say this. You are always so concerned that I be the proper lady. You even protested when I went riding last month."

"You were wearing pants and you rode astride," Canfield said. "Of course I protested, as would any husband concerned about his wife's reputation. But you are misunderstanding everything. What you wear in the discreet company of a private dinner and what you wear on the parade grounds are two different things. Now, I want you to wear the red dress, and I want you to be nice to the colonel."

"How nice?" Dolly asked. She didn't like the way the conversation was going, and she was purposely baiting him.

"I want you to be very nice," Canfield said. "Everything is considered when a promotion is at stake. *Everything*, do you understand? It's not only a man's performance of duty but other things, as well. It is important that the colonel like you. That's why everything has to be just right."

"And if the colonel insists upon staring, I am to grant him an eyeful?"

"You are an attractive woman, Dolly. I would think you would enjoy the appreciative stares of a man."

"What makes you think I would enjoy the lustful gaze of a lecher?" Dolly snapped.

"You forget, Dolly, that I know the kind of woman you really are," Canfield said flatly. "Your true nature is known to me and has been known to me since the day we were married. You are the type of woman who takes indecent pleasure in pursuits of the flesh."

"John, that isn't fair!" Dolly said, stung by his remark. "You are my husband! If I respond to you in bed it is because—"

"It is because you are a woman given to prurient behavior," Canfield interrupted. He laughed a small, evil laugh. "Do you think I flatter myself that you love me, my dear? I know that your heart is as empty of love for me as mine is for you. The pleasure you take from me in our nuptial bed you could take from any man. Now, I am merely giving you the opportunity to use your wantonness to our advantage. I insist that you wear the red dress, and I will not discuss this matter any further."

"Very well," Dolly said. "I shall wear that dress, and I shall put myself on display for the colonel. But remember, John, you asked me to do this."

"I thought you might see it my way," Canfield said with a sneer as he put on his hat and prepared to leave. "Don't wait lunch for me. I shall take my noon meal in the officers' mess."

Dolly watched her husband leave. Then she walked over to the armoire and took out the red dress, holding it up to look at it. Suddenly her anger moved her to an act of impetuousness. She removed the dress she was wearing, then her camisole. She slipped the red dress over her head and pulled it down over her bare breasts. The neck of the dress was cut so low that if she put her arms together and leaned forward, a careful observer would see not only the creamy tops of her breasts but perhaps even get a titillating glimpse of her nipples.

John wanted her to be nice to the colonel? If she were any nicer, she would be stark naked!

Four

That afternoon another boat arrived, the second in the same week. There was no mail from Sally, but Joe did get a letter from his old commanding officer back in New York. Captain Kirby, knowing that Joe enjoyed baseball, sent him an old copy of the *New York Mercury,* containing an article about a baseball match.

"The gentlemen from Philadelphia won the contest," Captain Kirby wrote, "but the newspaper man who wrote the article, Harry Chadwick, confided to me that had the New Yorkers a player of your caliber, they no doubt would have emerged victorious."

In another part of the newspaper was an article about a party given by a Mr. James Roosevelt. Among the names Joe found in a list of the party guests was Sara Delano's.

Joe interrupted his reading of the newspaper when he heard the bugler blowing officers' call.

"Lieutenant Murchison, sir," Sergeant Muldoon called back to him. "Did you hear the call?"

"Yes, thank you, Sergeant, I heard," Joe answered, folding the newspaper and laying it aside. This was an unscheduled officers' call, and he wondered about its purpose. Leaving Sergeant Muldoon in charge, he started toward post headquarters.

Out on the quadrangle three artillery crews were going through a "dry shooting exercise," with their twenty-four pounder fieldpieces. They were moving the guns around by horse teams, unlimbering them and setting them up, then loading them with ball but no powder. After that they would tip the barrel down so that the ball rolled out, hitch the gun to its team, then start the process all over again. The lieutenant who had been supervising the dry shooting exercise now left a sergeant in charge as he joined the other officers, all of whom were hurrying across the parade grounds from various points about the fort to respond to the bugler's call.

When Joe and the other officers went inside the headquarters building, Colonel Moreland was standing by the wall, looking at a large map of the Dakota Territory. The captain of the just-arrived riverboat was standing beside him.

"Thank you for coming, gentlemen," the colonel said, turning to greet his officers when the last one had arrived. It was a gratuitous courtesy, for the bugle had been blown and the officers had no choice but to report. "Failure to repair" was a court-martial offense.

Moreland's hair had been dark at one time, but now it was liberally dusted with gray. He had a round, owl-like face, made even more owllike by his beakish nose and the large oval glasses he wore. He nodded in the direction of the boat captain, a short, stout man with sideburns and chin whiskers. "Gentlemen, this is Captain Ethridge. He brought the steamer *Lucy B* in today."

Captain Ethridge nodded.

Colonel Moreland looked over at his cavalry commander. "Captain Barber, you may be aware that we were expecting twenty remounts for your troop."

"Yes, sir," the cavalry officer replied.

"Well, they didn't get here. Captain Ethridge made it as far as this point"—Moreland pointed at the map, to a spot on the river—"then he put in to shore to take on some wood and allow the horses to graze. While there, he was attacked by Wind in His Hair. Two of Captain Ethridge's men were killed, and every horse was stolen."

"We lost *all* the horses, sir?" Barber asked.

Captain Ethridge felt the need to defend himself.

"We didn't see the heathen bastards until they were upon us," he said. "We managed to fight them off, but not until they got what they came for."

"You can understand, I'm sure, gentlemen," Moreland continued, "what a serious situation this is. Now we are not only denied the use of those horses, but Lo is riding high, wide, and handsome, thanks to the U.S. Army."

There were a few angry curses from the officers.

"Believe me, I am as angry as you are," Moreland said. "But in the end, it may work to our advantage, for I have a plan that will not only recover the horses, it will also, I believe, trap the heathens who stole them. Gentlemen, this post is going to be a beehive of activity for the rest of the day. We are making all preparations to leave in pursuit of Wind in His Hair. I want the wagons loaded and rations and ammunition issued."

"Excuse me, sir," Captain Barber interrupted, "but if we make our plans so openly, will our intentions not be known to the Indians in the village?"

"I'm sure they will be, Captain."

Barber pointed toward the front gate. "Colonel, I know the Indians just outside our gate are supposed to be friendly, but isn't there a chance that some of them might be equally as friendly to Fool Dog or Wind in His Hair?"

"Oh, I hope so, and I hope word of what we are doing gets to them," Colonel Moreland said, grinning broadly. "Especially to Wind in His Hair. You see, Captain Barber, that's all part of the plan. Tomorrow morning at dawn we will throw open the gates and make a big show of sending out the cavalry. We'll have trumpets blowing and flags waving. You and your troops will make a big, noisy circle, and then you will come right back to the fort."

"That's all, sir?" Barber said.

"That's all, as far as your part of the plan is concerned. The rest depends upon Lieutenant Canfield." Moreland looked at Canfield. "Lieutenant Canfield, very early tomorrow morning, while it is still dark, you will leave the fort in command of one platoon of cavalry."

Barber looked surprised. "I beg your pardon, sir, but did you say you are putting Canfield in charge of a cavalry platoon?"

"That's what I said," Colonel Moreland answered.

"But shouldn't it be under the command of Mr. Murchison?"

"You would not deny Lieutenant Canfield this opportunity to prove himself, would you, Captain Barber? But if it makes you feel any better, I will be sending Mr. Murchison with Lieutenant Canfield. That way there will be a cavalry officer in the field." Moreland looked over at Joe. "I'm sure Lieutenant Canfield will be able to count on you for support, will he not, Mr. Murchison?"

"I'll help in whatever way I can, sir," Joe said, disappointed that he would not be leading the platoon on this, his first scout.

"Lieutenant Canfield, it is very important that you have the men leave behind everything that isn't absolutely necessary," Moreland continued. "I want nothing that will rattle or make noise. The Indians in the village will be sleeping at that hour of the morning, and I don't want them to see you go. Slip through their camp as quietly as you can, then head for Big Knife Creek. I want you and your men there by sunup." Moreland consulted his almanac. "The sun rises tomorrow at seven thirty-five. Will you make it in time?"

"We'll be there, sir," Canfield promised.

"Good. I must impress upon all of you that this is a complex plan that depends upon precise coordination and proper execution. You are the hammer, Mr. Canfield." Moreland looked over at the other captains. "Captains Taggert and Carter, you are the anvil. Before dawn and under cover of darkness, you will take your infantry company and your artillery battery down to the base of the bluff and load them onto the *Lucy B.* As soon as your men are loaded, have them get out of sight and stay out of sight. When Captain Barber and his cavalry leave in the morning, the Indians will be watching them. That diversion should be enough to allow Captain Ethridge to get his boat under way without Lo knowing that you and your men are aboard. You will then proceed downriver until you reach the point where Big Knife Creek empties into the Missouri River. There, you will off-load and take up positions for an ambuscade."

"Very good, sir," Taggert said.

"You won't have any trouble getting your guns into position, will you, Captain Carter?"

"No trouble at all, sir," Carter replied.

Moreland put his hand back on the map.

"Captain Barber, with you and the cavalry riding in a big circle up here, the Indians will be forced down along this natural draw to the vicinity of Big Knife Creek. That draw is almost exactly halfway between where Lieutenant Canfield will be with the cavalry and Captain Taggert and Captain Carter will be with the infantry and artillery. Wind in His Hair will be trapped in between.

"The whole plan depends upon precise timing. Which means, Lieutenant Canfield, that at exactly nine o'clock tomorrow morning, I want you and Mr. Murchison and all your men to start moving along Big Knife Creek toward Captains Taggert and Carter. Your mission will be to drive the Indians along the Big Knife until they are forced into the ambush."

Moreland looked up from the map with his eyes blazing in excitement. "Wind in His Hair and his warriors will be sitting ducks. When they come into artillery range, we'll cut them to pieces. Gentlemen, there are some officers who insist that artillery is not effective against the Indians. I contend that it is not a matter of ineffective artillery, it is a matter of ineffective commanders."

"I agree, sir!" Canfield said. "And your plan is brilliant!"

"Lo won't know what hit him," Captain Taggert added.

"Colonel Barber?" Colonel Moreland said. "Why is it that you haven't commented?" Moreland was using the brevet rank Barber had attained during the war. It was a courtesy use; Barber could still be addressed as *colonel* even though his actual military rank was captain.

"Colonel Moreland, I'm a little concerned about Lieutenant Canfield's platoon," Barber said. "As you may know, sir, Big Knife Creek is cut in a dozen or more places by draws and sloughs and gullies. What would keep Wind in His Hair from going up one of those draws and getting away? Or worse, setting up his own ambush for Canfield and his men?"

"We will depend upon shock and speed to keep Wind in His Hair off guard," Colonel Moreland said.

"I beg your pardon, sir?"

"Shock and speed, Colonel Barber. I shouldn't have to explain that to you. You are a cavalry officer, aren't you? You above everyone else should understand that Canfield's mission is one of classic cavalry deployment. Shock and speed." Moreland turned to Canfield. "However, Lieutenant Canfield, Captain Barber is right in suggesting that those cross gullies might cause you trouble. To minimize that possibility, it is absolutely imperative that once you get started, you move forward with all deliberate speed. Do you understand me? All deliberate speed."

"Yes, sir, I understand," Canfield replied.

"Colonel," Barber said, "request that Lieutenant Canfield and I change places."

"No, that won't work. Lo might get suspicious if he sees an entire cavalry troop being deployed with anyone but you at its head. When the Indians watch you and the cavalry ride out tomorrow, they must think they are seeing the real thing."

"What about the fact that it will be a platoon light?" Captain Taggert asked. "They may yet know something is amiss."

Moreland stroked his chin for a moment. "Good point," he said. "Captain Carter, you will supply Captain Barber with enough mounted men from your battery to bring his troop up to full strength."

"Yes, sir," Carter answered.

Moreland rubbed his hands together. "All right, gentlemen, get the word spread around the post, and let's get this operation going."

As the officers left the post headquarters, Barber walked with Joe toward the stables. "I don't like the idea of sending one of my platoons out under Canfield's command," the captain growled. "Joe, you be careful tomorrow."

"Yes, sir, I will."

"And before you leave in the morning, I want you to check the men, horses, and equipment, personally," Barber went on. "I don't want to leave anything up to Canfield."

"I will be most thorough, sir," Joe promised.

Amos Barber removed his hat and ran his hand through his receding hair. He wasn't a West Point graduate, but he was an experienced cavalry officer, having been a lieutenant colonel in command of a squadron of the Tenth Michigan Cavalry during the war. "I tell you what I'm going to do," Barber said. "I'm going to let you take Sergeant Muldoon with you. He's our most experienced noncommissioned officer. Maybe between the two of you you can keep Canfield out of trouble."

"Yes, sir," Joe said. "Thank you, sir."

Preparations for the mission to be conducted the next day did not prevent Lieutenant Colonel and Mrs. Moreland from hosting the dinner that evening, as planned. The two ladies and three officers dined by candlelight in the commandant's quarters, serenaded during their meal by a quartet of enlisted musicians who were paid a gratuity by Moreland to gather outside the dining room window and sing their renditions of "The Girl I Left Behind Me" and "Lorena."

The three officers were in their dress uniforms. Lieutenant Colonel Moreland, being a field-grade officer, wore a double-breasted tunic. Lieutenant Canfield's and Joe's jackets were single-breasted. As the officers represented three different branches, each uniform was piped with a different color. Moreland's uniform was trimmed in blue, as he was an infantry officer; Canfield's uniform was trimmed in red, for artillery; while the breast piping, leg stripe, and epaulets of Joe's uniform were yellow, for cavalry. Joe was a second lieutenant, which meant his epaulets were bare. Canfield's fringed epaulets had one silver bar, while Moreland's displayed a silver leaf. All three officers wore a crimson silk net sash beneath their saber belts.

The women were also elegantly dressed. Mrs. Moreland wore a "full-dress toilette" of coral and ivory. Ordinarily a simple dinner invitation would not call for such elaborate dress, but out here, Joe had already learned, the slightest occasion was used as an excuse to, in the words of Mrs. Moreland, "bring a little civilization to this bleak wilderness."

In accordance with her husband's wishes, Dolly had worn the low-cut red dress. And, true to her own plan, she wore it sans camisole. As a result, when she leaned over Joe to serve the apple pie that had been her contribution to the dinner, she afforded him a long look at the creamy tops of her breasts all the way down to her nipples.

Of course, Joe wasn't the only one treated to such a view. Colonel Moreland had been unable to take his eyes off her all evening long.

"Another piece of apple pie, Mr. Murchison?" Dolly asked, for this would be his second piece.

"I really shouldn't, Mrs. Canfield, but it is so good that I can't resist it. Yes, thank you," Joe replied.

"Aren't you cold, my dear?" Mrs. Moreland asked with a disapproving glance at Dolly's dress.

"Cold? Nonsense, how can anyone be cold?" Colonel Moreland said. "You've built the fire up to where it is so hot we can scarcely breathe."

"I was thinking more along the lines of providing the poor child with a shawl than in making the fire any hotter," Mrs. Moreland suggested.

Dolly realized then what Mrs. Moreland was suggesting, and she became very self-conscious about her dress. She knew she was making Mrs. Moreland very uncomfortable, which had not been her intention. Like

Eve confronted in the Garden, Dolly felt a sudden sense of shame.

"Yes, thank you," she said, putting her hand to her bosom. "I believe I would appreciate something to put over my shoulders."

Mrs. Moreland smiled broadly at her victory and, in victory, became most gracious. "It is a lovely dress, dear, but if men only knew what we had to go through to look nice for them. Whalebone stays, weighted skirts, burning up in the summer and freezing in the winter—all in the name of fashion."

Dolly looked at the older woman then, wondering if Mrs. Moreland suspected that she had worn this dress on specific instructions from her own husband to please Mrs. Moreland's husband. Then, seeing the look of long-suffering in Mrs. Moreland's face, she knew Mrs. Moreland *did* know.

Aware that the younger woman had just read her secret, Mrs. Moreland cleared her throat and smiled at Joe. "Mr. Murchison, you have been at our little post for nearly a month now," she said. "What do you think of duty on the frontier?"

"I find frontier duty very exciting," Joe said.

"But don't you miss the niceties of civilization?"

"There are some things I miss, yes, ma'am. But I shall learn to cope as has everyone else," Joe replied. "I must say, by the way, that you have done much to make your quarters attractive. Compared to the homey touches you have brought to your quarters, I may as well be living in the stable."

"Most bachelor officers live in quarters like yours," Mrs. Moreland said. "Wait until you get married. You will be amazed by what a woman's touch can do to even the drabbest of quarters."

"Speaking of marriage, tell me, Mr. Murchison, do you have you a lady friend back home?" Dolly asked sweetly.

"Dolly, that is not a question you ask a young officer," Canfield scolded.

"I only ask because everyone on the post is aware .

that earlier this week, he received not one but two letters from a certain young lady in New York."

Joe's cheeks flamed in embarrassment. He had not known that the inventory of his personal mail was such common knowledge.

"You are wondering how your personal life can be the subject for everyone's gossip, aren't you?" Mrs. Moreland asked, reading Joe's mind. "I'm afraid it is something you will have to get used to. You see, in a remote post such as this, we are like one big family, sticking our noses into everyone else's business. It will be disconcerting to you at first, but you must forgive us, for there is little else to occupy us. I hope you aren't offended."

"No, ma'am, I'm not offended," Joe replied. "But I'm afraid all the speculators are going to be disappointed. The letters were from a Miss Sally Delano. And although she is a friend, she is not what you would call my lady friend."

"I am sure Miss Delano must be lovely," Dolly said. "And why shouldn't she be? You are such a handsome young man, you could clearly have any girl of your choice." She smiled coquettishly and put her finger to her cheek, accenting the dimple she considered her prettiest feature. "Oh, dear me," she said. "Whatever has happened to my manners? I assure you, Lieutenant, I am not normally such a brazen person. I am a schoolteacher from Ohio, well-versed in proper deportment. I beg you to forgive my impertinence."

"There is nothing to forgive," Joe answered. "But I think I should tell you that Miss Delano is, in fact, quite young. She is still just a schoolgirl."

"Never underestimate the intensity of a schoolgirl crush, Lieutenant Murchison. They can be most formidable," Mrs. Moreland suggested.

"I'm sure they can be," Joe mumbled, not knowing what else to say and unwilling to tell them that Miss Delano was still just fourteen.

"My dear, both Mr. Murchison and Lieutenant Canfield have full days tomorrow. I think perhaps we had better stop this inquisition and let them go."

"Yes," Canfield said, standing quickly. Joe stood with him. "Mrs. Moreland, I thank you very much for the lovely evening. You have been a most gracious hostess."

"And may I add my own thanks, ma'am," Joe said.

"You were delightful company," Mrs. Moreland replied.

As Colonel Moreland walked them to the front door, he said, "John, I wonder if you would step into my office with me for a few moments? I want to go over a few final things with you."

"Yes, sir, of course," Canfield replied. "As soon as I see Mrs. Canfield home."

"I'm sure Mr. Murchison wouldn't mind escorting your wife home," Colonel Moreland said. "After all, his quarters are just next door to yours."

"Lieutenant Murchison?" Canfield said to Joe.

"It would be my pleasure, sir," Joe replied. He offered his arm to Dolly, who smiled broadly and took it. With a final good-bye to Colonel and Mrs. Moreland, Dolly allowed Joe to walk with her. Both Canfield and Colonel Moreland stared after them until they were swallowed up by the darkness. Then Colonel Moreland broke the silence.

"It will just take a few minutes," he said, motioning for Canfield to follow him to his office. Once in the office, Colonel Moreland lit a lamp. Then, offering Canfield a chair, he pulled a bottle of whiskey from the bottom drawer. Pouring two glasses, he gave one of them to Canfield.

"This operation tomorrow is very important," Moreland said.

"Yes, sir, I'm sure it is."

Moreland waved his hand and shook his head. "No, I don't think you realize just how important it is," he said. "There is talk of combining Fort Berthold and Fort Stevenson, making one post out of the two."

"Which post will survive, sir?"

"Ah!" Moreland said, holding up a finger. "That is the question, isn't it? That is the question." Moreland finished his drink, then refilled it.

"If Fort Berthold survives, we will go from a small post of three companies to a large post of three regiments. That would undoubtedly mean an eagle for me and captain's bars, maybe more, for you."

"More, sir? You mean there is a possibility I would skip over the rank of captain?"

"Why not? Certainly it has been done before," Moreland answered. "Hell, John, it could even lead to a lieutenant colonel's rank for you. On the other hand, if Fort Stevenson survives and Fort Berthold is closed, there is nothing ahead but ignominy for both of us. I will no doubt be forced into an early retirement, and you will remain a first lieutenant, perhaps for the rest of your military career."

"I assure you, sir, I will do all in my power to make tomorrow's mission a successful one," Canfield said soberly.

"I am sure you will."

Having walked Mrs. Canfield home, Joe was now in his own quarters. He lit a lamp and took off his sash, saber, and jacket. Then he began laying out the field uniform and equipment he would need for the next morning. The platoon was to assemble at four A.M., and such an early start meant he would need to get to bed soon.

He had not yet extinguished his lamp when a knock sounded on the door. Thinking it might be Lieutenant Canfield with some last-minute instructions, he opened the door without bothering to put on his jacket. He was surprised to see Dolly Canfield standing there.

"Mrs. Canfield! What are you doing here?"

"Aren't you going to ask me in, Joseph?" Dolly asked.

"Is something wrong?"

"Yes, something is wrong. I am freezing to death, and I don't particularly want to be seen standing out here, begging you to let me in," she said. "After all, how would such a thing look?"

"Well, I . . . uh, yes. Yes, of course. Come in," Joe invited.

As Dolly stepped into Joe's tiny quarters, Joe stuck his head out the door, then looked up and down the porch and across the quadrangle to see if anyone was watching. Although he didn't see anyone, he was well aware that someone could be out in the darkness of the quadrangle. And though he couldn't see them, they would be able to see him, backlit as he was by the lamp in his quarters. As soon as Joe stepped back inside, he closed his door, then reached for his jacket.

"Silly boy, you don't need to get dressed for me," Dolly said. She held something out, wrapped in a piece of cloth. "I'll only be here for a second. I brought this to you."

"What is it?"

"Another piece of the apple pie you seemed to enjoy so," Dolly said. "John hardly appreciates my cooking, and I certainly wouldn't want to throw this away. Dried apples are so dear."

"Mrs. Canfield, you shouldn't have."

"Oh, I know, it's all so terribly wicked, isn't it?" Dolly replied with a conspiratorial smile. "But I wanted to do it, so I did it. And if we keep it our little secret, no one will be the wiser. You will keep it our secret, won't you?" she purred.

"I won't speak of it," Joe replied.

"Good. Oh, my!" Dolly suddenly exclaimed, seeing a scar at the base of Joe's neck. She put her fingers on the raised puff of purple flesh. Somehow, though Joe didn't understand how it could be possible, Dolly's fingers had the effect of being hot and cold at the same time. "What a terrible scar," she murmured. She was now so close to him that he could feel her breath on his cheek. It was minty, and he realized she must have quickly chewed a mint leaf just before stepping over here, as if she knew she might be within a breath of him. "Did you get this when the steamboat exploded?"

"No," Joe answered. "I got it when I was a little boy, jumping in the barn."

Dolly chuckled. "What a darling little boy you must have been," she said. "And jumping around in the barn

like that. I'm sure you were a handful for your
mother."

"If Lieutenant Canfield returns and finds you absent,
this will be the first place he will look," Joe warned.

"Oh?" Dolly replied, raising one eyebrow. "And
what if he does look in here? Are we going to be doing
something that would shock him?"

"No, no! Of course not," Joe replied quickly. "I
didn't mean anything untoward was going to happen."

"Much the pity," Dolly said easily. She sighed. "I am
making you nervous, aren't I?"

"Yes," Joe admitted.

"Joseph, you are such a frightened little boy," Dolly
said, smiling again. "Very well. I shall go and leave you
in peace." She started toward the door, then suddenly
and unexpectedly, she put her right hand behind Joe's
head and pulled him to her. She kissed him full on the
lips, opening her mouth as she did so. By the time Joe
recovered from the shock of what she was doing and
began, almost involuntarily, to return the kiss, it was
over.

"Joseph," Dolly whispered. "Dear, sweet Joseph.
Please don't think me evil." She opened the door and
stepped outside before he could reply.

Dolly was already in bed when Lieutenant Canfield returned from his impromptu meeting with Colonel
Moreland. The idea that he might get promoted, and
not just to captain but perhaps to an even higher rank,
filled him with exhilaration.

"Are you awake, Dolly?" he asked as he sat down on
the side of the bed and began removing his boots.

"Yes," she replied.

"You will never believe what Colonel Moreland just
told me," he said excitedly. "There is a chance that
Fort Berthold will expand to three regiments." He continued to undress. "And if so, I am sure to command
one of the regiments. As a major—or maybe even as a
lieutenant colonel. Think of it, Dolly! A lieutenant colonel!"

"Then I did well for you tonight?" Dolly asked.

"You did very well," Canfield admitted. He was almost giddy. "Colonel Moreland was positively drooling."

"Do you like having other men drool over me, John?"

"No, of course not. But this was different. This was for my career."

"For your career?"

"Yes. The little show you put on tonight was harmless enough, but it might very well get me promoted."

"John, if going to bed with Colonel Moreland would get you promoted, would you want me to do so?"

"No, of course not."

"I think you would."

"No, I wouldn't."

"Yes, you would," Dolly said. "And I think you would want to watch."

"My God, woman! I've never known anyone as brazen as you," Canfield said. He was now completely naked, and he reached out in the dark for the hook where his nightshirt normally hung. "Where is my nightshirt?" he asked.

"I have it here, under the covers, keeping it warm for you."

"Give it to me."

"Get in bed to put it on. That way you won't freeze."

"Give it to me. I'm freezing now."

"Get in bed," Dolly said again.

Sighing, Canfield slipped under the covers and, almost as soon as he did so, he felt his wife's naked flesh press against him. She reached over to grab him.

"Woman!" he gasped. "What are you doing?"

"You had me showing my breasts to the entire post tonight, John," Dolly said in a husky voice. "Don't tell me you don't appreciate the fact that Colonel Moreland was enjoying the view. Besides, didn't my breasts do what you wanted them to do?" She began to stroke him, gently, and he felt himself growing erect.

"You shouldn't be doing this," Canfield said. "It isn't right."

"Ah, but think about it, John. Wouldn't Colonel

Moreland like to be here now? Wouldn't he like to have one hand here?"

She placed his hand on her breast, and while her skin felt soft and hot to him, her nipple was a hard little button under his palm.

"And wouldn't he like to feel this?" she asked, putting his other hand between her legs. She was incredibly well-lubricated.

"Woman, what has gotten into you?" Canfield asked.

"Don't blame me, John. If you are going to make me show myself like a brazen whore, then you shouldn't be surprised if it affects me. Just be thankful that I'm sharing my bed with you, not someone else."

Dolly was stroking him harder and faster now, and, no longer able to resist her, he began groaning in pleasure. When she knew he was ready, she pulled him over onto her, then spread her legs and lifted her knees slightly to facilitate his entry. When he went down into her, he felt as if he were dipping himself into a vat of hot wax.

Dolly closed her eyes as he made love to her. She let herself drift with the pleasant sensations he was evoking while, in her mind's eye, she wasn't seeing him in the dark above her. She was seeing Joe Murchison's naked chest. It wasn't her husband she was feeling in her, it was the young, virile lieutenant who lived next door.

Then, when she felt the orgasm happening, she let herself go, moaning and screaming as wave after wave of sensation broke over her. And if her husband disapproved of such wanton behavior, he was in no condition to protest, for he, too, was caught up in sexual paroxysms, groaning his own release as he thrust himself into her deeper and faster until the final burst left him spent and complete.

★★★

Five

It was four A.M. Joe would not allow any lanterns to be lit, so his platoon had to ready themselves by the dim light from the stars. The air was cold, and as the men and horses breathed, their breath formed vapor wraiths to curl about them.

Lieutenant Canfield had not yet shown, so Joe and Sergeant Muldoon were seeing to the preparations themselves, moving around, making last-minute checks of horses, men, and equipment. When Joe saw Corporal Todd, he stopped.

"What are you doing here?" he asked. "I thought you were in the second platoon."

Todd smiled. "Yes, sir, I was," he replied. "But I asked Captain Barber to let me come with you, and he did."

Joe put his hand on Todd's shoulder. "I'm glad to have you with me."

He continued to look over the platoon, examining arms and ammunition, girths, bits, and bridles, as well as the condition of the horses' hooves.

"Tenshut!" one of the men suddenly said, and everyone came to attention. Joe turned to see Captain Barber, his troop commander, coming toward them.

"Good morning, Colonel," Joe said, using his brevet rank. "You didn't have to get out of bed."

"I didn't want to let you and your men get away without wishing you good luck," Barber replied.

"Thank you, sir."

"Is Canfield here yet?"

"No, sir."

Barber pulled out his pocket watch and looked at it. "If the son of a bitch isn't here in five minutes, take the platoon out without him," he ordered.

"But Colonel Moreland said—"

"I'll square it with Moreland," Barber interrupted. "He's the one who insisted that the plan had to be precise to work. If this platoon is late getting into position, the whole operation will fall apart."

"Yes, sir."

"Listen, Joe, could I have a private word with you?" Barber asked.

"Yes, sir, of course." Joe followed Barber over to the edge of the barn, wondering why he was being so secretive.

"I saw you last night," Barber whispered when they were alone.

Joe looked confused. "I beg your pardon, sir. You saw what?"

"I saw Dolly Canfield go into your quarters."

"Then you must have also seen her leave, not more than two minutes later, sir," Joe replied quickly. "She brought me a piece of the pie served at Colonel Moreland's dinner last night."

"Joe, you don't have to explain anything to me," Captain Barber said easily. "You think I and every other officer—hell, every enlisted man as well—haven't looked at that woman and wondered . . ." He let the sentence hang. "But that's neither here nor there. The point I'm trying to make is, Fort Berthold is a small post. A very, very small post. There is nothing—absolutely nothing—that can go on without becoming common knowledge in a matter of hours. You are a young officer at the dawn of what I believe will be a brilliant career. Don't throw it all away for the likes of someone like Dolly Canfield."

"Believe me, Colonel, I have no intention of doing anything like that. And I thank you for the warning, sir."

As Joe and Barber walked back toward the others,

they saw Canfield approaching. "Well," Barber said under his breath, "I see the little pissant made it."

"There was no need for you to come out, Captain Barber," Canfield said. Canfield never addressed any officer by their brevet rank. "I am perfectly capable of handling a platoon of men."

"I'm sure you are," Barber replied dryly. "All the equipment has been checked and the men are ready to go. Take the command, Mister Canfield."

"Yes, sir," Canfield replied, saluting Barber. "Have we a bugler?" he asked.

"No trumpeter, sir," Joe replied.

"Buglers are for the rest of the army, Canfield," Captain Barber growled. "In the cavalry we use trumpeters."

"I'm aware of that, Captain. It was a slip of the tongue, that's all," Canfield said. He cleared his throat. "Officers and noncommissioned officers, post," he ordered.

Joe, Sergeant Muldoon, and Corporal Todd "posted," which meant to take their place at the extreme right end of the platoon.

"Prepare to mount," Canfield said. Then, "Mount."

As one, the men mounted.

"Remember," Canfield instructed them, "we must make our departure from here as quietly as possible. Left, by column of twos. Forward, ho!"

At his command, the platoon began moving. Joe rode behind Canfield; just behind him, Muldoon and Todd rode side by side. As there was neither trumpeter nor guidon bearer, the next two men were ordinary troopers.

The guards opened the gate to allow the riders to exit the fort, then pass through the sleeping tepees of the Indians. Following their orders to proceed silently, the men rode very, very quietly, with the only sound being the dull thud and brush of hooves in the dirt and dry grass, the twist and creak of saddle leather, and the subdued clink of bit chains.

* * *

By dawn, in accordance with Colonel Moreland's instructions, the platoon was in position on the banks of Big Knife Creek. The horses had been watered and the men were waiting around for their orders. Sergeant Muldoon and Corporal Todd were standing atop the highest knoll, looking eastward.

"There," Todd said. "Do you see it?"

"I'll be damned. That's some kind of a trick, all right," Muldoon said.

"What is it?" Joe asked, walking over to see what the two men were doing.

"Corporal Todd was showin' me a trick he learnt durin' the war, 'bout how to see riders up to ten miles away or more," Muldoon said.

"That sounds like a pretty good trick," Joe said. "How does it work?"

"It only works just after sunrise or just before sunset, when the sun is very low on the horizon," Todd explained, "With the sun at that angle, you can sometimes get a flare from the dust that's kicked up by a distant body of men. There is just such a flare out there now, about seven or eight miles distant."

Joe raised his field glasses and looked in the direction Todd pointed. He saw a tiny glow, far off.

"Yes," he said. "Yes, I see it. Think it's Lo?"

"It has to be, sir," Muldoon replied. "Cap'n Barber and the cavalry are some west of here. An' Cap'n Taggert an' Cap'n Carter ain't goin' to be doin' no walkin' to speak of."

"Mr. Murchison!" Canfield called. "What are you doing up there?"

"Sergeant Muldoon and Corporal Todd have spotted the Indians, sir," Joe said.

Canfield hurried up the slope. "Where?"

"About eight miles that way, sir," Todd said, pointing.

Canfield laughed. "I knew you were green, mister, but I didn't know you were that green. They are pulling your leg. You can't see anyone that far away."

"Yes, sir, take a look," Joe said. He raised his field

glasses, then sighed. "No, sir, you won't see them now. The sun has moved."

"The sun has moved? What are you talking about?"

"Tell him, Corporal Todd," Joe said.

Todd explained his theory.

"That's hogwash, Todd. Mr. Murchison, get the men mounted. It's time to get started."

"Sir, I volunteer to ride as point man," Todd offered.

"We won't be using a point man."

Joe and the two NCOs looked at Canfield in surprise.

"Beggin' your pardon, sir, but we have to use a point man," Sergeant Muldoon insisted. "Otherwise we could be riding right into an ambush!"

"We *are* riding into an ambush, Muldoon. That's the whole point," Canfield said. "An ambush for Mr. Lo." He laughed.

"Sir, with all due respect," Todd said, "Sergeant Muldoon is right. The Indians are ahead of us. We have seen them—which means they have seen us. So we must have someone riding point. The cavalry is the eyes of the army, and the point man is the eyes of the cavalry."

"Corporal, you may know cavalry tactics, but you clearly do not know the meaning of the word *respect*!" Canfield said. "When we return to the post, I intend to charge you with insubordination. I'll have those stripes back as quickly as you got them. Lieutenant Murchison, is this all the control you have over your men?"

"Sir, I don't think Corporal Todd meant any disrespect," Joe said. "He is an experienced cavalryman, and he was trying to give us the benefit of that experience."

"Can't any of you follow orders without arguing about it? Get mounted at once!"

"Yes, sir," Joe said as he, Todd, and Muldoon started back down the slope.

"All right, to horse!" Muldoon shouted at the soldiers, some of whom were napping to make up for the sleep they had lost this morning.

"Men," Canfield said, standing in the stirrups to address the platoon after they were mounted, "if you do your job today, we are going to get rid of Wind in His Hair once and for all. We are going to ride up the creek bed. We will start at a canter, continue the canter for ten minutes, then slow to a trot. Above all, keep it closed up and keep moving!"

"Sir, you don't mean the creek bed," Joe said. "Surely you mean we are going to be up on the ridge-line following the creek bed, don't you?"

"You heard Colonel Moreland's orders to me, Mr. Murchison," Canfield said. "Once we get started, we are to proceed with all deliberate speed. All deliberate speed, mister. We can move much faster by staying in the creek bed than we can by riding up on the ridge-line, where we will be constantly traversing gullies."

"Yes, sir," Joe replied.

"Forward, ho!" Canfield ordered, and the platoon started forward at the canter.

"Lieutenant Murchison," Sergeant Muldoon said to Joe about half an hour later. "Look up ahead, how the walls close in on the creek bed like that. Once we get in there, it'll be too narrow for maneuvering."

"You're right," Joe said. "Lieutenant Canfield! Sir, I recommend that we leave this creek bed and take the high ground until we are through that restricted canyon ahead."

"We will proceed with all deliberate speed, Murchison," Canfield called back over his shoulder. "All deliberate speed. We will ride through."

"Lieutenant, I am supposed to give you the benefit of my cavalry training," Joe said. "And my recommendation is—"

"I am aware of your recommendation, Mr. Murchison, and it will be noted," Canfield replied. "We will continue as before."

"Yes, sir," Joe replied.

They were halfway through the narrow canyon, and Joe was beginning to think that perhaps his worry was for naught. Perhaps they would make it all the way through without incident.

Suddenly there was a loud shout, followed by a horse whinnying in pain.

"Rockslide!" someone yelled.

Joe twisted in his saddle to see dozens of rocks of all sizes sliding down each side of the sheer rock walls. Because they were cascading down both sides, he realized instantly that this slide wasn't a natural occurrence.

"Injuns!" one of the troopers shouted immediately thereafter, and a cloud of arrows rained down on them. Most of the arrows clattered harmlessly off the steep, rocky walls that had now closed in on either side of them, but from the shouts and groans of fear and pain, Joe knew that some of the arrows had found their mark.

"Dismount! Dismount!" Canfield ordered.

"Sir, no! We can't dismount!" Joe shouted, shocked to hear Canfield give such an order. "We're in a confined area! We've got to get out of here!"

"Goddammit, Lieutenant! Quit questioning my commands!" Canfield screamed, his voice rising in pitch until it became falsetto.

Joe looked into Canfield's eyes and saw absolute panic.

"I said dismount!" Canfield ordered again.

The platoon was made up of seasoned cavalrymen, most of whom were "galvanized Yankees"—ex-Rebels who had fought in the Civil War. They knew that the moment a body of cavalry dismounted, it would lose one-fourth of its effective fighting force by virtue of every fourth man having to hold the horses of the other three. They also knew that if they dismounted here, they would be sitting ducks for the Indians up on the ridgeline. Nevertheless, they were soldiers and they had been given their orders, so they dismounted.

"Lieutenant, we've got to get the hell out of—uh!" That was as far as Sergeant Muldoon got before he was struck in the chest by an arrow. He looked down at it, as if surprised to see it there.

"Muldoon!" Joe shouted, reaching for the sergeant,

who by then had sunk to his knees. Joe knelt beside him.

"Lad, you've got to get the men out of here," Sergeant Muldoon gasped.

"Hang on, Muldoon," Joe said. He reached for the arrow.

"No, lad, don't pull it out, for 'tis in my heart!" Muldoon said.

"Lieutenant Murchison! They're picking us off like fish in a barrel!" Corporal Todd yelled, and as Joe looked around he saw that, in addition to Muldoon, at least two more men were down. By now the Indians were shooting rifles as well as arrows down on them.

"Lieutenant Canfield, we must get out of here!" Joe shouted. Then he turned to Muldoon. "Come on, Muldoon. I'll help you onto your horse!" Joe reached for Muldoon, then saw that it was too late. The sergeant's eyes were still open, but they were sightless, for he was dead.

Joe looked over at Canfield and saw that the lieutenant appeared to be in a state of shock. He was holding his pistol by his side, making no effort whatever to return fire.

"Joe, if Canfield doesn't do something quick, we're going to lose the whole platoon!" Todd shouted.

"Lieutenant Canfield, Sergeant Muldoon is dead! The Indians have us in an enfilade!" Joe said, his voice cracking under the strain. Canfield seemed not to hear. "Sir! *We have to get out of here!*"

Canfield threw Joe a frightened glance. He worked his mouth as if trying to talk, but no words would come.

"Very good sir!" Joe shouted back. "Platoon, mount!"

"I . . . I gave no such order," Canfield said weakly.

The rest of the platoon, obeying Joe's order, were already in their saddles.

"Lieutenant, get mounted, sir! We can't stay here!" Joe shouted down to Canfield, who had still not mounted. He realized then that Canfield was so immobilized by fear that he couldn't mount. "Todd! Help the lieutenant!" Joe shouted.

Todd leaped down from his own horse and grabbed Canfield. He put Canfield's hands on the pommel, then one foot into the saddle.

"Hold on, sir!" Todd shouted. As he lifted Canfield up toward his saddle there was a whacking sound, not too unlike the sound of a bat hitting a baseball. Joe was looking right at Canfield when it happened, and he saw a black hole appear in Canfield's forehead, then a little cloud of pink mist spray out of the back of his head. Canfield's eyes rolled up, and he fell onto his back, his arms flung to either side. His horse, already frightened and skittish, now bolted down the canyon, out of control. Canfield's foot was still hung up in the stirrup, and he was dragged behind the galloping horse.

"Column of twos, forward at a gallop!" Joe shouted, leading the men out of the narrow restriction in the same direction Canfield's horse was running. "Corporal Todd!"

"Yes, sir!" Todd was riding beside him now.

"When we get to the cross gully up ahead, take your column into the gully on the left! I'll take the right. As soon as you can, get out of the gully and circle back to charge the Indians on the ridge!"

"Yes, sir!" Todd replied.

They reached the cross gully in about a hundred more yards; then they split in two different directions. Joe was relieved to see the gully had shallow, sloping sides so that they were able to exit quite easily. Then, so quickly that it surprised even him, the soldiers were on top of the ridge at the same level as the astonished Indians. Here, too, was room to bring the troops on line.

"Now!" Joe shouted to his men. "Skirmish line front! Charge! Charge the bastards!"

This was Joe's very first charge, and he wished with all his soul that they had brought a trumpeter with them.

The galvanized Yankees suddenly reverted to the

Confederate soldiers they once were, and from the mouths of every trooper present came the rebel yell.

Joe had known of the yell, but this was the first time he had ever actually heard it used in battle. Spontaneously, he joined in, screaming at the top of his lungs.

Now the advantage belonged to the cavalry, for the Indians were shocked by the sudden and unexpected counterattack. They were also unnerved by the screams, for such was the tactic of the Indian, not the white man—certainly not any of the white men they had ever engaged before.

The troopers opened fire, and several Indians went down. The Indians, who had left their horses behind to effect the ambush, now had to flee on foot.

"Run them down! Run them down! Run the bastards down!" Joe shouted, caught up in the excitement of the moment.

His platoon was in two elements now, with skirmish lines on top of the canyon walls on either side of the creek. They charged the Indians at a full gallop until, finally, the Indians reached a very deep gully with walls much too steep for the horses to negotiate. Here the Indians regained some advantage, for they were able to slip into crevices and behind rocks as they scrambled down the canyon wall to the floor a hundred feet below.

"Dismount, continue to fire!" Joe ordered, and the soldiers dismounted, then hurried to the edge of the cliff where, taking up the kneeling position, they continued to pour lethal fire down onto the fleeing Indians.

Once they reached the canyon floor, the Indians were able to find draws and offshoot gullies that afforded them enough cover against the deadly accurate fire to get away. Then Joe saw one of the Indians standing defiantly on top of the far side of the gully, arms folded across his chest. The Indian was wearing a headdress of many feathers, and he was making no effort to take cover.

With a start, Joe realized it was Wind in His Hair!

The soldiers were still firing at the Indians below, though by now most of them had managed to scramble to safety, so there were no real targets.

"Cease fire, cease fire! You're wasting ammunition!" Joe shouted.

The firing fell off raggedly, with the last few shots echoing back from the canyon walls. For a long moment, Joe and Wind in His Hair stared at each other across the wide gap.

Joe put away his pistol. "Trooper," he said quietly to the soldier nearest him, "let me borrow your carbine."

"If you're thinkin' 'bout that there Injun, Lieutenant, he's too far away for a carbine. Now, iffen we had one of them infantry rifles, we could fetch him for sure."

"Let me have it," Joe repeated.

The trooper handed the carbine to Joe.

"That is Wind in His Hair," Joe explained as he raised the sight on the trooper's carbine, then set the elevation.

Wind in His Hair saw Joe taking very careful aim, but he stood defiantly, refusing to move an inch. Joe was sure it had something to do with the "medicine" the Indian claimed to have taken from him.

Joe took a deep breath, let half of it out, then touched the trigger. The carbine barked, then rocked back against his shoulder. At the top of the wall on the opposite side of the canyon, the ball managed to scatter a few feathers in Wind in His Hair's headdress.

"Whoooweee! Did you fellas see that?" the trooper who had loaned his carbine shouted to the others. "The lieutenant clipped Wind in His Hair's feathers!"

The cavalrymen on both sides of the creek cheered.

Wind in His Hair had not moved, even when the bullet passed so close by his head as to send his feathers flying. But now he pointed at Joe and shouted in English:

"You . . . cannot . . . kill . . . me! I . . . have . . . your . . . medicine!"

With that, Wind in His Hair turned, then disappeared on the other side of a small rise. By now all the

Indians were gone, leaving only the sound of a sighing wind.

Joe looked across the creek at Todd. "Corporal Todd, send four men down from your side to recover our killed and wounded. I'm going after Lieutenant Canfield."

"Yes, sir!" Todd called back.

"You four, come with me," Joe said. "The rest of you men, stay alert for any return of the Indians, and keep your eyes on the troopers below while they recover our fallen comrades. We don't want to leave them unprotected."

"What about the dead Injuns, sir?" someone asked.

"What about them?"

"Injuns don't like to leave their dead on the battlefield, but we come up on these heathens so fast, they didn't have no choice. Iffen we was to take the bodies with us, it would be bad medicine for 'em."

Joe thought for a moment. Before, he might have questioned the trooper's suggestion, but from his own experience he knew how important 'medicine' was to them. But he now had a greatly reduced platoon, deep in Indian territory. If he did take their dead, they would surely find a place to attack again—and this time it might not turn out so well for the cavalry.

On the other hand, if he left the dead and they took time to recover the bodies, it would give his platoon enough of a head start as to enable them to join up with Captains Taggert and Carter.

"No," he said. "I know you're right about the medicine, and ordinarily I would say it was a good idea. But this time I think we'll leave the bodies. That way it'll buy us a little breathing space."

The trooper realized immediately what Joe meant, and he smiled.

"You're all right, Lieutenant Murchison," he said. "You're goin' to make one helluva Injun fighter."

Joe saw Canfield's horse standing quietly about a quarter of a mile down the creek bed. Canfield was no more than a blue clump on the ground alongside, his foot still hung up in the stirrup. Joe urged his horse into a gallop and was there in a matter of a few seconds. Leaping down from his horse, he examined Canfield's body. It had been scarred and cut from being dragged across the rocky ground, but the black hole between the eyes and the gaping wound in the back of the head—through which much of his brain had spilled—indicated that Canfield was dead before the horse ever bolted. For that Joe was thankful.

"Is he dead, sir?" one of the men asked.

Joe stood up. "Yes," he said. "Throw him across his horse and let's get back with the others."

Ten minutes later, with the five dead troopers, including Sergeant Muldoon and Lieutenant Canfield, tied belly down on their saddles and with three more wounded being supported in their saddles by adjacent riders, the platoon was regrouped and ready to get under way again. Joe walked back to stand at the most elevated point and look over in the direction of the Indians' retreat. They had run away from the river, which meant they had run away from the planned ambush.

This hadn't been much of a battle—certainly not in terms of the great and desperate battles fought during the war. In addition to his own killed and wounded, there were eleven Indians killed that he counted. That was a total of fifteen dead.

Suddenly, and with no warning, Joe was overcome with nausea. Before he could stop it, he was throwing up.

"Here, Lieutenant, this will help," a voice said, and Joe turned to see Corporal Todd standing behind him. Todd had wet his handkerchief with his canteen and was holding it out to Joe.

"Thanks," Joe said. He wiped his mouth, then held it to his forehead. "I don't know what came over me just then. I was fine one minute, and then the next minute I was heaving my guts out."

"Yes, sir. I expect you'll be doing that quite a bit from now on."

"Have you ever thrown up?"

"More times than I can count," Todd admitted.

"But you get used to it, don't you?"

"Lieutenant, I don't ever want to get used to killing," Corporal Todd said.

"Yes," Joe said, nodding, and wiping his mouth again. "Yes, I see what you mean."

"By the way, I want to apologize for calling you Joe back there. But I figured I needed to get your attention. That fool Canfield was about to get us all killed."

"I usurped his command," Joe said. "If he hadn't been killed, I would have been court-martialed."

Todd shook his head. "I wouldn't say you usurped his command, sir. I'd say you took the initiative. If you hadn't, we would all be dead now. I'd say you handled yourself very well, for your first time in battle."

"How well can it be?" Joe asked. "Our mission was a failure. We didn't drive the Indians into the infantry ambush, and we didn't get our horses back."

"Come on, Lieutenant, I'm sure they taught you in that fine Yankee military school that no battle ever goes the way it's planned," Todd said. "The only thing you can do, once you are engaged, is to make the best of the situation, to seize the moment when it presents itself. And that you definitely did. As a matter of fact, if you were one of my officers, I'd be mentioning you in the dispatches today."

Despite himself, Joe laughed, then shook his head. "That's all the hell I need, Todd," he said. "To be mentioned in the dispatches of a Rebel colonel-cum-galvanized Yankee corporal. Why, I expect President Johnson himself would want to decorate me."

Todd laughed with him. "I expect you're right at that," he said.

"Come on, let's get these wounded men back to the boat. And these brave dead back to the post for a decent burial."

"Yes, sir. Prepare to mount!" Corporal Todd shouted, assuming the position of sergeant. "Mount!"

As they rode toward the rendezvous with the boat, keeping to the ridgelines this time, Joe thought of

Dolly Canfield. She was going to take her husband's death hard—the more so because she would be riddled with guilt over having kissed him last night.

As was he.

★★★

Six

"Are you Cadet Throckmorton?"

Throckmorton had been watching General Murchison so closely that he was startled by the unexpected voice. He turned to see an elderly woman whose bright, flashing eyes belied her years.

"Yes, ma'am. Cadet Throckmorton at your service, ma'am," he said when he regained his composure.

The woman chuckled. "My, it has been a long time since I made a young man jump so."

"I'm sorry, ma'am, I didn't hear you approach."

"I was told you could tell me where I might find—" Seeing General Murchison sitting on a stone bench overlooking the cemetery, the woman stopped and smiled. "Never mind. There he is." She started toward him.

"Excuse me, ma'am, but General Murchison asked not to be disturbed," Throckmorton called out, starting after her.

"Then I suggest you don't disturb him," the woman replied.

General Murchison, hearing the exchange, looked around. Recognizing the woman, he stood. "Hello, Sally," he said.

"Joseph, I think you should commend this young man for doing such a fine job," Mrs. Roosevelt said.

"I'm sorry, General," Throckmorton apologized.

General Murchison chuckled. "Never mind, Mr. Throckmorton. Mrs. Roosevelt has been doing things her own way for many years now. I don't suppose you and I can change her at this late date."

"Mrs. Roosevelt?" Throckmorton replied, puzzled by the name. This was obviously not Eleanor Roosevelt.

"I am the president's mother," Mrs. Roosevelt said, realizing what had the young man confused. "I am going to sit and talk with the general for a while. Now you have two old people to guard. Do you think you are up to the task?"

"Yes, ma'am!" Throckmorton replied resolutely.

General Murchison offered his arm, and Sara Roosevelt took it, then walked with him back to the stone bench where he had been sitting.

"Handsome young man," she said.

General Murchison chuckled. "Sally, you always were a sucker for a man in a uniform."

"You've guessed my secret, Joseph," she replied. "All these years, it wasn't you I found attractive. It was your uniform." She sighed. "Have you ever wondered about what might have been?" she asked. "I mean, how things might be if we had married?"

"For starters, if we had married, someone else would be president of the United States right now," the general replied. "And I don't think his name would have been Murchison."

"How do you know? How do you know Franklin didn't get his political presence from me?"

"Well, for one thing, he is not a Republican," General Murchison replied.

"Yes, I suppose you have me there," Mrs. Roosevelt admitted with a little laugh.

"Anyway, didn't you once write to me that such considerations were like looking in on the machinations of God?"

"I may have. Lord, I did write so . . . *dramatically*

in those days, didn't I? Still, it gives one pause to wonder."

Joe Murchison reached over to take her hand in his. "You were cut out to be the wife of a wealthy gentleman, Sally. You weren't cut out to be a soldier's wife. I'm afraid you would have been as miserable as Dolly Canfield."

"Dolly Canfield? Who is that? I don't believe I ever heard of her."

"No, you wouldn't have. She was my secret, my guilty secret—even though it was an innocent guilt, if I may be forgiven the oxymoron," the general said. "I haven't thought about her in a long time, but I must confess that I have been thinking about her this morning."

"Have you? My goodness, she must have made quite an impression on you."

"As I was young and impressionable then, I suppose she did. Ah, she was a beautiful woman, Sally, a rose among cabbages, as it were."

"Can you tell me about her now? Or are you going to be the quintessential gentleman and take the secret with you to the grave?"

"I suppose I have to tell you now, lest you think something scandalous happened," he replied. Briefly, he recounted the days at Fort Berthold, ending with a description of the skirmish that took Lieutenant Canfield's life.

"Oh, the poor woman, to be so cruelly widowed at such an early age," Mrs. Roosevelt said. "I wonder what happened to her. Did you ever hear from her again?"

"She wrote me a few times, yes," General Murchison admitted. "She returned to Dayton, where she resumed her teaching career. Later she married a judge and they had three children. One of her grandsons is now a congressman from Ohio."

"How interesting!" Mrs. Roosevelt said. "I may know him."

"I'm sure you do." The general stood, then held his

hand down to help Mrs. Roosevelt. "Come with me," he invited.

"Where are we going?" she asked, brushing off the back of her dress as she stood.

"Well, if you are going to stroll down memory lane with me, we may as well go all the way. I'm going to walk over and visit with General Custer for a few minutes."

"Custer, yes, I'd nearly forgotten that he is buried here. What a fascinating person he must have been. Some called him a hero, some called him a villain—but which was he, I wonder? A hero or a villain?"

"Oh, he was much too complicated a person to be placed in a pigeonhole as hero or villain," General Murchison said.

"Some call him General Custer. But he wasn't really a general, was he?"

"He was during the war. But when he died, he was only a lieutenant colonel. However, he wore the aura of his brevet rank with as much authority as if the stars of a major general were still on his shoulder." They reached the bas-relief shaft that marked Custer's grave. "Here he is."

"Oh, look!" Mrs. Roosevelt exclaimed. "His wife is here beside him. I didn't know that."

"It is right that she be here," Joe Murchison remarked. "General Custer's life belonged to him, but his myth belonged to Libbie. And long ago, the myth became larger than life."

"You know, I recall you writing me about the first time you ever met him," Mrs. Roosevelt said. "I can still remember something you said in that letter. You said, 'General Custer has an appointment with destiny.' Pretty prophetic words, as it turned out."

The general chuckled. "It would seem you weren't the only one who wrote overly dramatic letters. I do recall making that statement, but to tell the truth, I was thinking about a possible political future for him, not what eventually happened to him. Looking back on it now, it did seem prophetic, I suppose."

"I don't remember where you were when you met him," Mrs. Roosevelt said.

"I was at Jefferson Barracks. The army closed down Fort Berthold in early 1868, and those men who weren't mustered out or posted to one of the other upper-Missouri River posts were sent back to Jefferson Barracks for further reassignment. I was one of the latter."

ST. LOUIS, MISSOURI
JEFFERSON BARRACKS
SEPTEMBER 25, 1868

It was the bottom of the ninth inning, and the St. Louis Beer Brewers were leading the Jefferson Barracks Athleticals three to one. There were two men on base and two men out when Second Lieutenant Joe Murchison stepped up to the plate.

"Strike him out, Heinie!" the catcher called to his pitcher. "Let's send these soldier boys back out to Jefferson Barracks with their tails between their legs!"

"Hit the ball, Lieutenant!" one of Joe's teammates yelled.

Joe tapped the bat on the plate a few times, dug his feet into the dirt, then raised the bat as he stared at the pitcher.

The pitcher spat a wad of tobacco into his glove and worked it around. The result would be a ball that would come toward Joe somewhat like a corkscrew.

The pitcher went into his windup, then delivered his pitch. The ball caught the inside of the plate, and the umpire called strike one.

Not content with the juice he already had on the ball, the pitcher worked it over with another wad. He threw again, and this time Joe swung at it, only to have the ball drop away at the last minute. Joe missed the ball completely and nearly fell over from the force of his swing.

"Look at it this way, soldier boy," the catcher said as he returned the ball to the pitcher. "Just one more swing and you can go back out there to Jefferson Barracks for a nice supper. They still feedin' you soldier boys hardtack and beans?"

"That's the way it was in the old army," Joe replied. "Now we have steak and apple pie every day."

The pitcher delivered another ball, and this time Joe caught it on the fat part of his bat. It was a good, hard, level swing, and he felt the exhilarating explosion of power coming from his shoulders, back, and arms. The ball shot away from his bat as if fired from a cannon, and it was still climbing as it sailed over the center fielder's head.

To the cheers of his teammates, Joe rounded all the bases, stepping on home plate before the outfielder even got to the ball. As a result of one swing of Joe's bat, Jefferson Barracks won the game by a score of four to three.

Joe was the manager of the Jefferson Barracks baseball club. Although the other officers could accept the idea of Joe managing the club, they thought actually playing was beneath the dignity of an officer. Fortunately for Joe, however, the post commander didn't share the view of many of his junior officers. He looked upon a winning baseball team as a morale booster, not only for the players but for everyone assigned to Jefferson Barracks.

And the team was a winner. It had played, besides other army teams, half a dozen civilian teams like the St. Louis Beer Brewers, who were members of the Professional Base Ball Players Association.

When the team returned to Jefferson Barracks, they posed for a group photograph in front of the headquarters building. Although the other players wore their baseball uniforms, Colonel Beale had asked Joe to wear his army jacket and cap for all official photographs, to differentiate him from the others.

"You men in the front row, put your gloves on your knees," the photographer suggested. "And those of you in the back row, lean on your bats—like so." He demonstrated. When the pose was struck to his satisfaction, he put the plate in his camera, then stuck his head under the cloth.

"Look at me while I count to three, and it'll make a lovely picture don't you see. One, two, three," he intoned in a monotone.

When Joe stepped into the officers' mess for supper that evening, he saw that Colonel Beale was there with a lieutenant colonel whom he didn't recognize. The lieutenant colonel had long hair and a full, curving mustache, both reddish blond in color.

"Mr. Murchison!" Colonel Beale called. "Please, come here. I've someone I would like for you to meet."

Joe walked over to their table.

"Lieutenant Murchison, this is General Custer," Colonel Beale said.

"General Custer, sir, it is a pleasure to meet you. I have read much about your exploits during the war, about your bravery, and about the number of horses you had shot from under you."

Custer laughed. "I was a major general at twenty-one, and the most important thing you can remember about me is how many poor horses I killed."

"Oh, no sir, I didn't mean it like that . . ." Joe sputtered.

Custer laughed again and held up his hand. "I was only jesting with you, Mr. Murchison," he said. "Please, have a seat. Join us."

"Thank you, sir."

The waiter arrived and the three officers gave their orders. Custer ordered roast beef with horseradish, and roasted potatoes.

"That sounds good," Joe said. "I'll have the same," he told the private who was waiting tables.

"I suppose you are wondering what I am doing here, in view of my year's suspension," Custer said.

"Year's suspension, sir?" Joe asked. He shook his head. "I know nothing about a year's suspension."

A loaf of bread was already on the table, and Custer cut off a piece, then began buttering it as he talked.

"In that case, I may as well tell you," he said. "It is

best that you hear the truth from me, rather than some of the spurious rumors that are going around." His bread covered with a generous smear of butter, he took a bite, then continued to talk as he chewed.

"Last year I was court-martialed for absenting my post without proper authority and for the unauthorized shooting of deserters." A piece of bread snagged on Custer's mustache, and he used a napkin to wipe it and the resultant smear of butter away. "First, let me treat with the charge of absenting my post without proper authority, though in the chronology of events, that came after the shooting incident," he continued.

"Upon returning to Fort Hays from a long and hazardous scout against the hostiles, I learned of an outbreak of cholera at Fort Riley. Libbie—that is, Mrs. Custer—was at Fort Riley. As my post was Fort Hays, Libbie was occupying vacant quarters at the sufferance of the post commander. Since she was not sponsored, I feared that, should she be stricken with cholera, there would be none to tend her—indeed, perhaps no one who would even know of her condition.

"Accordingly, I placed everything in order at Fort Hays, then undertook a journey to Fort Riley to check upon the condition of my wife. Fortunately I found that she was in no danger. When I returned to Fort Hays, however, I learned my absence was being treated as unauthorized. This, though I had informed Colonel Smith of my intentions and had the freedom of movement as commander to go where I wished. Now, as to the other specification, the wrongful shooting . . ."

Custer took another bite of his bread and chewed it thoughtfully for a moment before he spoke again.

"During the scout, while in the vicinity of the Platte River, thirty-five men deserted the regiment within one twenty-four-hour period. As you might well understand, that left me most apprehensive for the rest of the command, especially as we had before us a long march through hostile country. Then, while breaking camp at about five P.M. one afternoon, thirteen more men, in the presence of the entire command, and in broad daylight, deliberately took off. Seven of the deserters were well-mounted, which gave them a distinct advantage, since only a few of the officers were saddled. I immediately directed Major Elliot and Lieutenants Cooke and Jackson, as well as my brother, Tom, to pursue the deserters. They were still visible, though by now they were more than a mile distant. I told them . . ." Custer paused and took a deep breath, almost as if testifying once again before the court-martial board. "I told them to bring back the dead bodies of as many as they could catch.

"The seven who were mounted had cleverly stolen our best horses, and thus were so far away as to make good their escape. Then one of those who were afoot did, while being pursued, present his carbine at Major Elliot. Before he could fire, however, he was brought down by another of the pursuing party. Two others were also brought down by pistol shots, while the remaining three threw themselves on the ground and feigned death, thus escaping being shot.

"The wounds of the others were not serious, and they recovered quickly, but the soldier who had presented his carbine died.

"Several chair-bound officers found my methods severe. But officers who have served in the field, who understand how one man must depend upon the other, were less harsh in their judgment. And all had to admit that my methods were effective, for there was not another desertion for as long as I remained with the command."

"And now, I understand, the suspension has been lifted?" Colonel Beale asked.

"It has indeed," Custer replied. Smiling, he pulled a telegram from his jacket pocket, then showed it to Beale and Joe. "I received this only yesterday."

SHERIDAN TO CUSTER, SEPTEMBER 24, FROM FORT HAYS, KANSAS:

GENERALS SHERMAN, SULLY, AND MYSELF, AND NEARLY ALL THE OFFICERS OF YOUR REGIMENT HAVE ASKED FOR YOU, AND I HOPE THE APPLICA-

TION WILL BE SUCCESSFUL. CAN YOU COME AT
ONCE?

"The moment I received the message, I stopped all
activity and hurried down to the depot to secure a train
ticket to Hays City, Kansas."

"That's all you have?" Beale asked. "No official orders?"

"Don't worry about that, Colonel. The official orders
will come," Custer said confidently. "General Sherman
himself has asked for me, which means that only President Johnson can override him. And as President Johnson missed conviction by only one vote during his trial
of impeachment, there is absolutely no chance he will
override General Sherman's request, lest he be forced
to go through another ordeal."

"Yes, I'm sure you are right," Beale agreed. "Have
you any idea what you will be doing when you return to
Fort Hays?"

"Yes, I do. This winter I will be leading eleven companies of the Seventh Cavalry on a scout against hostile
Indians from Medicine Lodge Creek toward the Wich-
ita Mountains," Custer answered. "As you probably
know from following the papers, Lo has had a summer
of barbarous behavior. He thinks he can now rest without fear during the winter. But this winter the Seventh
Cavalry shall disabuse him of that notion."

The meal arrived, and for the next several minutes
the three officers spoke only of inconsequential things.
Then Custer turned to Joe.

"Mr. Murchison, I understand you are a man of
some experience in fighting the Indians," he said.

"Very little, sir," Joe replied modestly.

"Oh? Is my information false? I was told you led a
platoon in a successful fight with Wind in His Hair."

"Lieutenant Canfield was in command."

"Canfield was killed, was he not?"

"Yes, sir."

"And if my information is correct, he was an artillery
officer, attempting to lead a cavalry platoon?"

"That is correct, sir."

"And he led that platoon down a streambed, between constricting bluffs?"

"Yes, sir."

"Why would anyone, even an artillery officer, commit such a tactical blunder?"

"We had been ordered to proceed downstream with all deliberate speed, General," Joe said uneasily. "I believe Lieutenant Canfield was following those orders as he saw them. He was a brave and conscientious officer."

Custer smiled. "And you are a good man, Mr. Murchison. A lesser man might well put the blame on his commander. Which, indeed, is where it belongs. I am glad to see, however, that you understand the meaning of loyalty. You will be a fine addition to the Seventh Cavalry."

"I beg your pardon, sir?"

"Tell him, Colonel Beale."

"This afternoon I received a telegraph communication from General Sheridan," Colonel Beale said. "In it he orders me to send an officer of my choosing with Colonel Custer."

"And you chose me, sir?" Joe asked happily.

"Yes. Unless you would rather stay here and play base ball for another year." He made two distinct words of *baseball*.

"No, sir!" Joe said. "Colonel Custer, when will you —that is, when will *we* be leaving?"

"Tomorrow morning," Custer replied. "Do you have a pressing need to delay the departure?"

"No, sir. Tomorrow morning will be just fine," Joe said. "But if you will excuse me, sir. I have much to do to get ready. Permission to withdraw."

"Permission granted," Colonel Beale said.

"Lieutenant?" Custer said as Joe stood.

Already several steps away from the table, Joe stopped and turned toward him. "Yes, sir?"

Custer smiled. "As our colleagues in the navy say, it is good to have you aboard."

Joe returned the colonel's smile. "It's good to be aboard, sir!"

FORT HAYS, KANSAS
ONE WEEK LATER

Joe was sitting at the desk in his room in the bachelor officers' quarters. It was unseasonably warm for so late in the year, and Joe had his window open to let in some air. Just outside the window he could hear the soft thump of moths fluttering against the screen, drawn by the bright light of Joe's kerosene lamp. Beyond the moths, insects and frogs serenaded the night. Over in the stable, a horse whickered and one of the pack mules brayed. Someone was playing a guitar somewhere, and he heard a burst of laughter from a group of enlisted soldiers who were gathered outside the sutler's store. He dipped his pen into his inkwell, then began writing a letter to Sally, informing her of his new duty station.

Fort Hays, Kansas
October 3, 1868

Dear Sally:
    As you have no doubt noticed by the above address, I am no longer at Jefferson Barracks. I am proud to say that I am now a member of the Seventh Cavalry, at Fort Hays, Kansas.
    The post is commanded by General Nelson A. Miles. Technically, the Seventh is under the command of Colonel A. J. Smith, though his position is administrative. The tactical commander, and the one who will actually lead us in the field, is Lieutenant Colonel (Brevet Major General) George A. Custer.
    You may have heard of General Custer. He fought brilliantly during the war and was promoted to the rank of Major General at the age of twenty-one. No one has ever occupied so lofty a rank at so young an age.
    I am much impressed with him. Under his command, the Seventh Cavalry has become a well-disciplined organization, wonderfully schooled at

the horse and drill. If they fight as well as they perform on the parade field—and I have no doubt but that they will—then I would declare the Seventh to be equal or superior to any regiment in the entire army. I truly believe that General Custer has an appointment with destiny.

I was pleasantly surprised to learn that my old friend Seth Todd was here. He is now a sergeant in Captain Hamilton's troop. I have been assigned to that troop and will, in fact, be in command of Todd's platoon.

It was good to see him again, for I think you know my opinion of him. I wish he could apply to the War Department for a commission—but, of course, having taken up arms against us during the late war, he cannot. Much is the pity, though, for he would be an excellent officer.

There are many officers here who were in the war and were with Custer at Sayler's Creek. What would they think if they knew that one of the Confederate commanders who fought so brilliantly against them was now with them in the ranks as an enlisted man? They do not know, of course, and for now they will continue to be ignorant of the fact, for Sergeant Todd has asked me not to share the secret of his background with anyone, and I am respecting those wishes.

Perhaps you would be interested in a description of Fort Hays. I will endeavor to make it come alive for you. The fort is laid out around a quadrangle, or parade ground, not too different from Fort Berthold—though this post, and the parade ground, is considerably larger.

The sally port, or front gate, is on the north side of the post. In the northeast corner of the fort, just to the left, as one enters, is a baseball field. It is empty during duty hours but filled with the more athletic of the enlisted men when the time is their own.

Just to the right of the sally port is the guardhouse, and one can often see a soldier's face looking soulfully through one of its barred windows. Seldom is the guardhouse occupied by desperate characters, however. Mostly its occupants are men whose crime was no greater than having had a little too much to drink in Hays City.

Next to the guardhouse, tucked into the northwest corner of the post, are the barn, stables, and wagon park. Our horses and mules are kept here, and I must say the Seventh is well-supplied with excellent stock.

Continuing south along the west side of the parade ground, one passes the magazine, where our ammunition and powder are stored, and then the commissary. The commissary is the quartermaster's domain, handling everything the men of our post might need, from blankets to water kegs.

After the commissary comes the sutler's store. Actually they are no longer called *sutlers* because earlier this year the War Department replaced sutlers with businessmen who secured franchises to set up permanent stores at army posts. The name sutler has stuck, however, and when someone says he is going to the sutler's, everyone knows what he is talking about. These stores give the officers and men an opportunity to buy whiskey, beer, tobacco, canned fruit, canned meats, shoelaces, needles, thread, soap, shaving brushes, and hundreds of other items. In the back of the store is a room where the men can relax with a deck of cards or a game of checkers. There are generally a few books there, as well as the latest issues of *Harper's Weekly* and *Frank Leslie's Illustrated Weekly*. As you might imagine, these magazines are eagerly consumed by officer and soldier alike, anxious to keep up with the news from back East.

Just beyond the sutler's store is the hospital and surgeon's quarters. Although the sutler's and the commissary are unpainted, the hospital and the surgeon's quarters are painted white, with a green-shake roof. They are actually very handsome buildings.

Just beyond the hospital is the post headquarters and the commandant's house, also painted white. The commandant's house is quite elegant and would be a fitting abode for the most substantial citizens in any town in America.

In the southwest corner of the fort are the married officers' quarters. Though not as elegant as the commandant's quarters, these are pleasant, white-frame houses of the kind one might find in the nicer neighborhoods of a civilian town. They are occupied by rank, which means that a newly arrived officer can take any house he wants by "ranking out" a junior officer's family. As a result of that process, some of the married junior officers seldom bother to unpack.

Going east along the south wall, one comes to where I live. There are three sets of bachelor officers' quarters, or BOQs as we call them. They are two-story, unpainted frame buildings with twelve rooms on each floor. Our rooms are large, well-lighted, and ventilated and provide us with most pleasant accommodations.

Next to the BOQs is the officers' mess where we bachelor officers take all our meals and where we hold parties. After the officers' mess comes the post chapel, which holds both Catholic and Protestant services every Sunday morning.

On the other side of the chapel is the officers' vegetable garden, and though all the vegetables have been harvested for the year, I understand it was a bountiful crop this season, and many things were canned for later use.

Beyond the garden, in the southeast corner of the fort, is Soapsuds Row. This is where the married NCOs are quartered and where the laundresses live and work. I don't believe I have told you of laundresses before. A military post is authorized laundresses at the ratio of 1 per 19½ men. The women receive $2 per month for each enlisted man and $5 for each officer they serve. Many of the laundresses are married to noncommissioned officers, and the combined household income of an NCO and his laundress wife can make the company-grade officers jealous. In addition, some of these sergeants are "twenty percenters," meaning they loan money to the privates for twenty percent interest. As a result of their various sources of income, a few NCOs have become quite wealthy by anyone's standards.

Soapsuds Row is followed by twenty sets of large, two-story barracks, providing housing for the unmarried enlisted men. In front of each set of barracks are the orderly rooms where the troop commanders and company-grade officers make their headquarters.

Set between the troop barracks and the four enlisted mess halls is a large, well-tended vegetable garden for the exclusive use of the enlisted men. The enlisted mess halls are very close to the baseball field—so close in fact that windows are constantly being broken by the better batters. And that, my dear Sally, brings us all the way around the post.

In your last letter you spoke of the impeachment trial for President Johnson. I am glad your father was opposed to impeachment, and I am glad he was not found guilty. I know little of politics, but I cannot but think that the removal of a sitting president by any means other than a ballot of the people would, in the long run, be harmful to our Republic.

Your friend,
Joe Murchison

Although Joe knew the mail would not go out until the next morning, he wanted to put his correspondence in the letter drop tonight because so doing would give him the illusion that it was already on its way. Sealing the envelope, he tromped down the stairs from his second-floor room, then walked across the dark quadrangle to the post headquarters and the mail drop.

A gentle breeze was blowing from the south, and it carried upon its breath the smell of lye soap from Soapsuds Row. From one of the married NCO houses he could hear the sound of a crying baby.

"Hello, Joe," a disembodied voice called from the darkness as Joe approached the post mailbox. "What are you doing out so late?"

Joe stared into the shadows toward the sound of the voice. "Who's there?" he asked.

"Just me." A figure stepped out of the shadows, and Joe recognized Custer's brother, First Lieutenant Tom Custer.

"Good evening, sir," Joe said, saluting.

Tom chuckled, then returned the salute. "Are you supposed to return salutes when you're drunk? I don't know," he said.

It wasn't until then that Joe noticed Tom was clutching a bottle of whiskey. He wiped the mouth of the bottle with his shirtsleeve, then offered it to Joe.

"Here," he said. "Have a drink."

Joe didn't want a drink, but he didn't want to offend Tom either—especially as he was Custer's brother. He took the bottle and turned it up, taking a much smaller drink than it appeared.

"Ah, good man, good man," Tom said. He held up his finger and wagged it back and forth. "I don't trust a man who doesn't drink." He took the bottle back and took another long swallow. "Course, that's no problem in the army. Pretty near ever'body drinks. Pretty near ever'body's a drunk. Hell, look at Captain Cooper. He's a bigger drunk than I am. Ever'body's a drunk, 'cept my brother." Tom looked at Joe conspiratorially. "Autie doesn't drink, you know."

"No, sir, I didn't know," Joe replied, not sure where the conversation was going, but not wanting to be rude.

"Not a drop," Tom went on. "Hell, he's a teetotaler. Took the pledge. He'd like me to, as well, but I told 'im go to hell. You can be a teetotaler if you want to, I said to him, but I aim to drink, and I aim to be friends with those who do."

He took another drink and offered another to Joe, who accepted.

"It's Libbie's fault, you know," Tom said. Again, he waved his finger back and forth. "Now, don't get me wrong. I love Libbie like a sister. I s'pose she is my sister, when you get right down to it. But she sure keeps a tight rein on my brother."

Tom giggled. "About some things," he added. "Other things, why, Autie pretty much does whatever he wants. You take a pretty girl, now. Autie can have her skirt up and drawers down quicker'n . . ." Realizing he might be saying more than he should, Tom let his voice trail off. "Well, you know what I mean," he added.

"Yes, sir," Joe said, not knowing what else to say.

"Autie's jealous of me, that's the problem. He's jealous 'cause I have two Medals of Honor and he, for all his bravery, has none. My 'baubles,' he calls them. 'Here is Tom and his baubles' he says when I'm in dress uniform and have the medals pinned to my chest. You never did answer me."

"I beg your pardon, sir?" Joe asked, surprised by the abrupt change of subject.

"I asked you what you were doing out here so late?"

"Oh, I've, uh, come to mail a letter, sir."

Tom smiled. "To your girl back home?"

"To a girl, sir. She's not my girlfriend."

"Then whose girlfriend is she? And what man would let another man write to his girlfriend?"

"It's nothing like that, sir. It's a simple friendship, that's all."

"Yes, well, you know what they say, Mr. Murchison. From little acorns, mighty oaks grow. Nurture it. It may yet develop into something."

"Yes, sir," Joe said.

Tom stood there looking at him for another moment, then killed the rest of his whiskey. "Carry on, Mr. Murchison," he finally said.

"Yes, sir," Joe replied. Quickly, he dropped the letter into the box reserved for outgoing mail; then, with one final nod to Tom, he started back across the dark quadrangle.

Halfway across the parade ground, a soldier appeared, carrying a trumpet. The trumpeter nodded quietly at Joe, raised the instrument to his lips, and blew air through it a couple of times. Joe stopped to listen as he played taps.

This was the official signal that it was time for everyone to be in bed, and Joe stood there listening as the mournful notes filled the air. Sweeter in sound from a trumpet than they were from a bugle, the notes rolled out across the flat, open quadrangle, hitting the hills beyond the walls of the fort, then bouncing back a second later as an even more haunting echo.

Of all the military rituals, the playing of taps was the one that most affected Joe. He never heard it without feeling a slight chill.

> Day is done.
> Gone the sun
> From the lake
> From the hill
> From the sky.
> Rest in peace
> Soldier brave,
> God is nigh.

The last note hung in the air for a long, sorrowful moment, and Joe thought of the things about the army that he liked—the loyalty of men to their country and their officers and the camaraderie of all members of the Seventh Cavalry—and he knew there would never be another thing in his life that he would love more than he loved being a member of this elite band of men.

"Corporal of the guard! Post number six, and all is well!"

The plaintive call from the furthermost guard came drifting across the post.

"Corporal of the guard! Post number five, and all is well."

The second call was a little closer. They continued down the line until post number two's call, and his call was so close that Joe felt a moment of embarrassment, as if he had intruded upon the quiet, lonely moments that were part of a sentry's privilege and duty.

Slowly, but with a sense of pride, Joe crossed the wide, dark parade ground to his own quarters. As the sentries said, all was well with his world.

Seven

HAMBY PLANTATION
KING WILLIAM COUNTY, VIRGINIA
SEPTEMBER 1868

Tamara Hamby sat on the veranda of her father's large colonial home, looking out over the beautifully manicured lawn. Down by the gate, Thomas Hamby was talking with one of the several black men who worked for him. The war had not changed things that much. The blacks who worked here now had always worked here, descendants of the black families who had worked on the Hamby plantation since before the Revolutionary War. They were no longer slaves, they were now paid employees—but that was the only difference.

Thomas Hamby was the oldest son of the late Richard Hamby, himself the great-great grandson of David Hamby, who had arrived in the Virginia Colony in the late 1600s. Over the years the Hambys had built a large plantation, and the law of primogeniture had preserved it intact until the present day.

Tamara could recite without pause her family's genealogy all the way back to England in the early 1600s. She liked doing that; she liked putting her name in that litany and knowing exactly who she was and where she belonged.

But now she had reason to believe that she didn't really know who she was at all.

This morning, while looking for a book she had misplaced, she came across a packet of letters her father had hidden. According to the return address, the letters were from a soldier named Todd. Curious as to why a soldier would be writing to Thomas, she began to read the letters. She was shocked to learn that the soldier, Todd, was her uncle Seth whom she hadn't seen in years. Except that he wasn't her uncle at all. He was her father!

Why had she never been told? And if he was her father . . . who was her mother?

Out on the lawn, Tom Hamby finished his instructions to his employees, then started back into the house. Seeing Tamara sitting on a chair on the veranda, he smiled and walked over to her.

"Hello, sweetheart," he said. "I'm glad to see you out taking a little air. You always have your nose buried in a book, and I think it's good for you to get out now and then."

"Why did you lie to me?" Tamara asked flatly.

Tom got a puzzled expression on his face. "I beg your pardon? Lie to you about what?"

"All these years you have let me believe that you are my father." She was hiding the packet of letters in the folds of her dress, and now she held them up for Tom to see. "But you aren't my father. And my mother isn't . . ." Tamara choked on the words and began sobbing aloud. "My mother isn't even my mother," she said.

The expression on Tom's face turned from confusion to hurt. "Tamara—"

But before he could finish, Tamara stood up. *"I hate you!"* she shouted with all the hurt and anger a seventeen-year-old could muster. She ran into the house.

"Tamara, please! Wait!" Tom called after her.

Crying so hard that she could scarcely see, she hurried up the stairs, then down the long hallway toward her room. Her mother—or rather the woman Tamara had always thought was her mother—was standing just outside one of the rooms, talking to the maid, when Tamara swept by with sobs in her throat and tears streaming down her face.

"Tamara, dear, what is it? What on earth has happened?" Ada Hamby asked.

Without answering, Tamara went into her room and slammed the door. Her mother started to follow her, but even as she reached the door she heard the lock being turned from inside.

By now Tom had also reached the second floor, and Ada turned to him. "What did you do to that child?" she demanded.

Tom held up the packet of letters. "She found these, Ada."

"Oh!" Ada gasped, putting her hand to her lips. She knew about the letters, thus no further explanation was necessary. She looked at the closed door. "Oh, the poor dear."

"I must talk to her," Tom said. "I have to explain." He twisted the doorknob, but it was locked.

"Doney," Ada said to the maid. She pointed to the lock and made the motion of turning a key. Doney nodded, then disappeared. A moment later she came back with a key and handed it to Ada.

"Thank you," Ada said. She put the key in the slot, turned it, then looked at Tom. "It's open," she said. "The rest is up to you."

Tom stepped into Tamara's room and found her lying on her stomach on the bed, crying into the pillow. He quietly walked over, then sat down on her bed. Tentatively he reached for her hand, and when she didn't jerk it away from him the moment he touched it, he felt a profound sense of relief. He held her hand for several minutes, just letting her cry but saying nothing.

"Who am I?" Tamara finally asked. "All my life I thought I knew exactly who I am. But I'm not that person at all."

"But of course you are," Tom said. "Tamara, in every way that matters, you the daughter of Tom and Ada Hamby. You are our daughter legally, and you are our daughter in our hearts and minds."

Tamara rolled over onto her back, then looked up at Tom with tear-filled eyes.

"Then what about Uncle Seth? Why does he say in these letters that he is my father?"

"Biologically, Seth is your father," Tom said.

"*Oh!*" Tamara whimpered.

"Shhh," Tom said soothingly. "All that means is that you are a Hamby, just as you always thought you were."

"And my mother?"

"Your mother was a nice young lady whose father owned a farm near here. Her name was Sue Ellen Wiggins. She died shortly after you were born. Ada and I had not been able to have children, so we asked if we could take you and raise you as our own. Sue Ellen's parents agreed that would be best for you."

"What about Uncle Seth?"

"He was in New Orleans. When he came back and learned what had happened, even he agreed that this was for the best. Then we had a judge confirm on paper what God had already confirmed in our hearts, and from that day until this, you have been our daughter."

"Why didn't Uncle Seth come back after the war was over?"

"I can't answer that question," Tom said. He sighed. "Seth always was someone who wanted to go see the elephant."

"Go see the elephant?"

Tom chuckled, then pulled out his handkerchief and dabbed at the tears on Tamara's face. "It is something your grandfather used to say about Seth. Seth was always anxious to see what was just on the other side of the hill or what was under the bridge. Your grandfather said he was always wanting to go see the elephant."

"Papa," Tamara said, and Tom felt his heart leap with joy over the fact that she was still calling him that. "Did you and Seth get on when you were young?"

"Oh, yes," Tom said. "You know, I actually envied Seth's aggressive spirit. I was always afraid of my own shadow for fear I would do the wrong thing, but Seth never gave it a second thought. And he was courageous, too. I remember when he was still just a boy, he took on a whole pack of bullies, all by himself." Tom chuckled. "Of course, he was whipped pretty good, but he got in enough licks that, individually, none of the bullies ever bothered him again."

"Do you think we will ever see him again?"

"I don't know, darling. I really don't know. Would you like to see your father?"

Tamara thought for a moment. "I would like to see Uncle Seth again," she said. She sat up and put her arms around his neck. "*You* are my father."

Tom, who had been so busy drying Tamara's tears, now found he could not stop his own.

HAYS CITY, KANSAS
EARLY OCTOBER 1868

Three army wagons were drawn up alongside the depot platform at the train station in Hays City. The soldiers who had brought the wagons into town were sitting on the ground under a spreading oak tree, playing a game of mumblety-peg. Sergeant Todd was the NCO in charge of the detail, and he walked over to the window to talk to the ticket agent.

"Is the train on time?" he asked.

"All I can tell you is they telegraphed that it left the last station on schedule," the ticket agent answered. He looked over his shoulder at a large clock. "It should be here in about another half hour or so."

"Thanks."

"Say, just what is it you fellas are a'pickin' up that it'll take three wagons?" the ticket agent asked.

"General Custer's wife and household goods," Todd answered. He walked back over to where the three soldiers were playing with the knife.

"Sarge, we got time to get us a drink before the train gets here?" one of the soldiers asked. He held the knife in his hand, trying to "spank the baby." He slapped it on the handle and missed.

"No drinking," Todd said.

"Come on, Sarge. What's one drink hurt?"

"Yeah, look at·Cap'n Cooper," one of the other soldiers said. "You think he ain't drunk by now?"

The others laughed.

"I'm not responsible for Captain Cooper," Todd said. "I am responsible for you. No liquor."

"Not even a beer? A beer ain't liquor."

"Not even a beer," Todd said.

The soldier "spanking the baby" made the knife stick on his "dare."

"Oh, you're one lucky sonuvabitch," one of the other soldiers said.

"Wish that train would come on," still another said. "I'm gettin' tired of waitin'."

"You mean you'd rather be back at the fort, shovelin' shit out of the stalls?" the mumblety-peg player asked.

"Yeah, I guess you got a point."

Leaving the threesome to their game, Todd walked over to the corner of the depot platform, then sat down to wait and took out his pipe. He thought about the men at Fort Hays who had their families with them. Not only officers, but several sergeants had their wives and children living right there on post with them.

Todd thought about his own situation. As a sergeant, he could now have his family live with him. That is, if he had a family. In truth, he had long ago given up any rights to claim Tamara as his daughter. Besides, she was no longer a little girl. She was a young woman now. Fort Hays, or any military post for that matter, would be a terrible place to bring a seventeen-year-old young lady who had no mother to look out for her. Even if she would come—which of course, she wouldn't—he couldn't bring her here. Still, it was pleasant sometimes to sit and fantasize about having her with him.

Todd was brought out of his reverie when, true to the ticket agent's promise, a whistle and a distant puff of smoke marked the arrival, exactly one half hour later, of the *Empire West*.

The train rumbled to a stop, then sat on the track, hissing, popping, and snapping as steam was vented and couplings and fittings began to cool. There was one freight car at the end of the string of "varnish," as the passenger cars were called. After the passengers were discharged, one of the brakemen ran over to a railway switch handle, moved it, then signaled for the engineer to back up. The engineer did so, and the freight car was disconnected. The train pulled back out onto the main line, the switch was closed, and the train gathered speed as it made its departure.

By now all the debarking passengers but three had been met or had gone off on their own. Three women were left standing on the station platform: Libbie Custer; Eliza, the Custers' maid; and Alice Patterson. Alice Patterson was the daughter of a United States Congressman, and she was to be a houseguest of the Custers until after New Year's Day, some three months distant.

Todd detailed two of the wagons for the household furnishings, while the third would be used to transport the women and their luggage out to the post.

Suddenly he became aware that Eliza, the black maid, was staring at him intensely. He tried paying no attention to it, but the more he tried to avoid it, the more intense the staring became. Finally, even Libbie noticed it.

"Eliza, what's gotten into you?" she asked. "Why are you staring at that soldier so?"

"I done seen him before," Eliza said. "Where have I seen you before?" she asked Todd.

"I was at the old Fort Hays," Todd said, referring to the original Fort Hays, which had been destroyed by flood. Several people had lost their lives in that flood, and the Custer household had barely escaped with its own. The present Fort Hays was some distance from the first—this one thoughtfully located on high ground.

"That ain't it," Eliza said. "I seen you somewhere before that, a long time ago."

"Maybe he was in the war," Libbie suggested. "Sergeant, were you in the war?"

"Yes, ma'am."

"The cavalry?"

"Yes, ma'am," Todd said.

"Well, then, Eliza. That's where you saw him."

"Yes'm, I s'pose so," Eliza said. "Only somethin' 'bout that man's botherin' me."

"Well, quit staring. It's very rude."

"Yes'm," Eliza said.

Once the women and their luggage were loaded, Todd sent the first wagon on into the fort, some one and a half miles away, while he stayed with the remaining two to supervise the loading of the furniture.

"Sergeant, be especially careful of the piano," Libbie called back to him as the first wagon drove off. "My husband loves it so."

"Yes, ma'am," Todd promised.

Todd watched the wagon drive away, knowing that Eliza would look back at him one more time. So he was not surprised when she did. He nodded at her, and she pulled her shawl about her shoulders, then quickly faced front, as if she had been caught doing something she shouldn't be.

Eliza was right, Todd thought to himself. She *had* seen him before, and she had seen him during the war. He could remember it vividly.

It was in June of 1864, near Louisa Court House, Virginia. A colonel in the Confederate cavalry then, Todd had attacked the Michigan Brigade. During the fighting he saw five caissons of artillery plus a headquarters wagon and a carriage trying to make an escape. Taking a few men with him, he hurried to run them down. When he overtook them, they stopped and surrendered without a fight.

"Who are you?" Todd had asked the Union captain who seemed to be in charge of the small detachment.

"I am Captain Nathan Greene of the Third Michigan Cavalry," the captain replied.

Todd rode over to the wagon, then pulled the flap back to look inside. The wagon contained tenting, bedding, a desk, and several items of clothing. A black woman sat on the front seat of the carriage, clutching a briefcase tightly to her. "Those are the general's things. You better leave 'em be," she warned.

"Who are you?" Todd asked.

"I'm Eliza, the general's maid," the woman answered proudly.

"By *general,* you mean whom?" Todd asked, for he had no idea whose headquarters he had just stumbled upon.

"Why, I mean General Custer, of course!" Eliza said, sounding indignant that she would have to explain.

Todd reached for the briefcase Eliza was holding. "Let me have that, please."

"No!" Eliza insisted. "This belongs to the general!"

"Not anymore it doesn't," Todd informed her. "Now it is part of the spoils of war. Let me have it."

"Mister, you want this satchel, you goin' to have to kill me for it," Eliza said.

Todd turned to one of his sergeants. "Get the satchel from her," he said. "If you can get it without killing her, do it. Otherwise, kill her."

Eliza gasped and, just as he knew she would, handed the briefcase over to Todd's sergeant without further struggle.

To Todd's disappointment, however, there was nothing of military value in the bag. But there were several letters from Custer's wife. That night, around the campfire, some of Todd's men were amusing themselves by reading the letters, which were surprisingly risqué. Embarrassed for Custer, Todd put a stop to it and ordered the letters burned.

Though Todd had seen Eliza at a distance when the Custers were at Fort Hays before the general's court-martial, he had not seen her close enough until today to realize that this was the same woman who had put up such a valiant fight for Custer's briefcase back during the war.

Would she realize where she had seen him before? Not wanting her to put it together enough to positively identify him, he decided he would stay away from her as much as he could.

"We're all loaded up and ready to go, Sarge!" one of the men called a few minutes later.

"All right, let's go," Todd said, mounting his horse and leading the wagons out of town.

Within two days after Libbie's arrival, General Custer hosted a dinner party for several of his officers, including Joe Murchison.

The long dining table was set for twelve, with enough silver, crystal, and china to do credit to any formal dinner anywhere. Adorning the menu were delicacies recently arrived with Libbie: Champagne, German chocolates, and tinned brandied peaches. For dinner they would be served French onion soup and curried lamb.

Libbie Custer, whose light-blue eyes were shining brightly with the excitement of the moment, pointed to one of the settings.

"Lieutenant Murchison, you will sit there, next to Miss Patterson."

"But, Libbie, I thought that was my seat," Tom Custer protested.

"Don't be hoggish, Tom, dear," Libbie replied sweetly. "You dine with us practically every evening. It won't hurt you to give your seat to a new guest. Mr. Murchison, will you help Miss Patterson to her seat?"

"But of course," Joe replied, holding the chair out.

"Thank you, Lieutenant," Alice Patterson said as she was seated.

Alice was very pretty, about twenty-one, of medium height, slender, and with hair the color of wheat straw. Her eyes were emerald and dusted with flecks of gold that, in the reflection of the candlelight, seemed to match her hair. She had a fine fair complexion, with cheeks and lips that achieved their color naturally. She was wearing a lime-green dress of silk, cut in the latest fashion to bare her shoulders. Joe also noticed that she had a beautifully formed neck.

Alice participated in the conversation at the dinner

table with the ease of one who was very self-confident though modest enough not to be intrusive. She had a delightful sense of humor and responded to the stories told by Custer with a laugh that had a lilting, music-box quality to it.

If Joe had expected an opportunity to engage Alice Patterson in a quiet conversation, however, he was disappointed. The meal was pleasant enough—the food was excellent and the conversation interesting—but the conversation was totally dominated by General Custer. Even Tom Custer managed to get in only a few words.

Joe wasn't the only dinner guest of the Custers. In addition to Tom Custer, also present for the evening were Major Barnitz and his wife, Jennie, Captain Hamilton, Major Elliot, and Captain Benteen. Lieutenants Keogh and Cooke rounded out the dinner party. Keogh was a big, affable Irishman, W. W. Cooke was Custer's adjutant.

The conversation was of battle tactics, and during the conversation, Custer made the remark that it was too bad the Indians were not better structured and more cleverly led.

"For then we could engage them in a battle worthy of the name," he suggested.

"Yes, I'm sure that's what Captain Fetterman thought," Tom Custer replied. "He always said he could take on the entire Sioux Nation with eighty armed men—and the whole world saw what happened to him."

"Surely, Tom, you are not comparing me with that pompous braggart," Custer said. "I could forgive you for that. But you are also implying a comparison between our regiment and the Eighteenth Infantry, and in so doing, you are impugning the fighting spirit of the men of the Seventh."

"I meant no disrespect for the regiment, Autie, and you know it," Tom replied.

"Then for whom did you mean the disrespect, Tom? Was it for me?"

"Autie, no. You know better than that."

The exchange between the Custer brothers brought all conversation to a halt.

"Who is Captain Fetterman?" Alice asked in the silence.

"He was just an army officer, that's all," Libbie said. "It's of no importance."

"No," Custer said. "I think it is important that Miss Patterson know who he was. Fetterman may have been a braggart and he may have been impetuous. But he was a regular army officer, and therefore he was one of us, one of our family. And he died a brave man's death, so he deserves more than to have his name dismissed so lightly."

"But who was he?" Alice asked again.

When Joe saw that no one was going to answer, he cleared his throat. "With the general's permission, I'll answer Miss Patterson," he offered.

"Please do," Custer said.

Joe began speaking in a low, matter-of-fact voice.

"Captain William Fetterman was part of the Eighteenth Infantry Regiment. They were en-garrison at Fort Phil Kearny, which is a post in the northern Rockies."

"They were there to guard the Bozeman Trail," Lieutenant Keogh added.

"Yes, sir, I believe they were," Joe said. He continued. "As General Custer indicated, Captain Fetterman was a brave man. During the Civil War he was breveted a colonel, and he was frequently mentioned in dispatches from the front. He even won the Medal of Honor. But he was also a man of absolute self-confidence, perhaps to the point of overconfidence. And he had nothing but contempt for the Indians. His contempt of the Indians caused him to make the remark that he could subdue the entire Sioux Nation with eighty armed men.

"Then, almost two years ago, on the twenty-first of December, 1866, a woodcutting party from the post was attacked by the Sioux. Captain Fetterman set out to rescue them, and, by an ironic twist of fate, he just happened to have exactly eighty men with him, the same number he had always espoused were sufficient to do the job.

"The Indians, seeing Fetterman approach, ran away, just as Fetterman knew they would. As it turned out, however, they weren't actually running. They were acting as decoys to draw the dismounted infantrymen into a trap.

"As Captain Fetterman and his men approached, the Indians stood on the crest of a nearby hill, yelling and gesturing down at them, drawing them farther and farther into their trap. Then the trap was sprung, and the eighty men under Fetterman's command suddenly found themselves surrounded by two thousand armed warriors. The battle lasted no more than twenty minutes. Toward the end, Captain Fetterman and his second-in-command, Captain Brown, stood up and held their pistols at each others' temples. They must have counted down, then fired simultaneously."

Libbie shivered, then wrapped her arms about herself and stood up.

"I . . . I don't like the way this conversation is going," she said.

"Sweetness," Custer said, "are you afraid such a fate awaits your boy? I am hurt to think you could believe I would ever maneuver my command into such a trap."

"I just don't want to talk about it, that's all," Libbie insisted.

"Then we shall talk about something else," Custer agreed. "Miss Patterson, are you familiar with the game of base ball?" He pronounced it as two distinct words.

"I know what it is," Alice replied. "I don't know much about it."

"I am told by those who know the sport that Mr. Murchison is as proficient as any who play the game professionally."

"Oh, my! How did you become so skilled?" Alice asked.

"I played the sport while a cadet at the academy," Joe replied.

"That reminds me, Mr. Murchison. I would like you

to peruse our ranks for others with base ball skills," Custer said. "Next summer we shall put together a team that can take the measure of any other army team on the frontier."

"I shall be glad to, sir," Joe replied.

"Do you see now, Libbie? We are talking about something else," Custer said. "Won't you please return to the table?"

"I'm sorry," Libbie apologized as she sat down.

"Never apologize for doing what your heart moves you to do," Custer said. He reached across the table to take Libbie's hand in his. "It warms a man's soul to know that he has a woman who loves him so." Custer looked over at Joe. "Mr. Murchison."

"Yes, sir?"

"If you are fortunate enough, some day you will have a woman just like that."

"I would be lucky, indeed," Joe agreed.

"Oh, no, Mr. Murchison. You do not depend upon luck to find such a woman. It is not by chance that the terms 'love and war' are so often linked, for the skills required in one will serve you well in the other. As if you are a battlefield commander, you must first reconnoiter your position, then strike with the all the aggressiveness of a cavalry charge."

"Yes, sir," Joe replied, not sure where Custer was going.

"Then do so," Custer said.

"I beg your pardon, sir?"

"Take Miss Patterson for a walk, my boy," Custer said. "Show her the base ball field and explain the game to her. Do I have to draw you a picture?"

The others around the table laughed.

"No, sir, no further explanation is needed," Joe replied quickly. He stood up and reached for Alice's chair. "Miss Patterson, would you care to take a walk?"

"I would love to," Alice replied sweetly.

"Take a wrap, dear," Libbie called. "The nights can be quite chilly at this time of the year."

Outside, Alice put her hand easily, comfortably,

through Joe's arm as they strolled across the now-dark quadrangle.

It *was* cool, though the air was more bracing than cold. The hospital, commandant's quarters, and even Custer's house—which was the most substantial of all the married officers' quarters—gleamed white in the moonlight. The officers' quarters were all well-lighted by kerosene lamps, and the windows shone brightly, projecting splashes of glimmering gold onto the ground outside. The sutler's store was also well-lighted, but beyond the store it was dark. On the far side of the quadrangle much dimmer lights shone from the enlisted men's barracks and from the married NCOs' quarters.

"Why are the lights so dim on the far side of the post?" Alice asked. "Is it to keep the Indians from seeing us?"

Joe smiled. "No, the army furnishes one candle per month per soldier, but lamps and kerosene must be bought, and that can get fairly expensive. Therefore, the enlisted men use candles almost exclusively."

"Oh, the poor things, to spend so much time in the dark."

"They don't seem to mind it too much," Joe said, and as if to underscore his comment, a loud burst of laughter rolled across the parade ground from one of the barracks.

"May I call you Joe?"

"I would be most flattered."

"Do you like the army, Joe?"

"Yes, I do like the army. I like it very much."

"What do you like about it?"

"I don't know that I can answer that," Joe replied. "A sense of belonging, I suppose. Although the army is not a surrogate for my family. I have a mother and father back in Illinois. But from the moment I set foot on the Plain at West Point, I knew I had found my calling." He shrugged. "That's not much of an answer, I suppose. But it is the kind of thing that if it has to be explained, then it cannot be explained."

The chording of a guitar and the words and melody

of a song, in four-part harmony, drifted across the quadrangle.

"Oh, listen to that. Isn't it beautiful?" Alice asked.

"Yes, it is. Sometimes at night I leave the window open in my BOQ room, and I am literally serenaded to sleep by the singing from the barracks."

"They are like children in a way, aren't they?" Alice said. "The enlisted men, I mean. Happy-go-lucky, no cares or worries."

"I suppose one can be lulled into thinking that," Joe replied. "And perhaps some of the more patronizing officers truly believe it. But the truth is far different."

"What is the truth?"

"An army post is like a city. The officers are the city officials and the employers. The enlisted men are the citizens of the city, and like the citizens of any city, they are a diverse bunch. We have heroes and villains, courageous and cowardly, virtuous and evil, living side by side, each with his own individual history."

"General Custer doesn't feel that way, does he?"

"Why do you say that? I think he has an enormous pride in the Seventh," Joe replied.

"Yes, in the Seventh Cavalry as a collective unit. Not in the individual soldiers. I have never heard him speak of them as you just did."

"To be fair, he cannot think of them in the same way," Joe replied. "He must only think of the Seventh as it can be utilized tactically. If he starts thinking of the soldiers as individuals, he will lose his effectiveness." They were passing a small bed of chrysanthemums, and Joe, eyeing a robust bloom glowing brightly in the moonlight, bent over and picked it. He handed it to Alice.

"Why, Joe, what a sweet thought," Alice said. "And what can I give you in return?"

He looked at her, her face radiantly beautiful in the moonlight, and, as if moved by some outside force, he brought his lips to hers.

At first his kiss was hesitant, a cautious testing of the waters. But Alice didn't resist him. In fact, her lips were soft and receptive; more than receptive, they were eager. She opened her mouth on his, then put her arms around him and pulled him to her.

Joe could feel her body pressing against his. Through the silk of her dress, every curve and mound was made known to him by their close contact. He felt a heat in his body, then the immodest pressure of his growing need for her. He tried to pull away, but Alice plied herself to him even more tightly, not shying away from his condition, but seeming to take pleasure in being its cause. Finally they separated, and Joe looked into her face.

"I . . . I'm sorry," he sputtered. "I had no right to force myself upon you in such a fashion. Please forgive me."

"Joe," Alice said quietly, "if I had not wanted you to kiss me, you couldn't have done it."

"Nevertheless, I feel I took an unfair advantage of you. Or if not you, then of the other single officers of this post. It is my understanding that you were brought out here for the morale of all."

"Oh, is that so? And what is to be done with me? Am I to be passed around from officer to officer like an old copy of *Harper's Weekly,* to be read, then discarded?"

"No, nothing like that!"

"Joe, do you know why General Custer asked you to walk with me and not one of the other officers?"

"Because he wanted me to show you the baseball field, and I am the only one who knows anything about the game," he replied.

"No, not at all," Alice said. "*He* chose you because *I* chose you."

"I beg your pardon?"

"At the parade yesterday morning, Libbie and I stood on the porch in front of the sutler's store, watching as the troops passed in review. We both agreed that you were the handsomest officer of them all, and I expressed a desire to meet you."

"Oh," Joe said. He didn't know how he should respond to such a statement.

"And here we are, met," Alice said. She smiled and

said playfully, "So you see, Mr. Murchison, when General Custer was talking about the art of tactics and maneuver, it is not only men who employ such devices."

"No, I . . . I suppose not," Joe said. If the relationship between men and women really could be described as battlefield tactics, then he had been outgeneraled from the moment he sat down to dinner this evening.

The next morning, Captain Hamilton called Joe into his office.

"So, how did you get on with Miss Patterson last night?" he asked.

"Just fine, sir. We had a most pleasant walk," Joe replied.

Hamilton smiled. "It must have been *very* pleasant," he said. "Especially for her."

"What do you mean, sir?"

"Well, she wants to go into Hays City today, and General Custer has asked me to detail you to be her escort. Have a 'pleasant' time in town, Lieutenant."

"Oh, sir, I don't know. . . ." Joe demurred. He pointed outside. "We're in the midst of mounted drill now, and—"

"Sergeant Todd can handle it."

"But I really should—"

"That will be all, Lieutenant. Miss Patterson is waiting."

"Yes, sir."

Hamilton chuckled. "What's wrong with you, Joe? Any other officer in this post would stand on his head for that duty."

Joe smiled. "It is an agreeable prospect, sir," he said. "But I thought it best not to appear too eager."

Hamilton laughed out loud. "Have a good time," he said. "But remember that you are not only an officer, you are also, by an act of Congress, a gentleman."

"I won't forget, sir."

Joe took Alice into town in a two-seat "country wagon," a small, well-sprung, and easily handled wagon that wasn't army issue, but belonged to General Miles, the post commandant.

Hays City consisted of two dirt streets. One street ran parallel to the Kansas Pacific Railroad track, and the other ran at right angles to it. Hays City had no street cleaners, therefore the street was packed nearly solid with horse droppings. It not only made footing treacherous, it smelled—even more so after a rain, such as the one early that morning. Most of the buildings were constructed of unfinished, whip-sawed lumber, though the Railroad Hotel and one or two of the numerous saloons were painted.

Fortunately a boardwalk had been laid along each side of the street, with plank crossings at each end. This allowed pedestrians some degree of mobility, and Joe and Alice made use of that convenience while she went shopping. She bought a bolt of blue cotton cloth and a spool of yellow ribbon. She also bought some handkerchiefs, buttons, and a few other items, moving from store to store to make her purchases while Joe walked from shop to shop with her, carrying the packages.

"Is there a nice restaurant in town?" Alice asked a female clerk in one of the shops.

"Oh, yes, dear," the middle-aged lady answered with a pleasant smile. "Why, you and your beau would have to go clear to St. Louis to find a place nicer'n Delmonico's."

"Thank you," Alice replied. "If I can talk my *beau* into it, we will eat there," she said, smiling at Joe as she referred to him as her beau.

"Are you sure you want to eat in town?" Joe asked as they stepped back outside onto the boardwalk. "Hays City isn't like any of the towns you're used to. It can be pretty rough."

"Nonsense, what can happen in the middle of the day?" Alice asked. "Besides, I'm tired of eating every meal with the Custers. I have no complaints with the food, you understand. Eliza is a very good cook. But it would be nice to dine out once, don't you think?"

Having cautioned her, Joe turned his thoughts to the

idea of having lunch with Alice. In fact, it seemed like a most pleasant prospect. "You're right," he said. "I think it would be a great idea."

He was surprised by the variety offered on the restaurant's menu, though he realized that, with the railroad, the finest delicacies from all over the country could be brought here, still fresh, in a matter of a few days.

"I think I'll start with oysters on the half shell," he said. "I haven't had any of those since I left New York."

Alice nodded. "Good idea. I'll start with the same."

Joe wasn't the only soldier in town. Just across the street from Delmonico's Restaurant was the Ace High Saloon. Inside, two troopers were standing at the bar. There were worried expressions on their faces, and as they stood together sharing a bottle of whiskey, they were trying to decide what to do next. Their worries came from the fact that they were absent without leave and had been since reveille that morning.

"Hell, Eddie, we could just go out there an' tell the first sergeant we overslept," one of them, a private named Ben, said. "He's a good man, he'd understand."

"He'd understand that we spent the night with a couple of whores and didn't even wake up until noon?"

"Yeah, well, the women promised they'd wake us up in plenty of time to get back," Ben said.

"And who was supposed to wake *them* up?" Eddie asked.

"I don't know," Ben admitted.

"We may as well go out there an' take our medicine," Eddie said. He reached for the bottle. "Only let's don't do it till we finish this. The way I figure it, we're goin' to get at least thirty days in the guardhouse, so this liquor's got to last us a long time."

"You're right, there," Ben agreed.

At the opposite end of the bar, a smallish civilian with a drooping mustache and cold, beady eyes slapped a coin down.

"Whiskey," he ordered.

"Afraid we got no blended whiskey left, Mr. Clay,"

the bartender said as he wiped the bar with a damp cloth. He nodded toward the two soldiers. "See them two soldiers down there? They bought the last bottle this morning."

The man called Clay pointed to the bottle in front of the soldiers. "I'll have that one."

"Can't, I told you. Them two bought the whole bottle," the bartender said.

"You two" Clay called. "Soldier boys! Slide that bottle down this way!"

The two privates looked at him, saw how small he was, then shrugged their shoulders and continued with their conversation.

"Didn't you hear what I said?" Clay called, louder this time.

"Bartender," Eddie said. "Pour the gentleman a glass on me."

"There, Mr. Clay," the bartender said nervously, trying to placate his patron. "Don't you think them soldiers are bein' reasonable?"

The bartender knew that the man called Martin Clay had a nasty disposition and a reputation for being a fast draw and a deadly shot. Some claimed he had already killed more than a dozen men.

"I don't want a glass, you sonuvabitch," Clay said to the bartender. "I want the whole thing." He walked to the two soldiers, reaching for the bottle of whiskey.

Eddie jerked the bottle back, then turned toward the civilian, squaring himself to face him. "Mister, I don't know who the hell you are, but you touch this bottle again and I'm gonna knock you on your narrow little ass."

"No!" the bartender cautioned, holding his hands out toward the two soldiers. It was obvious that they didn't know who Clay was. "Don't rile him."

"Don't rile him? The little pissant's rilin' *us*," Eddie said.

Clay grunted with contempt, then reached again for the neck of the whiskey bottle. Before his fingers could wrap securely around it, Eddie hit him. Clay caught the punch on his jaw and went down to the floor.

"Haw!" Ben said, pointing to Clay. "Ole Eddie told you what he was goin' to do. Why didn't you clean your ears out and listen?" He reached down to help the civilian up. "Come, let us buy you a drink."

Clay stood up, pushed away from Ben, then glared at Eddie. "Pull your gun, mister."

"What?"

"You heard me. I said pull your gun or give me the bottle."

Eddie looked bewildered. "What are you sayin', mister? You're wantin' to pull a gun over a bottle of whiskey?"

"Give him the bottle, Eddie," Ben said, uneasy now about the sudden turn of events.

"Hell, no, I ain't goin' to give it to him. Mister, I don't know what you got stuck in your craw," Eddie continued in a resolute voice, "but if you're wantin' to fight, I reckon I can oblige you."

"Leave it be, Eddie," Ben said again. By now his voice was highpitched with fright.

Clay was standing with his legs slightly bowed and with his hands hanging loosely by his side. There was a cold, killing glint in his eyes.

"Yeah, you're right," Eddie abruptly said. "There's no sense in fightin'." He picked up the bottle. "Come on; let's go where there's better company."

"Right," Ben said, relieved that Eddie had backed off.

"You two fellas are yellow-bellied cowards," Clay said coldly. "Is that what the yellow scarf around your necks stands for? Bein' a coward?"

Eddie stopped, but Ben continued.

"Come on, Eddie, let's get the hell out of here," Ben pleaded. Eddie looked back at the belligerent little civilian, as if thinking he might give him a fight after all. Then, thinking better of it, he shrugged and went out onto the front porch with Ben.

Clay followed them outside.

"Hold on, there. You two yellow-bellied soldier boys ain't goin' nowhere with that bottle," he said again.

"Oh, yes, we are," Eddie replied, his voice now

quivering with nervousness. "We don't want no trouble, so we're just goin' back out to the post."

"You won't reach your horse alive," the civilian warned.

Eddie and Ben stopped, and Ben turned to face the civilian.

"What are you goin' to do? Shoot us in the back?"

"Could be."

"Then you're goin' to have to do it, 'cause we're ridin' out of here."

"I'll make it easy on you," Clay said. "I'm going to count to three. You can pull your gun anytime you want, but you'd better do it before I get to three 'cause that's when I'm pulling mine."

"No! We don't want to do this!" Eddie said in a frightened voice.

Clay smiled evilly. "You ain't got no choice now," he said. "You gave that up when you wouldn't let me have the bottle." He began counting. "One . . ."

"My God, Eddie, he's goin' to do it!" Ben yelped.

With shaking hands, Eddie put the bottle down. Now he and Eddie stood on the porch looking back at the small man with the drooping mustache. Several others had gathered around as well, drawn to the scene by the promise of instant death.

Joe and Alice were just finishing their meal when the two shots rang out across the street—short, flat, and right on top of each other.

"What was that?" Alice asked.

"It sounded like gunshots," Joe said.

"Good heavens! Gunshots in the middle of town?"

"It's probably nothing," Joe said. "Out here the men quite often shoot off their weapons for no reason."

Even as Joe was trying to placate Alice, however, he had the feeling there was more to this than a drunk having a good time. The way the two shots sounded, coming so close together as they did, didn't bode well.

A moment later, Joe's premonition was borne out when a man wearing a star on his shirt stepped up to the table.

"Lieutenant, I take it you're from the fort?" the lawman asked.

"Yes, I'm Lieutenant Murchison. Is there something I can do for you, Sheriff?"

"Deputy," the man replied. "I'm Deputy Kyle Horner. You might'a heard the shots. We just had us a shootin' across the street. I was wonderin' if you'd come over an' take a look at the bodies. See if maybe you could identify 'em?"

"Why should I be able to identify the bodies?"

" 'Cause they're soldiers," the deputy answered.

Joe quickly wiped his mouth with his napkin and stood up. "All right," he agreed. "I'll take a look."

He followed the deputy across the street. There on the mud-spattered boardwalk in front of a saloon lay the two soldiers. They were on their backs with their legs spread wide and their feet turned out. One had a black hole between his eyes, the other a hole in his chest. At the opposite end of the porch two "soiled doves," as the prostitutes were called, stood with their hands on their hips, looking down at the dead soldiers with morbid curiosity.

"Oh, my!" Alice gasped.

Surprised that she had followed him, Joe turned to her. "Alice, go back," he said. "You don't need to see this."

"Those poor boys!" Alice said, holding a handkerchief to her lips.

"Do you know them?" the deputy asked.

"No," Joe answered.

"They're cavalry troopers, aren't they?"

"Yes, I've seen both of them at the post, but as they aren't from my troop, I don't know their names."

"Yeah, well, as long as I know they're from the post, I reckon we'll figure out who they are," the deputy said.

"What happened?"

"They got into a gunfight with a fella named Martin Clay. You ever heard of him?"

"I can't say as I have."

"Evidently these two boys hadn't heard of 'im, either. Else they wouldn't of been dumb enough to get into a gunfight with 'im.'"

"You're saying it was a gunfight? Look at their holsters." Joe pointed to the black, cavalry-issue holsters with "U.S." embossed on the closed holster flap. "The pistol flaps aren't even unsnapped."

"I didn't say they was good at it. I just said they got into a gunfight they ought not to have."

"Where is the man who shot them? This Martin Clay."

"Ain't no tellin' where he is now," the bartender said, stepping through the saloon door with a bar towel draped across his shoulder. "Soon's he shot 'em, he picked up the bottle of whiskey and rode out of here."

"The bottle of whiskey?"

"That's what they was fightin' over." The bartender explained what happened.

Joe shook his head. "Are you going after him?" he asked the deputy.

The deputy spit a stream of tobacco juice onto the porch beside the boot of one of the troopers, then shook his head.

"I don't reckon so."

"Why not?"

"I got no jurisdiction outside the county, and I figure he's long gone by now. Besides, ain't no one man goin' to bring in Martin Clay."

"Are you afraid of him?"

"Hell, yes, I'm afraid," the deputy said. "That's what I been tryin' to tell you. Now, what you want to do about these here bodies?"

"Get them off the street," Joe ordered. "They deserve better than to be gawked at like some circus attraction. I'll send a wagon back for them."

Joe escorted Alice back to their borrowed buggy and headed out of town. They were halfway back to the fort when he finally broke the silence.

"Are you all right?" he asked.

"I can't stop thinking about those poor men," Alice said. "Why, they may have been the very ones we heard singing last night, or laughing outside the sutler's store."

"Perhaps, but I doubt it. These men were downtown during the middle of a duty day, which means they probably spent the night in town. I'm sure we will find that they were absent without authorization."

"I'm glad you told the deputy to get them off the street," Alice said. "You're right, they shouldn't be left out like that."

"Yes, well, I just hope he did it."

"Oh, he did," she insisted.

"What makes you so sure?"

"Because you told him to," Alice said. She smiled, and put her arm through his, then shifted closer to him on the wagon seat. "And I have a feeling that people listen to what you say."

That weekend there was a dance at the officers' mess. But if Joe had any notion of dancing every dance with Alice, he was soon to discover that the notion was ill conceived. Alice, like every other woman at the dance, had her card completely filled. Even Mrs. Custer danced with the single officers as the handful of officers' wives did their best to sustain morale at the remote post.

By now Joe had learned the names of the two young soldiers who had been killed in town earlier in the week: Troopers Eddie Quinn and Ben Daniels. Todd told Joe that Quinn had been one of the troopers who came from New York with them a little over two years ago. Once Todd mentioned it, Joe remembered him, although he had forgotten until then. He felt bad that he had forgotten.

Joe did manage to have the final dance with Alice, and she was by his side at the end of the evening when General Custer offered up a toast to "the troopers who have gone on to Fiddlers' Green."

"To the troopers at Fiddlers' Green," the officers responded, holding their glasses high, then tossing down the drink.

"What is Fiddlers' Green?" Alice asked.

"It's a grassy glen beside a clear stream, where every cavalryman who has ever heard boots and saddles gathers after they die. There, they drink together and exchange barracks tales as they wait for taps to be played over the last trooper."

Alice smiled. "Oh, you mean it's a superstition, then."

"Not necessarily."

"But of course it is," Alice insisted. "It's a myth. You know there is no such thing as a place where all dead soldiers gather."

"Christians hold to the belief of a life after death, don't they?" Joe said. "Do you think heaven is a myth?"

"No, of course not."

"And isn't heaven supposed to be a place where everyone wants to go?"

"Yes."

"Then if cavalrymen want to go to Fiddlers' Green after they die, who is to say they don't? That might be their idea of heaven."

Alice laughed. "All right. I won't argue with you anymore."

"Band leader," Custer called.

"Yes, sir."

"Play 'Garryowen'!"

"Yes, sir!" the bandleader replied, and the jaunty tune that the Seventh Cavalry had adopted as its own was the final event of the evening.

* * *

Eight

Joe was on the parade ground, conducting mounted drill with the men of his platoon. The men and horses were going through their paces crisply and without complaint. Part of the reason was it had turned sharply colder within the last week, and brisk movement about the parade ground helped to warm the blood.

Joe had no such help, however; since he was conducting the drill, he was required to do nothing more than sit in his saddle and observe. Occasionally he would stand in his saddle to shout instructions or find some excuse to break into a gallop—more to warm the blood than to correct some mistake.

Also, he had thoughts of Alice to keep him warm. He had been seeing a great deal of her lately. They had gone picnicking on the last warm day, and he had called on her so many times at the Custer residence that Libbie jokingly asked if he didn't want his own key. Then, last evening, they had been out on the quadrangle in the cold night air, sitting on one blanket and wrapped in another as they listened to a concert given by the post band.

In the dark, and under the blanket, Alice had unbuttoned her blouse to allow Joe's hand to slip inside. It had moved easily under her lace camisole where he cupped her warm breast and hard nipple in his palm. It was the most exciting thing he had ever done, the more so because it was being done secretly while right in the midst of so many people.

Joe heard a rider approaching, and when he looked around, he saw the company clerk from D Troop. Realizing that he must have been sent by Captain Hamilton, Joe turned the drill detail over to Sergeant Todd, then rode out to meet the clerk.

"Captain Hamilton's regards, sir, and he asks if you would come to the orderly room," the clerk said, saluting.

"Mr. Murchison," Captain Hamilton said when Joe reported to him a few minutes later. "I have a mission for you and your platoon."

Joe smiled. "The men will be glad to hear that, sir," he said. "Anything to get them away from drilling."

Hamilton laughed. "I think the whole reason we drill them so much is so that no matter what we may ask of them, it is always an improvement over what they have been doing. But this I think you really will appreciate. I want you and your platoon to go to Fort Larned and escort the paymaster back here to Fort Hays."

"When do we leave, sir?"

"Just after parade, tomorrow morning," Hamilton said. "It will take you two days to get there and two days back, and I want you here in time to pay the troops by the end of the month."

"Yes, sir."

"Oh, and Joe, you have heard about Lieutenant Kidder, have you not?"

Lieutenant Kidder was a second lieutenant who, along with all ten of his men, had been killed and mutilated by Indians a year earlier while undertaking to deliver a message to Custer, in the field.

"Yes, sir, I have heard of him."

"Good. I don't want to have another second lieutenant wind up like him. So keep your eyes open out there."

"I will, sir," Joe promised.

* * *

A knock sounded on the door of Joe's room, and he sat up suddenly. Except for a silver splash of the moon, his room was in total darkness. What time was it? Had he overslept?

Quickly, he hurried to the door and jerked it open, expecting to see a trooper sent by Captain Hamilton to wake him. To his absolute shock, it was Alice Patterson.

"Alice!" he gasped in surprise. "Alice, what is it? What's wrong?"

"May I come in?" she asked.

Joe stepped back to let her in. "Of course you can come in." He looked behind her. "Are you alone?"

Alice giggled. "Of course I'm alone. You wouldn't expect me to bring someone with me when I call on my beau in the middle of the night, would you?"

"No, I guess not," Joe said. "But why are you here?"

Alice smiled at him. "If I really need a reason, I suppose I could say that I have come to tell you good-bye," Alice said.

"Good-bye?"

"You *are* going out on a scout tomorrow, aren't you?"

"Yes."

"Were you going to leave without saying good-bye?"

"No. We don't leave until after parade. I was going to tell you good-bye then."

"Yes, but then, I couldn't do this," Alice said. She slipped off her overcoat and Joe saw that she was wearing nothing but a silk-muslin chemise beneath. The moonlight through Joe's window highlighted the thin garment and made it shimmer as if by its own light. It draped her form like a filmy curtain, and the nipples of her breasts stood out in bold relief. She smiled when she saw Joe's reaction to her appearance.

"Do you approve of what you see?" she asked.

"Approve is not quite the word," Joe said. "But you shouldn't be here."

"Joe, don't you think I haven't been telling myself that all night long?" Alice asked. "I know what I am doing is wrong. I know, too, that if the Custers found out about it, I would be sent back in disgrace. I even know that I am taking an awful chance with you. You might find my behavior so unseemly that you won't want to have anything more to do with me. And yet, despite all those good reasons for staying away, I couldn't stop myself from coming here."

Joe smiled at her, then put his hand on her shoulder. "I'm a coward," he said. "You shouldn't have had to brave the night to come to me. I should have gone to you. Only, I didn't know if you'd have me." He leaned down and kissed her.

"Oh, Joe," Alice whimpered, and her quivering lips opened on his in a kiss both tender and urgent. "Joe," she whispered in his ear, "I've made the first move. The rest is up to you. I've no will of my own, no courage to go on nor strength to resist."

Joe needed no further urging to take the lead now. His desire had taken charge, sweeping away all barriers, forcing him into bold moves. He kissed her again, more urgently than before, and again she made a strange little sound deep in her throat and plied her body against his.

He reached down and picked her up, then carried her to the bed he had so recently abandoned. He lay her on the covers that were still warm from his own body and kissed her again, this time pressing against her, pulling her body to his, feeling her softness against the hardness of his muscles. His kisses became more demanding, and Alice became more responsive, positioning herself here and moving herself there to accommodate him. The tip of her tongue darted across his lips, then dipped into his mouth. The warmth Joe had felt erupted now to a raging inferno, and he began to pull at the hem of Alice's chemise and his own sleeping shirt until suddenly they were naked against each other.

Joe moved his hard, demanding body over her soft, yielding thighs and, poised above her, paused for one last moment, as if giving her one last chance to resist. When she offered none, he went on.

* * *

When it was over, Joe lay on her for a while, not pressing down with all his weight, but just feeling the softness and the warmth of her body beneath his. Alice stroked his shoulders until, eventually, Joe rolled to one side to lie beside her.

"Alice," Joe finally said. "Will you marry me?"

Alice was silent for a long moment.

At last she raised up on one elbow and looked down at Joe. Her breast on that side swung forward, and the nipple touched Joe's chest, causing a tingling, pleasurable sensation.

"Joe, I can't," she said. "Please, don't ask."

"What?" Joe asked in surprise. "But, I don't understand. After this, I thought . . . that is . . ."

"Joe, my sweet, sweet Joe," Alice said, running her fingers lightly across his lips. "Did you think to make an honest woman of me?"

"Well, I . . . I don't know," Joe said.

Alice smiled. "Don't you know it's too late for that?"

"No, it's not too late. What just happened was an act of love. No one can hold that against us."

Alice chuckled. "Oh, Joe. Oh, you sweet, sweet, innocent. Did you think this was my first time?"

He looked away.

"You did think that, didn't you?" Suddenly Alice gasped and put her hand to her lips. "Oh, my God, I just realized. It was *your* first time, wasn't it?"

"Let's don't talk about it any more."

"Oh, Joe, I'm so sorry."

"Why? It had to happen sometime. I couldn't stay a virgin forever."

Alice, who was still supporting herself on one elbow, now moved down onto Joe, mashing her breasts against his naked chest. She put her finger to his cheek and turned his head toward her.

"You're right, I'm not sorry," she said, smiling broadly. "I'm glad I was your first. And if you're up to it, I'd like to be your second, as well." She slid her hand down across his stomach. "Oh!" she said. "I see that you *are* up to it."

* * *

The next morning the entire regiment was formed into a regimental parade front for Joe's departure. Joe's platoon was broken out of the regiment formed in front of them. He was on horseback, standing in his stirrups. For the moment there was absolute silence, the only audible sound that of the snapping and flapping of the garrison flag, flying high overhead.

Joe surveyed the assembled platoon of thirty-two mounted cavalrymen, sitting tall and proud in their saddles and stretched out in a long, single line facing him.

"Sergeant Todd, prepare to move out!" Joe shouted to his platoon sergeant.

Sergeant Todd moved out of the line, then turned back to face the men. "Platoon, form column of twos!" he yelled, his strong command voice echoing across the fort.

The men executed the command.

"Guidon, post!" he yelled again, and a soldier carrying a red-and-white swallowtail pennant galloped to the head of the column.

"Sir," Sergeant Todd said, saluting and reporting to Joe, "the platoon is formed."

"Thank you, Sergeant," Joe said, returning Todd's salute. He turned to face Custer, then saluted sharply.

"Colonel, I have the honor, sir, of reporting that the detail is ready to depart in accordance with your command."

"Execute your marching order, Lieutenant," Custer replied, returning Joe's salute.

Joe turned back to Todd. "Move them out, Sergeant," he said quietly.

Sergeant Todd stood high in his stirrups. "Forward ho!" he yelled.

The platoon started through the gates as, beneath the flagpole, the regimental band began playing "Garryowen."

Colonel Custer held the regiment in parade formation so they could watch as Joe's men passed by. Colonel A. J. Smith, his staff officers, and the ladies of the post were assembled just inside the sally port, watching as the platoon departed.

As Joe passed, he drew his saber and gave the command, "Eyes right!" He held the hilt of the sword at his chin, with the blade pointing up and out at a forty-five degree angle; then he turned his head to the right to pay his respects to the officers and their ladies. Colonel Smith and the staff officers returned his salute. Alice smiled at him privately, and from the look in her eyes Joe knew she was recalling their time together last night. Joe almost felt as if everyone on the post could read her expression, and his cheeks burned a little as he looked forward and returned his saber to its scabbard just as he and his men passed through the gates.

It was midway through the second day, and the column was on the beaten trail, moving slowly but steadily. The plains stretched out before them in motionless waves, one after another. As each wave was crested, another was exposed and beyond that another still.

The march was a symphony of sound: jangling equipment, squeaking leather, the dull thud of hoofbeats. Those same hoofbeats stirred up grasshoppers to whir ahead of them in awkward flight. Underneath, the dusty grass gave up a pungent but not unpleasant smell. Joe took out his watch. Since it was time for another break, he held up his hand.

"Sergeant, give the men and horses a short blow," he ordered.

"Yes, sir," Todd replied, and he passed the order on to the men, then dismounted.

The soldiers dismounted as well. Some of them stretched out on the ground for a moment, while several others used the opportunity to relieve themselves.

"Bet you I can piss that grasshopper off that-there weed," one of the soldiers said.

"A nickel says you can't."

The soldier issuing the challenge directed his stream toward the grasshopper, knocking him off.

"Sonuvabitch, he did it! Guido pissed off a grasshopper!"

Several men offered their humorous congratulations, and Guido picked up the immediate nickname of Deadeye Dick.

Joe couldn't help but chuckle at their antics. Then he handed the reins of his horse to one of the soldiers, and, taking his field glasses, he climbed the hill to scan the horizon. He saw only dusty rocks, shimmering grass, and more ranges of hills under the beating sun. He started to drop the glasses when he noticed one outcropping of rock that looked slightly different from the others. He examined it more closely.

"Sergeant Todd!" he called. "Would you come here, please?"

Todd ran up the hill, so that he was puffing quite audibly by the time he reached Joe.

"What is it, sir? What do you see?"

"Have you made this journey before, Sergeant?"

"Yes, sir, several times."

"Then it may be nothing." He handed his field glasses to Todd. "But if I'm not mistaken, there's a burned-out wagon out there. Was it there the last time you were here?"

"No sir, it was not there," Todd said. "Nor has it been reported, for it would have been marked on Captain Hamilton's map."

"That's right, it would be, wouldn't it?" Joe said. Every item of any significance was annotated on Hamilton's map—a farmhouse, an abandoned way station, even a broken wagon wheel. Joe had studied the map carefully and had not seen a burned-out wagon. Surely a burned-out wagon would be listed if anyone knew about it.

"Well, we'd better make a note of it so we can—" His words were interrupted by Todd.

"Oh, sweet Jesus!" Todd exclaimed. He was still looking through the glasses. "Sweet, sweet Jesus!"

"What is it, Todd? What do you see?" Joe asked.

Todd returned the field glasses. "Look to the rear of the wagon and tell me what you see, sir," he said. "For I hope I have made a mistake in what I think it is."

Joe looked at the wagon again, then moved the

glasses to the back. There, lying on the ground behind the wagon, he saw two clumps of red.

"What is it? I can't quite—" Suddenly Joe knew what he was seeing. He was looking at bodies—women's bodies. The red he saw was the fabric of their dresses.

"Let's get the men mounted," Joe said.

Sergeant Todd ran back down the hill. "Mount up, men! We've seen something ahead!"

"What is it, Sergeant Todd?" someone asked, and half a dozen others repeated the question.

"It's something the lieutenant wants to investigate," Todd replied without saying anything more. "Now, would you get mounted, please? Or do you need an engraved invitation? *Mount up!*" he shouted, much louder this time.

Joe reached his own horse, then swung into the saddle, wondering what they would find when they reached the wagon. Would the bodies be swollen and purple? Would they be hacked to pieces? Had the women been abused before they were killed?

"Forward at a trot, Sergeant," Joe said.

The column broke into a trot at Sergeant Todd's command. Sabers, canteens, mess kits, and rifles jangled under the irregular rhythm of the trotting horses, and dust boiled up behind them. Joe held the trot until they were within a hundred yards of the burned-out wagon.

"At a gallop!" he called, and he stood in his stirrups and drew his saber, pointing it forward. The saber wasn't drawn as a weapon, but rather as a signaling device, for a drawn saber meant that carbines should be pulled from the saddle scabbard and held at the ready.

Every nerve in Joe's body was tingling as the group of soldiers swept down on the wagon. Joe was alert to every blade of grass, every rock and stone, every hill and gully. He was not about to be another Second Lieutenant Kidder.

They reached the wagon and Joe held up his hand, calling the men to a halt.

"Line of skirmishers, front and rear!" he ordered, and two squads of horse soldiers moved into position.

Joe swung down from his horse, and Sergeant Todd started to dismount as well.

"No, Sergeant," Joe said, holding up his hand. "I think one of us should be ready to assume mounted command."

"Very good, sir," Todd replied, taking the reins of Joe's horse.

Joe walked toward the two red clumps on the ground. As he approached, he could hear the buzzing of flies. He gasped when he got there.

It was a woman and a little girl, lying side by side in the grass. Both bodies were penetrated by several arrows. A short distance beyond the wagon was a man lying on his back. He was stripped naked, and the top of his head was cut away. Brains were spilled onto the ground. His heart had been removed and penis and testicles cut off.

"Sergeant, assign a burial detail," Joe ordered as he walked back to the horses.

"Yes, sir," Todd said. He called for half a dozen men, and the men, moved by morbid curiosity, didn't even protest the order as they took shovels and began to dig the graves.

Some time later, as the dirt was being packed down into three mounds, Todd walked over to Joe and asked, "Lieutenant, did you notice something about those bodies?"

"What do you mean?" Joe asked.

"They weren't swollen by the sun. They were probably killed this morning—no more than a couple of hours ago."

"Damn!" Joe said. "If we had just gotten started a little earlier this morning, we could have prevented this!"

"Yes, sir," Todd replied. "But, of course, we had no way of knowing."

"Sarge! Sarge, we found somethin'!" one of the troopers shouted.

Sergeant Todd went over to see what it was, while

Joe stood over the three graves. He tried to say a little prayer, but no words would come. All he could think of was that had he been a couple of hours earlier, he might have been able to save them.

Todd returned. "You might want to take a look at this, sir," he said. He was holding a small leather-bound notebook, which he handed to Joe. "It appears one of them was keeping a diary."

Joe opened the little book and read aloud from the front page.

"OUR TRIP WEST,
OR A THRILLING ACCOUNT OF THE
EXCITING JOURNEY OF THE FAMILY CARMODY.
RITA CARMODY, AUTHOR.
"April 15th, 1868, Corinth, Mississippi. My father has just told us that we are moving to the West. He says there is good farm land there for free, and we are going to get our share."

"Damn!" Todd said. "Folks hear the word 'free' and they go crazy. They'd have to be crazy to come out here like that, in one wagon, travelin' alone."

"Real pioneers will withstand any hardship or brave any danger," Joe said. He remembered hearing stories of his own grandfather fighting Indians when Illinois was first settled. There were no Indians in Illinois now . . . evidence of the inevitability of civilization. Someday, no doubt, there would be no hostile Indians in Kansas. But that would come too late for the Carmodys.

"Trumpeter, sound to horse," Joe called. "We'll be getting underway again."

The trumpeter blew the call, which summoned the troopers back to their horses, and a few minutes later the column was on the march again. They maintained a steady pace for the rest of the day, until they made camp that night.

Sergeant Todd assigned a detail to see to the horses and a few others to start the cooking fires for supper and coffee. A guard was posted, and Joe sat down near one of the fires and began reading more from the diary.

"Oh, damn," he said, softly. "Todd!"

"Yes, sir, what is it?"

"How many did we bury back there?"

"Three, sir."

"I think there may have been four of them, including another girl, an older sister." He showed the diary to Todd.

> Emma has been pining ever since we left Fort Riley because she met a beau there. She told Papa she wanted to get married, but Papa said he didn't want any of his daughters marrying anyone who wore a blue uniform.

"Doesn't that sound like another girl was with them?"

"More a young woman, than a girl," Todd agreed.

"What happened to her? Could we have overlooked her?"

Todd shook his head. "No, sir. We looked all over the area. There were no more bodies."

"That leaves only one inescapable conclusion," Joe said.

"The Indians have her," Todd replied.

Joe nodded. "The heathen bastards."

A few days later, with the paymaster riding with them, Joe and his platoon returned to Fort Hays. There was no parade to greet their return, but Joe could feel all eyes on them as they rode through the sally port and passed under the shadow of the flag. All over the post, training and work details halted as the men watched the soldiers return.

Joe had telegraphed word back to Fort Hays from Fort Larned, telling about the wagon they had found. As soon as he dismissed the detail, he hurried to render a report to Custer.

Custer, having already followed up on the information, told Joe, "Her name is Emma Louise Carmody. She is nineteen."

"Has she been found, sir?" Joe asked anxiously.

Custer shook his head. "No. But the people at Fort Riley remember the family. It seems that the young woman was going to elope with one of the troopers there. Her father found out about it and stopped it at the last minute."

"Is it possible she could have run away to rejoin her beau before the wagon was attacked?" Joe asked hopefully.

"If so, no one at Fort Riley has seen her," Custer replied. "And the soldier in question is still there."

"Then she *is* with the Indians."

"It looks that way. One of my scouts, California Joe, is out there right now, trying to find out what happened."

"Sir, if we find that the young woman has been captured, are we going after her?"

"Absolutely," Custer replied.

"When that occurs, I very much want to be in the rescue party."

"Rescue party? There won't be a rescue party, Mr. Murchison. We will be going out in strength. I intend to lead eleven companies of the Seventh against those heathens."

"Very good sir," Joe said. "And now, if you will excuse me I'm going to go get cleaned up and—"

"Joe," Custer said. It was the first time Custer had ever called him by his first name, and there was something ominous about it.

"Yes sir?"

"I think perhaps you had better have a look at this." Custer held an envelope out toward Joe.

"What is it, sir?"

"It's a letter from Miss Patterson."

"A letter? Why would she send me a letter when we see each other just about every day?"

"She's gone, Joe. She left Fort Hays yesterday morning."

"Gone? But why would she leave? I thought she was going to stay until after the first of the year."

"The only thing she told us was that she felt it best if she left before you came back from your scout. I don't know what happened between the two of you," Custer said. "And I suppose it is none of my business. All she said was that after you read this letter, you will understand." Again, he offered the letter to Joe.

"Thank you, sir."

Joe put the letter in his tunic pocket, saluted, then excused himself to find the privacy to read.

Dear Joe,

It is as difficult for me to write this letter as it is for me to leave this place. I don't want to do either, but I must do both.

Joe, dear, sweet Joe. I fear I may have hurt you cruelly, and I certainly had no intention of doing so. But things got out of hand so quickly. I thought our relationship would be no more than a few shared intimacies, a source of memories when this episode of our lives had passed. But you misunderstood. Now you want to get married, and I am not yet ready for marriage. Even if I were, I would not marry a soldier. And you are so enamored of your army that I know you could not give it up. Indeed, I would not ask you to give it up for fear of it always coming between us.

Therefore, to prevent any more hurt to either one of us, I think it best that I take my leave of this place while you are gone, for surely if I were to see you right now, I would lose my resolve and remain here, to be drawn more deeply into the pit.

Good-bye, Joe. I hope someday you find a woman who truly deserves you, for I surely do not.

With fondest affection,
Alice Patterson

Nine

Joe had to hold the hurt inside, for his duties left him no time for a broken heart. That was because although the paymaster was in charge of the transfer and overall accounting of funds, the officer who actually paid the soldiers was drawn from the regiment. And, as the newest officer of the regiment, that task fell to Second Lieutenant Joseph T. Murchison.

Joe set up a table in the regimental headquarters building. In base pay, or "pay proper," as it was called, a private's pay was $19 per month. Sergeants received from $30 to $50. Second lieutenants drew $65; first lieutenants, $80; a captain, $120; a major, $180; and a lieutenant colonel about $230 per month. In addition, officers had certain entitlements, or emolument, such as separate rations, quarters allowance, et cetera, which increased their pay. As a result, the total amount of cash needed to pay the regiment was quite substantial. Altogether, Joe was carrying a satchel with over $20,000, and he was glad to have two armed guards with him.

Joe paid the officers first. They drifted in one or two at a time until all were paid. Then, at about a quarter of ten, the sutler came in with his debit book. He took a chair right beside Joe so that he could deduct what was owed to him before a soldier even drew his pay.

The sutler had every right to do this, but Joe couldn't help but harbor some resentment toward the man. He knew, for example, that the sutler could buy

tinned oysters for twenty-nine cents a can, yet he sold
them for a dollar. Tinned fruits received an even higher
markup. But the soldiers, and the officers, willingly
purchased such items to supplement the beans, hardtack, fat pork, beef, and coffee that was their normal
staple.

Precisely at ten o'clock, the trumpeter blew pay call
and the soldiers, dressed in their best uniforms, poured
out of the barracks to line up alphabetically according
to rank. The pay line stretched all the way across the
quadrangle, but no one complained, not even those at
the rear. There was always an air of excitement on payday, and the soldiers would joke with each other as the
line slowly progressed.

"Wilson, you're so far back in line, there won't be
any money left by the time you get there," a private
named Anderson joked with one of his friends.

"Don't you worry none about me, Anderson. You'll
have done spent your money on booze an' whores by
the time I get paid. Then you'll be broke and I'll be
flush."

"Yeah, when you go downtown, make sure you save
some for us," another soldier called.

"Save what? Booze or whores?" Anderson replied,
and several laughed.

In addition to the sutler, others were after the
soldiers' pay. The "twenty percenters," sergeants who
loaned money during the month at twenty percent interest, set up their own tables outside the headquarters
building. They also hired the biggest and strongest men
to go after the ones who owed them, to remind them of
their obligation to repay their debt.

The ritual for paying was the same for each man,
and after three hundred or so men, Joe found he was
mouthing the words by rote. Despite that, he had to be
very careful that each man was paid the right amount,
for at the end of the day, the pay book had to balance.

For a soldier to get paid, he would first have to pass
inspection by a sergeant detailed for that specific task.
Hat, jacket, trousers, boots, belts, all underwent the
sergeant's scrutiny, and if he found a soldier wanting,

the soldier would have to return to the barracks, get himself in order, then start the process all over. As a result, there were always several men with last names early in the alphabet who were occupying positions at the end of the line.

After a soldier passed the sergeant's inspection, he would then approach the pay table, stop two paces away, and salute.

"Sir, Private Saunders, reporting for pay."

Joe would return the salute, then look at Saunders's name on the pay roster.

"Private Saunders. Nineteen dollars, less two dollars for laundry and"—Joe looked over at the sutler's book —"three dollars for the sutler. That makes a total of fourteen dollars."

Joe would then count out the fourteen dollars so that Saunders could count with him.

"Thank you, sir," Private Saunders would say, picking up his money. Saluting a second time, he would then do a sharp about-face and exit the building as the next private approached the pay table.

Sergeant Seth Todd had his own room at the end of the D Troop barracks building. He put a twenty-dollar bill in an envelope that he had addressed to his daughter. This was the first time he had written her since receiving an unexpected letter from her. In it, she said her father had told her how to write to him. Before that, she had believed he was dead. She asked if he would ever come back to Virginia to see her again.

"Some day I am sure I will come," Todd wrote her. "But for now my duties keep me here. In the meantime, please take this money and buy yourself something nice."

Sealing the envelope, Todd walked over to the letter drop to post it. Then he went down to the stables. As this was payday, Custer had authorized a twenty-four hour relaxation of procedures. As a result, there were no stable details being performed, other than a punishment detail. It was to check upon the men of the punishment detail that Todd went into the barn.

"Boy, get yer ass outta my way an' let my horses have some o' them oats," someone was saying.

"I can't do that, sir. These here is U.S. Army oats," a soldier answered. Todd recognized the soldier's voice as one of those being punished.

"That's okay, boy. I'm a U.S. Army scout," the first voice said.

Hurrying to investigate, Todd found a young soldier holding a pitchfork at port arms as he protected the platoon's store of oats from a tall, scarecrow-thin man with long white hair and a full white beard.

"What is the problem here?" Todd asked.

"Hell, they ain't no problem here, Sergeant," the man replied. "I'm California Joe, scout for the Seventh Cavalry. I just come back offen a scout an' my horse is hungry, but this mule-headed buck here won't get outta my way."

"It all right, soldier," Todd said.

"All right, Sarge, if you say so," the private replied, lowering his pitchfork and stepping aside.

California Joe chuckled. "Hell, what's the matter, boy? Don't I look like a scout to you?" he asked.

"I don't know, sir. I've never seen a scout," the soldier answered.

"Well, they all look like me," California Joe insisted. "Only most of 'em ain't nigh as handsome as I am." The scout looked at Todd while he fed his horse. "Was you one of them that found the Carmody wagon?" he asked.

"Yes," Todd replied. "Did you find the missing girl?"

"Yep."

"Well, where is she? Is she still alive? Is she all right?"

"She's still alive," California Joe said. "But I reckon I'd better give the rest of my report to General Custer a'fore I start blabberin' it all over the place."

Having finished paying all the soldiers, Joe heard officers' call sound approximately one hour later. Todd had told Joe about the scout's arrival, and figuring the officers' call must have something to do with the scout's report, he hurried over to the regimental head-quarters, anxious to hear whatever Custer had to say.

General Custer had a stern expression on his face as the officers of his command gathered around him. When all were assembled, he cleared his throat and began to talk.

"Gentlemen, last week Lieutenant Murchison, while on escort duty for the paymaster, discovered a burned-out wagon and three slaughtered civilians. This was the Carmody family, and certain evidence taken from the scene suggested that a fourth Carmody, a young woman, might yet be alive.

"Today our scout, California Joe, brought us absolute proof that she is alive and is a captive of the Indians."

The assembled officers reacted in anger.

"Damn their hides!"

"Those heathen bastards!"

"How is she?"

"Has she been harmed?"

Custer held up his hand to call for quiet, and when the officers responded, he showed them a letter. "California Joe brought a letter from the young woman," he said. "I propose now that I read it to you."

The officers stood absolutely quiet as Custer began to read from the letter he held:

"Kind friend. Whomever you may be, if you will only buy me from the Indians with ponies or anything, and let me come and stay with you until I get word to my friends, they will pay you well. And I will work for you also, and do all I can for you.

"The Indians tell me, as near as I can understand, they expect traders to come, to whom they will sell me. Can you find out and let me know if they are white men? If they are Mexicans, I am afraid they will sell me into slavery in Mexico.

"If you can do nothing for me, write,—for God's sake!—to W. T. Carmody, Corinth, Mississippi. He is my grandfather and the only kinfolk I

have left, the Indians having murdered my
mother, father, and younger sister. Tell my grandfather what fate has befallen me, and he will raise
the money to buy my freedom.

   If you can, let me hear from you. Let me know
what you think about it. Write to my grandfather.
Send him this. Good-bye!"

Custer looked up at the men. "She signed it Emma
Carmody, then she appended a P. S., stating that she
was as well as could be expected."

"General, what are we going to do about this?" Captain Hamilton asked.

Custer smiled—the first smile to cross his face since
officers' call had sounded. "What are we going to do
about it? Why, we are going after her. We are going
after her, and we are going to destroy the Indian village where she is being held."

"Good!"

"Hurrah for the general!"

"Let the heathens feel some hot lead and cold steel,
and it will be a while before they capture any more
white women."

"Gentlemen," Custer interrupted. "Prepare your
troops for departure first thing tomorrow morning.
Take food and equipment sufficient for a march of six
weeks."

"Shouldn't we leave sooner than tomorrow, General?" Captain Benteen asked.

Custer shook his head. "She's been their captive for
several days now," he said. "Hopefully one more day
won't matter—and I fear that many of the troops, having just been paid, will be in no condition to leave today."

"Yes, sir, I believe you have a point there," Major
Elliot said.

"Tomorrow morning, gentlemen," Custer said by way
of dismissal.

FORT HAYS, KANSAS
EARLY DECEMBER 1868

The next morning Joe was in position just behind Captain Hamilton in regimental parade-front formation. The entire post was turned out to watch, officers' ladies and enlisted men's wives and unmarried laundresses, their dresses covered with coats, blankets, and robes as they braved the cold to watch, standing on the porches as the Seventh made all preparations to leave.

Joe was shivering, though he didn't know if it was from the cold or from excitement. They were heading for a battle, not merely an encounter nor even a skirmish of the type he had fought against Wind in His Hair. This would be a planned attack on an enemy-held position. Such an operation could only result in a full-scale, precisely executed battle, of the kind fought during the Civil War. And this would be Joe's first such battle.

There was a great deal of activity still going on. Men were riding at a gallop to and fro, delivering messages or attending to last-minute details. Aside from the rustle of horses and the murmur of men, however, the parade ground was relatively quiet.

Major Elliot, General Custer's second-in-command, was already in position just under the flagpole. Some of the messages were being delivered to him, and a horseman would ride up, salute, exchange a few words, salute again, then ride back, all at a gallop. Also at the flagpole, getting in position to play, were the members of the regimental band.

"Here comes the general now," Joe heard someone say in the ranks behind him, and Joe looked toward Custer's quarters to see the general and Libbie, riding side by side toward the parade ground. When they reached the edge of the parade ground, Custer continued on while Libbie stopped and dismounted. A nearby soldier took the reins of her horse, and she joined some of the other ladies to watch the departure.

Custer rode to the flagpole, then received the salute from Major Elliot. He looked out over the parade ground at his assembled troops. A total of eleven companies were ready for the march, divided into three battalions.

From the regimental trumpeter came the clear, sharp notes of assembly.

Now the shuffling around stopped, and the regiment grew quiet. Custer stood in his stirrups and called to his battalion commanders.

"Form into line of march, column of fours to the right!" he shouted.

The battalion commanders issued the commands, and the entire regiment turned to the right.

"Guidons, post!"

The battalion and troop color bearers moved into position at the heads of their respective units. The regimental color bearer rode at a gallop to a position at Custer's left. For a long moment, there was absolute silence as the horses and men held their positions. The only sound to be heard was the snapping of the guidons and the American flag.

"Battalion commanders, pass in review!" Custer ordered.

"Forward!" the battalion commanders shouted, and the troop commanders picked up the supplementary commands.

"Forward!" the eleven troop commanders called, the word echoing itself all up and down the line.

"Ho!" the battalion commanders called, and, as one, the regiment began to move.

As the first horse stepped out, the band began playing. The lead battalion did two left turns, then passed in review with all officers rendering the saber salute to General Custer as they rode by. The gates were opened, and the Seventh left the post to begin their march.

For miles piling upon miles, the Seventh Cavalry moved toward the Washita, whereupon, according to California Joe, they would find the Indian village. At each break, the battalions would switch positions so that the battalion in the lead would move to the rear, the battalion in the middle would move to the lead, and so forth.

After a full day's march, covering some thirty miles, a scouting party was sent ahead to find water and wood, and once a suitable place was located, the men established their camp for the night. They ate beans and bacon and drank coffee, then pitched their tents. Two troopers could bivouac together to make a two-man tent of their shelter halves. Two officers bivouacked together as well, but they shared the much larger Sibley tents. Joe's tent mate was Captain Hamilton.

By nightfall it was considerably colder than it had been, and a damp wind was coming down from the northwest. Inside the tent he was sharing with Captain Hamilton, however, Joe was sheltered from the wind and warmed by his bedding so that he was, in spite of everything, quite comfortable.

"Do you think we'll reach the Indians tomorrow?" he asked.

"California Joe says we should reach the village around midnight tomorrow," Hamilton answered.

"I hope the woman is all right."

"I suppose that depends on what you mean by all right," Hamilton remarked.

"Do you think the Indians have raped her?"

"I expect by now that she's been ridden so many times she's got saddle sores," Hamilton said.

"Damn. I wish we could've gotten to their wagon in time to save them," Joe said. "If we had only started earlier that day."

"And if a frog had wings, he wouldn't bump his ass every time he jumped," Hamilton replied. "Listen, Joe, you can't go through the rest of your life worrying about ifs. You've got to just take things as they are."

"Yes, sir, I'm sure you're right," Joe said. "I just pray that she has the strength to withstand all she has been through."

There was silence for a moment, then Hamilton asked, "Joe, how many people do you know at Fiddlers' Green?"

"At Fiddlers' Green, sir? Well there's Sergeant Muldoon and Lieutenant Canfield. And there's my roommate from West Point, Lieutenant Dixon, though he died in an accident, and not in battle. Why do you ask, sir?"

"By the time the regiment returns to Fort Hays, some of us will be at Fiddlers' Green," Hamilton said.

"Yes, sir, I suppose so."

"Do you think about that much?"

"No, sir."

"Good. It's good that you don't."

"Do you think about it, Captain Hamilton?"

"No," Hamilton said resolutely. "I never think about it."

Joe held in check the obvious question: If Hamilton never thought about it, why had he brought it up?

Lying in the cocoonlike warmth of his bedding, lost in his own thoughts, and with the gentle snoring of Captain Hamilton in the background, Joe finally drifted off to sleep—oblivious to the large flakes of snow that, just after midnight, began tumbling down through the blackness.

When reveille sounded the following morning, the officers and men of the Seventh emerged from their tents to a world covered in a pristine blanket of snow. There were no trails, no footprints, no hoofprints. Everything was covered in a world of white, as if man had never been here before.

Breakfast was a cup of coffee and a piece of bread; then the trumpeter played general, which was the call to strike tents, and then boots and saddles; which ordered the men to saddle their mounts, and finally to horse, which put every soldier standing at the head of his horse. After that the orders prepare to mount and mount were given verbally, and once again the Seventh was on the march.

The march element was one battalion smaller than it had been the day before, Joe discovered, because Major Elliot and his squadron had left at three A.M. They were going ahead to make certain the Indians didn't get wind of the advancing cavalry, pull up their village, and leave.

Their march continued on through the day. Movement was much more difficult today than it had been yesterday because they had to break the crust of the newly fallen snow, which quickly tired horses and men. Twenty minutes of every hour the men dismounted and led their horses for ten minutes, then let them rest for ten minutes. Behind them, stretching now almost as far as the eye could see, was a long black smear across the plains, showing clearly the path they had taken through the snow.

"I have Major Elliot in front of us," Custer said. "If he locates the village, he will send a courier back."

"He won't try and attack without us, will he now, General?" Lieutenant Keogh asked in his thick brogue. "I mean, you do know Major Elliot. Sure an' he's just the kind of firebrand who would do something like that."

"He has the strictest orders not to," Custer replied. He smiled. "Don't worry, gentlemen, we will all get our crack at Lo."

" 'Tis the lass I'm worried about. I hope we are there in time," Keogh said.

"We will be," Custer promised. He looked up at the sky. "It is such a bright, clear day that had we a balloon, we could find the village in no time."

"If we had one, who would go up in it?" Captain Benteen asked.

"Why, I would, of course," Custer answered. "You may be unaware of this, Benteen, but I was one of Professor Lowe's first aeronauts."

"General, you mean you went up in a balloon?" Hamilton asked.

"That I did," Custer said. "It was in 1862, before I married Libbie." He chuckled. "She has told me that she does not want me to make any more ascensions, but had we the means to do so now, I assure you, gentlemen, I would do it."

"What is it like from up there, sir?" Joe asked, fascinated by the idea.

"It's wonderful," Custer answered. "You feel as if you are master of the world—although you're a prime target for everyone to see."

Shortly after that break, the regiment resumed the march. It was nine o'clock that evening when at last they reached the point where Major Elliot and his three troops were found halted.

Nearby was a stream of good water with deep banks. Also, the valley was quite heavily timbered at this point. Therefore, by building their fires under the edge of the bank, the men were able to prepare coffee without giving away their position to any Indians who might be looking. A handful of hardtack crackers supplemented the coffee and served as their supper. The horses were unsaddled, their bits were removed, and they were given a full portion of oats.

They had been at rest an hour when Custer gave word that they were to resume the march. From here on there would be no bugle calls and no loud commands. Orders were given to tie down all loose equipment, thus minimizing the danger of being given away by making too much noise. The men were also forbidden to light their pipes, not only for fear of the glow of fire being seen but also because the Indians might be able to smell the aroma of smoking tobacco. When they resumed the march, it had fallen to Captain Hamilton's troops to take the lead.

California Joe and a handful of Osage scouts rode a quarter of a mile in front. Custer was at the head of the column that followed behind him, silent save for the muffled crunch of snow. Captain Hamilton was just behind Custer, and Joe was just behind Hamilton, so he had a clear view of everything that was going on.

For some reason that he couldn't understand, Joe suddenly recalled the time when, as a cadet at West Point, he had gone to New York City with the entire corps of cadets to march in Abraham Lincoln's funeral cortege. With black mourning bands around their arms, the cadets had marched to muffled drums on that sad day. Then Joe realized why he was having such a memory: The muffled fall of horses' hooves in the snow reminded him of those funereal drums.

A couple of the Osage scouts rode back.

"Me smell fire," Joe heard one of the Osages say.

"I don't smell anything," Custer replied.

"Look there," the other Osage said, pointing to the edge of a tree line.

Looking in the direction the Indian pointed, Joe saw a faint glow of embers. "Captain Hamilton, have someone check that out," Custer said.

"Mr. Murchison, take one man with you and have a look," Hamilton ordered.

"Yes, sir. Sergeant Todd, with me," Joe said, breaking ranks. He and Seth Todd rode quickly over to the edge of the timber to examine the fire. There were no more than three or four embers left.

"How old you think that is?" Joe asked.

"Can't be much over a couple of hours," Todd replied. "My guess is someone was out here, probably watching the ponies or something."

"Then the village has to be close," Joe suggested.

"Damned close," Todd agreed.

They galloped back to the formation, and Joe gave his report.

"All right, gentlemen, the village can't be more than a couple of miles from here," Custer said. He spoke to one of the scouts. "Hard Rope, you and the others go have a look. We'll wait here."

Hard Rope, the oldest of the two Osage scouts, nodded, then rode off without a word.

"Shall we dismount, sir?" Hamilton asked.

"No," Custer replied. "We will remain mounted until we hear."

The moon came out from behind a cloud, then touched the snow-covered valley with a light so bright that, even though it was nearly midnight, the entire line of cavalry could be seen sitting motionless on their horses, awaiting further orders.

After several minutes the guides returned.

"Heap Injuns down there," Hard Rope said.

Quietly, the command resumed the march. Just over

a mile later, they crested a hill. The Osage guides signaled to Custer, and he dismounted, then crawled up to look over the top of the hill.

Joe could see them, but from this distance he couldn't hear what they were talking about. After a moment or two, Custer came hurrying back, his feet making crunching sounds in the snow.

"Pass the word," he said quietly. "I want all officers to report to me immediately. Tell them to leave their sabers behind. I don't want any sound."

It took almost five minutes before all the officers were assembled. Then Custer outlined his plan to them.

"I'm going to divide the column into four detachments of equal strength," he said. "Captain Barnitz, you take one to the woods below the village; Benteen, you take another to the timber above it; Major Elliot, you occupy the crest just to the north of the village; and Captain Hamilton, your men will remain here, with me. We will attack simultaneously."

"General, would you be tellin' us our signal for attack?" Keogh asked.

Custer smiled. "I'll have the band play 'Garryowen.' That will not only provide everyone with the signal, it should also wake the heathens up."

He agreed to give the other detachments four hours to get into positions. In the meantime Hamilton's troops were permitted to dismount, but they couldn't stamp their feet or even pace back and forth to get warm, for fear it might give away their position.

About two hours before dawn, the moon went down, and the night, which had been so bright before, became pitch black. Suddenly a brilliant light appeared in the sky, and for a moment everyone thought it was a rocket. After looking at it more closely, however, they realized that it was just the morning star.

"An interesting omen," Hamilton said quietly, to Joe. "I don't know if it portends good luck or a terrible misfortune."

"What are you talking about, sir?"

"The morning star," Hamilton said. "It may be some

sort of omen. Don't you know what the Indians call Custer?"

"No, sir."

"They call him 'Son of the Morning Star.' "

"Captain Hamilton," Custer suddenly called.

"Yes, sir?"

"Have your men discard their overcoats and haversacks. It's time to go."

On the one hand, discarding the overcoats meant the men would be even colder and more miserable than they were now. On the other, however, it meant that they were about to see action—and that had to be better than standing around waiting the whole night through.

A rifle shot echoed from the far side of the village, indicating that all troops were in place. Custer nodded at the band director, and the night air was suddenly filled with the jubilant strains of "Garryowen."

Whether actually inspired by the music or anxious, at long last, to get moving, the soldiers from all four elements of Custer's command rushed forward, firing as rapidly as they could at the tents that rose up in the darkness before them.

"Keep calm, men!" Hamilton shouted to his troop. "Keep calm and fire low!"

Almost immediately after that, Joe heard Hamilton give a strange-sounding grunt, and he looked over at his commander. Hamilton jerked convulsively, then stiffened in his stirrups. He was carried for a distance of several yards before he fell from his horse.

An Indian suddenly burst from a tent in front of Joe, firing his rifle. Joe, who was carrying a pistol, swung it at the Indian and pulled the trigger. The ball hit the Indian in his right eye, and he went down instantly. Though Joe may have killed one or more Indians in the fight with Wind in His Hair, this was the first time he had ever observed his bullet actually hitting another human being. He didn't have time to contemplate it, though, because an arrow buried itself in his horse's shoulder at almost that precise moment, and Joe turned to fire at the Indian who had shot the arrow.

Off to Joe's left, Captain Barnitz, who had led one of the other elements, was engaged in a one-on-one skirmish with an Indian. They exchanged fire from point-blank range, and the Indian went down. Barnitz was hit in the stomach, the entry of the bullet clearly visible because the Indian had been so close when he fired that the muzzle blast had scorched a ring on Barnitz's coat. Barnitz rode on another two hundred yards, then dismounted and lay down while the fighting raged on around him.

A young Cheyenne in his early teens suddenly burst out of one of the Indian lodges. Jumping on an unsaddled and unbridled pony, he attempted to escape. Captain Benteen went after him. The boy wheeled his horse around and fired, killing Benteen's horse and dropping the soldier into the snow. The boy fired two more times before Benteen returned fire, killing the boy with one shot from his revolver.

Several warriors did manage to get mounted, and they rode off downstream. Major Elliot held up his hand. "Here's for a brevet or a coffin, boys!" he shouted. "Who is with me?" He started after the Indians, and almost a score of troopers, including the regimental sergeant major, went with him. Joe was going as well, but his horse, suffering now from the arrow wound, suddenly broke stride, then quit running altogether. Realizing that any further riding might kill his horse, he dismounted.

When the last batch of warriors fled downstream, the immediate fighting stopped.

With the fighting stopped, the soldiers began to look after their wounded. Joe went first to Captain Hamilton and knelt beside him. His tunic was open, and Joe could see the entry wound just over his heart. There was very little blood, first because of the cold and secondly because he had died almost instantly after receiving the wound, so the heart had quit pumping immediately, and thus no blood was flowing.

"Sir, over here!" someone called to Joe. "Captain Barnitz is still alive!"

Joe left his commander and hurried over to look into Barnitz's condition.

"Get one of those buffalo robes over here," Joe ordered. "Get him warm."

"Bless you, Mr. Murchison," Barnitz said. "But you're wasting your time, lad. I'm gutshot. You ever know anyone who survived being gutshot?"

"I'm sure many have survived," Joe said. "And you're as tough as any man. So, hold on, sir. You can do it."

"Maybe," Barnitz said. "Maybe not. Just in case, would you let me dictate a letter to you for my wife, then see that she gets it?"

"I'll write it," Joe said. "But you can deliver it yourself."

While Joe took Barnitz's dictation, the Seventh Cavalry went about its business of tending to the wounded and cleaning up the village. Included in this action was the shooting of several hundred ponies. It was a task the men undertook with little enthusiasm, but, as Custer explained to them, it would make it more difficult for the Indians to make their raids against innocent settlers next summer.

Emma Carmody was found in the midst of the women and children prisoners. Too frightened by everything that was going on around her, she didn't even identify herself but was recognized when one of the soldiers saw that she wasn't Indian.

The Seventh spent the rest of that day and that night bivouacked in the Indian village, warming themselves by large fires. The next day, according to plan, they started not for Fort Hays, but for Camp Supply.

Just before they left, Custer called all the officers together.

"Gentlemen," he said, smiling broadly and rubbing his hands together in glee, "we have just taught Lo a lesson he won't soon forget. We have recovered a white captive, and we have taken away the wherewithal for any nefarious activity the Indians might have planned for the future. The trains, stagecoaches, way stations, farms, and ranches of the white settlers in this part of the country are now secure, thanks to the Seventh Cavalry!"

The officers cheered.

"We are all saddened by the death of Captain Hamilton and the nineteen enlisted men. In addition, we have three officers and eleven enlisted men wounded. Is there any update to these figures?"

"What about Major Elliot, sir?" Joe asked.

"What about him?" Custer replied easily.

"During the fight, I saw him lead several troopers downstream after a group of fleeing Indians."

"Aye, sir, the lad is right," Keogh said. "I saw him, too. And he took the regimental sergeant major with him."

"Anybody else know anything about it?" Custer asked.

None of the officers did.

Custer stroked his chin for a few moments, then said, "Gentlemen, it is my belief that Elliot has returned to Camp Supply."

"Why would he do that, General?" Benteen asked.

"Why? Why not? Our business is finished here. If he pursued the Indians some distance, it would be an economy of movement for him to go directly to Camp Supply rather than return here."

"But don't you think we should send someone to look for him?"

"No," Custer said. "We have wounded to tend to. And we need to get Miss Carmody back to civilization. The poor woman has surely suffered enough. Prepare to move out."

Custer sent a courier ahead, carrying news of their victory to General Sheridan, who had promised to meet them at Camp Supply. Now, halfway back, a courier arrived from General Sheridan, bearing a message for Custer and the Seventh. Upon reading the message, Custer broke into a big smile, then ordered the troops to be formed into a parade-front formation so he could read the message to them.

" 'The energy and rapidity shown during one of the heaviest snowstorms known to this section of the country, with the temperature below freezing, the gallantry and bravery displayed, resulting in such signal success, reflects highest credit on the Seventh Cavalry,' " Custer read. " 'The major general commanding·expresses his thanks to the officers and men engaged in the Battle of the Washita, and his special congratulations to their distinguished commander, Brevet Major General George A. Custer, for the efficient and gallant service opening the campaign against the hostile Indians north of the Arkansas.' "

Although there were too many men spread too wide for everyone to hear him, enough heard so that the message seeped through all the ranks.

"Gentlemen!" Custer shouted. "I salute the men of the Seventh Cavalry. And when we return to Fort Hays, I promise you forty-eight hours without duties."

"For the general!" someone shouted. "Hip, hip . . ."

"Hooray!"

Doffing his hat, as he so often had during the Civil War, Custer returned to the front of the column.

"Bandmaster!" he called.

"Yes, sir!"

"When we reach Camp Supply, the band will play 'Garryowen.' We will return in triumph."

"Yes, sir!" the bandmaster agreed.

★★★

Ten

THE U.S. MILITARY ACADEMY
WEST POINT, NEW YORK
JUNE 1941

"Excuse me, General Murchison, Mrs. Roosevelt?" Cadet Throckmorton said, walking quietly up to the Custer burial plot.

"Yes, Mr. Throckmorton, what is it?" General Murchison asked, turning to him.

"The ceremonies are beginning, General, and they have asked that all the VIPs be in their places."

General Murchison chuckled and turned to Sara Roosevelt. "West Point hasn't changed much, Sally," he said. "Even as a VIP, I am told when and where I must go."

"I'll walk with you, Joseph," Mrs. Roosevelt said. "I wonder . . ." Her sentence trailed off, but General Murchison finished the question for her.

"Whatever happened to Alice Patterson?"

Mrs. Roosevelt chuckled. "I wasn't going to ask about her," she said. "But since you obviously want to tell me . . ."

"If you can believe it, Alice married a missionary."

"No!" Mrs. Roosevelt said, laughing.

"That's the gospel," General Murchison said, laughing over the double entendre. "She spent forty years in China. Then, when her husband died, she came back to the United States. The last I heard, she was living in a church home for missionary widows, somewhere out in California."

"Actually, what I was going to ask was, what happened to Major Elliot?" Mrs. Roosevelt said.

"Ah, yes, poor Major Elliot. It turns out that there were many more Indians in that encampment than we realized. When Major Elliot chased that band of warriors down the riverbed, he and his men rode into a hornet's nest. It was nearly two weeks before we found them. They were surrounded by empty shell casings, so we know they put up a fight, but they had no chance. As a matter of fact, when we found out later how many Indians were actually gathered at that place, the wonder is that *we* weren't wiped out as well. That we pulled off a victory is a credit to Custer's surprise and daring. Unfortunately, there are some historians today who want to call that battle a massacre, and compare it with the Sand Creek Massacre of Colonel Chivington. But they don't know what they are talking about. And they conveniently forget that we rescued a young woman who went on to live a full and productive life."

"I have also heard some criticism of the abandonment of Major Elliot," Mrs. Roosevelt said.

"Yes, I've heard it, too," General Murchison replied. "I think the criticism is unfounded. Custer maintained, and with justification, that he believed Elliot returned to Camp Supply on his own. Most, if not all of the 'abandonment' criticism stems from Captain Benteen. None of the other officers who were present that day have maintained such a charge. But Benteen made criticism of Custer his life's work. By the way, I think it is significant to note that not even Benteen, as bitter an enemy of Custer as he was, ever criticized the battle itself. Even he regarded it as a victory, not a massacre."

"What caused all the animosity between Custer and Benteen?" Mrs. Roosevelt asked.

"I think there were a lot of reasons Benteen didn't like Custer. Custer was younger and more vibrant. And, of course, everyone knows about his flamboyance. Benteen was put off by that. Also Custer was given command of the Seventh. Benteen, who had been in the army much longer and had himself been a brevet colonel during the war, felt bitter about being returned to the rank of captain while Custer retained the rank of lieutenant colonel."

"Mrs. Roosevelt, there you are," a young man said, hurrying over with a concerned expression on his face. "The president has been worrying about you."

"Nonsense, Franklin knows better than to worry about me," Mrs. Roosevelt replied.

"Please, Mrs. Roosevelt, won't you come with me? They have asked that all dignitaries be in their seats."

"Yes, young man, I'll come with you," Mrs. Roosevelt said. She put her hand on General Murchison's arm and smiled up at him. "Thank you, for allowing me to visit General Custer with you," she said. "I know it was a very private moment, and I am deeply honored to have been able to share it with you."

"Sally, you have shared much more than just a moment. Don't you realize that through your letters, you shared my entire career?"

"I suppose I did, didn't I?" Mrs. Roosevelt replied. "Though I know there must have been times when you felt that the immature letters of a schoolgirl with a terrible crush were an unwanted intrusion."

"Never," General Murchison replied. "I'm almost embarrassed, even at this late date, to tell you how welcome they were."

General Murchison and Sara Roosevelt parted company, and the general was led by Cadet Throckmorton to the auditorium.

"General, would you sit here, please?" a colonel said, meeting him as he stepped into the auditorium. "Cadet Throckmorton, I thought you were informed of the time schedule," he added, scolding the cadet.

"Don't be angry with Cadet Throckmorton, Colonel," General Murchison said. "Mr. Throckmorton has performed his duty admirably. But I am not a bouquet of flowers to be moved from point to point. I am a major general—no longer on the active list I'll admit, but a major general nevertheless. And if I choose to divert from the schedule you have worked out, there is nothing Mr. Throckmorton can do about it."

"Yes, sir," the colonel said, chastised. "I'm sorry, sir, we don't wish to be overbearing. But we do have a lot to accomplish and—"

"And you want me in my seat," General Murchison said, waving the colonel aside. "Very well, I shall go to my place like a good soldier."

"Thank you, General," the colonel said with obvious relief.

General Murchison took his seat, then leaned back and watched as the others began to file into the room to listen to an address by intelligence expert William Donovan. The subject of his speech was "Why the French Army Failed."

General Murchison couldn't help but smile wryly over the title of the speech. He had once written a report with the same title.

JUNE 1870

Fort Hays, Kansas
June 15, 1870

Dear Sally,

General Custer has been asked by his publisher, Galaxy, if he will come to New York to discuss the idea of making a book from his articles and to speak at a few events they have set up for him. If you have never read any of the articles, may I recommend them to you? He is an excellent writer, and one cannot read the articles without a feeling of actual participation in the scouts of the Seventh Cavalry.

General Custer has agreed to go to New York, and he has asked me to go with him. I realize that it will not be possible for me to call on you—given the fact that your father would not approve. I do not blame him for this. You are barely eighteen, so there is some justification to your father's concern. And as you have appointed me your "big brother" I also feel protective of you.

Should you feel adventurous, however, I know that General Custer will be speaking at a meeting that will be open to the public on the afternoon · of June 25th, in the Times Building. I will be there as well.

With fondest regards,
Your friend, Joe Murchison

Having gone to Castle Gardens to visit with some of his old friends, Joe made arrangements to meet Custer at the Times Building. But his visit had taken him longer than he anticipated, and now he was a few minutes late. It didn't really matter if he was late, other than the fact that this was the one place he had told Sally he would be, and if she was going to come, he certainly wanted to be there for her.

He hurried across the street, picking his way carefully through the steady stream of coaches and wagons, and finally pushed through the entrance doors of the Times Building.

"Go on up to the fifth floor," a man said as Joe stepped inside.

"I beg your pardon?"

"You are with General Custer's party, are you not?" the man asked, indicating Joe's uniform.

"Yes, I am."

"Take the elevator," the man said, indicating the conveyance. "Or, if you are frightened by the device, as some are, you may use the stairs."

"Thank you," Joe said. He entered the elevator, and the operator, who was reading a paper, stood up and closed the doors, then turned the handle to operate the steam-powered drum and weights by which the elevator moved up and down. In just a few moments he was on the fifth floor. He was going to ask the operator where the reception was being held, but he didn't have to. Even as the operator was opening the doors to let him out, Joe could hear several people talking and laughing. He merely followed the sound.

At the end of the hall Joe saw a large room with open double doors. Inside the room, many people were milling about beneath a low-lying cloud of bluish tobacco smoke. Most were holding glasses of wine or stronger drink, and—or so it seemed to Joe as he approached the hall—they were all talking at once.

He couldn't miss Custer. His commander was wearing a black-velvet tunic grandly trimmed in gold and fringe. He was speaking, and everyone present, men and women alike, were hanging on his every word.

Joe moved closer.

". . . as I wrote to my dear Libbie, last night, my behavior since I arrived in New York has been above reproach. However the maid who is taking care of my room at the hotel sometimes looks at me with suspicion whenever she comes to make the bed in the morning with it not having been slept in. I'm sure she believes I do not pass my nights in the most reputable manner. In fact, circumstances, as she sees them, are clearly against me."

Everyone laughed at Custer's words, then one of the women spoke.

"Your wife evidently knows little of the worldly ways of New York women," she said. "For a New York woman who sets her cap for a man is perfectly willing to project herself as boldly as is necessary to achieve those ends."

Custer looked at the young woman who had spoken. She was a very pretty dark-haired woman with an inviting smile and challenging eyes. Custer held his glass up toward her in a modest toast.

"Oh, to be a bachelor amidst such women," he said, and again his comments were greeted with laughter.

Joe stood just on the periphery of the group for a moment longer; then Custer happened to notice him.

"Ladies and gentlemen, allow me to introduce Lieutenant Joseph Murchison. Mr. Murchison was with me during the Battle of Washita, and I must say he acquitted himself most gallantly. He is here as part of my staff."

"Part of your staff?" one of the women said. "Oh, how perfectly marvelous! How perfectly military!"

"Isn't he a handsome young man, ladies? And he is a bachelor."

Joe smiled sheepishly as several of the women moved toward him.

"What is it like to fight against Indians?" one of the women asked.

"It's interesting," Joe answered, not really knowing what to say.

"Tell me, Lieutenant," a woman's throaty voice asked, "how many Indians have you had to kill?"

Joe looked at the woman who had asked the question. She might have been attractive, but her face was so heavily made up with rouge, lip paint, and eye darkener that any natural beauty she possessed was well concealed. Her dress was cut shockingly low, and Joe noticed she tended to lean toward him slightly, as if deliberately providing him with an enticing view of her breasts.

"Never mind that. Tell us about the woman you rescued from the Indians," another woman said. "Had she been—well, you know . . ." The woman paused in midquestion.

"Yes, tell us about it, Lieutenant. Had the woman been *used* by the Indians?"

Joe knew that Emma Carmody had, in fact, been used and passed around from Indian to Indian. It was the shame of that degradation that had prevented her from calling out to them when they first arrived, and that same shame kept her speechless until after they returned to Camp Supply. Even though Miss Carmody had since returned to Mississippi, Joe had no intention of adding to her shame by telling her story here.

"I don't know," he lied.

"Well, you know the Indians made her their concubine," one of the other women said. "Why else would they have captured her? I've heard that Indians favor white women, because their own women are so ugly." The woman who was speaking was tall and gangly, with close-set eyes and a hooked chin. Joe couldn't help but compare this woman with Wind in His Hair's sister, Quiet Stream.

"Well, let's ask Mr. Murchison," another woman suggested. "Lieutenant, in your opinion, are any of the Indian women pretty?"

Joe looked over at his commander for help. Custer, eating a cookie from the refreshment table, was smiling, obviously enjoying Joe's predicament.

"Some are prettier than others," Joe said. He smiled graciously. "Though I must say that there are few women anywhere who can compare with New York women."

"Oh, my!" one of the women said, touching the back of her hair. "How gallant you are!"

"Ladies and gentlemen!" someone called. "If you would kindly take your seats, it is time for General Custer's address!"

"Oh, I don't want to miss that!" one of the women said and she and the others hurried to find seats so they could listen to Custer speak.

Unconsciously, Joe pulled at the choke collar of his uniform, glad that something had diverted the women's attention. It had been an uncomfortable moment for him.

Joe heard a light, lyrical laugh. "My, you *do* seem to have the women buzzing around you."

When Joe turned toward the voice's source, he saw Sally Delano. She was taller and more mature-looking than she had been the last time he saw her, but it was definitely her. And the beauty that had promised in youth, had, at eighteen, come to fruition.

"Sally!" Joe said.

"Hello, Joseph."

"So you managed to come after all."

"Oh, yes. Did you think I would miss this opportunity to see you again?"

"Shhh!" someone in the back row hissed as General Custer was being introduced.

Joe pointed toward the double doors at the back of the room and, nodding, asked her to step outside with him. She agreed, and they started out of the room.

"Once the general starts speaking, I will close the doors and you won't be allowed back inside," the doorman whispered as they stepped through the still-open doors.

"That's all right," Joe whispered in reply. "I've heard the general speak before."

True to the doorman's words, the doors were closed almost immediately, leaving Joe and Sally alone in the hallway.

"There are a couple of chairs down at the far end, by those potted plants," Joe invited. "Why don't we have a seat and talk?"

"All right," Sally agreed.

Joe held the chair for Sally; then he sat opposite her.

"Look at you," Joe said, opening the conversation. "You have certainly grown into a pretty girl."

Sally smiled. "Biologically, I'm no longer a girl. I'm a woman. There are many my age who are married, many who are already mothers."

Joe cleared his throat. "Yes, I . . . I suppose that's true. Still, you are quite young yet. I certainly hope you aren't serious enough about any of your beaux to contemplate anything like that."

"Only one beau," Sally teased.

Joe knew she meant him, and he was at loss as to how to answer. Her charm, beauty, and flirtatious nature were almost more than he could handle, and he had to use the strictest self-discipline to resist her. He held up his finger and wagged it back and forth.

"I thought we agreed that I was to be your big brother and not your beau," he said lightly.

"But of course you are," Sally replied.

At first Joe was confused. Did she mean, of course he was her brother? Or, of course he was her beau? Then, observing the sly smile on her face, he realized she was being purposefully vague, so he decided to let it go at that.

"How long will you be in New York?" she asked.

"I think just through the weekend," Joe replied. "From here we go to Washington for the general to appear before a congressional committee, and from there we shall return to Fort Hays."

"I find Washington to be very exciting," Sally said. "Don't you?"

"I'm sure it will be," Joe replied. "But this will be the first time I've ever visited there."

The two talked for several more moments, though Joe thought the conversation rather stilted. It was much easier, he decided, to write to Sally than it was to speak to her. Whereas the letters were vessels for his innermost thoughts, he found it quite impossible now to say anything to her of a personal nature.

Throughout their visit they were aware of Custer's speech. Though he was on the other side of closed doors, his muffled voice could be heard if not understood. They could also hear the reactions of his audience, as his speech was frequently punctuated with their laughter. Then there was a particularly loud burst of laughter, followed by applause, upon which the doors were thrown open and the crowd began filing out. Sally stood.

"I think I had best be going before someone recognizes me and word gets back to my father," she said.

"What does your father think of our correspondence?" Joe asked.

"At first he was not pleased with it," Sally said. "But I have assured him that you are just a long-distance friend. Also, he has read about some of the exploits of the Seventh Cavalry in the newspapers, and I think he is even secretly pleased that, through me, he has some inside information. He likes to be able to go to his club and say such things as: 'Custer used the regimental band as a signal to launch the attack at the Washita Battle.' And when the others ask him how he knows something that hasn't been reported in the papers, he just smiles and says, 'I have my sources.'"

Joe walked Sally to the elevator. Just before she got on, she leaned toward him and impulsively kissed him on the cheek.

"Good-bye, big brother," she said. "Please keep writing. I love your letters so."

Before he could even respond, Sally was swallowed up by the crowd leaving Custer's talk. Joe watched until the elevator doors closed, then went back into the room where Custer had spoken. The general was standing near the podium, talking with two men. One was short, fat, and bald. The other was tall, with dark hair and a sweeping mustache that extended at least two inches from either side of his nose. The mustache was twisted and waxed, and as he listened to Custer, he twirled it. He was wearing the much bemedaled uniform of a French lieutenant colonel. Joe recognized both the uniform and the rank from a class he had taken at West Point on "Armies of the World."

"Ah, there he is now," Joe heard Custer say. "Mr. Murchison, would you come here, please? I have a couple of gentlemen I would like you to meet."

Joe joined the three men.

"This is Colonel Phillipe Arnaud of the French army," Custer said, indicating the one in uniform. "And this is John Helm of our own State Department."

"Colonel Arnaud, Mr. Helm," Joe said.

"Lieutenant Murchison, I was honored to meet the gallant General Custer, and now the honor extends to one of his officers, as well," Arnaud said. Though he spoke English quite well, there was a distinct French accent to his speech, particularly in the softening of the *g* in the word *general.*

"Colonel Arnaud is over here to learn what he can about our cavalry tactics," Custer said. "As you may know from reading the newspapers, the situation between France and Prussia has become quite strained."

"But aren't negotiations going on?" Joe asked.

"Negotiations, *oui,*" Colonel Arnaud replied. "But the negotiations have done little to make the situation better. They have, in fact, made conditions worse. Consider this. Last week we received this message from Prussia, and I quote, 'His Majesty the King has decided not to receive the French ambassador again and has told him, through the aide-de-camp on duty, that His Majesty has nothing further to communicate to the Ambassador.' "

Joe whistled. "That's hardly the language of diplomacy."

"*Oui*, I am glad you understand," Arnaud replied. "And I am sure that the world will understand that our government has been so insulted by this insolent dismissal that we cannot allow it to pass."

"You say you cannot allow it to pass, but what are your options, sir?" Custer asked.

"War, General," Arnaud replied. "The Prussians have left us no choice."

"I don't know," Custer said. "It seems to me that war should always be the final option."

"But you are a warrior yourself, General Custer. Surely you can understand why the blood of patriotic Frenchmen would boil over such an insult. Our army is anxious to fight—and our people, as well."

"We came here today just to meet you," Mr. Helm interjected.

"*Oui*. When I read in the paper that you would be speaking, I had to come. I would like for our cavalry to perform as brilliantly as the Seventh Cavalry has performed."

Joe shook his head. "That wouldn't be possible, Colonel. The tactics we employ are totally different from those you would deploy. In the case of the Indians, we are fighting a highly mobile and lightly armed enemy. But in a battle against the Prussians, you will be facing artillery and countless legions of entrenched infantry. Our tactics would be useless to you."

"But *non*, Lieutenant," Arnaud insisted. "Your cavalry operates on courage and daring, does it not? Those two elements would be assets to any army."

"Here, here," Custer said.

"Colonel Arnaud, we must be on our way," Mr. Helm, said.

"*Oui*," Arnaud said. Smiling, he extended his hand again, first to Custer, then to Joe. "Again, let me express my pleasure in meeting two officers who possess the very things we were discussing: courage and daring."

* * *

"It's all politics," Custer was saying to Joe a few moments later as they glided grandly down Park Row, sitting comfortably in the overstuffed leather seats of the beautifully appointed phaeton. Ahead, two perfectly matched horses pulled in powerful unison, and a liveried driver sat quietly on the high front seat.

"Politics, General?" Joe asked. "I'm not sure I follow you."

"Politics," Custer said again. "It is the oil that lubricates the life of man." He hooked his thumbs into his black velvet tunic. "Do you think I enjoy being turned out like some popinjay court lackey? I would much prefer to be in my buckskin jacket and fatigue trousers." He was quiet for a moment, and Joe made no effort to fill the silence. Custer fingered the sweeping feathers of his hat.

"You know what many here do not know. You know that the Custer whom people see depicted in the illustrateds or written up in the newspapers is not the real Custer," he said, speaking of himself in the third person. "Look not for Custer at the sound of giggling women and foolish men. Look for Custer at the sound of battle. He is only complete when he is in the field with the Seventh Cavalry!"

There was more silence, and Joe realized that Custer didn't expect a response.

"Ah, but therein is the rub, you see," Custer went on. "There are some in Congress who would cut back the army and eliminate the Seventh Cavalry altogether. Do you know there is a strong movement afoot to allow the state militias to handle their own defense against the Indians? Can you imagine that? Store clerks, farmers, and mechanics trying to do the work of soldiers? If we aren't careful, we'll find the army cut back to forty privates and a captain to guard the stores at Fort Pitt, just as it was after the War of Independence." He looked outside the carriage for a moment, then pounded his fist into his hand.

"Well, by all that's holy, I don't intend to let that happen. If it means I have to play the lackey to every newspaper and illustrated editor in America, I will do that. If it means I have to make speeches to every society in the country, then I will do that. And if I have to go to every party in the United States, dressed like a . . . a damn peacock," he spouted, indicating his uniform with his hand, "then, by Godfrey, Lieutenant, I will do that, too."

"I understand fully what you're talking about, General," Joe said, "for I started my career doing the same thing." He explained how, as a member of the military unit of the immigration department, he had to attend so many parties.

Custer laughed. "I knew that you, of all my officers, would understand what I am doing," he said.

Joe thought that he had seen all there was to see of New York during his tour of duty here. But in the week he spent with Custer, he was introduced to more of the city than he had ever dreamed existed. Custer had the ability to maximize the opportunities afforded him, and on the days he would go to the theater, he would see not one play, but two and sometimes three. His enjoyment of the drama did not limit him to being an inert member of the audience. Custer and his party would always occupy a box of some importance, normally made available to him by some admirer. And he would always be introduced to the audience before the curtain, during which times he never failed to introduce Joe as well, embarrassing him by telling the audience that Joe was "one of the bravest officers it has ever been my pleasure to command." After the final curtain, Custer and Joe were invariably taken backstage, there to meet the members of the cast.

Among the many entertainments they attended was a ballet, and during the performance Joe was particularly struck with the grace and beauty of the prima ballerina of the troupe. He passed a no-more-than-casual remark to Custer that he thought she was an exceptionally pretty woman. Later, when they went backstage after the performance, Joe saw that same woman standing apart from the others, watching with curious detachment as the corps de ballet gathered around Custer.

The woman was slender, with a long neck, high cheekbones, and large, almond-shaped eyes. Her eyebrows were high and arched, and her hair was pulled back into a bun, which had the effect of highlighting her delicate features. She had a towel draped across one shoulder, and she was standing, rather peculiarly, on one leg, much like a stork. Custer, seeing where Joe was looking, smiled, then said something to the director.

"But of course," Joe heard the director reply, though as he had not heard Custer's comment, he didn't know what the director was replying to. "Monique," the director called to the girl Joe had been watching. "Monique, please, do come here."

Monique patted the towel against her face, then tossed it to one side and walked over in response to the director's bidding.

"Monique, this is the famous General George A. Custer," the director said. "I'm sure you have heard of him. General, this is Monique Mouchette, our prima ballerina."

Monique smiled and curtsied. "I am sorry I did not know who you were, Monsieur General," she said, softening the *g* in the same way as had Colonel Arnaud. "But I am just visiting your country and know none of your heroes."

"Well, then, let me introduce you to one of our most gallant heroes," Custer said. He held his arm out toward Joe. "This is Lieutenant Joe Murchison."

"Lieutenant Murchison," Monique said, curtseying again.

"You might be interested in knowing, Mademoiselle Mouchette, that during your brilliant performance, my young friend here leaned over to tell me that he thought you were the most beautiful woman he had ever seen."

"You make me blush, Monsieur," she said.

"So, I thought you might like to have dinner with us tonight," Custer invited. He took in the other dancers with a wave of his hand. "And, just to keep things on the up and up, why, we'll have one of these ladies come with us as well."

"I would be most honored, Monsieur," Monique replied.

"Now," Custer said, stroking his mustache. "Which one of you beauties would like to go with us?"

To Joe's surprise, at least a dozen hands went up. Custer looked them over, then chose a very young girl from the corps de ballet, who introduced herself as Lydia Burke.

Like the theaters, the finest restaurants and social clubs also threw their doors open to Custer, and when the two officers and the ladies they were escorting stepped into The Lotos Club,* they were given preferential treatment.

At first Joe had been somewhat amused by all the attention Custer received. But after a few days his amusement changed to wonder, for he saw that the attention was freely offered and that Custer did nothing to garner it. Nor, he noticed, did Custer do anything to discourage it.

During dinner, Joe learned that Monique was from Paris, she had been in New York for six weeks, and she had two more weeks to go before she was to return to France. No, she said, when Joe asked her, she had never heard of Colonel Phillipe Arnaud.

Joe knew very little about ballet, and Monique knew nothing about the U.S. Army, so there was very little for them to talk about. It didn't matter, though, because Custer, as was his habit, kept them all entertained with his stories, including one about his being the best man at the wedding of a West Point classmate.

"Now, being the best man at a classmate's wedding is not in and of itself an unusual thing," Custer explained. "But this particular classmate happened to be a captain in the Confederate army. And, in order to attend his wedding, I had to approach the lines under a flag of truce, then be blindfolded and escorted to the place of

* Actual restaurant visited by Custer.

the wedding. Well, you can imagine the thoughts that
went through my mind. Here I was, a Major General in
the Union forces, behind the rebel lines. Had they
wanted to capture me, I'm sure I would have made
quite a prize."

"But weren't you frightened?" Lydia asked.

"Not a bit," Custer replied. "You see, I depended
upon honor. My classmate had given his word that I
would not be harmed, and I was not."

"What a wonderful story!" Lydia said, clapping her
hands.

After dinner they walked out onto the street, and
Custer summoned a cab. "I'll take Miss Burke home,"
he said to Joe, "while you show Mlle Mouchette the
same courtesy."

"Yes, sir," Joe replied, realizing then that Custer
meant for them to separate.

Joe watched the cab with Custer and Lydia drive off,
heard another squeal of laughter from Lydia, then
summoned a cab for himself. He helped Monique into
the carriage, then climbed in beside her.

When they reached her building, Joe escorted her to
the front door. He could go no farther because she was
staying in a woman's boardinghouse. After she went
inside, he returned to the cab and gave the driver the
address of the hotel where he and Custer were staying.

Custer's room was right across the hall from Joe's.
No light showed in the translucent transom above the
door, and it was silent, which meant that Custer had
not yet returned. Joe went into his own room, adjusting
both the transom and the windows to draw in a little
air to cool the room. Then he turned up the gas lamp
and went to bed to read for a while. After several
pages he realized he was reading the same passage
over and over again, so he extinguished the lamp and
went to sleep.

He didn't know how long he had been asleep when
he heard Custer returning. He started to get out of bed
to speak to him, then heard Custer make a shushing
noise, followed by a woman's laughter.

"You must be very quiet and not wake up my lieutenant," Custer said. "For what would he think if he knew his commanding officer was entertaining a woman in his room?"

"I'll be quiet," Lydia hissed so loudly that Joe could hear her quite easily. A moment later a lamp was lit in Custer's room, the light reflecting off Custer's open transom, across the hall onto Joe's transom, and down into his room. As Joe lay in his bed looking up at the transom, he saw an amazing thing: Not only was the transom reflecting light, it was reflecting images as well, for he clearly saw Lydia take off her dress, then slip out of her petticoats and camisole! For a moment, and a moment only, he could see her small, perfectly formed breasts. Then the light in Custer's room went out, and Joe saw nothing more.

WASHINGTON, D.C.

Joe leaned back in his chair as he watched Custer at the witness table. Across the room from the witness table was the long desk of the Military Appropriations Committee, behind which sat the honorable members of the committee. One of them was shuffling papers, looking for something to validate a remark he had just passed.

"Yes, here it is," the congressman said, picking up the paper. He slipped his glasses on and read it.

"The yearly cost for keeping the Seventh Cavalry— including all pay, allowances, food and equipment—is one million, two hundred and thirteen thousand dollars. Last year there were two hundred and seventeen hostiles killed." The Congressman looked up. "That means, General, that it is costing the United States five thousand five hundred eighty-nine dollars and eighty-six cents to kill each Indian." The congressman put the paper down, then stared at Custer over his glasses. "Now, I ask you, General, do you consider this an effective utilization of federal money?"

Custer stared at the congressman for a moment, gathering his thoughts before he answered.

"Mr. Congressman, if you consider the Seventh Cavalry to be nothing but bounty hunters, then I would agree that too high a bounty has been placed on the head of each Indian. If, on the other hand, you regard the Seventh as a peace-keeping organization, then I would ask you to turn your figures around. There are approximately three quarters of a million white men, women, and children in the Department of the Missouri who were not killed last year. I ask you, sir, if you consider the lives of these American citizens to be worth a dollar and sixty-three cents apiece?"

The gallery first exploded into laughter at the congressman's expense. Then they applauded Custer heartily. The applause continued until the committee chairman quieted the gallery with his gavel. When order was at last restored, the chairman, who happened to be one of Custer's supporters, spoke up.

"General Custer, I want to thank you for taking time out from your busy schedule to appear before our committee. No doubt your testimony will be helpful to those members who have not yet made up their minds. You are excused, sir."

Custer tossed his hat onto a table, then settled into a chair with a long, audible sigh. He ran his hand through his hair and looked over at Joe, who was adjusting the windows to provide a soft breeze.

"What do you think?" Custer asked. "Did we accomplish anything before the committee today?"

"I walked back into the cloakroom, as you asked," Joe said. "And, under cover of reading a newspaper, I overheard the conversation of several of the congressmen. I think you've made quite a favorable impression on them, General. I believe they will act to save the cavalry."

"I'm not interested in just *saving* the cavalry," Custer said. "I also want my men to be well-fed and -equipped. I wonder what these . . . gentlemen"—Custer purposely set the word *gentlemen* apart—"would think if they were suddenly told that all they would have to eat for the next week would be army hardtack first issued in 1861?"

Joe chuckled, remembering that on one scout last year, that was the date on the hardtack issued as field rations for the men. "I think they would lose their appetites," he said.

"I think so, as well," Custer replied. "And it isn't just the food. You know the weapons we carry. Our breech-loaders are of such inferior quality that it is almost criminal to distribute them. After three or four rounds, the firing chamber gets hot, and it causes the spent cartridge to swell so that it gets lodged and the extractor won't pull it out. Then, because the cartridges are made of soft copper, the extractors pull the lip off, leaving the empty casing in the chamber."

"Yes, sir," Joe said. "It is precisely for that reason that I have ordered all my men to wear a bent nail on a string around their neck. With the nail they can jab through the back of the shell casing and eventually dislodge it."

"In the meantime, fully two-thirds of the Indians are well-armed, half with revolvers and half with repeating rifles . . . Winchesters and Henrys. I'm telling you, Mr. Murchison, we have got to sell ourselves to Congress, or there is going to be hell to pay out on the plains."

"Yes, sir," Joe said. "I agree."

Custer stroked his chin and stared at Joe for such a long moment that it made him uneasy.

"I'm glad you agree," Custer finally said, "because I believe there is something you can do to help."

"I'll do anything I can, sir," Joe promised.

"Do you remember Colonel Arnaud?"

"The Frenchman, yes, sir," Joe said.

"He's in Washington. I saw him yesterday."

"Yes, sir?" Joe had no idea where the conversation was going.

"As you know, war has now broken out between France and Prussia. Colonel Arnaud wants to take an American cavalry officer to France to act as an advisor to their cavalry."

"Can we do that, sir?" Joe asked. "I mean, wouldn't that be in violation of our neutrality or something?"

"Oh, he wouldn't be called an advisor," Custer said. "He would be called an observer, and that is quite common. As a matter of fact, we had several military observers with us from practically every country in Europe during our Civil War." He chuckled. "And more than one of them took a hand in the action, too, I must say. Anyway, I have spoken with Mr. Helm in the State Department. He has told me that if our army will agree to send a cavalry officer to France for the duration of the Franco–Prussian War, we would be able to count on the full support of the State Department in our battle with Congress. I would like for you to go."

"Me, sir?"

"Yes. I think you would be ideal. You were the top graduate in your class at West Point, and you have proven yourself on the field of battle. Would you like to go? I really do believe it would help us."

"Then how can I refuse?" Joe asked. "Of course I'll go. That is, if the army will approve."

"I have already spoken with Generals Sheridan and Sherman. They offer their wholehearted approval."

"When do I leave, sir?"

Custer laughed. "I told them that would be the first words out of your mouth. You will leave just as quickly as we can get your promotion approved."

Joe smiled. "I'm to be promoted to first lieutenant for this duty? Well, that is an unexpected and pleasant surprise."

Custer shook his head. "Not first lieutenant," he said. He stuck out his hand to shake Joe's. "Congratulations, Captain Murchison."

★★★

Eleven

Observation report filed by:
Joseph T. Murchison
Captain, U.S. Cavalry
On special duty as observer with French Forces
August 16, 1870:

It has been two days since the battle of Borny.
Although the French are claiming victory, it is my
belief that the battle was, at best, inconclusive.
What is obvious, however, was the bloodiness of
the fight. The Prussians lost, in killed and
wounded, 5,000 officers and men, the French
about 3,500, including General Decaen, the commander of the 3rd Corps.

Since the battle, both armies have broken contact. The French army has withdrawn to a line
across the Verdun road between the tiny villages
of Vionville and Mars-la-Tour. Here, in the farmers' fields on either side of the road, the cavalry
has unsaddled their horses and the infantry
soldiers have erected their tents. It is obvious that
they do not expect another battle soon.

It was still early in the morning, and after finishing
his report, Joe poured himself a cup of coffee, then
walked across the road and stepped into the large command tent to watch as the French commanders consolidated their reports from the field and updated the
situation map. Still sipping his coffee, Joe stepped over

to have a closer look at the map, Arnaud, seeing him, came over to explain the situation in English.

Though Joe had only been in France for a few weeks, he and Arnaud had already become very good friends. The two had crossed the Atlantic together, and Joe liked both Arnaud's sense of humor and his frankness.

"We have one cavalry division in camp here at Vionville," Arnaud said. "A few miles east, at Rezonville, camped along the Verdun road, are the Second and Sixth Corps. The Third Corps is a little further north, at Verneville. General Ladmirault is moving up the Fourth Corps by every available road."

"And the Prussians?" Joe asked.

Pointing to the map, Arnaud continued his briefing. "We believe that the Prussian First Army and Ninth Corps are east of the Moselle, and the Second Army is south of Pont-à-Mousson. Immediately opposing us is Von Bredow's cavalry division, half of the Tenth Corps and the entire Third Corps."

As Arnaud described the situation, Joe suddenly realized it presented a great opportunity for the French. "Colonel," he said, "look at this." He pointed to the map with his finger as he spoke. "The Prussians are isolated here and here, whereas the French troops are massed all through here. By skillful maneuvering, you can choose your battlefield and be 'the fustest with the mostest,' " he suggested, chuckling.

"I beg your pardon?"

"It's a quotation from Confederate General Nathan Bedford Forrest of our late war," Joe explained. "He was an illiterate man but a brilliant tactical commander. What that means is that even though the Prussians have more total men in the field, the French are in position to have the superior forces at the point of contact, if the assets are maneuvered properly. You could crush one element before the Prussians can bring up reinforcements; then you can turn your full force on the Prussians' reserves, destroying them one element at a time."

"*Oui,*" Arnaud said, seeing at once what Joe was

suggesting. "You are right, my friend," he said. "I will point this out to Bazaine, but if you do not mind, I will take the credit for it," he added, smiling. "After all, you cannot be promoted in our army, but I can."

"It's all yours, Colonel," Joe said, grinning.

Twisting his mustache, Arnaud walked over to where General Bazaine was holding a conference with another group of officers. He stood by patiently until Bazaine recognized him. They began talking animatedly, then, and Arnaud stepped over to the map to explain the plan of taking on the Prussians, piecemeal. As they were speaking in French, Joe couldn't understand the words, but he could follow Arnaud's finger across the map and was able to keep up with them. At one point he had to laugh, for he heard in clear English the words, "fustest with the mostest."

A few minutes later, however, Joe began to realize by both the expressions on their faces and in the tone of their voices that General Bazaine was dismissing the plan out of hand. Finally Arnaud gave up his effort, then came back to speak with Joe.

"He refuses to take the initiative," Arnaud said. "He believes such a command can only come from Emperor Napoleon himself."

"But Bazaine is the field commander, is he not? Surely he does not lack the authority," Joe said.

Arnaud shook his head. "It is not lack of authority that delays him. It is fear," he said.

"Bazaine is not a coward," Joe insisted. "I've seen him on the battlefield, willingly exposing himself to danger."

"His fear is not of the Germans. His fear is of his own inadequacies," Arnaud replied.

"What is he going to do, then? Just sit here?"

"We are waiting for the arrival of the Fourth Corps," Arnaud said. "Until then, we do nothing."

"Then I suggest we send out cavalry patrols to make certain the Prussians stay put," Joe said.

"I have suggested this as well," Arnaud replied. "But the general is afraid that the cavalry patrols might become engaged, thus drawing us into another battle."

"What?" Joe replied incredulously. He barked the word out more sharply than he intended, thus halting all conversation. General Bazaine looked over at him sternly. Joe ran his hand through his hair, then sighed. "Colonel, if you will excuse me," he said, "I'm going to step outside for a little air."

"Oui," Arnaud replied. "I think perhaps that is a good idea."

Outside the command tent, the French soldiers were completely relaxed. Several dozen fires were going, over which hung soup kettles and coffee pots. Privates were passing bottles of wine and long baguettes of bread back and forth, laughing and talking as if they were spending an afternoon in the park. Weapons were stacked, and an amazing number of the men were absolutely naked, pouring water over themselves in an effort to gain some relief from the heat. A card game was in progress on the back of a wagon, which was parked in a patch of blooming cosmos, the purple blossoms adding to the air of gaiety.

Joe saddled a horse and had just mounted when Arnaud came out of the command tent and saw him.

"Where are you going, Joe?"

"Someone has to have a look around," Joe replied.

"Wait and I will go with you," Arnaud suggested.

"I don't think Bazaine would approve."

"But you cannot go alone."

"On the contrary, it would be better if I did," Joe explained. He pointed to the armband around his American uniform. "This says 'neutral observer.' If I'm by myself, even if I encounter the Germans, I'll be all right."

"Unless they realize that you are helping us," Arnaud replied. "In which case you will be executed as a spy."

"I'll take my chances," Joe said, riding away.

He rode down the road to Flavigny and beyond, toward Gorze. He had gone about two miles when, off to his right, coming through a valley and spilling out into the broad, flat plateau, he saw thousands of men. He reached for his field glasses case for a closer look, then discovered, in frustration, that his glasses were gone. Someone had stolen them.

"Damn!" he said aloud. He moved as close as he could get without exposing himself, then sat on his horse, watching the troops maneuver for a while longer. They were still too far away for him to see their uniforms clearly, but he was certain, by the way they moved, that they were Prussian. Jerking his horse around, he started back up the road at a gallop. It took only five minutes to return to Vionville.

The sight of the American officer galloping into camp on a lathered horse aroused not the slightest stir of interest among the French soldiers. Over in the wagon by the purple cosmos, the card game was still under way. Joe leaped down from his horse and ran into the command tent.

"Colonel Arnaud!"

Arnaud was putting symbols on the map, and he looked up. *"Oui?"*

"The Prussians are moving on our positions!" Joe shouted. He hurried over to the map and pointed out where he had seen the troops.

"But that can't be," Arnaud said, looking at the map. "We have no account of any Germans there."

"You may not have an account of them being there, but they *are* there," Joe said. "I just saw them!"

General Bazaine came over to see what they were talking about, and Arnaud pointed to the spot on the map where Joe said he had seen the troops maneuvering.

Bazaine dismissed it with a wave of his hand, then said something to Arnaud.

"What did he say?" Joe asked.

"He says that is only our Fourth Corps moving up to join us."

"Damn it, General, that isn't the Fourth Corps! It's the Prussians, and if you don't do something about it, in about one hour they are going to be on you like a duck on a junebug!"

"General, if Capitaine Murchison says he has seen

German troops approaching, I believe him," Arnaud said in English.

Bazaine stopped, then turned to look at Joe.

"You should stick to fighting Indians, Capitaine Murchison, where the enemy always wears feathers," Bazaine said. Until this moment, Bazaine had never spoken a word of English and Joe was surprised to learn he knew the language. "As Europeans do not wear feathers, it is no doubt difficult for you to tell French from German."

Joe held in check the impulse to say anything else. Instead he pushed his way out of the tent, then walked over to sit on a large rock. One of the card players had just won a hand. He laughed out loud, then fielded the good-natured jeers and taunts of the other players.

"General Custer, what the hell did you get me into?" Joe muttered under his breath. "Any trooper in the Seventh would be a better commander than this idiot." He found himself wishing Sergeant Todd were here. He knew that Todd wouldn't be able to do anything to change the situation, but at least Joe would have someone he could talk to about it.

Suddenly there came a rushing sound, like a disconnected freight car rolling down a track. The laughter and conversation stopped as every soldier looked up at the sky with eyes wide in fear. They had heard this sound before, and they knew what it was: incoming artillery!

The Prussian artillery fired shells with point-detonating fuses, which meant they exploded on contact. The shell Joe heard coming in hit the wagon where the men were playing cards, but the wagon didn't offer enough resistance to detonate the fuse, so it passed through intact.

Joe watched the entire thing as if time had somehow been magically slowed. He saw the black object plunge down from the sky to pass through the wagon, and he saw the expressions of shock and fear on the faces of the card players. So vivid was the scene that he was able to examine the expression on the face of each of the men in this, their last split second on earth.

The shell hit the ground just below the wagon and exploded with a roar, sending up a large blossom of flame and smoke. When the smoke cleared, there was nothing left but bloody chunks of flesh and broken pieces of the wagon.

That shell was followed by another and then another as the soldiers ran for cover. Finally the artillery barrage quit, and gradually the soldiers began to emerge from their places of cover. Under the urging of their officers, they grabbed their rifles and took up positions to repel the enemy attack when it came.

Despite the heavy and deadly accurate artillery preparation, the German infantry could make no progress in their attack against the French because, as Joe had pointed out, the French had, by a peculiar set of circumstances, superior forces at the point of contact. The German infantry was turned back, suffering heavy losses from French fire. The only advantage the Prussians had was in their artillery. Their batteries were in commanding positions and were able to pour a killing fire into the closely packed French troops.

The battle continued for some two hours—the Prussians advancing to within a few hundred yards, only to be driven back, whereupon their artillery would commence shelling again.

Then, at about noon, Colonel Arnaud found Joe and asked if he would please come with him. Joe, who had located a place from which he could observe the battle, gave up his vantage point and followed Arnaud down into a ravine, which was acting as a bomb proof for the French high command.

"Capitaine Murchison, I would like your opinion on something," Bazaine said.

"All right, sir."

"General Bataille has been wounded at Mars-la-Tour, and the Germans are about to break through," Bazaine explained. "I intend to send the cavalry up there to launch an attack against the German Infantry at that point. Colonel Arnaud has advised me against it. You are a man of boldness. What do you think?"

"I agree with Colonel Arnaud, General. I would strongly advise you against that," Joe said.

"But you do not understand," Bazaine replied. "A cavalry charge is our only hope! We must hold the line at Mars-la-Tour, even if it means the sacrifice of a regiment."

"General, if you launch a cavalry attack, you will sacrifice a regiment or a brigade or an entire division, if that is what you send out. A mounted cavalry charge right into the face of well-positioned infantry and artillery is sheer madness."

"*Oui, monsieur!*" Bazaine said with his eyes shining brightly. "But that is precisely the kind of madness that wins battles. Colonel Arnaud, prepare the cavalry for a charge!"

"Very well, General," Arnaud replied. "Request permission to lead the charge."

"I thought you did not agree with the plan."

"I do not agree with the plan, General, but the order has been given, and I now intend to do my duty. I wish to lead the charge myself."

General Bazaine put his hand on Arnaud's shoulder. "France is privileged to have such men as you," he said. "You may lead the charge."

Arnaud started off to issue the necessary orders, and Joe quickly chased after him.

"Phillipe!" Joe called to him. Arnaud stopped and Joe caught up with him. "Phillipe, don't do this. You are riding to your doom. You will be leading good men to their death!"

Arnaud looked at Joe, and Joe saw a sense of total resignation in the French colonel's eyes. It was as if he had already accepted whatever fate awaited him.

"I know I will be, Capitaine," Arnaud admitted. He shrugged. "But we French have a saying. *C'est la guerre.* Such is war."

Joe followed Arnaud out of the ravine and over to where the cavalry was dismounted and fighting as infantry. Arnaud shouted several orders, and the Lancers and the Cuirassiers cheered, then abandoned their positions and hastened to saddle their horses. Joe began to saddle his horse, as well.

"What are you doing?" Arnaud asked.

"I am going with you," Joe said.

Arnaud put his hand on Joe's arm. "No, Joe, you are not."

"Do you expect me to stay back here while the rest of you go off on some wild charge?" Joe asked.

"That is exactly what I expect," Colonel Arnaud said sternly. "Listen, Joe," he added more softly, "this isn't your war. If a man is going to die in a cavalry charge, he should at least die in his own war."

Joe stopped with his saddle halfway up to the horse's back. He paused for a moment, then put the saddle back down. Putting one arm around the horse's neck, Joe leaned his head into the animal's withers and stood that way for a long moment. His blood was hot, and he was ready to ride to victory or death—with the odds particularly greater on the latter. But Colonel Arnaud was right. This was not his war. Finally he sighed. Then he picked the saddle up and began saddling his horse.

"You are not going, Capitaine, and that is an order," Arnaud said.

"I'm not going to make the charge with you, Phillipe," Joe said. "But I am going to ride to the line of debarkation with you. I am an observer. I intend to observe."

Arnaud smiled. "Very well, my friend," he said. "But you must promise me that all you will do is observe."

Joe nodded. "I promise."

He located another pair of field glasses and was wearing them on a strap around his neck when he reached the line of debarkation. Once there, the cavalry was formed in a skirmish line facing the Prussian positions about a quarter of a mile away, on the other side of a large, open area that was broken into several plots of tilled ground. Arnaud, who was in front of the line of troops and facing them, now pulled his saber and held it over his head. The cavalrymen did the same. Arnaud looked at them for a long moment; then he turned toward the Germans and brought his saber down, point facing the enemy.

"Vive l'Empereur!" Arnaud shouted at the top of his voice, and the call was repeated in the hoarse screams of a thousand men.

Again, Joe felt an almost overpowering compulsion to go with them, but he fought the impulse and remained behind as the horses thundered out across the large, open field with screams of defiance and challenge issuing from the throats of all the cavalrymen.

The broken agricultural land over which the cavalry was charging disturbed their perfect alignment, so that by the time they were halfway across, they were no longer an orderly attack wave, they were a ragged bunch of individual riders.

The German infantry commander held his troops in check, refusing even to answer the sporadic fire of the cavalrymen who were now shooting from their saddles as they drew closer. Not until the French cavalry was right on top of them did the German infantry open up. One devastating volley checked the charge and cleared the saddles of fully half the attacking force. After a second volley, the remaining riders were so dispirited and disorganized that they galloped wildly over the battlefield. Then, with the French charge broken, German hussars counterattacked.

Through his field glasses, Joe was able to watch the battle unfold, though there was little to see other than a confused and swirling melee of sabers and horses. Then suddenly the German cavalry withdrew, leaving the remaining French cavalrymen to return to their lines as best they could.

To charge against guns that were firmly established was not the normal duty to ask of a cavalryman, but Arnaud's regiment had done it, and they had done it without complaint. Joe stood by as, one by one, the men returned, some unscratched, some slightly wounded, and some barely able to stay in the saddles. Colonel Arnaud was one of the latter, for though he survived the charge, he was badly wounded.

"Phillipe!" Joe shouted, and he spurred his horse

into a gallop, catching up with Arnaud just as he was about to tumble from the saddle. Joe got down from his own horse, then helped Arnaud down.

"Doctor!" Joe called. "I need a doctor over here! Phillipe, how badly hurt are you?"

"I will live long enough to see my name in the newspapers for leading a bold charge," Arnaud replied. "It was a bold charge, was it not?"

"The boldest," Joe agreed. He watched as Arnaud was taken from the field in a stretcher and put into the back of an ambulance wagon for evacuation back to Paris.

At two o'clock that afternoon, six squadrons of the German cavalry under Von Bredow reversed the tables and launched a charge against the French positions. Whereas the French cavalry had been in the open for the entire quarter mile, giving the enemy time to wait and take careful aim for their deadly volley, the Prussians, during their attack, were partially concealed by a depression just north of the French lines. As a result, they were able to approach to within just over one hundred yards of the French batteries. Then, like ghost riders, the horsemen suddenly and unexpectedly burst out of the smoke a thousand strong, slashing and firing at the French troops from point-blank range. Their objective was to take out the French artillery, and this they did, chasing the gun crews away, then spiking the guns they left behind.

By the time the French were able to organize a counterattack, the Prussian cavalry had withdrawn from the field. They had, however, been as successful in their mission as the French cavalry had been unsuccessful in theirs.

By seven o'clock that evening, daylight was beginning to fade. The fighting had run the full length of the line that day, beginning with the morning attack on Vionville and Flavigny, then the failed French cavalry attack at Mars-la-Tour, then along the slopes north of the Verdun road where Von Bredow's Prussian cavalry had destroyed the French artillery, then along the

Tronville ridge and to a field above the Yron. As the flame of battle subsided, it left the lines in comparative quiet. The better marksmen of the infantry continued to snipe at one another, sometimes reaching out across the distance to kill an unsuspecting soldier who was smoking a pipe or drinking a cup of coffee. It created dozens of tiny, personal tragedies but did nothing to change the outcome of the battle. Then, mercifully, it was too dark even for sniping, and during the night Bazaine withdrew his army to St. Privat.

$$\bigstar\bigstar\bigstar$$

Twelve

Paris, France
September 12, 1870

Dear Sally,

Was it just three months ago that we had our little rendezvous in New York? The calendar tells me this is so, but so much has happened in the interim that I could believe it was years ago and that it happened to someone else.

I have a confession to make. I have often lamented the fact that I was too late to participate in the Civil War. Indian battles aside, I have always wanted to lead men in a great and desperate battle involving tens of thousands, with all the attendant panoply, machinery, and maneuvering.

I no longer have that desire. Though my position here is observer rather than commander, I have now been a party to such a battle. I tell you with all sincerity, Sally, only a journey into the bowels of hell itself could be more terrible. At the battles of Borny, and Vionville, for which we just now have statistics, the Prussians engaged nearly 190,000 men and 732 artillery pieces against 115,000 French soldiers and 530 guns. The combined losses, killed and wounded, for the two battles are 20,000 for the Germans and 15,000 for the French.

There have been other battles since those, just as terrible, and the killing has gone on.

You remember that I wrote to you of my friend Phillipe Arnaud. He is a lieutenant colonel in the French cavalry and I met him first in New York and again in Washington. In addition, we shared a stateroom on the ship coming to France. I regret to say that he was badly wounded at Mars-le-Tour while gallantly leading his men in what could only be described as a suicide charge. I am pleased to report, however, that he is now in a hospital here in Paris and is recovering quite nicely.

That these men charged boldly forth in the face of near-certain death, speaks more of their bravery than their tactics. Not even General Custer, whom I believe to be a man totally without fear, would have led the Seventh Cavalry on such an undertaking.

As an observer I am prohibited by the rules of war from taking an active part in the fighting—and I knew the attack was folly. But I must tell you that seeing those brave men prepare to go forth engendered in me the strangest longings. It was not my regiment, country, or president, yet I had an almost overwhelming desire to go on the charge with these men, even though I knew better than they what they faced. I cannot explain to you why I had such a desire, for I don't understand it myself.

Somehow I found the strength to resist that unhealthy urge, and I remained behind at the line of demarcation as those gallant young men charged into the jaws of death. I watched through field glasses as the first Prussian volley emptied the saddles of the horses. The second volley halved again the remaining cavaliers. Watching this terrible battle while refraining from participating was one of the most difficult things I have ever done. What is there about mankind that finds war so appealing? Why is it that in all the animal kingdom, only man and ants conduct war? Are we no better than the ants?

I do not know who is at fault in this war. I know that France invaded Prussia, but I know, too, that it was with great provocation, for it is said that Prussia hopes by this conflict to unite all the German states into one greater Germany. The right and wrong of it is for politicians and historians to decide. I know only that I have become a cipher, a participant at the most basic level, with regard not for states or principalities, but for men like Phillipe Arnaud and the other officers with whom I shared the mess.

With fondest regards,
Your friend, Joe Murchison

After writing Sally, Joe wrote a letter to his parents and another to Seth Todd. He also wrote to General Custer, sending him a copy of the report he was required, by the orders that brought him to France, to send to the War Department.

Then, with the letters sealed and posted, he went to the hospital to visit Colonel Arnaud.

There had been so many wounded in such a short time that the hospitals of Paris were overwhelmed by the numbers of patients. Because of that, several other buildings were pressed into wartime use as emergency hospitals. Phillipe Arnaud was in such a building. Until the war it had been a convent, a redbrick, two-story building surrounded by a mortised stone wall. This particular convent was chosen because the nuns were also nurses. They willingly put up a long row of cots for themselves in the cellar, giving up their own quarters so that the patients could have rooms.

Joe walked through the open iron gate and passed a splashing fountain. One of the novitiates was on her knees, tending zinnias. Recognizing Joe, she raised up and tucked a tendril of hair back beneath her cowl, leaving a smudge of dirt as she did so.

"Bonjour, Capitaine Murchison," she said, brightly.

"*Bonjour,* Sister Marie," Joe replied. "How is your Mother Superior?"

"She is well, thank you," Sister Marie replied.

Mother Superior was just inside the door. A robust and healthy-looking seventy-year-old, she got up from her desk and shuffled around quickly to meet Joe.

"*Bonjour,* Joseph," she said. "You have come to visit Colonel Arnaud again. You are a good and loyal friend."

"I brought something for you," Joe said, holding out a small package.

"Licorice," Mother Superior said, smiling broadly. "Thank you. I shall put it aside until after vespers."

"How do you know it's licorice?"

Mother Superior smiled. "Because you know I have a taste for the confection," she said. She opened the package and looked inside. "Maybe I shall have just one now," she said, "and I will save the rest until after vespers."

Joe laughed, then started up the narrow set of stairs. A young woman was coming down the stairs, carrying a bundle of bedding. Seeing Joe, she started to go back up, for there was not enough room for them to pass on the stairs.

"No, please," Joe said, stepping back and motioning for her to come down. The young woman came down with a shy smile, looking away at the last moment so that she would not have to meet his eyes.

Joe heard Arnaud's voice as he reached the top of the stairs. It was insistent sounding, and he thought he recognized the word *wine.* The nurse replied in a quiet but just as insistent voice.

"Phillipe, are you causing trouble?" Joe asked as he stepped into the room.

"Joe!" Arnaud said. "It is good to see you, my friend." He nodded at the nurse. "I'm just trying to talk this woman who has no heart into bringing me a bottle of wine. She wants to serve me tea. Tea—as if I were an Englishman."

"I can only bring you wine if the doctor prescribes it," the nurse said, also in English.

"Do you think there is a doctor anywhere in France who does not understand the medicinal benefits of wine?"

"I do not know."

"You want to know what I think, Joe? I think she is a spy for the Germans."

"I am not a spy."

"Yes, you are, you are a spy. Suppose I ask for beer? That you would bring me, yes? Beer and sausage. Say nothing of any military importance around her, Joe. Every day I see her looking through that window, spying on Paris. At night she writes messages on little pieces of paper and ties them to the legs of pigeons, which she releases from the roof. *Bier und Wurst, bitte?*"

Despite herself, the nurse laughed. "You are impossible, Colonel. Very well, one glass of wine—but just one," she agreed.

"And for my American friend, as well," Arnaud shouted as the nurse left on her errand. "She is pretty," he said when she was out of sight. "Don't you think she is pretty?"

"Yes," Joe agreed.

"And she is a nun. Such a waste. Nuns are the brides of Christ, you know. It isn't fair. Christ doesn't care whether his brides are pretty or ugly. Wouldn't you think he would leave the pretty ones for us?"

Joe laughed. "How is your leg? Is it still hurting?" Arnaud's right leg was being held up by a sling.

"Sometimes more than others," Arnaud said. "Now, not so much. Last night they decided to take the bandage off and leave the wound open so the pus will drain. Last night it hurt very much."

The nurse returned with a bottle of wine and two glasses. She poured each of them a glass, then started to leave with the bottle.

"Leave the bottle," Arnaud said.

"I can't do that," the nurse answered.

"My friend may want more. What sort of host would I be if I had no wine for him?"

"I think the wine is for you more than it is for your friend."

"After the grievous wound I have received in defense of our country, would you deny me this small pleasure?" Arnaud asked.

"I will get into trouble."

"If anyone asks, I will tell them that my friend brought the wine," Arnaud promised. "Leave it, and I will testify on your behalf at your court-martial when they discover you are spying for the Prussians."

"I wish I could get an audience with Napoleon," the nurse said, laughing. "I could tell him how to end the war. 'You do not need men with guns,' I will tell him. 'You need only send Colonel Arnaud over to talk to the Prussians. He will talk them into going back home.' " With a sigh of surrender, she put the bottle on the table, then left again.

"The war is not going well for us," Arnaud said as he took the first swallow of the second glass. "And I fear that it will get worse."

"It's too early to tell," Joe lied. He had already come to the conclusion that Prussia would defeat France.

"Even in victory, we lose," Arnaud said. "Our generals do not know how to take advantage of the victories our soldiers give them."

"Your soldiers are fine men," Joe said, not knowing what else to say.

"Yes. Even if we lose this war, the soldiers need feel no shame, for it is their commanders who have betrayed them."

"Not all their commanders," Joe said, smiling. "No one can deny that you have fought well."

Arnaud smiled. "Thank you, my friend. But tell me, why have you come to the hospital again?"

"What do you mean, why have I come? Why do I always come? I have come to see my friend."

"I want you to do something for me," Arnaud said. "Since I cannot do it myself, I want you to go out and chase the beautiful women. The women of Paris are beautiful, are they not?"

"Yes, indeed," Joe said.

"Then why do you not chase the girls and have a good time?"

"It is very difficult for me," Joe explained. "I must find a girl who speaks English."

"English? Who needs English when you can speak love? *Amour* is the universal language. You are a handsome man, you find a pretty girl, what is there to talk?"

Joe shrugged.

"I have a plan for you," Arnaud said.

"What sort of plan?"

"Open that drawer," Arnaud directed, pointing to a small bedside table. He poured himself another glass of wine as Joe opened the table drawer. "Do you see what is there?"

Joe took out an envelope, then looked inside. "It is a ticket of some sort."

"*Oui*. It is to the Paris Opera House. Go. See the show and have a good time. And if you see a pretty girl there and you do not know what to do . . . just ask yourself, What would Phillipe do?"

Joe smiled and put the ticket in his pocket. "All right, Phillipe," he said. "Tonight, just for you, I will chase the pretty girls."

The ticket was for the ballet, and as Joe looked through the programme, his eyes fell upon the name Monique Mouchette. She, he remembered, was the young woman he had met in New York.

Joe waited impatiently through the overture. Then, as the show began, he studied each dancer as they made their appearance. He didn't have to look too hard to find Monique. She was the prima ballerina, and the audience applauded her the moment she came on stage.

Joe had never considered himself to be particularly fond of the ballet before. But tonight, as he watched this sylph of a girl glide around, he could almost believe that she had discovered the secret of flight. So graceful were her movements that she was like a feather borne by a breeze. When the performance was over, he was on his feet, cheering and applauding with the crowd.

A few minutes later, as Joe was moving with the crowd through the lobby on his way out of the opera house, an usher stepped up to him and asked, "Monsieur Capitaine Murchison, would you come with me please?"

Joe stepped out of the stream of people to stand to one side. "You want me?" he asked, surprised to hear himself summoned by name.

"Oui," the usher replied. "You are Capitaine Murchison, are you not?"

"Yes," Joe said.

"Come with me, please."

Joe's first thought was that something had happened to Arnaud. That had to be it, for Arnaud was the only one who knew he was here.

"Did something happen to Phillipe?" Joe asked. "Has his condition worsened?"

"This way, please," the usher said without providing any more information.

With Joe following him, the usher pushed upstream through the exiting crowd until they broke into the clear inside. They moved quickly to the front of the auditorium, going through a small door that led backstage. "Wait here, Capitaine," the usher said.

As Joe waited, wondering what this was all about, he bided his time by looking at the several ropes and pulleys that controlled the stage flies. They were each labeled with a series of numbers and letters that, as far as Joe was concerned, made the whole thing even more incomprehensible.

"Allô, Joseph," a soft voice said.

Joe turned and saw Monique standing there, looking as beautiful as she had the first time he saw her in New York.

"Mlle Mouchette!" he said. "How did you know I was here?"

"Everyone knows you are here, Joseph," she said.

"Everyone?" Joe asked. "How could that be?"

Monique smiled. "Do you recall when I was introduced to your General Custer in New York, how I said that I did not know your country's heroes?"

"Yes."

"Now you are one of *my* country's heroes."

Joe laughed.

"No, I am sincere," Monique said. "It is written about you in all the newspapers."

"What on earth could be written about me?"

"It is said that before the battle of Vionville, you took a great risk to reconnoiter the Germans. You brought word of their presence back to General Bazaine, and it was that information that enabled France to win a great victory."

There was very little in that story that was not greatly distorted. Joe did ride out to scout the Prussians, but he took no risk. And when he did see them and brought word back to Bazaine, the French commander didn't believe him. In addition, the battle could hardly be called a French victory. However, Joe gave voice to none of these thoughts. Instead, he just sighed and ran his hand through his hair.

"Don't believe everything you read," he said. "I am not a hero."

"Oh, but you are. And you are modest as well," Monique insisted. "I saw you in the audience tonight," she added.

"You saw me? You picked me out of all those people?"

Monique laughed. "It was not hard. You were the only one in an American uniform."

Joe laughed with her. "Yes, I guess that's right."

"Did you enjoy the performance?" Monique asked.

"I enjoyed it very much."

"I am glad. Have you had your dinner?"

"No," Joe answered. "I was going to get something after the performance."

"Wait until I change," Monique suggested. "I will go with you."

It was funny, the anticipation Joe felt at going out to have dinner with Monique. It was almost as if she were an old friend from home, even though he had met her only once—and then the evening had been dominated by General Custer.

Tonight, there would be no one but the two of them.

★ ★ ★

Thirteen

The coach was moving rather briskly, and its wheels threw up little rooster tails of dirt to hang in the air and mark its passage down the road. Sergeant Seth Todd, who was riding behind the stage, couldn't help but admire Pearl Coltrain's expertise in handling the team. Although driving a stage was usually a man's job, Pearl was in no way masculine. On the contrary, her brown hair fell softly to her shoulders from beneath the felt hat she wore, her amber eyes flashed brilliantly from beneath long lashes, and her skin was olive complexioned without a blemish. She was slim of form but well enough rounded so that even the bulky clothes she wore while driving did little to hide the fact that she was a woman.

Sergeant Todd, and the four men under his charge, were escorting the stage between Hays City and Larned. That was a distance of about eighty miles, and it could be covered by the stage in two days, including a night layover at Rush Center.

When the army had first started escorting the coach, the cavalry horses had trouble keeping up with it since the coach took on a fresh team every twenty miles. Then Todd made the suggestion that the army keep remounts at the coach way stations so that they would have horses as fresh as the teams that pulled the stage. With General Custer's approval, the plan was adopted.

Western Kansas had been growing rapidly, ever since the Battle of Washita. With the Indians held in check, the citizens were opening new businesses, building new towns, and establishing communication and transportation links between them.

Recently, though, an Indian named Hard on His Ponies had jumped the reservation, taking six young bucks with him. Hard on His Ponies and his handful of followers seemed to be trying to start their own war. They butchered some cattle, burned several barns and ranch houses, and last month they attacked a wagon, killing a rancher and his wife. Hard on His Ponies's group wasn't large enough to warrant a full-scale military operation, but both Fort Hays and Fort Larned had patrols out looking for it and had established escort details for the scheduled stage lines.

The sun was half a disk down on the western horizon, and Todd knew it would be dark soon. They were still an hour away from Rush Center. The train from Kansas City had been late this morning, and the mail contract specified that the stagecoach could not depart Hays City until after it arrived. That made the stagecoach run behind schedule. They should have reached Rush Center before sundown.

Todd didn't like being out on the road at night. The coach would be particularly vulnerable then. And though the Indians seldom fought at night, they would fight after darkness if they had a distinct advantage.

The sergeant broke formation and moved his horse up alongside the coach. He had escorted the stage enough times now that he and Pearl were on a first-name basis, so he called to her.

"Pearl, stop the stage."

She hauled back on the reins, then applied the brakes. The stage came to a halt. As soon as it did so, one of the horses began to urinate.

"What is it, Seth?" Pearl asked.

Todd stood in his stirrups and looked ahead. "It's going to be dark soon. I think it might be a good idea to use the patrol to screen the coach."

"Do whatever you think best," Pearl replied without

protest. She put her foot up on the kickboard, then stuck her hand down in the top of her boot to scratch. The action gave Todd a good look a her well-shaped leg, and seeing that it caught his attention, Pearl smiled coquettishly. "Better keep your mind on your business, Sergeant Todd," she teased, speaking in a voice so low that only he could hear her. Todd returned her smile, then called back to his men.

"Alsup, you and Gooch ride screen on the right side of the coach; Carter, you and Wilson ride screen on the left." The men did as he ordered, and Todd watched them move into position.

One of the passengers, an overweight man with a walrus mustache, stuck his head out the window of the coach. He was a whiskey drummer who had made this same run with Todd before. "What's going on, Sergeant Todd? Is there anything wrong?" he asked anxiously. "You haven't seen any Indian sign, have you?"

"No, sir, Mr. Ring," Todd answered politely. "Everything is fine. I'm just repositioning my men, is all."

In addition to the drummer, there was Mrs. Hardesty, a rancher's wife, and her seven-year-old boy, Timmy. There was also a young woman going to Larned to get married. Before they left Hays City this morning, Pearl told Todd that the woman was a mail-order bride. Todd had looked her over as she got on the coach. She was rather plain-looking, with a misshapen nose and a very weak chin. Todd had also seen the fear and uncertainty in her eyes, and he found himself hoping that things would work out for her. He saw her now, looking through the coach window, and he felt moved to say something comforting to her.

"Don't worry about it, miss," he said, touching the brim of his hat. "Everything is going to be all right."

The woman stared at him, as if wondering whether he was talking about the Indians or about her personal situation. Then she smiled at him, and the smile softened her features.

"You've got a nice smile, ma'am," Todd said. "You should do that more often."

The woman's smile deepened, and her cheeks flushed.

"Pearl," Todd said. "If you don't mind, I'm going to tie my horse on back, and ride up there with you."

"Sure thing, Seth. I'd appreciate the company."

Todd tied his horse onto the boot, then crawled across the top of the stage and dropped down onto the seat where the shotgun guard would normally ride. Pearl released the brake, slapped the reins against the horses, and the stage got under way again.

As the sun slipped completely below the horizon, the stage wheels rolled over the packed dirt road with a soft, rhythmic crunch. Todd could feel Pearl's closeness as she sat next to him, working the team. He was aware of her in a way that he had not been aware of any woman for a long time.

He knew her history. She and her husband, Angus Coltrain, had taken advantage of the improved situation after the defeat of the Indians at Washita by starting a stagecoach line to connect Hays City with Larned. A U.S. Mail subsidy helped them through the rough spots until the line actually began to show a profit.

Then suddenly and unexpectedly, Angus Coltrain had suffered a seizure of apoplexy. The malady left him confined to a wheelchair and unable to speak. Nearly everyone believed Pearl would close the stage line or sell it or at the very least hire someone to run it for her. She shocked them all by not only keeping it going but by running it herself.

"Angus worked too hard to get it started," she told anyone who questioned why. "I don't intend to let it go now."

Pearl had been operating the stage line for almost six months now, so no one even bothered to question her anymore.

"That was a nice thing you did," Pearl said, interrupting Todd's thoughts.

"What?"

"With the mail-order bride," Pearl answered. "Poor

thing, she's frightened to death—and not of the Indians. I think you made her feel better."

"I hope she has a good life," Todd replied.

There were no street lamps in the little town of Rush Center, though splashes of light spilled out onto the street from the small cluster of buildings that made up the town: a hotel and restaurant, a general store, two saloons, and a livery stable that also served as the stage station. In addition to the handful of commercial buildings, there were perhaps a dozen or so houses.

The coach clattered into town, the light from its twin kerosene side lamps illuminating the dusty street. Finally it drew to a stop in front of the livery stable, where the lantern that illuminated the livery sign also provided enough light for the passengers to disembark. Todd climbed down from his seat and unlatched the door for the passengers.

"Timmy, wake up, honey, we're going to spend the night here," Mrs. Hardesty said to her son.

"Where are we?" the little boy asked, rubbing his eye.

"We're in Rush Center, and we're going to go down the street to have supper, then get a room in the hotel," the boy's mother said. Mrs. Hardesty turned to the mail-order bride. "Would you like to eat supper with us, my dear?"

"Yes," the young woman said, smiling gratefully. "Yes, thank you, I would like that."

The four troopers dismounted, stretched, then started unsaddling their horses. They had pulled this detail before and knew there would be no hotel for them. They would be throwing their bedding in the livery stable itself. But that was better than many of the places they had slept, for here, at least, there was straw, and the barn would keep back some of the cool night air.

"Sarge, can we go down to the Brown Dirt Saloon and get us a drink or two?" Alsup asked.

"Why don't you just go across the street to the Alhambra?" Todd replied. "It's closer, and you could also get something to eat."

"Don't need to buy supper; I got jerky in the saddle-bag," Alsup said. "Besides which, the Alhambra ain't got no—" Looking over at Pearl, who was unhitching the team, he abruptly stopped.

"What?" Todd asked.

"Uh, it ain't got no . . ." Alsup nodded toward Pearl. "You know," he said. "I don't want to say it in front of the woman."

"He's tryin' to say the Alhambra ain't got no whores," Gooch explained.

Todd chuckled. "Oh, so that's the problem. All right, you men can go down to the Brown Dirt if you want. But stay out of trouble. I can't escort the coach if you're in jail."

"We ain't goin' to get in no trouble," Alsup promised.

"Get your horses taken care of first."

"You don't got to tell us that, Sarge. Hell, a cavalry-man don't do nothin' till he's got his horse took care of."

Because the soldiers had only one horse apiece to tend to while Pearl had six, the troopers were headed up the street, laughing and talking, before she was even half finished. Todd went over to help her.

"I figured you'd be going off with the boys down to the Brown Dirt," she said.

"No, I'm going over to the Alhambra. You can get ham and eggs and fried potatoes there."

"Would you like some company?"

"I'd love some company," Todd replied. "But I thought you always ate in the hotel restaurant."

"Normally I do," Pearl said. "But I heard Mrs. Hardesty invite the mail-order bride to eat with her. That means Mr. Ring will expect me to sit with him, and I'm too tired to listen to any of his stories tonight."

Todd and Pearl turned the last of the team out into the corral. "Well, then," Todd said, offering her his arm, "what do you say we step across the street?"

As they left the livery, Pearl shivered slightly and said, "It's turning colder."

"If you're cold now what are you going to do this winter when you have to drive through snow and ice and a cutting north wind?" Todd teased.

"Oh, I've got some really warm buffalo robes," Pearl answered. "I'll wrap up in them and I'll be as snug as a bear. And if you're still riding escort, you can climb into my robes with me."

Todd cut a glance at her. Was she issuing some kind of invitation? He thought it best to let the remark pass rather than make a comment without a clear understanding of what she meant.

A woman's high-pitched shriek, followed by the laughter of a dozen or more men, came from the Alhambra as they approached. After that a piano began playing, and the notes spilled through the batwing doors and out into the street. One man came out of the saloon and started up the boardwalk, while two others seemed to materialize from out of the darkness in front of the saloon, pushing their way through the doors to go inside.

The Alhambra, and the other saloon just down the street, the Brown Dirt, were the two most brightly lit buildings in town. The brightness seemed to draw people to them with the same magnetism as the gleaming kerosene lanterns here and there drew fluttering moths.

Inside the bubble of light and sound, the piano player was grinding out "Old Folks at Home." A drunk was leaning on the back of the piano, singing off-key, but he was the only one paying attention to the music. At all the other tables and along the bar, the patrons were engaged in so many loud and animated conversations that the piano and singer were barely audible.

"Look, they've got the stove lit," Pearl said. "Let's sit beside it."

"All right. Take that table, I'll get our beer and order our supper."

Todd stepped up to the bar and ordered two beers, and two ham-and-egg specials.

"You escortin' the stage, Sarge?" the bartender asked.

"Yes."

The bartender pulled a brown envelope out from beneath the bar. "Mr. Silverthorn was in here a while ago. He's our telegrapher. He told me if I seen anyone with the stage, to give 'em these telegrams he worked for Fort Larned."

"He couldn't send them on?"

"The wire's down. Been down since early this morning."

"All right," Todd said, taking the envelope and the two beer mugs over to the table.

"I don't like the sound of that," Pearl said, when Todd told her about the downed wire.

"It could be anything," Todd said. "It could be the wind blew it down." Todd didn't add that it could also mean that Hard on His Ponies cut the wire. He didn't have to add it. Pearl knew that was a distinct possibility.

The bartender brought over the two ham-and-egg plates, and Todd and Pearl continued to talk as they ate. Todd tried to measure where he stood with her. She had made the comment about sharing her buffalo robes with him. Was it an innocent remark that intended no more than the words meant? Or did *buffalo robes* mean something else? Buffalo gals was another name for whores, since they often plied their trade on buffalo robes. Todd knew that Pearl knew this. Which was not in any way to imply that she was a whore . . . just that she knew what use could be made of buffalo robes, other than warmth.

The biggest obstacle, of course, was the fact that Pearl was married. She was not only married, she loved her husband. Todd knew that she loved him because of the way she talked about him. And it was for him that she was keeping the stage line going. On the other hand, Pearl was a woman who had known a man and who undoubtedly experienced the same sort of needs that Todd felt. With Angus unable to perform his husbandly duties, it couldn't be easy for Pearl. There were no "buffalo men" to whom a woman like Pearl could go. And because the penalties of a woman committing adultery were so harsh, both by societal ostracism and actual incarceration, a woman like Pearl would have to be extremely circumspect if she actually was contemplating such a thing and careful with whom she committed the act.

Todd wondered if he should ask her outright if she would spend the night with him. Could he do that without jeopardizing their friendship? He valued her as a friend beyond any carnal relations they might establish, and he didn't want to lose that through some misunderstanding on his part.

As Todd was thinking such things, a man approached their table. He was wearing a shirt that was so dirty, one could only guess at the color. He had a three-day growth of beard and a puffy mass of scar tissue that caused him to keep one eye half closed. He hitched up his trousers.

"How about a little dance, miss?" he asked Pearl.

Pearl smiled at him sweetly. "Thank you very much for asking me," she replied. "But I just drove the stage down from Hays City today, and I'm pretty tired."

"Just one little dance."

"I'd really rather not."

"Lady, I ain't takin' no for a answer," the man said, reaching for her.

"No, get away! Leave me alone!" Pearl said, recoiling from him. "Seth!"

"Don't ask your boyfriend. He can't do nothin'," the man said.

From beneath the table Todd's boot suddenly flashed out, kicking the man in the groin. The man let out a large expulsion of air, then a groan of pain as he staggered back, doubled over and holding himself.

No one had paid any attention to them when the man first approached the table, but now Todd, Pearl, and the man who had accosted her were the focus of everyone's attention.

The room grew very quiet, and Todd heard someone say, "That there's Deekus Zoller. He ain't the kind of man you want to irritate."

Slowly, Deekus straightened up, then glared at Todd. "Soldier boy, all I done was ask, real friendly-like, if your woman would like to dance," he said. "You didn't have no call to kick me like that."

"I'm sorry," Todd apologized. "But you seemed to be having trouble understanding the word *no.*"

Deekus grinned, showing a mouthful of stained and crooked teeth. "That's 'cause I ain't the kind of man you can say no to," he said. "Now, I'm goin' to ask the lady one more time, just real polite, if she'd like to dance with me. And if you stick your nose into it ag'in, I'm goin' to have to invite you to go for your gun."

"No invitation is needed, friend," Todd replied. "You see, I've already got my gun out. It's under the table—pointed at you—right now."

There was a collective gasp from the others in the saloon.

"Now, see here," Deekus sputtered, pointing a finger at Todd. "That ain't no kind of fair."

"Who said anything about being fair?" Todd asked. "Killing isn't a sport with me, mister. It's a profession. That's what we do in the army. We use artillery, Gatling guns, mines, mortars, hand bombs, swords, bayonets—whatever it takes. Right now, I figure all it's going to take is one forty-four-caliber bullet in your belly."

Deekus's eyes grew wide and his nostrils flared in fright. He held both hands out in front of him, palms extended, as if trying to hold Todd off. "You ain't got no call to shoot me. Look, I ain't even goin' for my gun."

"Take your gun out," Todd ordered. "And do it slow."

Deekus did as he was instructed.

"Now, empty the cartridges and drop them on the floor."

Again, Deekus responded, and the extended stillness

of the saloon room was interrupted by the sound of heavy .44-caliber cartridges hitting the floor.

"Is your pistol empty?"

"Yes," Deekus replied.

"All right, open the door to the stove and throw it in the fire."

"*What?* Hell, no, I ain't goin' to do that!

"Do it, or I'll kill you here and now," Todd said calmly.

"No! No! Wait! Here, here, I'm doin' it, see?" Deekus opened the stove, then tossed his pistol into the flames.

Todd smiled. "Well, now that's much more like it," he said. "This way I figure you and that pistol will cool off at about the same time." Todd brought his hand out from under the table so that everyone could see what he was holding. It was his fork.

"Why you . . . you sonuvabitch! You was runnin' a bluff!" Deekus bellowed. With an angry roar, he lowered his head and charged at Todd, who stood up quickly, snatching up a chair as he did so. He stepped out of Deekus's way, like a matador executing a pass before the charge of a bull, and, as Deekus swept by, Todd brought the chair crashing down onto the man's head. Deekus hit the floor, then went out like a light.

"Let me through, let me through!" a new voice was saying. Todd looked around to see the sheriff pushing his way through the crowd. The sheriff's name was Meechum, and Todd knew him to be a fair and honest man.

"What's goin' on here? Sergeant Todd, I just left your men down at the Brown Dirt," Meechum said. "They ain't givin' me no trouble a'tall. Now, how's it goin' to look if I have to lock up their sergeant?"

"It ain't goin' to look like nothin' a'tall, Sheriff, 'cause you ain't goin' to do it," the bartender said. "Hell, there ain't a person in here who wouldn't testify that it was Deekus who started the whole ruckus. He started it, an' the sergeant here finished it."

"You're a little late, Meechum," Todd said to the sheriff. "It's all over now."

"Where's Deekus's gun?" Meechum asked, pointing to the empty holster. Deekus, who had come to, was now on his knees, shaking his head.

"It's in the stove," Todd said.

Sheriff Meechum looked up in surprise. "The hell you say! How did it get in there?"

The sheriff's question was an open invitation for everyone in the saloon to start telling what happened, and they began doing so, sometimes all talking at once and sometimes talking in relays. Their story was interspersed with a great deal of laughter, including the sheriff's. Finally, Meechum looked over at Todd.

"You pullin' out in the morning?" he asked.

"With first light," Todd said.

"All right, I'll tell you what I'll do. I'll throw his carcass in jail tonight for disorderly conduct, and I won't let 'im out until after you've left. That way you won't have to keep looking over your shoulder all night. By the time he sobers up tomorrow, he'll forget all about it."

"Thanks, Sheriff, I'll take some comfort from that," Todd admitted.

Todd and Pearl left the saloon a few minutes later, and he walked her down to the hotel.

"Feels like we're going to get some rain tonight," Todd said.

"Yes, it does," Pearl agreed. "I hope you and the boys can stay dry there in the stable. I'm going to be thinking about you while I'm in my bed."

Was that another example of her meaning more than she was actually saying?

They reached the hotel, and Todd hesitated until Pearl started through the door before he called out to her. "Pearl?"

She stopped and looked back at him.

"Yes?"

"I wouldn't want anything to come between us," he said. "I value our friendship."

"So do I," Pearl answered, a confused look on her face. "Seth, do you think something might interfere with our friendship?"

"I don't know. I hope not," Todd answered. "But if I happened to misunderstand something—uh, you know, figuring you might be saying something that you aren't —I wouldn't want you to think bad of me."

Pearl smiled, then came back a few steps and reached out to take Todd's hand in hers. She leaned forward and kissed him, then pulled quickly away before the kiss could deepen.

"You aren't misunderstanding me, Seth," she said. "But when it comes right down to it, I don't think I have the courage to go through with it. Please don't be angry."

"I'm not angry," Todd said.

It was about three A.M. when Todd was awakened by the rain. He got up from the bedding he had unrolled in the straw, then walked down the wide, center corridor to the end of the barn, where he stood for a moment looking outside. It was very dark because the rain obscured the moon and the stars, and at this late hour not one lantern remained lit anywhere in the town.

The rain drummed hard against the roof of the barn, cascaded down from the eaves, and covered the hoof-scarred paddock, overflowing the several puddles so that the whole corral was turned into a small lake.

The smell of horse dung was quite strong.

Todd felt the need to urinate, but rather than go outside and get wet, he relieved himself as he stood in the doorway, arcing his own stream out to mingle with the falling rain.

He walked back through the barn to the door at the opposite end and looked over toward the hotel. From here he could see the window to Pearl's room. It was dark, and closed against the rain. She had done a man's work for better than ten hours yesterday, and she had another ten hours to go today. He hoped she was resting comfortably.

The rain had already stopped the next morning when Pearl left the hotel and hurried through the predawn darkness to the barn. Removing a match from a waxed, waterproof box, she lit a kerosene lantern. When the flame was turned up, a small golden bubble of light cast long shadows inside the barn. She looked over into one of the stalls and saw the five makeshift beds of the escort detail. The men were still asleep, snoring softly.

Because they had arrived late last night, Pearl had unhitched the horses herself. The new team this morning would be put in harness and connected to the coach by the liveryman, but it was by Pearl's choice that she herself give them their morning feed. She believed the team responded better to her if they were dependent upon her for their food.

There were some people who criticized Pearl for keeping the stage line going herself. She addressed their criticism by saying she had an obligation to Angus. But the truth was, she loved it. She thrilled to the sound of her trumpet as she blew it to announce her approach to a way station. She liked the smell of leather and cured wood, and the feel of power when she held the reins of six spirited horses. She liked to see the daily parade of passengers and guess about their backgrounds and hope that, in some way, she was making life better for them.

The horses moved expectantly toward the trough to await their morning meal of oats.

"Good morning, horses," Pearl said. "I hope you slept well and had pleasant dreams."

As Pearl spoke to the horses, the memory of her own dream returned. It had occurred in that last hour before awakening. On the one hand, she felt a sense of shame, for the dream was surely a manifestation of what she had been thinking about just before she went to sleep. Passions and desires that had lain dormant since her husband's incapacitation had been reawakened by a dream lover.

The lover in her dream was Sergeant Seth Todd.

"I hope you stayed dry last night," Pearl said, forcing the dream out of her mind.

"You look nice and fresh this morning," a man's voice said.

Pearl was startled by Todd's unexpected appearance,

and she brushed a fall of hair back from her face, then smiled. "I was talking to the horses," she said.

"So was I," Todd replied with a little laugh.

"Then why don't I just leave so you and the horses can have a nice conversation?" Pearl teased.

"How long before we get under way?" Todd asked. "Do we have time to make some coffee?"

"It'll be about an hour," Pearl answered.

"All right!" Todd shouted to his men. "Up and at it, men! Get your coffee going. We're out of here in an hour."

In the stall halfway down the barn, the four troopers began to awaken.

It was late morning. The ride today had been harder, made more difficult by the mud from last night's rain. The coach wheels slipped and slid through it, and the horses pulled their hooves out of the ooze with little sucking sounds. Todd could tell that his horse was exhausted, and for the animal's sake he would be glad when they reached the next way stop so they could get fresh mounts.

When they finally approached the stop, Pearl blew a loud bleat on her trumpet. She blew it a second time, then a third, before Todd rode up alongside to see what was wrong.

"Why hasn't Bert answered me, Seth?" Pearl asked with a worried expression on her face.

"I don't know," Todd said. "It could be 'most any reason, I guess. Maybe he's misplaced his trumpet."

"Come on, Seth, you know he keeps it right by the door all the time."

Todd took off his hat and ran his hand through hair that was beginning to gray. "I know," he said. "All right, I'll tell you what. Why don't you just take a break here? Let the passengers out to stretch a bit, and I'll ride down to see what's going on."

"All right," Pearl agreed.

"Gooch," Todd called, "you come with me. You other three stay here with the coach and keep your eyes open. If everything's all right, I'll give you a bleat on the trumpet myself."

Pearl smiled. "Now, that I would like to hear."

The way station was not visible from this point because of a low ridge that lay between them. Todd and Gooch crested the ridge, then started riding toward the way station, some one-half-mile away. As they drew closer, they saw a freight wagon tipped over on its side. A short distance from the wagon, a man lay sprawled on his stomach with the top of his head missing.

"Ain't that Bert Tanner, Sarge?" Gooch asked, pointing to the body.

"Yes," Todd said. He pulled his pistol. "Keep your eyes open, Gooch."

"If I open 'em any wider, Sarge, they're goin' to fall out," Gooch said.

Slowly, ready to jerk their horses around and gallop off at the slightest notice, the two men rode the rest of the way. They stopped just as they came onto the grounds.

"You stay mounted, Gooch," Todd said, swinging down from his horse. "If anything happens, get back to the coach as fast as you can and help defend it."

"All right," Gooch agreed.

Gingerly, Todd began looking around the station, straining his eyes to peer into the shadows and behind the corners. It was quiet . . . and dead still. When the windmill, answering a breeze, suddenly swung around with a loud squeak and clank and started spinning, Todd swung his pistol toward the stable, only to see the windmill whirling into life.

"Oh, shit!" he said.

"What is it, Sarge?" Gooch asked anxiously.

"Look at the stable," Todd said. "The sonsabitches killed all the horses."

"All of 'em?"

"All the ones they didn't take with them," Todd replied.

Todd walked toward the main house. On the ground behind the porch were the two stable hands who worked here. Like Bert, they had been killed and scalped. Unlike Bert, the two stable hands had been stripped. Their genitals had been cut off.

A careful search of the place showed clearly that the Indians who had done this were gone.

"What do we do now, Sarge?"

"Let's get these bodies covered with a piece of canvas so the women and the little boy won't have to see them," Todd said. "Then I'll bring the stage on in."

It was another ten minutes before the coach arrived. Todd rode out to meet it just before it rolled onto the way station grounds.

"Is everything all right? You blew the horn," Pearl said.

"I blew the horn, but everything isn't all right. Bert's dead. So are the two stable hands."

"Oh, those poor men!"

"At least the Indians are gone," Todd said. He sighed. "But we're going to have to make the next part of our trip with the same horses and without food. The Indians stole all of the food and some of the horses. And what horses they didn't steal, they killed."

"Without a fresh team, it's going to take us a lot longer to get there," Pearl cautioned.

"I'm sure it will," Todd agreed. "But I don't see that we have any choice."

With a tired team, Pearl had to stop twice as often to give the horses a breather. They had been gone from Bert's station for the better part of three hours. It was midafternoon, and the sun seemed to hang halfway through its western arc. Todd had tied his horse to the back of the stage and was riding atop. He had done this not for comfort, but because he felt that the elevated position would give him a better view, and as he stood up and looked around, he was proven correct.

"Pearl, stop the coach!" he shouted, and Pearl hauled back on the reins. "We've got company," Todd said, when the coach slid to a stop.

"Where?" Pearl asked, looking around. "I don't see anything."

"They're off to our right about two hundred yards,"

Todd answered. "They've been riding just on the other side of the ridgeline." Even as he pointed them out to her, he saw an Indian slipping behind a clump of rocks. "Did you see him?"

"Yes," Pearl said.

"Mr. Ring!" Todd called down. "Are you armed?"

"No," Ring answered nervously.

Todd picked up the shotgun lying at Pearl's feet and passed it and a box of shells in through the window.

"If they get close enough, you can do a lot of damage with this," Todd said. "But you could do just as much damage to me or any of my men, so be careful."

"I will be," Ring promised.

"Sergeant, if you have a couple of revolvers you could spare, Miss Miller and I would be grateful," Mrs. Hardesty said.

Todd took one pistol from his saddlebag, and another from the boot of the coach. He passed them in through the windows.

"Here you are."

"I know. You don't have to tell me," Mrs. Hardesty said, taking the weapons. "We'll save the last bullet for ourselves.

Todd thought of the Carmody woman the Seventh Cavalry had rescued at the Battle of Washita. She returned to Mississippi, and someone said she was now married.

"Don't be too quick to do anything like that," Todd cautioned. He met the eyes of the rancher's wife and the mail-order bride with a direct gaze of his own. Both women nodded as if they understood.

"You men, move in close," he called to his troopers. Though the Seventh had fought several campaigns, these men were new. Todd knew that if action occurred, it would be the first time for any of his men. "All right, Pearl, let's go," he said.

Pearl clucked at the team and the coach started out again. The Indians continued to trail alongside for about half an hour longer; then, as the coach approached a ford in a creek, Pearl called back to Todd.

"They're going to have to do something soon," she

said. "On the other side of the ford ahead the land is flat for more than a mile to either side. They'll have to show themselves."

"We're ready for them," Todd said.

The coach rolled through the ford, kicking up sand and bubbles of water. When it came out on the other side, Hard on His Ponies and his little group made their first attack. They dashed toward the stage at a full gallop, bending low over their horses. From several yards away one of the Indians shot an arrow, and Todd watched it approach, almost hypnotized by the majestic arc of its flight. At the last instant he realized the graceful-looking missile was dangerous, and he pulled aside just as the arrow thunked into the roof of the coach.

"Hold your fire!" Todd shouted. "Hold your fire until they're so close you can't miss!"

"All right, Sarge!" one of his men yelled back, his voice tinged with fear.

Todd waited until the Indians closed to within thirty yards.

"Now!" he ordered. He had drawn a bead on the nearest Indian, and when he squeezed the trigger, he saw the Indian pitch from his saddle. One of the other Indians dashed right up to the side of the coach, shouting. Todd heard the blast of the shotgun from below and saw the Indian's face turn to pulp.

The Indians broke away from the coach, galloping off until they were just out of range. They trailed the coach for a while; then one of them broke off for an individual charge, riding hard and bending low behind his horse so as not to present a target.

"Sarge, I can't get a shot at the sonuvabitch!" one of his men yelled.

"Shoot his horse!" Todd called back, and almost immediately there was a volley of carbine fire from the men. The Indian's horse went down headfirst. Its rider hit the ground and rolled, then, yelling, got up and ran back toward the other Indians. One of them reached down and helped the unseated Indian onto the back of his own pony.

The Indians charged again, and this time Todd took long, careful aim at the one he was sure was Hard on His Ponies. He touched the trigger, and the Indian grabbed his chest, then fell off his pony. The two Indians who had been forced to ride double had made an attractive target to the troopers, and they went down as well.

The one remaining Indian suddenly realized he was alone, and he wheeled his horse about and galloped away while bullets whistled by just inches from his head. The troopers let out a cheer, then started shouting insults toward the Indian, who was pulling away rapidly.

During the entire skirmish Pearl had kept the horses at a gallop. Now with the threat relieved, she pulled them to a halt and let them stand there, blowing hard in their harness.

"Whoooeee!" Gooch said, slapping his knee happily. This was his first encounter with the Indians. "That's the best goddamned time I ever had in my life! We was killin' them red sonsabitches like they was flies!"

"Do you think he'll get some others and come back?" Pearl asked.

"No, I believe we killed Hard on His Ponies, and that buck has had enough," Todd answered.

"So what if he does round up some others and come back?" Gooch asked boisterously. "If he does, we'll kill ever' damned one of 'em! We're the Seventh Cavalry, by God!"

It was after dark when they reached Larned. The stage depot was at the end of the single street, nearest Fort Larned. With the coach safely at its destination, Todd waved good-bye, then took his men into the fort, where they would be fed and billeted for the night. There, too, Todd turned over the brown envelope of telegraph messages the bartender had given him back in Rush Center and reported that, to the best of his knowledge, Hard on His Ponies was dead.

"He *is* dead, Sergeant Todd," the officer of the day replied. "The telegraph is working again, and we got confirmation of that fact earlier tonight. You did an excellent job."

"Thank you, sir," Todd replied. He looked over at the mess hall and saw the four young troopers following a cook inside. "I hope our late arrival doesn't too inconvenience the cookie."

"Don't worry about that," the OD replied. "I'm going to go over there personally and see that they are very well treated."

"Again, I thank you, sir."

"And as for you, Sergeant, why don't you go on into town and treat yourself to a restaurant dinner and a few drinks?"

Todd looked back at the young officer of the day; then he smiled. "Lieutenant," he said. "You have the makings of a fine officer. I think I'll do just that."

After a much-appreciated supper of pork chops and sweet potatoes, Todd stepped into the nearest saloon for a drink. A card game was in progress at the back of the room, and because soldiers were often easy marks for gamblers, Todd was invited to join.

An hour and a half later, and nearly one hundred dollars richer, Todd quit the game. The other players around the table learned the hard way that Todd was an expert card player, his skills honed in the gaming establishments of New Orleans when he was a very young man.

With one more drink to see him on his way, Todd left the saloon, mounted his horse, and began riding out of town. It was nearly midnight, and except for the lights and noise from the two saloons that were still going, all was quiet. The hollow *clomp* of hoofbeats echoed back from the dark houses and false-fronted stores.

He rode past the depot and saw the coach sitting empty. Next door to the depot was the Coltrain house, and when Todd glanced at it, he was surprised to see a lamp burning downstairs.

He stopped and studied the house for a long minute. What was Pearl doing awake? He knew how exhausted she must be. Surely she would be asleep now. But if so, why was the lamp burning?

Maybe she had forgotten to extinguish it.

Todd urged his horse toward the house, then dismounted in front. Maybe he should knock on the door to see if everything was all right.

As he started for the house, the front door opened and Pearl stepped out onto the porch.

"I saw you ride into town earlier tonight, and I've been waiting for you to leave. I hoped you would see the lamp," she said.

"Pearl, is anything wrong?" Todd asked.

"Yes, something is wrong."

"What?"

"Seth, I can't go on like this," she said. "It's eating me up inside. There's only one way to handle it, and that is to have the courage to go through with it," she said. Pearl was wearing a robe that buttoned at her neck. Now she unfastened the button and opened the robe. Beneath the robe she wore nothing. "I think I have found the courage."

Todd was on the porch in two steps. He took her in his arms, then kissed her deeply, feeling her naked skin against his hands. After a long moment they separated, and Pearl chuckled.

"However, I don't have the courage to do it out here on the porch," she said. She pulled him into her house, and through an open door off the living room he could see a bedroom. He could also see a bed with the covers already turned down.

"Angus?" Todd asked quietly.

"He's asleep, upstairs," Pearl answered. "If we're careful . . ." She let the sentence hang.

Todd looked up, almost as if he could see through the ceiling. "Pearl, if you feel uneasy about this . . . "

"Yes, I feel uneasy," she answered.

Todd turned toward the door. "Maybe I'd better go."

"No!" she said, hissing the reply so loudly that they both looked up in alarm to see if there was any response from above. Pearl dropped the robe off her shoulders and let it fall to the floor so that she was now totally naked before him, her body shining golden in the reflected light of the lamp. "It's too late," she said. "I can't back out now." She put her arms around his neck. "Oh, dear, what you must think of me! But I can't back out now."

Todd scooped her up into his arms, then lay her on the bed while he began undressing. He looked at her as she watched him, her eyes growing smoky, her tongue darting across her lips. When he was naked and fully aroused before her, she let out a little moan and reached for him as he came down over her.

"Yes," she said. "Oh, yes."

PARIS, FRANCE
JANUARY 7, 1871

Observer's Report to General W. T. Sherman
From J. T. Murchison, Captain, U.S. Cavalry

Paris is under siege. Official estimates are that civilian food supplies will last until the tenth, instant (three days from now), while army supplies will last for another two weeks.

Yesterday I accompanied Minister of War Jules Favre as he drove out to General Trochu's headquarters. The French army is in near-total collapse. The troops are dispirited and the commanders pessimistic. The defense positions before Le Bourget are a shambles.

General Trochu has offered to resign, but his most likely successor, General Ducrot, is even more defeatist. With an air of resignation, Mr. Favre urged General Trochu to attempt "extraordinary efforts beyond all orthodox military principles," to turn the tide of war. General Trochu replied that the troops were too exhausted for any further efforts, but he would certainly deliver battle as soon as he could.

Such was the French state of mind when, two days ago, the Germans began bombarding Paris.

There appears to be no military justification for this attack upon civilians other than to create panic. In this, the Prussians have been most successful, for the bombardment is having an extremely demoralizing effect.

The range of the German siege guns is astonishing! They are able to throw a shell from the Châtillon heights to the Ile-Saint-Louis, a distance of over eight miles! As the French have no way of retaliating against this long-range shelling, the citizens of Paris can only sit and wait until their food supply is exhausted.

I have been invited to make a balloon ascension for the purpose of viewing the German artillery, and tomorrow I shall do so.

Joe put down his fountain pen and looked through the window of his apartment. The sky was low and heavy tonight, the clouds underlit by an orange glow. Joe didn't know if the glow came from fires burning in the city—he had heard the distant crump of German shells a few minutes earlier—or whether it was just the normal reflection of the city's lights.

In the kitchen, Monique Mouchette was standing over a wood-burning cookstove, stirring the contents of a large pot. The three-room apartment was permeated by the rich aroma of a simmering stew. Joe walked into the small kitchen and sniffed loudly.

Monique laughed. "You remind me of a pet poodle I once had, sniffing for food."

"I am not a poodle," Joe said. "I am a wolf."

"A wolf, are you?"

"Yes," Joe said. He put his arms around her. "A timber wolf—and you are my mate."

She kissed him, then turned back to the stove. "Can you smell the ragout?" she asked.

"Of course I can smell the ragout. Everyone in the building can smell the ragout. What I want to know is, where did you get the meat? There is nothing coming into the city." Joe dipped out a spoon of broth and blew on it to cool it.

"Monsieur Garneau killed Lili and divided her up among the members of the dance troupe."

Joe sprayed out the broth. "He killed *who*?" Garneau was the director of the ballet troupe.

Monique laughed out loud. "He killed Lili," she said. "Lili was a cow who no longer gave milk. Did you think, perhaps, Lili was one of the corps de ballet?"

"It could be. You said that Monsieur Garneau was a stern troupe master."

Monique laughed again. "He is stern, yes, but not so that he would shoot someone and eat them if they did not dance well."

"I've known first sergeants who would," Joe joked.

Joe and Monique were living together. Living together without benefit of matrimony was not something Joe had ever thought he would do, and yet he had fallen into it so easily that it seemed a perfectly normal condition. Indeed, since he and Monique had moved in together, Joe learned that, in Paris at least, cohabitation without marriage was not all that rare.

"Many men and women become husbands and wives, have children, and raise families without ever knowing true love," Monique told him, justifying the idea. "Is it not better for a man and woman to live together in love without marriage than to have a union blessed in the grandest cathedral, yet there be no love between that husband and wife?"

Joe agreed with her because he wanted to agree with her. He realized that Monique's liberal point of view was in great part shaped by the fact that so many of her fellow dancers and actresses were involved in arrangements similar to her own. Though in many cases they were not actually living full time together, but were keeping a separate apartment, as the men with whom they were involved were already married.

Joe had asked Monique to marry him. He was far less naive now than he had been when he proposed to Alice Patterson. He had asked Alice to marry him because he had felt obligated, thinking he was the first man to compromise her. He knew he wasn't the first man to share Monique's bed, but it made no difference to him. He was in love with her, and he wanted to marry her.

Monique said yes, but it was a conditional yes. She would marry him only if he would leave the United States Army and move to France.

"But what would I do in France?" Joe had asked. "How would I support us?"

Monique laughed. "Silly boy. Do you not know that I make a great deal of money as a prima ballerina?"

Joe was adamantly against that. "No, I could not let you work while I did nothing."

"Then you could go into the French army," she suggested. "I know many ministers in the government. And you have met many generals. I am sure you could get a commission."

Joe had no doubt but that he could get a commission in the French army, but he didn't want one. The French officers' corps was not only poorly paid, it lacked an esprit de corps and a sense of respect from the civilian population. In addition, the fortunes of war were such now that Joe wasn't entirely certain there would even be a French army when the fighting was finished.

Monique didn't want to go to America to live, and Joe didn't want to come to France. As a result, their marriage plans were at an impasse. They decided to deal with it by not dealing with it at all. They both knew that at sometime in the future, Joe's duty in France would end, and then he would return to the United States. But they never spoke about it.

Joe had not mentioned Monique in any of his letters —not to his parents, nor Sergeant Todd, nor General Custer, and especially not to Sally Delano.

Once, he almost told Sally. His letters to her had become a means of venting his most personal thoughts, as if he were writing a diary. But he was afraid she wouldn't understand the relationship he had with Monique and would, perhaps, break off the correspondence in disgust. And he realized now that what had started as a curiosity, and as a favor to a young girl, had now become a very important part of his life.

"I saw you writing to your government," Monique said. "Did you say in your report how the Germans are shooting their cannon at civilians?"

"Yes."

"And did you tell them how the Prussians have our beautiful Paris in a siege and how our people are starving?"

"Yes, I told them that also."

"Perhaps your government will do something to help us."

"What could they do?"

"I don't know. But did France not help the United States in its revolution? I have read this."

"Yes," Joe agreed. "France did help."

"Then perhaps the United States will help us now."

"Perhaps so," Joe said, not wanting to argue about it.

"But I think it will be too late," Monique said.

"Yes, I think so as well."

"The ragout is ready. Are you hungry?"

"I'm ravenous."

"We can eat now."

In the bedroom after dinner, Monique stood by the bed, waiting for Joe to get undressed. She was already naked, her body subtly lighted by the ambient light coming in through the windows. Monique had a slender, dancer's body, her legs smooth and tapered, though remarkably muscled, her breasts small, firm, and well-rounded. Right now the nipples were drawn tight from their exposure to the cool air. At the junction of her legs the tangle of hair curled invitingly. Joe looked at her appreciatively for a long moment before removing his clothes.

"I'll get your boots and trousers," Monique offered, motioning for him to sit on the edge of the bed, then kneeling before him.

As soon as she finished undressing Joe, she raised up to him and kissed him hungrily, opening her mouth on his. Joe sent his tongue darting against hers, then pulled her down onto the bed and rolled on top of her.

Monique received him easily, wrapping her long, well-toned dancer's legs around him, meeting his lunges by pushing against him. Joe lost himself in the pleasurable sensations until a few minutes later, when Monique began a frenzied moaning and jerking beneath him. He let himself go then, thrusting against her until at last he played out his own passion.

They lay together for a long time after that, holding each other but not speaking. Joe felt the chill of the deepening night in an apartment with only residual heat from the cookstove. As the room grew colder, they snuggled closer, sharing each other's body warmth.

In the distance they heard the heavy thumping sound of crashing shells. When one sounded nearer than the others, Monique whimpered in fright and drew even closer to him.

"Don't be afraid," Joe told her. "The shells are falling as randomly as lightning bolts. They are no threat to us."

Monique sighed. "I am not afraid as long as you are here."

"I am Gaston Tissandier, Capitaine Murchison," the tall, slender man said, extending his hand. Though his hair was short, he had a full mustache very much like that of General Custer's, even to the coloration.

"I am honored to meet you, Monsieur Tissandier," Joe said, taking the Frenchman's hand. "I am told how you have used your balloon to carry mail and dispatches over the German lines."

"*Oui,*" Tissandier replied. "And if the government had listened to me when I made my plea, we would now have an air corps of many balloons that could carry not only mail and dispatches but enough food to relieve Paris. And a few bombs to drop on the Germans' heads, for good measure."

"But are you not dependent upon the winds for such voyages?" Joe asked.

"*Oui,* but so are the sailing ships dependent upon winds," Tissandier said. "And yet with wind power alone, man has traversed the globe." He pointed to the balloon, which was even then being filled with gas. "Some day, my friend, there will be giant balloons that will carry freight and passengers as easily as trains and ships do today. There remains only the means of controlling the vessels in the air—but as sailors have learned to tack against the wind, so shall aeronauts."

Phillipe Arnaud, out of the hospital now but requiring a cane to walk, came over to talk to Joe.

"Are you really going aloft in that thing?" he asked.

"Yes," Joe said. "I am an observer. What would be better than a *vue à vol d'oiseau*?"

"The view from a balcony seat at the opera house perhaps?" Phillipe teased. "You cannot say that you did not enjoy *that* view."

Joe laughed. "You are right. I very much enjoyed that view."

"Such a fool I was to give the ticket to you," Phillipe said. "Had I gone to the ballet, the beautiful prima ballerina would have fallen in love with *me*."

"You are certain of that?"

"But of course, *mon ami*. What woman could not fall in love with a wounded war hero?" Phillipe bantered.

"Capitaine Murchison," Tissandier called, "the balloon is ready for the ascent. Would you step into the gondola, please?"

As Joe approached the gondola, Tissandier gave him a fur cap and a fur muffler.

"You will need these," he said.

Joe waved them aside. "I'll be all right," he said. "It isn't that cold today."

Tissandier smiled. "Monsieur, you would need this on the hottest summer day, for as we climb higher, it gets much colder."

"Oh," Joe said. "Well, in that case . . ." He took the proffered items; then as two men held the wicker basket steady, he climbed over the railing. Tissandier climbed in right behind him.

"In the event I become incapacitated for some reason, pull this cord," Tissandier explained. "It will release the gas and allow the balloon to descend."

"What will keep it from falling like a rock?"

Tissandier laughed. "Do not worry, Capitaine. The gas will not be able to escape so quickly as to allow a too-rapid descent," he explained. He pointed to where he wanted Joe to be, and Joe moved into position.

Tissandier began calling out orders to the ground crew, and ropes were released and ballast cut free. The balloon began to rise. At first Joe thought it was rising slowly, though he was amazed at how quickly he was looking down upon first the trees and then the tallest buildings. As the balloon drifted up higher still, he could see more of the city, and he found himself looking for the building where he lived. He found it, then saw someone hanging wash on the clothesline on the roof. Recognizing a blue flannel shirt he knew was his own, he realized he was seeing Monique, and he gasped.

"What is it?" Tissandier asked.

Joe pointed to the building. "That is my . . . my friend," he said, not knowing how else to describe her. "I can see her so clearly, yet she is so far away."

"Yes, that is the beauty of these devices," Tissandier said.

As they climbed higher, Joe was able to see to the outer limits of the city. He could see the French and the German armies, and, from this perspective, they seemed amazingly close together.

"Do you see there?" Tissandier said, pointing to an elevation to the southeast of the city.

"Yes."

"It is from there that the Germans are shelling Paris."

Joe raised his field glasses and looked toward the ridge. He saw a line of one hundred or more guns—huge machines, bigger than any artillery piece he had ever seen. He saw also that the guns were being readied for action.

"I think they are about to start shelling again," Joe said.

A few moments later he saw, in a rippling effect, the flash and smoke of several guns being fired almost simultaneously. Several seconds later he heard them, like a distant roll of thunder.

Quickly, Joe moved his glasses back toward the city to watch the shells fall. He watched them explode in the streets and against the buildings, then heard the crumping sound of their impact.

"The bastards!" Joe said. "They are making no attempt to aim their guns. They are just shooting into the city at random."

"*Oui,*" Tissandier said. "And there is nothing we can do to stop them."

The wicker-basket gondola continued to be borne aloft in a broad blue sky laced with cirrus clouds. True to Tissandier's prediction, it became much, much colder, and Joe welcomed the fur hat and muffler Tissandier had insisted he bring. It was worth the discomfort, however, for the view from up here was more breathtaking than anything Joe had ever seen or imagined. For the first time in his life he could visualize Earth as round, as from horizon to horizon he could see the suggestion of a dipping curve.

Joe was startled by a hissing sound, and he quickly looked around to see Tissandier opening a valve.

"What are you doing?" Joe asked.

"I am venting gas," the aeronaut explained. "We have reached a height of four kilometers. There is no air above this altitude. Should we attempt to go higher, we would die of asphyxiation."

Joe had noticed that he was breathing a little harder, but he had attributed that to excitement.

"Good," Tissandier said, a moment later. "The wind forces are perfectly balanced here. We shall be able to descend well within our own lines."

From aloft, Joe could see how completely the Germans had invested Paris, for their lines ran from the Châtillon heights to the south—where their huge siege guns were even now bombarding the city—in an unbroken arc to Brie on the east, continuing up to Le Bourget to the north, around to Montretout to the west of the city, then back down to Châtillon. Joe studied the entire line carefully, trying to determine where the

French army might be able to break out. He saw no such place.

Slowly, he lowered the field glasses, then stuck his freezing hands into the muffler.

"Have you seen enough, Capitaine?" Tissandier asked.

Joe nodded.

Tissandier pulled the cord, opening the gas relief valve, and almost immediately the balloon began descending.

One hour and forty minutes after lifting off, the balloon touched down again, very near the French fortress of Charenton. Recovery wagons were sent out for the balloon, while a carriage took Joe and Tissandier back to the military headquarters inside Paris.

Though Joe's observation had shown just how tenuous the French position was, the ascension itself had been so thrilling that Joe was practically euphoric as they rode back to the city, describing one sensation after another.

"Careful, Capitaine Murchison," Tissandier said, "lest you catch the disease."

"The disease? What disease?" Joe asked.

Tissandier chuckled. "The disease from which so many aeronauts, including myself, suffer. The disease that makes you feel as if you are not complete unless you are aloft."

When the carriage stopped in front of French military headquarters, Joe hurried to find Phillipe. In excited tones, he began to describe the excitement he had felt during the balloon ride. Then he saw that Phillipe was not listening to him. His friend's eyes were sad, his face gaunt. It was an expression that stopped Joe cold.

"Phillipe, what is it?" he asked. "Why are you looking like that?"

"I am so sorry," Phillipe said.

Joe felt a constriction in his chest and a hollowness in the pit of his stomach. "Phillipe, tell me—what has happened?"

"The worst possible thing, my friend." Phillipe put

his hand on Joe's shoulder. "The boche. Their hellish cannonading. This morning, while you were aloft, a German bomb hit your apartment building. Monique was killed."

★★★

Fourteen

William Donovan finished his address to polite applause. After he sat down, a major introduced the West Point Glee Club. In richly harmonizing voices that struck resonant chords in the hearts of all who were present, the cadet chorus sang "The Battle Hymn of the Republic," followed by "Army Blue." They concluded with a stirring rendition of "Garryowen," the marching song for the Seventh Cavalry. Their choice of that particular song was by coincidence only, but it caused Joe to resume his own memories. Or, were they memories? The sensations were so strong that he could almost believe there must be some sort of parallel existence. He was here, in this time, and yet the incidents of the past weren't simply being recalled . . . they were being relived.

FORT LINCOLN, DT
MAY 12, 1876

The Seventh Cavalry was no longer in Kansas. They were now in the Dakota Territory, having come to Fort Lincoln in the summer of 1873 to protect the construction engineers of the Northern Pacific Railroad as they surveyed and built their track. The railroad was completed now, but the Seventh remained in the Dakota

Territory with a changed mission: Now they were here to protect the whites moving into the territory. What was particularly agitating the Indians, and causing difficulty for the army, was the number of whites who were streaming into the Black Hills in search of gold. More than a thousand miners and prospectors were already in the hills, despite the fact that the Black Hills had not only been ceded to the Sioux by treaty but were also considered sacred by them.

Joe did not return directly to the Seventh Cavalry after his tour in France. For the first two years he was in Washington, D.C., assigned to the Bureau of Ordnance. Both the Army and Naval Ordnance Departments had expressed a keen interest in the long-range siege guns with which the Germans had bombarded Paris. As a result of Joe's first-hand observation of such weapons, he found himself in great demand. He began helping both branches of service as they developed and tested many different calibers and designs of guns, both rifled and smoothbore, as well as muzzle- and breechloaders.

Joe also worked on advanced models of a Gatling gun that used the same caliber cartridge as the Cavalry carbines, thus greatly simplifying the supply system. With a redesigned ammunition feeder, a smoother barrel rotation and cartridge extractor, and cleaner-burning powder, the performance of the guns improved markedly.

Then, in a monumental blunder, the United States Congress adjourned without passing the Army Officers' Compensation Act. Although the enlisted men of the army would continue to receive their pay, the officers would not. It took several months to straighten out the oversight, during which time the officers were left to shift for themselves. For the summer of 1872, Joe managed to support himself by playing baseball on a professional team. Ironically, he made considerably more money in that three months than he had earned in the previous two years on his military salary.

Even though Joe spent two years in Washington, for the entire time he was there he was carried on the Seventh Cavalry table of organization chart. Thus, when the Seventh moved to Fort Lincoln, Joe was able to rejoin them without the necessity of cutting further orders. He was welcomed back warmly and promptly given command of M Troop. To his pleasant surprise he discovered that the First Sergeant of M Troop was none other than his old friend Seth Todd.

There followed three years of campaigning with the Seventh, including a summer-long expedition into the Yellowstone in the summer of 1875, during which Joe fought in the battle that subsequently became known as the Battle of Agee's Island. And though he did not forget Monique Mouchette, time and activity finally managed to heal his grief.

Joe was at his desk in the M Troop orderly room when Sergeant Quinlin knocked on the door. Quinlin was temporarily filling this position of first sergeant because Todd had gone to Jefferson Barracks, Missouri, to escort back ten new recruits to bring the Seventh up to strength for the upcoming expedition against the Sioux.

"Yes, Sergeant Quinlin?" Joe asked, looking up from his ammunition inventory. "What is it?"

"Sir, we've got sort of a problem," Quinlin said.

"What kind of problem?"

"Well, sir, First Sergeant Todd isn't here."

"I know he isn't here, Quinlin. I'm the one who sent him to Jefferson Barracks, remember?"

"Yes, sir. Well, sir, this mornin' I sent Trooper Bernstein into Bismarck to meet the train an' pick up the mail, since it was our time to do so." Quinlin paused.

"Well, go on, man. Do I have to drag every word out of you?"

"The thing is, sir, the mail ain't the only thing he brung back. He brung back a young woman."

Joe stood up with a puzzled expression on his face. "Who is this young woman?"

"She's the first sergeant's niece, sir. Her name is Miss Hamby. She's waitin' out here to see you, sir."

Joe stepped to the door, then peeked through it into

the outer office. A young woman was standing over by the wall, examining the manning chart. She was strikingly pretty, with light brown hair, a smooth complexion, high cheekbones, and a tall, willowy form.

Joe opened the door wide and cleared his throat, and the girl looked around, then smiled, showing her dimples. The dazzling beauty of her smile made his breath catch.

"You must be Captain Murchison," the young woman said. "I'm Tamara Hamby." Her voice was soft, well modulated, and with a decided southern accent.

Joe regained his composure. "Yes," he said. "Yes, I am."

The young woman crossed the space between them with her hand extended. "My uncle has told me all about you."

"He has?"

"Well, only in letters, of course. It has been many years since I last saw him. I was very disappointed to learn he isn't here."

"He will be absent for a short time only. He went to Jefferson Barracks to collect some new soldiers. Miss Hamby, was Sergeant Todd expecting you? I could have sent someone else to Jefferson Barracks so that he would have been here to meet you."

"He isn't *exactly* expecting me."

Joe smiled. "What do you mean by 'he isn't exactly'?"

"He sent me a letter inviting me to come out here for a visit"—she smiled, again flashing her dimples—"but instead of answering the letter, I just came ahead. I hope my impetuousness won't cause a problem."

"I hardly see how the presence of a lovely young lady on an army post could ever be a problem," Joe said. "However, we must find some place for you to stay."

Tamara's eyes knitted in question. "Why, I assumed I would be staying with my uncle."

Joe shook his head. "That's not possible. Your uncle has a single room in the back of the barracks—hardly a fitting place for you."

"Oh, dear."

"Don't worry, Miss Hamby," Joe said easily. "If you'll just come with me, I'll take you over to see Mrs. Custer. They frequently host guests, and I'm sure she will be able to find a place for you with no problem at all."

"Of course I can take care of finding a place for Miss Hamby," Libbie Custer said, answering Joe's question. She smiled at the young woman. "Why, she'll simply stay right here with the general and me."

"I don't want to be any trouble, Mrs. Custer," Tamara said.

"Nonsense, you'll be no trouble at all. Why, I was just lamenting to the general the other day that, what with his recent trip to Washington and New York, we failed to make any arraignments for a summer visitor this year. When you consider that, you can see what a fortuitous event your unexpected arrival is."

"It so happens you have arrived at a very good time, Miss Hamby," Joe said. "Tomorrow night there's a dance at the officers' mess."

"Yes, that's right," Libbie said enthusiastically. "Oh, it will be wonderful having you attend the dance."

"But I'm sure all the plans have already been made. I wouldn't want to impose."

"Don't be silly, dear," Libbie said. "You won't be an imposition, you will be a wonderful addition. And this dance is very special, for it is to celebrate the general's reinstatement."

"Reinstatement?" Tamara asked.

"It's nothing," Libbie said with a peremptory wave of her hand. "Oh, we can laugh about it now, though I suppose it had the potential to be quite serious. You see, my husband got into some difficulty recently. It was no more than a silly misunderstanding, really— something about Autie not paying a courtesy call on the president before he left Washington.

"Autie immediately got in touch with General Sheridan and explained he had attempted to see the president but that the president sent word that he would not receive him. Why, what was Autie to do? Wait in Washington all summer until the president could fit him into his busy schedule?

"Anyway, it is all worked out now, and tomorrow night we are having a dance to celebrate. Oh, I know!" Libbie said, clapping her hands together as if she were a schoolgirl. "We'll make the dance do double duty. Not only will it be to celebrate the general's reinstatement, it will also be to welcome you to Fort Lincoln."

"Will my uncle be back in time for the dance?" Tamara asked.

"I'm afraid not," Joe answered. "He won't be back for another three days." He didn't bother to tell her that as the dance was for officers only, even if her uncle had been here, he wouldn't have been allowed to come. He didn't tell her because he feared that she might consider the dance so exclusionary that she would be too uncomfortable to attend. And he very much wanted her to attend.

Joe knew what Libbie had referred to when she said that the general had gotten into some difficulty. He knew also that she had made an understatement when she said it was nothing more than his failing to pay a courtesy call on the president.

Custer's problems had started during a long and involved trip to Washington, D.C., where he testified before Congress, bringing charges of graft and corruption against Secretary of War Belknap, the "Indian Ring" of corrupt Indian agents, and even against the president's own brother, Oliver Grant. But because Custer's charges were based upon little more than rumor and unsubstantiated hearsay, all he had accomplished was to make official Washington angry with him.

Then, while on his way back to Fort Lincoln, the train had stopped in Chicago. Custer stepped off the train to stretch his legs during the train stop and was immediately arrested. The arrest was no more than the vindictiveness of President Grant, who was angry at Custer for the charges he had made. It was more to get his attention than anything else, and when Custer protested the arrest, pointing out that he had made numerous attempts to call on the president, Grant relented, and the arrest order was rescinded.

But the president wasn't yet through with Custer. He hit him with another reprimand even more devastating than the arrest had been. By presidential order, Custer would be prohibited from accompanying the Seventh Cavalry on their expedition this summer. This expedition promised to be the most involved of any the Seventh had ever participated in, and Custer desperately wanted to go.

Custer was desperate enough to make a direct "soldier's appeal" to the president:

The Adjutant General,
Division of the Missouri, Chicago

I forward the following:
To His Excellency, The President:
(Through Military Channels)

I have seen your order transmitted through the General of the Army directing that I not be permitted to accompany the expedition to move against the hostile Indians. As my entire regiment forms a part of the expedition and I am the senior officer of the regiment on duty in this department, I respectfully but most earnestly request that while not allowed to go in command of the expedition I may be permitted to serve with my regiment in the field. I appeal to you as a soldier to spare me the humiliation of seeing my regiment march to meet the enemy and I not share its dangers.

G. A. Custer

Custer also appealed to General Terry, who had been placed in command over Custer. General Terry sent along his endorsement to Custer's request.

In forwarding the above, I wish to say, expressly, that I have no desire whatever to question the orders of the president or my military superiors. Whether Lieutenant Colonel Custer shall be permitted to accompany the column or not, I shall go in command of it. I do not know the reasons upon which the orders given rest, but if these reasons do not forbid it, Lieutenant Colonel Custer's services would be very valuable with his regiment.

Alfred H. Terry
Commanding

Custer's urgent plea, endorsed both by General Terry and General Sheridan, was heard by General Sherman, who took up Custer's cause directly with the president. Sherman was successful, and he replied by telegraph on the very next day.

TO GENERAL A. H. TERRY:
GENERAL SHERIDAN'S ENCLOSING YOURS OF YESTER-DAY TOUCHING UPON GENERAL CUSTER'S URGENT REQUEST TO GO UNDER YOUR COMMAND WITH HIS REGIMENT HAS BEEN SUBMITTED TO THE PRESIDENT, WHO SENT ME WORD THAT IF YOU WANT GENERAL CUSTER ALONG HE WITHDRAWS HIS OBJECTIONS. AD-VISE CUSTER TO BE PRUDENT, NOT TO TAKE ALONG ANY NEWSPAPER MEN, WHO ALWAYS MAKE MIS-CHIEF, AND TO ABSTAIN FROM PERSONALITIES IN THE FUTURE.

W. T. SHERMAN
GENERAL

Custer returned from his trip, if not completely vindicated, then at least conciliated.

On the night of the dance, the officers' mess was gaily decorated with bunting and flags and brightly glowing chandeliers. There were not only American flags but other flags as well, including the regimental flag—a blue banner with an eagle clutching arrows in its claw —and Custer's personal standard, a swallowtail pennant, blue on top and red on bottom, with crossed white sabers in the middle. Also on Custer's flag, though not readily seen unless someone looked closely, was the name *Libbie* embroidered in white. Libbie herself had made the standard that her husband had been given special permission to carry, as such standards were not normally authorized to lieutenant colonels.

Each of the companies had their own guidons at the dance. These were swallowtail pennants that resembled the Stars and Stripes and which were marked by the crossed sabers, the number 7, and the letter of the troop to which it belonged.

The ballroom of the officers' mess was bursting with life as the band played dance tune after dance tune to the delight of the officers and their ladies. A banner on the wall read WELCOME HOME, GENERAL CUSTER, for, as Libbie had explained, that was one of the purposes of the dance. Libbie also managed to make Tamara one of the special reasons for the dance, though Tamara quickly learned that the underlying reason, even surpassing the general's welcome back, was to say farewell. The regiment would soon be leaving on an extended scout.

As the dance went on, a beaming Custer stood by the refreshment table, eating smoked oysters and drinking non-alcoholic punch. He was explaining to those officers gathered around him why he had never worried, not even for a moment, about the ultimate outcome of his application for leniency.

"I, of course, knew that Sheridan would see to it that I was restored to my command," he said, "for he is, and always has been, my most ardent supporter. Captain Murchison, you will be interested in this, I am sure. Did I tell you that I met General Sheridan in New York, shortly after he returned from his own visit to Europe to view the Franco–Prussian War? I believe he visited there while you were still in France."

"Yes, sir, it was while I was there," Joe said. "Although his schedule was quite busy, he was gracious enough to extend a dinner invitation to me one evening."

"Yes, he is a fine man," Custer said. "But to get back

to the meeting he and I had in New York—at that time, the general told me that he had no doubt that I, and the Michigan Brigade that I commanded during the war, would have been able to capture Prussia's King William several times over. Now, Captain, because you know more about that war than anyone else in America, I would be interested in your opinion of Sheridan's assessment."

Joe thought of his friend Philippe Arnaud's ill-fated cavalry charge at Vionville.

"I am sure that your Michigan Brigade would have acquitted itself very well, General," Joe said, noncommittally. "As would the Seventh," he added.

"Here, here," the other officers said, and several held their glasses up in a toast.

Captain Benteen and his wife approached the group. Mrs. Benteen was carrying a tray of pastries, which she put on the table with the other refreshments.

"I hope all of you single officers have had the opportunity to meet Miss Hamby," she said. "She is such a lovely girl."

"So we've noticed," Tom Custer said.

"Aye, an' that's a fact," Keogh added. "All the young men are making fools of themselves over her, when 'tis plain as the hair on your head that 'tis only this Irishman the bonnie lass has eyes for."

The others laughed at Myles Keogh, because he, like Tom Custer, fancied himself a ladies' man—and not without some justification, since both officers were often seen with beautiful young women on their arms.

With a chuckle at their antics, Mrs. Benteen excused herself, but Captain Benteen stayed back with the other officers.

"You know, Myles, I think Joe might take issue with you," Tom Custer suggested. "He certainly has monopolized her since she's been here."

Joe had to admit to himself that he had been smitten with her almost from the first moment he saw her. Because of that, he didn't join in the banter of the other single officers. Let them tease each other about it; he preferred to keep his own counsel.

"What about that, sir?" Lieutenant Hodgson asked. "Have you laid claim to her? Or is she still open game for the rest of us?"

"I have no claim on the young lady," Joe replied. "I feel a degree of responsibility for her until her uncle returns, that's all."

The conversation moved on to other things, but Joe didn't take his eyes off Tamara. He couldn't help but admire the effortless way she had fitted into an environment that was so new to her. At this particular moment she was dancing with Lieutenant Godfrey. The dances were allocated strictly by dance card, and no one officer could have more dances than any other—though Joe did find some compensation in the fact that he had danced with her first and that he had still two more dances with her, including the last dance. He watched as Lieutenant Godfrey surrendered to Lieutenant Sturgis, and he saw the ease and graciousness with which Tamara moved from partner to partner.

"Don't you agree, Joe?" Custer was saying.

Joe, who had been lost in his observation of Tamara, now looked around, surprised to find that Custer had been talking to him.

"I beg your pardon, sir?"

"Gathering wool, Captain?" Custer teased.

"'Tis more like silk he's gatherin', from the looks of things. Green silk, I'd say," Keogh suggested.

The reference was to the green silk off-the-shoulder dress Tamara was wearing. The others laughed, and Joe smiled self-consciously.

"I'm sorry, sir," Joe said. "Perhaps there is more truth to Keogh's suggestion than I care to admit."

"That's quite understandable. I think we have all agreed that Miss Hamby is a lovely young woman. But, back to the point, I merely remarked that sometimes a person can become bigger than the person himself, and I wondered if you concur."

Joe looked confused. "I'm afraid I don't understand the question, General," he admitted.

Custer picked up another smoked oyster with his fingers, contemplating it for a moment as he gathered his thoughts.

"I shall try to explain," he finally said. "Let us consider George Washington. He is many things to the American people. He is the hero of the Revolution, the Father of our Country, the first president . . . and yet, through it all, he was merely a man. Now, I submit that the persona of George Washington as general, hero, president, and so forth was much bigger than the rather plain-looking man with the wooden teeth."

Tom Custer laughed. "History teachers all across the country would be scandalized to hear such disrespect, Autie."

"But you miss the point, Tom. I don't mean it as disrespect. I think I am being very realistic about it, and I cite myself as an example. Already the Custer persona that I am forced to bear is larger than life. Here, you see me as the simple soldier that I am, trying to do his duty as God gave him eyes to see his duty. And yet I know beyond a shadow of a doubt that my name will be spoken in the next century with as much awe as those in this century bespeak the name George Washington."

"There are some major differences between you and George Washington, General," Benteen suggested.

Custer held up his finger. "Yes, so it would appear on the surface, Benteen. But I venture that a closer scrutiny will show more similarities than differences."

"An interesting observation," Benteen said, baiting Custer. The dislike between the two men that Joe had noticed before seemed even more pronounced now. "But how would you deal with the fact that George Washington was a president, while you are but a lieutenant colonel?"

"Quite easily," Custer replied. "Like Washington, I was a major general when our country was at war. And like Washington, I shall be president."

The other officers looked at him in surprise. Custer sucked the smoked oyster, then looked at the men and smiled.

"Why is everyone looking at me so? Have I suddenly turned green?"

Lieutenant Cooke laughed. "You may as well have, General, for I don't think you could shock us any more than you just did."

"How so did I shock you?" Custer asked. He chuckled. "Oh, you mean in that I suggested I might become president?"

"Aye, sir, 'twas a bit of a surprise, I'd say," Keogh said, speaking for them all.

Custer smiled conspiratorially, and it was now obvious that he had been leading the conversation just to advance it thus far.

"Gentlemen, what do you think I was doing in New York and Washington this spring?" he asked. Before anyone could respond, he answered his own question. "Well, I will tell you that there was much more afoot than the theater and testifying before Congress. I made a whirlwind round of receptions and parties, meeting the right people and persuading those with power as to my viability as a candidate. As a result of my efforts, and the offers of a few well-placed friends that I made, I can now say that at the Republican National Convention in Cincinnati this year, my name will be placed into nomination by Senator James G. Blaine!"

"Congratulations, General!" Lieutenant Cooke said, being the first to offer his hand.

All the other officers extended their congratulations as well, though Joe noticed that a few of them, most notably Benteen and Reno, were considerably less enthusiastic than the others.

"So you can see," Custer continued, "why this expedition is so important. We must strike quickly, we must strike hard, and we must have a resounding victory over the Indians. It cannot hurt to have my name in all the papers at about the same time the campaign is getting under way."

"But you have a problem, do you not, General?" Benteen asked.

"What sort of problem?"

"You will not be the commander in the field. That

honor belongs to General Terry. You are no more than a subordinate officer."

"Don't you worry about Terry," Custer said. "I'll cut loose from him and swing out on my own. Gentlemen, after this summer the Seventh Cavalry will be forever linked with George Armstrong Custer and the destiny that awaits us!"

Whatever conversation followed Custer's remark was lost to Joe as he excused himself to claim Tamara for the next dance.

"I lost count," she said as he approached her. "I thought you had the dance before this, and when young Lieutenant Hodgson showed up instead of you, I was disappointed."

Joe smiled. "No, it is this one . . . and the last one," he added. He was pleased that not only did she admit to counting the dances, she also confessed disappointment when she thought he had missed his appointment. "Are you having a good time?" he asked as the music started.

"I'm having a wonderful time," she replied. "Though I have just learned that the entire regiment will soon be leaving on a long field expedition."

Joe nodded. "I'm afraid that's true."

"I can see now that I made a huge mistake by not answering Uncle Seth's letter. He could have told me that now is not a good time to come."

"Oh, but I don't agree," Joe said. "Now is an excellent time to come."

"How can you say that, if everyone is going to be gone?"

"Well, I, uh . . ." Joe paused, then chuckled. "I don't know," he admitted. "I'm just glad you did come, no matter what the timing may be."

Tamara looked up at him and smiled. "Then I am glad, as well," she said, and it seemed to Joe that she moved a little closer to him as they danced.

That dance ended all too soon, and Joe waited patiently for the last one. After the last dance of the evening, the band played "Garryowen." Then it was all over.

"May I walk with you to the Custers' house?" Joe asked.

"You had better, or I shall be shown the liar," Tamara answered.

"I beg your pardon?"

She chuckled. "I have already turned down three other invitations by saying that I had accepted yours, even though you hadn't asked."

"I didn't wish to be presumptuous," he said.

Exchanging good-nights with the others, Joe walked outside with Tamara on his arm.

"What was the name of that song they played? The last one?"

" 'Garryowen,' " Joe said. "It has become our own regimental song. It's a good, bouncy tune that's easy to march or ride to. Do you like it?"

"Yes, I do," Tamara said. "There's an excitement to it." She pointed to the signal cannon under the flagpole. "Oh, Joe, can we walk out to that cannon?"

"Sure." It did not escape his notice that she had called him Joe, rather than Captain Murchison.

"I find it very moving how they fire that cannon every evening, then play the bugle so beautifully as they lower the flag," Tamara said.

"That's called 'retreat,' " Joe said. "And it *is* an impressive ceremony. Only it isn't a bugle they play, it's a trumpet. Bugles for the rest of the military, but trumpets for the cavalry."

"Aren't they the same thing?"

"No. A trumpet has the greater musical range needed for the additional calls that are just for the cavalry. Also the sound carries farther. And I think it's a more impressive instrument."

"There are many things about the military that I find impressive," Tamara said. "For example, the Custers' guest bedroom is upstairs, overlooking the parade ground, and this morning I watched all of you come together. There was a lot of excitement and shouting going on. I watched you, particularly." She saluted, then quoted, " 'Troop M all present and accounted for, sir!' "

Joe laughed at her mimicry. "That was the reveille formation," he explained. "The clerks make out their morning reports from that formation."

"Did you miss your regiment while you were in France?"

Joe looked at her in surprise. "How did you know I was in France?"

"Oh, I know almost everything there is to know about you, Joe Murchison," Tamara replied. "I know that you were the top graduate in your class at West Point, Class of '66. I know that you are considered some sort of ordnance expert," she laughed, "though I'm not all that clear on what ordnance *is*. My uncle has written all about you."

"I see. What else do you know?"

"I know you are a very good baseball player. And I know that Uncle Seth thinks you are one of the finest officers he has ever known."

"I take that as a sincere compliment, coming from him," Joe said.

Tamara looked up at Joe and smiled coquettishly. "He has really managed to pique my interest about you. I know also that you write to a girl named Sally Delano but that there is no romance between you."

"Hmm. I think Sergeant Todd writes too much," Joe said.

"Don't blame him. I think he writes such things as one would write in a diary. I don't think he feels he is betraying any confidences."

"That's funny," Joe said.

"What's funny?"

"That's exactly the way it is between Sally and me. She is more like my diary than an actual correspondent."

"Then you aren't angry with Uncle Seth?"

"No," Joe said. He smiled. "How can I be angry with him if he has, as you say, piqued your interest in me?"

Tamara put her arm tighter through his, then leaned her head against his shoulder as they walked under the spreading vault of stars. "Mrs. Custer has asked me to stay with her while all of you are gone. She said I would be good company for her in what is going to be a lonely time."

"You *would* be good company for her," Joe said. "Are you going to stay?"

"Would you like for me to stay?"

"Very much," Joe admitted.

"All right," Tamara said. "I'll stay."

At that very moment, First Sergeant Seth Todd was on a train returning from Jefferson Barracks with two other Seventh Cavalry sergeants; Mickey McDonald and Galen O'Braugh. The three sergeants were bringing back ten new recruits. Todd's ten years of uninterrupted service with the Seventh Cavalry made him one of the most senior NCOs in the regiment, and the three stripes and diamond on the sleeve of his jacket reflected that.

When the Seventh Cavalry left Fort Hays to come to Fort Lincoln, however, Todd almost didn't come. By coincidence, he had just reached the end of one of his tours of enlistment, and he had the opportunity to take his discharge and stay back in Kansas to drive a stagecoach for Pearl. Pearl had begged him to do so, offering him a full partnership in the stage line and assuring him that his staying behind would infer no additional promises to her.

Todd almost took her up on her offer, but in the end the same restless spirit that had brought him to the army in the first place was still too strong to allow him to settle down. Reluctantly, he had turned her down, and now he needed only to close his eyes to see her face when she heard him turn down her offer. She had been composed but obviously disappointed.

"Seth, one of these days you are going to regret this decision," she had told him.

"I think I already regret it," Todd had answered.

They had kissed, a kiss that reminded him of the pleasures they had already shared and mocked him with the pleasures he was denying himself by his decision. It was almost as if she had burned the kiss on his lips, for even now he could feel it when he thought about it. He put his fingers to his lips.

" 'Twould sure be nice to have somethin' to drink," Sergeant McDonald said.

Todd had been deep in thought, and McDonald's words brought him back.

"Yeah," he agreed. "It would be nice."

The front door to the car opened, and the conductor came walking through, balancing himself skillfully against the rock and sway of the train.

"Jamestown!" the conductor called. "Jamestown! If you folks want to get out and stretch a bit, we'll be here 'bout an hour and a half."

"Would you be wantin' to go over to the saloon and have a drink or two while we're here?" McDonald asked his fellow Irishman, Sgt. O'Braugh. "Sure'n we've plenty o' time."

"Mickey, m'lad, 'tis totally without funds I am," O'Braugh replied. "You go."

"Sure'n how'm I to go when I don't have any money either?" McDonald said.

"No money, you say? Then why is it you brought it up in the first place?"

"I was thinkin' maybe himself would buy us a drink. What about it, First Soldier? 'Tis always flush you are. Would you be wantin' to go us a round or two?" McDonald asked.

"I've only got enough for one drink apiece," Todd said. "Then what? The saloonkeeper will have our money, and we'll still be thirsty."

"Aye, and do you know who runs the inn?" O'Braugh asked. " 'Tis Carl Jensen, that's who. And after what that blackheart did to me last time I was through here, 'tis none o' my business I'll give him, for all that I'd like a drink."

"What did he do?" McDonald asked.

"Do you not remember, Mickey? I bought a bottle with a twenty-dollar gold piece, I did, and when I asked for my change, he said I had none comin'. None comin', mind you, and here I'd given him twenty dollars! The lyin' bastard said all I'd give him was a silver dollar. When I lodged my complaint, 'tis a shotgun he took after me. Told me that if I'd take my bottle and get out, he wouldn't call the sheriff."

" 'Tis pure robbery, that is!" McDonald said.

"Aye. Robbery I calls it, and robbery it is," O'Braugh agreed.

"And was there nothin' you could do about it, Galen?"

"What could I do? Was comin' back from a furlough I was," O'Braugh said. "The only soldier in town and, aye, the only Irishman besides. Where could I have gone for support?"

" 'Twas a fix you were in, sure enough. And I'll wager the bastard has done to lots of soldiers and a few Irishmen."

"For sure. Comes right down to it, folks are goin' to believe a civilian before they believe a soldier, no matter what."

Todd listened to the two sergeants bewail the many tribulations of being a soldier and having to contend with people like the crooked saloonkeeper.

"And the evil thing is, lads, 'tis nothin' to be done about it." O'Braugh went on. "Not a blessed thing."

"Maybe there is," Todd suggested, as the train drew to a halt in the station.

"How?"

"Evans, Slaper," Todd called to two of the recruits. When they responded to his summons, he pointed through the train window to the saloon. "Gather up about six or seven canteens. I want you to take them over to that saloon and offer to trade your pistols and carbines for whiskey."

"*What?* Top soldier, have you gone daft, now?" McDonald gasped.

Todd smiled. "Trust me," he said. He looked back at the recruits. "Just do what I say."

The two recruits looked at the other sergeants. They paused for a minute, then shrugged.

"If the first sergeant says do it, lad, you do it," O'Braugh said.

"But if we get into trouble?" Evans protested.

" 'Twill be his ass, not yours," McDonald told them. "Now, you heard himself. Do what he said."

Evans and Slaper shrugged again, then began gathering canteens. The rest of the soldiers, wondering what was going on, watched anxiously through the window as the two men, canteens clanging and weapons dangling, started across the street to the saloon. They went inside, and there was a long, anxious moment while the soldiers on the train wondered what was going on. Finally they saw their friends emerge from the saloon. The young recruits still had the canteens but no weapons, and they were smiling broadly as they came back across the street.

"We got the whiskey!" Evans said, holding up one of the canteens. "And it ain't rotgut, neither! We made 'im pour the bonded stuff!"

"Yahoo!" someone yelled, and another reached for one of the canteens.

"Just a minute!" Todd said.

"What is it? What's wrong?"

"You two men are under arrest."

"What?"

"Here, now, First Sergeant. And would you be tellin' me what is goin' on?" McDonald asked.

"Form an armed detail and place these two men under arrest," Todd said. Then, as everyone looked at him in shock and anger, he smiled. "I believe Mr. Jensen has some weapons that belong to the U.S. Army, and we're going to get them back."

Now McDonald and O'Braugh saw what Todd had in mind, and they laughed out loud.

"Aye, now, you heard the first soldier! There's none smarter in the battalion—nor the regiment, either, I'm thinkin'. Let's go!" McDonald said.

With Todd walking alongside his detail and Sergeant O'Braugh calling cadence, the fully armed troopers marched across the street from the depot, then up onto the boardwalk in front of the saloon. Their boots tramped in rhythm as they hit the boards, and by the time they pushed through the batwing doors of the saloon, they had already attracted the attention of everyone inside. The piano music stopped, falling off in a few ragged, discordant notes.

"What the hell is goin' on here?" the man behind the bar roared. "This ain't no goddamn drill field. What did you march them men in here for?"

"Is your name Jensen?" Todd asked.

"So what if it is?"

"Prisoners Evans and Slaper, is this the man you gave your weapons to?"

"Yes, First Sergeant," Evans and Slaper replied in unison.

Todd looked at Jensen. "You are in illegal possession of U.S. Army weapons," Todd said. "I am here to confiscate them."

"The hell you are! I traded good whiskey for those guns."

"First four men," Todd commanded, "order arms."

"What are you doing?" Jensen asked.

"Turn over those weapons."

"I told you, I traded for them guns, fair and square."

"Ready!" Todd ordered, and the four men opened the trap-door breeches of their Springfield carbines and inserted the copper-cased .45-caliber cartridges. They slammed the breeches shut.

"What . . . what the hell is going on here?" Jensen asked, more nervous now.

"Hand over the weapons," Todd said again.

"You go to hell!"

"Aim!" Todd said, and all four men raised their carbines to their shoulders, pulled back on the hammers, and sighted down the barrels.

Todd raised his hand.

"No! Wait! *Wait!*" Jensen yelled. "Have you gone crazy? You can have the guns! They're under the bar!"

"Order arms." The four men lowered their carbines. "Evans, Slaper, retrieve your weapons!"

Quickly, the two men did as directed.

"Sergeant O'Braugh, take these prisoners and their guard detail back to the train," Todd ordered.

"Sure'n the lads won't be gettin' away from me, First Sergeant!"

"Hey!" Jensen said, pointing at O'Braugh. "Hey, I know you! You're that big mick caused me trouble once before!"

"About face! Forward, march!" O'Braugh said, marching the men out.

"And you! You can't come in here like that! Ridin' roughshod over innocent civilians!" Jensen shouted at Todd.

Todd pointed to the blustering saloonkeeper. "You got off easy this time, Jensen" he said. "Cheat any more soldiers and I will personally see to it that you are put before a firing squad."

"Get out of here! Go on, get out of here and don't come back! I don't need no soldiers' business!" Jensen screamed in frustrated rage.

It was all the troopers could do to maintain military discipline as they marched to the train. Once they were back on board, they began whooping and laughing at the good trick their first sergeant had put over on the civilian. Todd passed the whiskey-filled canteens around, and by midnight they were all feeling pretty good.

Todd knew he was violating the tenets of military command by letting the men get drunk. He not only let them get drunk, he had helped them through the trick he played on Jensen. But why not let them have a little fun, he thought? This summer promised the biggest campaign yet in the Indian wars, and the Seventh Cavalry was going to be a major part of it. The Seventh, and these men, were going to see some hard soldiering, and it would be a long time before any of them got a chance to relax again. Some of them, he knew, would never get another chance, for they would die this summer.

Fifteen

General Sheridan developed a simple plan to crush the Indians, once and for all. It called for General George Crook to lead a column north from Wyoming, while Colonel Gibbon would bring a column east from Fort Ellis, in Montana. A third column—including the Seventh Cavalry and led by General Terry—would drive westward from Fort Abraham Lincoln in the Dakota Territory. The three columns would converge in southern Montana and the Indians would be caught in the middle. Any one of the three columns, Sheridan believed, would be enough to do the job.

After much preparation, the Seventh Cavalry set out from Fort Lincoln on the morning of May 17, heading for a rendezvous with General Terry on the Yellowstone. The regiment was augmented by artillery—including Gatling guns, infantry, pack mules, scouts, civilian mule skinners, wagons, ambulances, and, despite General Sherman's warning against them, a small army of reporters. When lined up in full order of march, the army of soldiers and animals stretched more than two miles.

For the first few miles of march, Custer had authorized the wives and women of the post to accompany the men, and riding beside General Custer in formation was his wife, Libbie. She was riding Dandy, while Custer was riding Vic. When they separated, Libbie would switch to another horse, leaving Dandy with her husband so that he would have two of the finest horses in the regiment.

Tamara rode out with the column as well, riding alongside Seth Todd and just behind Joe and his executive officer, Second Lieutenant Benny Hodgson.

It was early morning and, behind them, the sun was just peeping over the horizon as they headed west. In front of them a billowing cloud of morning mist appeared, and in an optical phenomenon, its water crystals coalesced into a gigantic concave mirror that spread over the head of the marching column. As a result it not only reflected the soldiers, its concavity reversed the mirror image so that it was an exact reproduction of the army on the ground.

Joe was alerted to the mirage by the gasps and exclamations of the men of his command. Then the Indian scouts, believing it to be an omen, grew frightened and started to chant. To Joe's surprise, even the most hardened soldiers were disturbed by it, and many swore they could pick out comrades who had been killed, riding in the sky.

"That's old Fred Wyllyams there, riding point. Damn me if it ain't!" one of the soldiers said. "He was kilt near Pond Creek back in '67!"

"There's Cap'n Hamilton!" another pointed out. "You recollect, we lost him at Washita."

"My God!" one of the soldiers said, almost reverently. "Boys, we're lookin' right into Fiddlers' Green!"

"Uncle Seth, what is it?" Tamara asked, awed by what she was seeing. "Have you ever seen anything like that?"

"It's nothing, child," Todd said, reaching his hand across to lay on hers. "A mirage, nothing more."

The soldiers continued to grow more and more uneasy.

"Benny," Joe finally said to his lieutenant.

"Yes, sir?"

"This thing doesn't have you spooked, does it?"

"It's pretty strange, Captain," Hodgson admitted. He smiled. "But I don't think it means I'm going to get killed or anything."

"Good. How about riding back along the line of march and explaining to everyone that it's only a mirage, an optical illusion caused by the sun and the mist?"

"All right, sir," Hodgson agreed, pulling his horse out of the formation.

In addition to Tom Custer, General Custer's brother, and Lieutenant Jim Calhoun, who was married to Custer's sister, Maggie, two more members of the Custer family were present for this scout. They were Boston Custer, the general's youngest brother, and Autie Reed, even younger, who was Custer's nephew. Boston and Autie weren't in the army, and thus subject to no officer's command except for that of the general himself—and for all his discipline with his men, Custer was known for leniency toward members of his own family.

Like a pair of young colts, Boston and Autie slapped their legs against the sides of their horses, urging them into a gallop, dashing ahead of the column, racing each other toward the mirage as they tried to catch up with it.

A galloper came up alongside the column to hail Joe. "Captain Murchison, Lieutenant Calhoun's compliments, sir, and he asks if he could speak with you for a moment?"

"First Sergeant, take command," Joe said, turning it over to Todd because Lieutenant Hodgson had not yet returned. Breaking ranks, Joe rode back along the side of the column until he saw Calhoun coming out to join him. Calhoun's wife, Maggie, who was riding alongside him, started to come as well, but Calhoun held up his hand to stop her. "I'll be right back, Maggie," he said.

"What is it, Jim?" Joe asked.

"Joe, I don't know how to say this without it sounding somewhat foolish," Calhoun said, "so I guess the best way is to just come right out and say it. But if anything happens to me during this scout I would like to think that you'll help Maggie get resettled somewhere."

Joe laughed it off. "What do you mean, if something happens to you?"

"If I don't come back," Calhoun said. "If I'm killed."

"Come on, Jim, don't tell me you're spooked by the mirage," Joe said.

"No," Calhoun answered. "No, it isn't that. Actually, I've been feeling this way for a long time. I don't know how to explain it. It's . . . it's like a feeling of doom." Calhoun shivered.

"Well, I'm not going to make light of it," Joe said. "I know that those feelings can be very unsettling. But I know, too, that they are just that—feelings—and I'm sure there's nothing to this one. It'll go away and then you'll be just fine." He smiled reassuringly. "But in the meantime, if it will ease your mind, of course I'll help Maggie. Though I'm sure you know that the general will do everything that needs to be done. After all, she is his sister."

"No," Calhoun said, shaking his head, "that's just the point. I don't think he'll be coming back, either."

"Hey, it's gone!" someone said. "Look, everybody! The mirage is gone!"

The men broke into a cheer, and the mood changed quickly from grim to glad.

Calhoun smiled as well. "Maybe it's nothing," he said. "But I did want to mention it. I guess I'd better get back to Maggie. She'll be wondering what we're talking about, and I'm not very good at hiding things from her."

"Hide this if you can," Joe advised. "There's no sense in making her worry for nothing."

Calhoun smiled, then slapped his hat against the side of his horse. "You're right," he called back over his shoulder. "Forget I said anything, will you?"

Joe waved, then rode back to his own position in the line of march.

The band was riding at the front of the column, and Custer had them play several numbers. Boston and young Autie continued to cavort around like the schoolboys they were, and any mood of melancholia that Joe might have experienced from his conversation with Calhoun was quickly dispelled.

The column of march, including the ladies from the post, continued until noon, at which time Custer stopped them on a beautiful overlook that afforded a view not only of the Missouri River but of the sweeping grandeur of the plains, as well. The fields were covered with new spring growth, white-and-yellow oxeye daisies, slender white-and-blue columbines, and brilliant red Indian paintbrushes. In the distance rose a great range of snow-capped mountains.

The women had prepared a special picnic lunch for the officers, and they feasted on roast duck and wine. Mr. Ingersoll, a photographer, and Mark Kellogg, a reporter, were invited to dine with the officers and their ladies, and from the laughter and gaiety, no one would guess they were men embarked upon a military campaign.

"Oh!" General Custer said, as he wiped his mouth with a fine linen napkin. "Never in the history of warfare have soldiers been sent to battle with more contented stomachs—or with lovelier attendants to see to their needs. You ladies have truly outdone yourselves."

"Autie, back at the fort they are loading the *Far West* with supplies for your expedition. I know Captain Marsh would make accommodations for me on board. If I came on the boat, it would work no particular hardship, and I could be that much closer to you during this scout," Libbie said.

"I know, old girl, and I wish it could be so," Custer replied. "But some things cannot be. You have obligations here. In my absence, you are the head of our little post family. Think of the wives who will be depending on you for advice and help." He looked over at Tamara. "And don't forget that we have a lovely houseguest for you to look after." He smiled. "I know what I will do. I will give you ladies a parade. Major Reno!"

"Yes, sir," Reno answered.

"Major, take command of the column and pass in

review. I will stay here with the ladies until the entire column has passed; then I shall return to the head."

"Very good, sir," Reno replied. He got to his feet and shouted for the trumpeter.

"Joe!" Custer called as Joe started for his horse.

"Yes, sir?" Joe replied, coming back to him.

"Before we leave on this scout, I would like for you to know that I have written to Washington, recommending that you be promoted to major."

Joe knew this because the regimental sergeant major had told Todd, and Todd had told Joe. But he wasn't supposed to know, so he pretended ignorance.

"I am honored by your confidence."

"You have earned my confidence. And with Generals Terry and Sheridan's endorsements, I have no doubt but that your promotion will come through. In addition, you impressed quite a few important people with your mission to Europe. The only thing is, I wish you were already a major. If you were, I would give you command of Reno's battalion. I don't know about him."

"He seems like a capable officer, sir," Joe said.

Custer shook his head. "He isn't one half the officer Benteen is. But Benteen is so disagreeable, and he dislikes me so much. Still, I wish I had more like him . . . and you. I'm going to keep my eyes on Reno during this entire expedition, and if I perceive that he is following my orders with less than unbridled enthusiasm, I am going to relieve him of his command and turn the battalion over to you. Are you prepared to take it?"

"I'm prepared for any order you may give me, sir," Joe replied. Again, he started toward his horse, but Custer put out his hand.

"Let Lieutenant Hodgson take the troop," he said. "You stay here and watch the parade. I think Miss Hamby might appreciate your company."

"Thank you, sir," Joe said.

Joe, Custer, and the ladies formed a reviewing stand as the column marched by. The band played, the flags and guidons snapped, and the troop commanders saluted with their sabers.

"Joe," Tamara said quietly, so quietly that only he could hear her. He turned to her. "You will look after my father, won't you?"

Joe stared at her in surprise. "You mean you know that he's your father?"

"Yes, I know. He doesn't know that I know, but I do."

"You should tell him that you know."

"I will. When the time is right."

"Captain Murchison, we had better get mounted," Custer called. "We're going to have to ride like the wind to catch up to our places."

"Yes, sir," Joe answered, reaching for his horse.

"Joe?" Tamara said, just before he mounted. He stopped, and she came over to him, kissing him lightly, but on the lips. "Take care of yourself, as well."

At that moment the last unit rumbled by. With a touch to the brim of his hat, General Custer said good-bye to the ladies, and he and Joe rode at a gallop to rejoin the column. They had to ride hard for several minutes, but finally they were back in their assigned positions. Joe twisted in his saddle for a look back, hoping for a last glimpse of Tamara, but she had disappeared from his view.

Lieutenant Hodgson saw Joe rejoin the column, so he moved over to give him the command position. Todd moved up beside Joe.

"It's good to see you back, sir," he said.

Joe chuckled. "Did you think perhaps I wouldn't be coming back?"

"I wasn't sure," Todd admitted. "I think Tamara would have kept you with her if she could."

"Seth, I don't mind telling you that I would *stay* with her if I could. She is a fine and beautiful young woman, and you should be very proud of her."

"I am, sir," Todd replied.

Joe looked over at him and smiled. "And I appreciate the buildup."

"Beg your pardon, sir?"

"She told me how you have been selling me to her in your letters."

Todd grinned sheepishly. "Captain, if things would happen to work out so that she stayed out here . . . for any reason whatever . . . I wouldn't be unhappy."

"Well, you've done your part, First Sergeant. I guess the rest of it is up to nature."

"Yes, sir, I suppose it is."

"Tell me, First Sergeant, do you think the men were disappointed because they weren't paid before we left the post?"

Todd chuckled. "That's putting it mildly," he answered.

"We're going to pay sometime during the expedition," Joe said.

"What good will that do the men? There's no place out here to spend the money."

"That was the whole idea," Joe said. "Custer was afraid the men would all go across the river to the Point and catch the doxy's disease, or get drunk and into trouble. This way, not a single man has been left behind with the clap or broken bones from a fight." Joe was referring to the collection of saloons, dance halls, and prostitutes' cribs that, kept out of the town of Bismarck, managed to flourish right across the river from Fort Lincoln itself on a place called "the Point."

"Yes, sir, but it also means that some of the married troopers weren't able to leave any money with their wives."

"The wives will get along all right," Joe said. "You know the sutler will carry them until the regiment returns."

"Yes, sir. At twenty percent interest," Todd grumbled.

The column was in the field for nearly three more weeks before the men were paid. At first Joe wondered why Custer waited so long; then he recalled the incidents of desertion back in Kansas. Perhaps Custer felt that if the men had been paid on the first few nights out, while still close enough to civilization, they might break and run. With twenty-two days of hard marching behind them, they were now so far away from anything

resembling civilization that any deserter would have
nowhere to go and no place to spend his money.

That didn't mean the soldiers didn't still manage to
enjoy their payday. On the night they were paid, scores
of poker games broke out around the hundred or more
campfires, and thousands of dollars changed hands.
The men ate well that evening, too, dinner consisting
of beans, freshly killed elk, and crushed chili peppers.
It was spicy, but very good, and Custer returned to the
pot to fill his mess kit a second time.

"Enjoy it while you can, gentlemen," he said. "I fear
we won't be eating this well much longer. Soon we
shall be on forced marches and taking our meals in the
saddle."

"If you gentlemen ate this way all the time, I would
be only too glad to accompany you the entire summer,"
the reporter Kellogg said, following Custer to the pot
of simmering beans and meat.

"Mark, did I notice that you received some news dispatches with the courier this evening?" Custer asked.

"Yes, I did, General," Kellogg replied. "They came
with my mail."

"I would be quite interested in knowing what the
eastern newspapers are saying about our summer exercise."

"They are following it, to be sure," Kellogg said.
"But I must be honest with you. Most of the news is of
the Republican National Convention."

"Is that a fact? What do the dispatches say?"

"All I know is that the first ballot has been advanced," Kellogg replied. "But I have been so involved
with the expedition that I haven't had time to read
them."

"You mean you have the dispatches from the convention and you haven't even read them?" Custer said.
"Well open them, man. Open them, and read them at
once."

"Shall I read them aloud?" Kellogg asked.

"Yes, please. I'm sure we are all interested."

Custer sat on a log, then raised his leg and wrapped
his hands around his knee, to allow him to lean back.

He looked over at his brothers and winked as they moved in closer to hear.

Kellogg cleared his throat and began to read:

"The Republican National Convention opened its activities by discussing the rules of the nominating procedure.

"As Governor Rutherford Hayes is from the Midwest, it had been rumored that Senator Blaine intended to nominate a judas goat, also from the Midwest, hoping thereby to split the delegations of the states of that region of the country. But the rules committee, having heard of Senator Blaine's plan, refused to allow the name of this unknown person to be entered unless Senator Blaine declared the nominee to be a serious candidate, fully backed and supported by Senator Blaine himself.

"Upon hearing that ruling, Senator Blaine stated that he would not be placing any name in nomination, whereupon he left the convention and went home, thus allowing his own name to be put into contention.

"The first ballot, as expected, went to Senator Blaine, though Governor Hayes garnered enough votes to keep Blaine from being nominated. More balloting will come tomorrow."

Joe watched Custer's face as Kellogg read the dispatch. He saw the smile leave, to be replaced by hurt, then embarrassment, and finally a cold, hard, anger. When Kellogg was finished, Custer stood up and brushed off the seat of his trousers.

"Would you gentlemen excuse me, please? I think I shall take a walk."

Kellogg watched Custer in surprise as he walked away.

"Is the general all right?" he asked.

"He's fine, Mark," Tom Custer replied. "Don't worry about it."

Joe waited for a moment. Then he got up and

walked out into the dark, taking the same directio
Custer had. A few minutes later he saw Custer stand
ing at the crest of a small hill, looking out over th
plains to the west of them. Joe approached him quietl
then cleared his throat. Custer looked around at him

"Did you dig a drainage trench around your ten
Joe? It's going to rain tonight."

"Yes, sir, I did," Joe replied.

"The rain will bring more mosquitoes."

"Yes, sir, it always does."

"Well, I don't recall anyone ever promising us that
soldier's life would be easy."

"No, sir," Joe agreed.

Custer was silent for a long moment, and Joe knew
he had run out of small talk.

"Joe, I have made a fool of myself," Custer finall
said. "I have made a fool of myself in front of you an
the other officers."

"No, General, you haven't at all," Joe insisted
"What would make you say such a thing?"

Custer laughed a small, self-mocking laugh. "I ha
such plans of grandeur," he said. "I would be presi
dent? I must have been temporarily insane!"

"General, there is nothing foolish about having you
name considered for president. There is only honor."

"A judas goat," Custer said. "You heard what th
paper said. Had my name been submitted, it woul
have been as a judas goat!"

"General, a judas goat is only effective if others fol
low," Joe said. "By definition, a judas goat is a leader."

Custer looked over at Joe in surprise, then he
smiled. "By Godfrey, that's right, isn't it?"

"Yes, sir, it is right. Besides, there will be other op
portunities. If you weren't nominated this time, per
haps you will be nominated in the next convention
four years from now, or even eight years from now
And if not by the Republicans, then by the Demo
crats."

Custer looked at Joe for another long, silent mo
ment, then put his hand on Joe's shoulder and sighed

"Perhaps it is for the best" he finally said. "I don'

believe I am well-enough known to be elected now. The best thing for me to do is to bide my time and do those things that will create a public demand for my candidacy."

"That's the way I see it, General," Joe said.

"Then I shall start with this expedition," Custer declared. "Captain Murchison, you can count on it. I will not let anything stand in the way of the Seventh Cavalry getting all the credit for what lies before us."

That night in his Sibley tent, on his camp desk, by the light of a kerosene lantern, Joe wrote to Sally.

June 9, 1876
In the field, 20 miles from mouth
of Powder River
Montana Territory

Dear Sally,

The weather is most disagreeable right now. It has been cloudy all day, and now it is raining, the rain drumming hard against the canvas of my tent. Do not worry about me, though. The tent is well constructed and without leaks, so I shall spend the night quite dry, thank you. I worry about some of the men, for the little two-man tents they erect are not as weatherproof as the larger tents used by the officers and some of the noncoms.

The one hazard that strikes us all, from the lowest private to General Custer himself, is mosquitoes. They, and what the men call buffalo gnats, are particularly bad after a rain. The gnats are so small that the Indian scouts call them "no-see-ums." They can be quite pesky, but the mosquitoes are worse. They are very large. The men have a good humor about it, however, for I heard one of them say that they would give the next mosquito they killed to the cook so that he might bake it, as one would a turkey.

I am told by our scouts that we are in territory

never before visited by white men. The men have a song they sing sometimes while on the march: "This is the way we go . . . Forty miles a day on beans and hay . . . in the regular Army-O."

Well, yesterday we didn't go forty miles, but we did make thirty-two through some of the roughest terrain I have yet seen. There is, however, a beauty in its ruggedness, and I do not blame the Indians for fighting to keep it theirs.

I am sure the time will come when the Indian and the white man can live together in peace. If you look at it objectively, we do not compete for the same thing. The white man looks for gold, the Indians care nothing for it. Why could the Indians not let the white man pass this way in peace? The white man farms, the Indians care nothing for agriculture. Why could they not let our people farm in peace? The Indians hunt, as do we, but game is so plentiful and we take so few of the animals that there is plenty left for both races. Only the buffalo have been overhunted, and perhaps we do bear some of the blame for that.

I wish you could see the Seventh Cavalry on the march. It is really quite impressive. There are 28 officers and 747 men. In addition, there are two companies of the Seventeenth Infantry and one company of the Sixth Infantry, these making up 8 officers and 135 men. We have one platoon of Gatling guns, with two officers and 32 men. We have had several spirited discussions as to whether to take the Gatling guns with us. I feel we should, for one Gatling gun can put out as much firepower as an entire platoon. Some of the officers, however, feel the guns are too unwieldy, and I believe Custer is in that number.

The marching formation of the Seventh is divided into two columns, with Major Reno commanding the right wing and Captain Benteen the left. Reveille sounds at 3 A.M. and we are breakfasted and on the march by 5 A.M. Some of the men complain of the hard travel, but nothing seems to bother Custer. He thrives on hardship and cannot understand those who do not.

Some disingenuous men, with political ideas of their own, convinced General Custer that they would nominate him for president at the Republican National Convention this summer. As it developed, they had no intention of ever making a serious nomination. However General Custer is too decent and honest a man to have seen through such duplicity, and I believe he was deeply hurt by the injustice that was done to him.

I do not worry about him, though. He will shake it off and dedicate himself even more to a successful operation against the hostiles. If you have not yet read of our expedition in the New York papers, I have no doubt but that you soon will.

Your friend,
Joe

Joe reread the letter before he sealed it, noticing that he had not mentioned Tamara to her. He had not consciously omitted her name, but now that he thought about it, he decided that it wasn't yet fitting to mention her. For the time being his thoughts about her were still his own, too private even to commit to his "diary."

In his own tent, First Sergeant Todd was also writing a letter to be sent out with tomorrow's courier.

Dear Tamara,

How surprised I was to see you when I returned from Jefferson Barracks—and how thrilled, as well. I am grateful to your parents for letting you come to visit me and grateful, too, that through these years they have allowed me to write to you.

You seem to have taken an interest in Joseph Murchison, and I couldn't be more pleased. As I told you in some of my earlier letters, Captain Murchison and I have served together for ten years, and I have never met a finer gentleman. He is a wonderful officer. I only wish there were more like him, and should anything develop between you, know now that such a relationship would have the blessings of a loving uncle.

Soon we will join with General Terry, then close the trap that has been set for the Indians, not only by our expedition but by two other armies also in the field. We will have a great victory over the Indians, of this I am sure. But that will leave the question, What is to become of us— Indian and soldier alike? If we defeat the Indians in this last major battle, they will be finished forever on the plains. But then, so will we, for with no Indians to fight, what need is there for the army?

Your loving Uncle,
Uncle Seth

FORT LINCOLN

"Are you writing to your uncle, dear?"

Tamara turned at the sound of the voice and saw Libbie standing in the door of her bedroom. Tamara smiled.

"No," she said. "I am writing to my family, back in Virginia. I'm telling them what a wonderful place this is, and how exciting everything has been."

"I'm sure they will be thrilled to get your letter," Libbie said. "And what about Captain Murchison? Have you written him?"

Tamara shook her head. "I feel it might be too soon. I wouldn't want him to think me too bold."

"Oh, my dear, he is a cavalry officer," Libbie said. "Boldness is their stock in trade. I think such men admire spirit, be it in a horse or a woman."

"Have you known Captain Murchison long?"

"I have known him for eight years," Libbie replied. "He is as fine an officer as I have ever met. Autie thinks the world of him."

"So does my father."

Libbie looked puzzled. "Your father?"

Tamara smiled. "The man you know as my uncle is actually my father. My natural mother died when I was born, and my uncle and aunt adopted me. They have been my parents, and out of respect and honor to them, I have always referred to them as such. But Seth Hamby is my natural father."

"Hamby? But I thought his name was Todd."

"He was an officer in the Confederate army during the War between the States," Tamara said. "I think he felt that would be held against him."

Libbie gasped. "Oh, my! Your father is Colonel Todd Hamby!"

"Yes. You have heard of him."

"Indeed I have. Autie has often remarked that Colonel Hamby was the most proficient cavalry commander he faced during the entire war." Libbie gasped again. "That means Eliza was right."

"I beg your pardon?"

"Eliza—you know, my maid—said that she had met your father somewhere before, but she couldn't remember where. Now the mystery is solved. During the war, she was captured and then paroled by the Confederates, but not until she had been relieved of Autie's satchel. That satchel contained several of my personal letters."

"I'm . . . I'm sorry," Tamara said.

"Oh, my dear, it wasn't your fault. It was an act of war. Besides, I later received word that Colonel Hamby proved to be the gentleman by burning all the letters before they could be used for sport."

"I'm sorry your letters were lost," Tamara said.

"It is actually quite ironic that we should be discussing such things as the privacy of letters at this moment," Libbie said. "Especially in light of the reason I have come to your room."

"Oh? What reason is that?"

"I . . . I had a dream last night. A nightmare. In it I saw Autie lying facedown on the ground. A half-naked Indian was standing over him, holding up"—Libbie stopped, then took a deep breath—"holding up a scalp," she finally managed to say.

"Oh!" Tamara gasped.

Libbie quickly smiled, as if dismissing her own dream as something silly. "Yes, well, I'm sure that the dream is constructed of nothing but the apprehensions of an anxious wife, though I must confess it has me somewhat unnerved."

"After such a dream I can understand why you would be," Tamara said.

"The problem is," Libbie continued, "I have just written a letter to Autie, and I would not want to add my foolish fears to the terrible burden command has already placed upon his shoulders. So, I would like you to read it before I send it. In all the years I have shared the dangers with Autie, I don't think I have ever written one quite so . . . so full of my own fears. Or perhaps I just perceive it to be so. At any rate, I would like your opinion as to whether or not I should send it."

"All right," Tamara said. "If you are sure that you don't mind having a relative stranger read such a private letter."

"No, I ask that you please do," Libbie said. She handed the letter, written in blue ink on light brown stationery, to Tamara, who began to read:

My dearest Bo,
  I still feel that I could have come upriver on the *Far West* and, while some distance from any danger, would be that much closer to you—indeed, would have been with you much longer. I feel an emptiness during this expedition that transcends anything I have ever felt before. I cannot but feel the greatest apprehensions for you on this dangerous scout. Oh, Autie, if you return without bad news, the worst of the summer will be over.
  Carter has returned and is chief trumpeter. He really sounds the calls beautifully. But his long-drawn notes make me heartsick. I do not wish to

be reminded of the cavalry just now, for it only increases my feeling of nervousness.

The papers told last night of a small skirmish between General Crook's cavalry and the Indians. They called it a fight. The Indians were very bold. They don't seem afraid of anything. Please, do be careful, Autie.

The Belknap case is again postponed. Of course, that also worries me. The prosecution is going to call you as a witness. Politicians will try to make something out of you for their own self-ish ends, as we have only too-well learned by your betrayal at the convention. Yes, my darling Autie, if you have not yet heard, then it pains me to tell you that Senator Blaine, despite his promises, turned his back on you.

I am perfectly delighted with your *Galaxy* arti-cle on the war, but I wish you had not spoken for McClellan so freely. Still, I don't see how you could have consistently given your opinions on the war without giving him his just due. I fear it means the finish of Mr. Chandler as a friend and I am sorry for that, as he can be a most tenacious enemy and, of late, he has been only a passive friend. A cautious wife is a great bore, isn't she, Autie?

You improve every time you write. There is nothing like the McClellan article for smoothness of style. I think to ride as you do and also to be able to write is a wonderful gift. Nothing daunts you in your wish to improve. I can only wish that your destiny had fallen in the literary field, and yet, Autie, I wouldn't have you anything but a sol-dier.

I want you to do something for me. I want you to take special care of Captain Murchison. We have known him for so long and have always con-sidered him a fine man, lacking only a wife to complete his life. I know it is very early to make such a prediction, but you may say that I, too, have a gift, and that is intuition. I believe that young Tamara Hamby, our houseguest, is destined to be the wife of Joe Murchison. So you see, you have quite a responsibility on your shoulders to see to his safety.

Autie, I know you must be disappointed at the news from the convention, but do not despair. You are of positive use to your day and generation. Do you not see that your life is precious on that account—and not only because an idolizing wife could not live without you?

I shall go to bed now, and dream of my dear Autie.

Libbie

Tamara handed the letter back to Libbie. "I think it is a beautiful letter," she said. "I only hope that when I get married, it will be as wonderful as your marriage is."

"Yes," Libbie said. Suddenly, as if purposely trying to break the melancholia, she smiled. "I must confess, I don't know if these long absences make the marriage sweeter or more painful. I do know, however, that the reunions are . . ." She paused, then smiled again, more broadly this time, and almost blushing. "Well, one day you'll learn about the happy reunions of a wife and her husband."

"I'm sure I will. I wonder, though, if your prediction will come true, and if that husband will be Joseph Murchison?"

"Would you like it to be?" Libbie asked.

Tamara nodded. "Yes, I would very much like it to be."

★★★

Sixteen

IN THE FIELD

The steamer *Far West* was specially equipped to support the expedition against the Sioux. Its wheelhouse was reinforced with two-inch boilerplate, and its lower deck was protected by oak planking backed up by bales of hay. The riverboat, under the command of Captain Grant Marsh, had pushed farther up the Yellowstone than any boat had previously gone, and it was almost a surprise to the men of the Seventh Cavalry when, after several days of hard trailing, they suddenly came upon a boat lying almost leisurely at anchor.

On the night of June 21, General Terry held a strategy conference in the great cabin of the boat. The cabin was large, as boat cabins go, stretching all the way across the width of the boat, but there were too many officers for all to sit, so many stood. Custer was among those who stood, even though his rank would have allowed him to sit, had he wanted. It was his restless energy that made him stand.

"Now, Custer, look at this map,". Terry said. "I have marked your route with pins," Terry adjusted his glasses to stare at the map. He leaned closer, then sighed in frustration. "I can't see those damned pins. Does anyone have a pencil?"

"I have a blue pencil, General," Joe replied.

"Trace along these pins with your pencil, would you, Captain?"

Joe did so, and for a moment there was no sound save the voices coming into the cabin from the soldiers resting on the riverbank and the quiet whisper of the current as it slapped against the hull.

"There," Terry said, when Joe was finished with his work. "Now, General Custer, what I want you to do is take your troops up the Rosebud and—well, perhaps it would be best if I had your orders read aloud. That way there will be no misunderstanding. Ed?"

General Terry's adjutant, Capt. E. W. Smith opened a folder, and then began reading:

"Lieutenant Colonel Custer, Seventh U.S. Cavalry. Colonel: The brigadier general commanding directs that as soon as your regiment can be made ready for the march, you will proceed up the Rosebud in pursuit of the Indians whose trail was discovered a few days before. It is, of course, impossible to give you any definite instructions in regard to this movement, and even if it were, the department commander places too much confidence in your zeal, energy, and ability to impose upon you precise orders, which he feels might hamper your success. He will, however, indicate to you his own views of what your action should be and desires that you should conform to them unless there is sufficient reason for deviating from them."

Captain Smith paused in his reading and looked up at Custer, as if charging Custer with the specific instruction that he was to conform to Terry's orders.

"Yes, yes, I'm quite prepared to do that," Custer said impatiently. "Go on, Captain."

Captain Smith resumed reading.

"He instructs you to proceed up the Rosebud until you ascertain definitely the direction in which the aforementioned trail leads. Should it be found, as it appears almost certain that it will be, to turn toward the Little Bighorn, you should continue southward, perhaps as far as the headwaters of the Tongue, and then turn toward the

Little Bighorn, feeling constantly to your left so as to preclude the possibility of the escape of the Indians to the south or southeast by passing around our left flank. The column of Colonel Gibbon will head for the mouth of the Bighorn. As soon as it reaches that point, it will cross the Yellowstone and move up at least as far as the forks of the Big and Little Bighorn. Of course, its movements will be controlled by circumstances as they arise, but it is hoped that the Indians, if upon the Little Bighorn, will be outflanked by two columns so that their escape will be impossible.

"The department commander desires that, on your way up the Rosebud, you should thoroughly examine the upper part of Tulloch's Creek, and that you should send a scout through to Colonel Gibbon's column with the results of your examination. The lower part of this creek will be examined by a detachment from Colonel Gibbon's command. The supply steamer will be pushed up the Bighorn as far as the forks of the river are navigable, and the department commander, who will accompany Colonel Gibbon's column, desires that you report to him there, not later than the expiration of the time for which your troops are rationed, unless in the meantime you receive further orders."

Captain Smith cleared his throat, then handed a copy of the orders he had just read to Custer.

"By my reckoning," Terry said, "we should make contact with the Indians on the twenty-sixth. With our two columns converging, there will be no way for them to escape. Do you have any questions?"

"No questions, General," Custer replied. "And I thank you for your confidence in me."

"I'm certain that my confidence is well-placed, Custer. But remember, the most important part of the entire plan is for us to reach the Indians by the twenty-sixth, and in concert. I have to inform you that the scouts tell me the signs are for the largest encampment they have ever seen. We may very well be going up against a thousand or more armed warriors."

"Even so, General, I don't think we are likely to encounter any more than the Seventh could handle," Custer said.

"Any more than the *Seventh* can handle? I hope, with that attitude, you aren't planning on handling them alone, General," Colonel Gibbon said.

"I will be following my orders, Colonel," Custer replied.

"Very good," Terry said, straightening up from the map. "Any more questions, gentlemen?"

"Just one," Custer said. "It's not a question as much as it is a request. I plan to leave the Gatling guns behind."

Although Custer had said it was a request, it sounded far more like a peremptory statement.

"Leave them behind? Why would you want to do that, Custer? Why, just four of those guns can put out as much firepower as an entire company."

"Yes, sir, if we are in a static position," Custer replied. "But they must be pulled by horses—and I remind you that the horses we have pulling these guns are marked *IC*: inspected and condemned."

"But that just means they are condemned for riding. They're quite capable of pulling the gun caissons," Gibbon said.

"Maybe so, but the terrain we'll be going through is not suited for wheeled vehicles. Already we have had them flip over several times. I feel that the impedance to our progress outweighs the questionable advantage of their firepower."

"All right, Custer, if you don't want to take the Gatlings, you may leave them behind."

Custer smiled. "Thank you, sir."

Joe knew that Custer had a point, as far as the mobility of the guns was concerned. But he had seen them operate and knew how effective they could be. He had no doubt but that four of the guns would be able to stop a full-blown charge of practically any number of

Indians. And with the guns' range of nearly a mile, the Indians wouldn't be able to even get close. Nevertheless, Custer was in command, and it was his decision to make.

"General Terry, with your permission, sir, I would like to salute you by having the Seventh pass in review."

"Permission granted," Terry said. "Oh, and Grant," Terry added to Captain Grant Marsh, "you may want your roustabouts to watch this. A pass in review by a full cavalry regiment can be quite impressive."

"Thank you for the invitation, General," the steamboat captain replied. "I'll have them assembled on the Texas deck."

Half an hour later, with trumpets blaring and guidons flying, the entire Seventh Cavalry passed in review. As Joe, at the head of M Troop, passed by, he commanded, "Eyes right!" Every man in the troop, except for those riding on the right file, snapped their heads in a quarter turn to the right. The troopers riding on the right file continued to stare straight ahead. The guidon bearer dipped his colors as Joe and Lieutenant Hodgson rendered the hand salute. Ordinarily at this point, the salute would have been given by saber, but like the Gatling guns, the sabers were being left with the *Far West*.

Custer, mounted, had taken the review with Terry and Gibbon. He didn't stay there for the entire review, but started toward the front of the column just as M Troop passed by.

"Custer!" Joe heard Gibbon call. "Now, don't you be greedy! You save some Indians for us!"

"No, I won't," Custer said enigmatically.

For the march, Custer divided his command into three separate units plus the supply train. Because Custer wanted no wheeled vehicles to impede his march, the supply train was made up entirely of pack mules.

Joe was the senior officer after Reno and Benteen, and as such, he was given the additional duty of regimental operations officer. In that capacity he kept a field report, or a diary, of their movements.

At the end of the day he began making his entries:

> June 22. The Seventh Cavalry Regiment, under command of Lieut. Col. George A. Custer departed its camp on the Yellowstone and moved upriver 2 miles to the mouth of the Rosebud, crossing the latter near its mouth. At that point the Rosebud is 30 to 40 feet wide and 3 feet deep, clear with slightly alkaline water and a bottom of gravel. Because of delays to the pack train, we marched only 12 miles today, selecting for our campsite a place at the base of a steep bluff on the left bank of the river. Here we have plenty of wood, grass, and water.

Joe had just finished his entry when Trumpeter Martini approached him. "Capitano Murcho," he said, which was as close to Joe's name as the recent Italian immigrant could come. "The General Custer, he want'a to see all'a officers."

Joe closed his field diary and shoved it into his saddlebag, then walked upstream to Custer's headquarters to answer the officers' call. Several officers were already there, others were appearing out of the fading twilight. Custer was standing by a small mulberry tree, watching the assembly grow until it was completed. He had pulled a twig from the tree and was sucking on it, almost passively. Cooke had his hand down inside the canvas part of his kersey trousers, shamelessly scratching his crotch. Though the trousers appeared all blue from a distance, their inner thighs, crotch, and seat were reinforced with canvas.

Tom Custer took a pull of whiskey from a bottle, then passed it over to Jim Calhoun. Boston Custer and Autie Reed were sitting on a large rock away from the others—but close enough to satisfy their curiosity as to what was going on.

"Gentlemen, up until this point we have been what you might call in transit," Custer began, "but from here on, we shall consider ourselves in the Sioux's backyard. I would like to keep our presence a secret for as long as possible. That means no more trumpet calls. From now on I want all orders issued verbally or by hand signals. Also, have your men secure all loose equipment. An approaching cavalry regiment makes as much noise as a band on parade."

The officers all nodded assent.

"As you know, we have a schedule to keep, so it is up to you officers to see to it that the men respond quickly to all orders. I want them up and breakfasted in time to be on the march when I give the word. Do not let anyone straggle behind. We are, as I explained, in Sioux country. The hostiles would like nothing better than to catch one or two of our men by themselves. Death wouldn't be easy, gentlemen, and you might use that as an incentive to keep the men moving to orders."

Again, the officers nodded.

"Now," Custer said, "I have something I would like to get off my chest. It has come to my knowledge that my official actions have been criticized by some of the officers of the regiment at department headquarters. Gentlemen, I am willing to accept recommendations from the most junior second lieutenant of the regiment, should that recommendation be given to me in a proper manner. But the regulations are quite clear concerning criticisms of commanding officers, and I will take all necessary steps to punish whoever might be guilty of such an offense, should there be a reoccurrence."

"General, may I speak?" Benteen asked.

"Go ahead."

"It seems to me that you are lashing the shoulders of all to get at some. Now, as we are all here, wouldn't it be better to specify which officer or officers you are accusing?"

"Colonel Benteen," Custer said, using Benteen's brevet rank, "I am not here to be catechized by you. But, for your own information, I will say that none of my remarks have been directed toward you. Now, gentlemen, reveille is at three A.M. To horse at five."

June 23. Under way at five A.M. A very broken bluff obliged us to follow the valley for some distance, crossing the stream 5 times in but 3 miles. We then proceeded up the right side of the stream for 10 miles, where we halted to allow the pack train to close up. Soon after starting we recrossed to the left bank and continued on for another 15 miles, crossing back one final time to camp on the right bank at 4:30 P.M. Total distance covered today was 30 miles.

Today we began encountering Indian sign for the first time since leaving the Yellowstone. All indications are that the number of Indians ahead is much larger than the numbers given us by the agents on how many have jumped the reservation.

June 24. Underway at 5 A.M. Followed right bank of the Rosebud, crossing the first two running tributaries seen. Stopped at 1 P.M. for lunch of coffee and hardtack. Indian signs easy to read as they are making no attempt to conceal their trail.

At first Joe was puzzled as to why the Indians were making no attempt to cover up after themselves. As they continued on, though, he realized that the Indians weren't covering their trail because they *couldn't* cover their trail. There were just too many of them. He also realized that they didn't even care whether they were being followed or not. The Indians were supremely confident of their strength.

Todd moved up alongside Joe. "Captain Murchison, I've never known Lo to be overconfident," he said. "If they aren't showing any fear of us, you can believe they must have every reason not to be afraid."

"Dorman," Joe called, and the big black scout guided his white horse over to Joe. Isaiah Dorman was the only black man in the entire expedition. He had been a scout for some two years and was considered particularly valuable because of his ability to speak Sioux. He had lived with the Sioux for two years, knew Sitting Bull and Crazy Horse personally, and had married a Santee woman.

"What do you make of the sign we've been seeing?" Joe asked.

"Take a look for yourself, Captain," Dorman said, sweeping his hand over the ground around them. "All the grass has been eaten by their ponies, the ground is left littered with horse turds, buffalo hides, bones, and carcasses. We're not following a village . . . hell, we're following a city."

Some time later Custer halted the column for a water break. Joe walked down to the river to fill his canteen alongside Custer and several of the other officers. He overheard Jim Calhoun talking to Custer.

"General, have you been paying attention to the sign?" Lieutenant Calhoun asked as he dipped his own canteen into the stream. "I wouldn't be surprised if there weren't four or five thousand Indians ahead of us."

"Oh, that might be stretching it a little," Custer replied easily.

"Not according to all the scouts. I've never seen them so nervous. I don't mind telling you, General, I, for one, will be glad when we join up with Terry again."

"We aren't going to join him," Custer said.

"I beg your pardon, General?" Calhoun replied.

"Think about it, Jimmy," Custer said, taking his hat off and running his hand over his hair, which, just before this campaign, had been cut uncharacteristically short. "If we join forces with Terry, who will be the commander in the field?"

"Why, General Terry, I suppose," Calhoun answered.

"Oh, there is no 'suppose' to it," Custer replied. "Since General Terry is senior officer, the command would be his. As would be the glory, even though it would be the Seventh who would bear the brunt of battle." Custer put his hat back on. "I don't intend to let that happen."

"General, may I raise a point?" Joe asked.

"Certainly. I'm not an ogre, unwilling to listen to my officers."

"Consider this, sir. Perhaps the Seventh Cavalry *is* strong enough to handle the Indians—".

"No perhaps about it. We *are*," Custer insisted.

"Yes, sir, but is Gibbon's regiment?"

"What do you mean?"

"What I'm getting at, sir, is that General Terry and Colonel Gibbon will be proceeding with the belief that they can depend upon the Seventh to be in a certain place at a certain time. If they run into Lo and we aren't there to help them, I fear they may be wiped out."

Custer tapped his mustache for a moment.

"You do have a point, Captain," he said. "All right, suppose we do this? Suppose we increase our rate of march so that we make contact tomorrow? That way we will be certain that Gibbon and his men will be out of harm's way. And if, for some reason, we don't make contact tomorrow, then we will return to the plan as drawn up by Terry. Will that take care of your worry?"

"About Colonel Gibbon? Yes, sir," Joe said.

"But you still have some concern."

"I was just wondering," Joe said. "In view of the strength of the Indians ahead of us, would it not be better to keep the regiment together? I agree with you, General, that the Seventh Cavalry can handle anything we might encounter. But if we divide our forces so that, by circumstance, the Indians find themselves with superior numbers and position on the field"—Joe remembered his discussion with Colonel Arnaud three years earlier when the French failed to take advantage of just such a situation—"they'll have a classic case of Nathan Bedford Forrest's 'fustest with the mostest.' "

Custer chuckled. "Forrest was quite a military man, that is true," he agreed. "But what made him successful was his boldness. And that's what we shall exhibit. Believe me, Joe, when Lo sees three well-led and well-disciplined units attacking from three different directions, they will become so demoralized that we'll be able to pick them off at our leisure."

"Autie," Tom Custer said, coming down the steep riverbank then, his boots dislodging the loose rocks as he almost slid down. "Take a look at this." He held out a stick from which hung two scalps, obviously from white men.

"There!" Custer said, pointing to the scalps. "I ask you, gentlemen. Do we need any more justification than that for what we are doing here? No doubt these men were poor prospectors, doing no more harm than poking around in the rocks and dirt. I only wish we could identify them so we could let their families know of their fate. Have someone bury them, Tom. It's the closest thing to a Christian burial we can give to the poor creatures who once wore them."

"All right," Tom said.

"General Custer," Major Reno called from a short distance up the stream. "Bloody Knife has found something that I think you ought to see, sir."

Custer and his officers climbed up the bank of the river, then down into a little ravine, where they found a sweat lodge.

"A sweat lodge," Custer said, nodding. "Why the big interest, Marcus? We've already seen a dozen or more of them." He turned and started to leave.

"Yes, sir, but not like this. Take a look inside."

Custer turned back, then pulled aside the flap to look in. There he saw three red stones in a row, then a circle of rocks with the skull of a buffalo bull on one side and the skull of a cow on the other. A stick was aimed at the cow.

"What does that mean?" he asked.

"It means the Indians will fight like bulls and the white men will run like women," Bloody Knife explained.

Custer grunted. "Big talk from a race of people who have done nothing but run from me my entire life. We will rest here until midnight. Then we will get under way again. I do not intend to let them get away from me this time."

"General, you don't seem to be getting the point," one of the civilian scouts, Mitch Bouyer, said. "They ain't runnin'."

The Seventh made their camp and started their supper. Custer's striker erected his tent and then Custer planted his flag in the alkali dirt out front. A sudden gust of wind blew it down. Lieutenant Godfrey picked it up and replanted it, but it blew over a second time. When he put it up the third time, he used some sagebrush to support it.

The Indian scouts, seeing the flag blow over, exchanged long, silent glances. Joe watched them, and though they said nothing to each other, he knew that the symbolism of Custer's flag blowing over wasn't lost on them.

The regiment got under way again at midnight. On through the night they went, with no lights permitted, not even the faintest glow of pipes or rolled cigarettes. They were able to keep their bearings by following the dust clouds that billowed up before them. Also, the rearmost soldiers of each element had to violate Custer's edict of silence by pounding their tin cups on the saddle horns to guide the troop behind them.

As the night sky grew gray in the east, any hope of discovering the village before daylight faded. Since that opportunity was lost anyway, Custer finally decided to stop the march and give his troops a chance to rest until full daylight.

The soldiers concealed themselves in a wooded ravine between two slopes. A few even unsaddled their mounts, but most simply lay down where they were to sleep the sleep of the exhausted.

They had not selected a very good campsite. What little grass there was for the horses had been cropped very close by the Indian ponies. Here, too, the water was so alkaline that the horses refused to drink it. Even the coffee the men made with the water was practically impossible to drink.

During the night, Custer had sent Lieutenant Varnum and his scouts ahead to see if they could find the village. Varnum returned at daybreak, just as Custer was eating his breakfast.

"Have a seat," Custer invited. "What did you see? Did you find the village? Or have they skedaddled like they always do?"

Before Varnum answered, he pulled a bottle of whiskey from his saddlebag and took a long, Adam's apple-bobbing pull from it. He wiped the back of his hand across his mouth and looked at Custer with flat, expressionless eyes.

"What is it, Varnum? What have you seen?" Custer asked again.

"General, if you want my advice, you will halt this march right now and wait until General Terry's column reaches us. With both columns combined, we might be able to escape."

"Escape?" Custer barked with a little laugh. "Escape what?"

"Annihilation," Varnum replied.

Custer snorted. "Oh, come now, Varnum. Annihilation? Aren't you being a bit overly dramatic?"

"General, you have to see it to believe it. The entire valley on the other side of Crow's Nest is covered with tepees. It's white with the damn things. And there are so many campfires that smoke covers the whole basin. You tell him, Dorman."

Varnum passed his bottle to Dorman, sharing it as easily with the black scout he had come to respect as he would share it with any of his fellow officers. Dorman took a deep swallow before he spoke.

"General, there are more warriors ahead than there are bullets in all the belts of all the soldiers in this command."

For just an instant Custer looked shocked. Then he smiled at all the officers who, upon seeing Varnum and Dorman return, had gathered around to hear the report.

"Well, then I guess we are in for the fight of our life,

eh, gentlemen?" Custer said. "But I guess we shall get through them in one day."

Custer stood up and stretched, then pitched out more than half a cup of undrunk coffee. He slapped at the mosquitoes that had prevented him from getting any rest as he looked out over his soldiers sprawled about the campsite. They were all exhausted, thirsty, and driven nearly insane by the same mosquitoes that had bothered him so badly.

"Colonel Benteen, do you see those hills over there?" Custer pointed to the low-lying rolling ridge, stark against the bright sky. The flank riders had already brought back a description of the country just on the other side—an endless procession of jagged draws and long, narrow coulees.

"I see them, sir."

"Good. I want you to take your battalion over there. You will parallel our course, continuously feeling to your left, to make certain that the hostiles don't try to run. Beyond that, you may use your own judgment as to any action you need to take."

"Hadn't we better keep the regiment together, General? If this is as big a camp as they say, we'll need every man we have."

"You have your orders, Colonel," Custer said curtly.

"Very good, sir," the Missourian replied, duly chastised.

"Shall I pass the word to break camp, General?" Lieutenant Cooke asked.

"No, Cookie," Custer replied. He walked over to his horse Dandy, then hesitated. "Striker, saddle Vic. I'll ride him today. Then I'll pass the word around camp myself. I want the men to see that I am just as exhausted as they are. That way they will realize I am not asking anything of them that I am not asking of myself."

Thirty minutes later, with Benteen and his three companies scouting the other side of the hills as directed, the column got under way again. The men rode like zombies, exhausted from twenty hours of marching in the previous twenty-four. They had barely gotten started when one of Varnum's scouts returned with word that the huge camp they had located in the valley ahead was showing signs of moving.

"Damn!" Custer swore. "We've come this far: We can't let them get away now. Cooke, ride back to the rear of the column and tell Reno to report to me at once!" The lieutenant started to turn his horse. "Cooke!" Custer called again.

Cooke jerked back on the reins so hard that the horse reared. "Yes, sir?"

"Have Captain Murchison and First Sergeant Todd come up with Reno."

"Yes, sir."

Moments later, Cooke and the three men he had summoned returned, their horses lathered from the exertion.

"Major Reno, I have just received word that the Indians are trying to get away. We can't let that happen. I want you to take your battalion across the river at once to engage them."

Reno blinked in surprise, then looked squarely at Custer.

"General, do you mean make a feint?"

"No, Major. I want you to engage them. Charge right through. You attack the village at the south end of the valley, and I will support you."

"Very good, sir," Reno said.

"Joe, I am going to take your first sergeant away from you," Custer said. "Sergeant Todd, you are now Sergeant Major Todd. I want you with me."

"Very well, sir."

"I hope you don't mind, Joe, but I think I'd like to have the colonel who nearly whipped me at Sayler's Creek on my side this time."

Todd took his hat off and ran his hand through his hair. "How long have you known, sir?" he asked.

Custer smiled.

"Hell, Colonel, I've known for eight years," Custer replied. "During the war I tried to learn everything I could about the commanders against me. So when Eliza said she thought she had seen you before, I hired

a Pinkerton man to check you out. When I found out
who you were, I was going to confront you and have
you kicked out for fraudulent enlistment, but I liked
the idea of my one-time enemy having to come down
from a colonel to a trooper. Then it wasn't too long
after that that I decided you were one of the best damn
soldiers I'd ever served with, officer or enlisted, Union
or Confederate. So I just let things stay as they were."

"General, you are full of surprises," Todd said.

Custer smiled. "That's what makes life interesting."
He turned to Joe. "Captain, you'd better return to your
command. You'll be going into battle very soon."

"Yes, sir," Joe said. He took a long look at the man
who had been his commander for the last eight years.
Custer was wearing the field uniform that had become
his trademark: buckskin trousers and a buckskin shirt,
the shirt affixed with epaulets bearing the silver-leaf
insignia of a lieutenant colonel. His pants were tucked
into his boots, his shirt was open at the collar, and his
broad-brimmed, cream-colored hat was turned up on
the right side, the brim fastened by a small hook and
eye to the crown.

"Do you have something more, Captain Murchison?" Custer asked.

"No, sir. Good luck to you, General. And good luck
to you, Sergeant Major," Joe said, turning his horse.

"Joe!" Todd called, and Joe stopped. Neither he nor
Custer commented on Todd calling him by his first
name. "I want you to be good to my daughter . . .
and my grandchildren."

Before Joe could answer, Todd spurred his horse and
darted up to the head of Custer's column.

As Joe rode back, he saw Boston Custer and Autie
Reed going forward.

"Boston, Autie!" he called. "Don't go up there. Get
back with the pack train!"

"The pack train?" Boston called back. "Nothing is
going to happen back there! We're going to where the
action is! Wait!" he yelled to his brother. "Wait for us!"

MEDICINE TAIL COULEE

Custer's troops, about two-hundred fifty strong, were formed in a long skirmish line at the top of the hill. The men were sitting tall in their saddles, all signs of weariness drained away. They were holding their carbines at the ready. Red, white, and blue guidons snapped in the breeze, and Todd felt a chill pass over him as he looked at the men. Some of them had served with him for many years, others were raw recruits on their very first scout. He noticed four of the men were part of the group he had brought back from Jefferson Barracks, including Trooper Evans, one of the two men he had sent to trade his weapon for whiskey. Todd smiled at Evans and, nervously, the young trooper smiled back.

"All right, men, we've got the heathens right where we want them!" Custer shouted to his troops, standing in his stirrups. "They're just beyond the ridge on the other side of the river, and they damn well know we're here! The bastards are sitting over there, waiting for us!"

"Well, if they're wishing to throw a party, General, I suppose we can go!" Tom called back, and the men laughed.

"Martini!" Custer called. "Where's the trumpeter?"

"Here, General."

"Ride back to Colonel Benteen. Tell him to come quick and bring packs."

"Be quick? Come back?" Martini repeated.

"Here, Martini!" Lieutenant Cooke said, scribbling on a pad. "Take this to him."

Cooke wrote: *Benteen. Come on, big village be quick, bring packs. W. W. Cooke. P.S. bring packs.*

Martini took the message, then left at a gallop.

Custer turned in his saddle and looked at Todd. When he did, Todd saw deeper into Custer's soul than he had ever seen into any human being. It was as if the weight of the world rested upon his shoulders. Their eyes held for a long, agonizing moment. Then Custer turned away and gave the command to go forward.

* * *

The first thing Joe noticed when he reached the south end of the valley after a hard ride of just over a mile was that Reno had not yet issued the orders for the attack. Many of his men were still dismounted, some were even lying down.

"Major, we are to attack, sir!" Joe shouted. "The general is about to commit his forces! We must attack, at once!"

"Captain, I am not going to take three companies against a force that large. To do so would be pure folly," Reno replied.

"Major, you must! If you don't, General Custer and every man with him will be killed! Don't you understand? They will be wiped out to the last man! You *must* attack!"

"Very well," Reno said reluctantly. "I will make a demonstration against the village, but it will be a demonstration only. Trumpeter, sound boots and saddles."

The trumpeter sounded his call, and the men, realizing then that they were about to go into action, let out a cheer. Reno cut them short at once.

"Stop that cheering!" he ordered. "You are no better than wild Indians when you do that."

"Major, let them yell!" Joe said. "It is good for their morale."

"They are soldiers," Reno replied. "And, by God, they will act like soldiers."

"Yes, sir," Joe said. He brought his troop onto the skirmish line, then took his position at their head. Reno's battalion was made up of 112 men, spread out in battalion front on the ridgeline where Ash Creek emptied into the Little Big Horn River. They were looking across the river at a village of as many as 10,000 Indians, at least 4,000 of whom were warriors. Joe saw Dorman move up alongside Bloody Knife, the other scout with Reno's battalion. The two men exchanged a few words, then Dorman pulled out his rifle. It wasn't the government-issue Springfield carbine the soldiers were carrying, but a customized Winchester. He operated the lever, jacking a round into the chamber. Then he spit on the sight and rubbed it with his thumb. The men waited for a long moment, and the tension built.

"Major?" Joe said. Reno looked at Joe, and Joe could see fear in his superior's eyes. Then, summoning his courage, Reno stood in his stirrups.

"Trumpeter, sound the charge!" Reno shouted.

The trumpet blew its thrilling clarion call, and the men swept down the ridge, across the river, and toward the village.

IN THE BLACKFOOT CIRCLE OF THE INDIAN CAMP

Quiet Stream was scraping the hide of a freshly killed antelope. Scores of other antelope hides dotted the prairie, pegged out to dry in the sun. As she raised up, she could see several horses hobbled within the camp itself, while to the west, on a plateau that rose some two hundred feet above the river, thousands of ponies grazed, attended by young boys from all the tribes of the camp.

This was the largest gathering of Indians Quiet Stream had ever seen. The camp extended along the banks of the river for four miles or more. Thousands of tanned buffalo-hide tepees were pitched in seven great camp circles, each circle more than half a mile in diameter. Dogs of all sizes and types slinked around the tepees, protecting their staked-out territory from all intruders by bared fangs and low growls.

To the uninitiated, the arrangement of the village might appear to be haphazard, but Quiet Stream knew that ancient customs governed the placement of each camp circle, allotted a place for each band within the circle, and established the location of every lodge and tepee. This gave every Indian a definite address that was known to all so that though the camp had just been erected, a friend could call upon a friend without having to ask directions.

At the northernmost end of the village were three hundred lodges of the Cheyenne. Camped with the

Cheyenne were a few families of Gros Ventre. Next came the Oglala Sioux. Then came the Brulé, then the Sans Arcs, then the Miniconjou. Quiet Stream's Yankton were camped with the Blackfoot Sioux, which also included the Assiniboin, Yanktonai, and Santee. At the southernmost end of the village was the largest camp circle of all, the three thousand Hunkpapa Sioux.

A short time earlier there had been a fight with the soldiers under Crook. The Indians had won a great victory, and throughout the night they had danced and beaten the drums in celebration. Because of that the village was only gradually coming awake this morning. Quiet Stream had already been at work half the morning when she saw Sitting Bull coming back into camp. He had not celebrated with the revelers last night but had, instead, spent the night upon the ridge overlooking the camp, praying and meditating.

Sitting Bull was, Quiet Stream thought, a very imposing figure. Today he was wearing a tanned buckskin shirt decorated with green porcupine quillwork and tassels of human hair. His leggings and moccasins were also smoke tanned, though his long breech clout was deep red. He was wearing a single feather at the back of his head, and his face was painted red, for good luck.

Quiet Stream was nearly finished with her task when she heard shooting coming from the south end of the camp. Looking in that direction, she saw dust rising, then saw her brother, Wind in His Hair, emerge from his tepee and run for his horse. Wind in His Hair's wife and child stood just outside the tepee, watching as he galloped toward the sound of the guns.

"Soldiers are coming! Soldiers are coming!" someone yelled as he ran through the camp. His warning was totally unnecessary, though, as everyone in the camp already knew they were being attacked. Quiet Stream hurried over to the tepee of her brother to help his wife, Capture Heart Woman, tend to the children.

"Look! The soldiers making the attack are few," Capture Heart Woman said. "Why would so few attack so many?"

"Who can understand the ways of the white man?" Quiet Stream replied anxiously.

As the soldiers approached the village, the battle came much closer, and bullets began whizzing through the camp, rattling off the tepee poles and peppering the lodgeskins with holes.

"Be brave!" Sitting Bull shouted. "We have much to fight for. If we lose the battle we have nothing to live for! Fight like brave men! Be brave!"

Two children, wet from swimming in the river, ran by. A crippled old man, supporting himself on a crutch, came hobbling along. A bullet cut his crutch in two and he fell. Quiet Stream ran out to help him to his feet, then pulled him over to the relative safety of a small depression.

Warriors—by the few, then by the dozens, then by the scores—rushed to join the battle.

"Hoka hay!"

"It is a good day to die!"

WITH RENO

"My God!" Reno said as he led his battalion toward the village. "My God, Joe, they aren't running away! They're charging us! Bugler! Sound dismount!"

"Marcus, no!" Joe screamed. Dismounting would decrease their fighting strength by one fourth, since every fourth man would be designated to hold the horses. "You can't dismount!"

Despite Joe's shout, Reno discontinued the attack and dismounted in a clump of trees in a gully. "Take cover!" he shouted. "Take cover and fire from the ditch!"

At that very moment Joe had his horse shot from under him, and, afoot, he had no recourse but to take cover with the others. Already he saw soldiers struggling to remove the swollen cartridges from the breeches of their weapons, and he realized that not only were they outnumbered by the Indians, many of the Indians possessed Henry and Winchester repeating rifles.

"Major, we can't stay here!" Joe shouted. "We've *got* to get mounted!" Even as Joe spoke, he knew he would have to catch a mount somewhere to replace his own mortally wounded animal. A cloud of arrows dropped into the ditch then, and half a dozen men shouted out in pain as the arrows found their marks.

"You're right!" Reno said. "Mount up! We're going to move back. Move back! Go back across the river!"

"Look! Sioux warriors leave now!" Bloody Knife said, pointing toward the village. Just as he had said, the Sioux were leaving, heading toward the other end of the village. Joe believed that by now Custer must have attacked, and the Sioux were going to join the battle with him.

"Major, Custer's plan is working!" he shouted. "We've got to press the attack!"

Suddenly Bloody Knife's head practically exploded as a bullet crashed into it. Blood and brain tissue splattered onto Reno's face, some of it getting into his mouth. Reno gagged and began spitting.

"Dismount!" he shouted, and half the troopers who had mounted on his first command dismounted again, though Reno himself did not.

"Withdraw to the river!" he ordered, and he led the retreat, leaving behind several of his men, now totally disoriented by the confusing and contradictory orders. They stayed behind in the gully and watched as their comrades and all the horses left. They were trapped.

Without a horse, Joe was left behind when Reno retreated. He watched Reno's men hit the river. The bank was several feet above the water, and the men had to urge their horses over. Once in the water, the horses started across, while the Indians continued to work the levers of their repeating rifles, pouring a high volume of fire at the fleeing soldiers. The climb up the other side of the river was as steep as the jump down had been on this side. Joe saw Lieutenant Hodgson being pulled across the river, holding on to the stirrup of a trooper's horse. As the horse started climbing up the other side, Hodgson was hit by several bullets, and he let go, then slid back down into the water.

"Benny! Damn," Joe said under his breath as he saw his executive officer floating downstream, facedown and motionless.

Joe looked around the thicket and found he was the only officer in charge of a small group of frightened, trapped soldiers.

"Captain Murchison, what will we do? What will we do?" one man asked in a frightened voice.

"First, everyone check your weapon to make sure it is loaded."

The troopers did as they were told.

"Now, lay low, here in the thicket," Joe said. "Don't fire unless you're fired on. Perhaps the Indians will overlook us."

Joe and the others took cover in the little thicket of trees and waited. The Indians who had swooped by in pursuit of Reno's retreating soldiers now returned laughing and shouting. Several of them were brandishing freshly taken scalps.

"The heathen devils," one of the men sobbed and started to stand up. But Joe reached for him and pulled him back down.

"Quiet!" Joe cautioned, holding his finger to his lips.

"We are all going to be killed!" one of the others said fearfully.

"Yes," Joe said. "We probably are. But we all have to die sometime. If it's to be now, let us at least die as brave men."

They lay there for quite a while longer. Joe occupied the time by thinking pleasant thoughts.

He remembered a baseball game in New York, when his home run won the game and upwards of twenty-thousand people stood to cheer his name.

He thought of his mother and father back in Illinois, and of what the farm looked like at sunrise.

He thought of the many letters he had exchanged with Sally, and he wondered if anyone would tell her what had happened to him.

He thought of Monique, and he visualized her dancing.

He thought of Tamara, and how Todd had asked him to be good to his daughter and his grandchildren. And he knew at that moment that if he survived this, he would marry her.

Toward noon, several Indian women came out and began walking around, picking up their own dead and wounded. The women were crying over the bodies of their men and Joe, despite the danger of the situation, couldn't help but feel a degree of pity for their grief. The pity he felt was soon dispelled, however, for the bodies of the soldiers were stripped of their clothes and severely mutilated. Then one of the women discovered Isaiah Dorman and she shouted at the others. Though badly wounded, the black scout was not yet dead when the women raised him to a sitting position.

Joe thought the women were going to help him, but one of them slit his throat, then stuck Dorman's own tin mug under the jugular vein, filling it to overflowing with blood. Another took a sharpened stake and drove it through Dorman's testicles. Dorman opened his mouth to scream, but the slice across his throat prevented any sound from coming out. Joe watched the silent scream, fighting hard to keep from screaming out his own rage.

The Indians moved around the thicket all afternoon, riding back and forth, running, shouting at each other, and sometimes even coming through the thicket. Fortunately, they had no idea that Joe and the others were still there, for they didn't appear to be searching for anyone.

In the meantime, Joe realized, Reno had probably taken a position on the far side of the river, in the bluffs, for he could hear sporadic firing from that direction.

WITH CUSTER

When Custer crested the hill on the opposite side of the river from the village, he saw that the Indians would not run from him as he expected, but would stand and fight. He also realized for the first time that there were many more Indians than he, or anyone else, had expected. At first he couldn't see the entire village because his view of the section farthest downstream was obscured by the bends in the river and the timber growing along the banks.

"Damn, Autie, look at that!" was all Tom Custer could say.

"It looks like New York City, only with tepees, doesn't it?" Custer replied. He held his hand up to stop the column.

"Oh, my!" Boston Custer said, and the general, surprised to hear his young brother's voice, turned around.

"Boston, what the hell are you . . ." He then saw young Autie Reed coming up beside him, and he pinched the bridge of his nose. "I wish you boys hadn't come," he said.

"What? And miss the fun?"

"Colonel Hamby," Custer said.

For just a moment, Todd didn't realize Custer was speaking to him. Then, with a start, he answered. "Yes, sir?"

"Colonel, I want you to take my brother and my nephew back to the rear, out of harm's way."

"General, I'll do anything you ask," Todd replied. "But do you really think we'd make it more than a quarter of a mile from here?"

"We have no chance here, Hamby, and you know it," Custer said.

Gunfire sounded from the south end of the village.

"Reno is committed," Custer said. "We have no choice now but to attack."

"What do you want of me, General?" Todd asked. "Do I stay with you? Or do I run with the boys?"

"We want to stay!" Boston said.

Custer looked over at Tom.

"Let them stay, Autie. Hell, Todd's right, we're all going to die, anyway. We may as well die together."

"So it has come down to this," Custer said. "The man who would be president is going to end his life in a remote valley in Montana. No cheering crowds, no fawning politicians—nothing but Indians."

"Yeah, and the hell of it is, they don't even have the vote," Tom said, laughing.

At first, Custer scowled at his brother; then, suddenly, he, too, broke into laughter. "Well, brother Tom. I am pleased to see that you have maintained a sense of humor through it all." He stood in his stirrups and looked back over his command. "Trumpeter!" he called.

"Y–yes, sir?" the trumpeter stammered.

"Sound the charge!"

The trumpeter lifted the instrument, but he was so frightened he couldn't make a sound. Quickly, Todd rode over to him.

"Blow your horn, boy," he said.

"I . . . I can't. I'm too scared!"

"Son, whatever happens to us is going to happen to us all," he said. "Now, what do you say we get this shindig over with? I've got some friends waiting for me in Fiddlers' Green."

The young trumpeter smiled, then raised his trumpet. Todd had never heard the charge blown more thrillingly.

IN THE INDIAN CAMP

The notes of the bugle call drifted down across the stream and into the village. Quiet Stream felt a cold chill traverse her body at the sound. Now she knew the answer to the question everyone was asking: Why had so few attacked at the southern end of the village? Because the main attack was to come at the northern end.

She hurried toward the north end of the camp, arriving in time to see the soldiers charging down the hill toward the village. At first she could hear only the beat of shod hooves. Then came the jangle of gear and the rattle of bits. Finally she heard the soldiers themselves, shouting and screaming at the top of their lungs as they approached. Closer and closer they came, until the great blue mass became distinguishable as horses and riders, then closer still until even the individual faces were visible.

But the ruse of the soldiers had not worked, for Quiet Stream could see hundreds of Indians waiting in ambush, holding their fire until the soldiers hit the stream. When the first horse entered the river, the Indians raised up and fired. Several soldiers were hit and the column was divided. A few men in front managed to cross the stream and make it all the way to the edge of the Cheyenne circle, but the soldiers on the opposite side of the bank were caught in a murderous crossfire and were driven back.

"General! Our line has been cut!" Quiet Stream heard one of the men shout to their leader. Unlike the soldiers, who were dressed in blue, the leader was wearing buckskins.

"Damn! They must come across," the leader replied. He turned his horse and with his hat began to wave his troops over, but the soldiers were unable to cross.

"General, we have to get back with the men!" a man with stripes on his sleeve shouted. With a start, Quiet Stream realized that she knew this man. He was Soldier without Shoes, one of the two who had come into their camp ten years earlier, barefoot, half naked, and nearly dead from starvation.

"Damn!" the leader shouted. *"Damn!"* Turning his horse, he dashed back into the river, followed by the few who had crossed with him. They rode hard across the shallow ford, the hooves of their horses kicking up a silver spray of water.

The soldiers on the opposite side of the river rallied when their leader returned, and he began leading them in an organized withdrawal. Gradually the soldiers started working their way up to the north end of the ridge, but at that moment nearly all the warriors who had gone to the south end of the village came up to take part in the fight. They rushed across the river to join the others, and as they swarmed around the soldiers, it reminded Quiet Stream of a swiftly flowing river streaming around a handful of pebbles.

Gradually the volume of shooting diminished, and then even the women and children crossed the stream and climbed up the hill to witness the final stage of the battle. One by one the remaining soldiers were gunned or clubbed down, until finally there was absolute and total silence.

The Indians merely stood around for several moments afterward, too shocked by what had happened to do anything. There was no celebration of victory, nor wailing for the dead. No one spoke a word as they began methodically stripping the bodies.

NIGHTFALL, IN A WOODED GULLEY JUST SOUTH OF THE VILLAGE

The moon came out, but there was a heavy overcast so it wasn't too bright. Joe knew that if they were ever going to escape, they would have to do so now.

"Let's go," he ordered, and, in a crouch, he led his little group of men toward the river. They got about halfway there when they saw a mounted band of Indians. Joe signaled the others, and they all dropped to the ground, remaining very still. The Indians, laughing and talking, rode right past them but didn't see them in the dark.

Finally the soldiers reached the river's edge, and one by one they slid down the bank. They dropped their heads in the water and drank deeply, satisfying the thirst that had bedeviled them during the long, hot, terrifying afternoon.

They were able to drink from the river, but they discovered they couldn't cross here, for the water was too deep and the current too swift.

In the rear, upriver, Joe could see and hear great circles of the Indians holding a war dance around burning piles of wood and brush. The flames lighted the village with an eerie, flickering glow, and in that light Joe could see that the Indians were grotesquely painted, and many were carrying the severed heads of slain soldiers.

After exploring numerous places along the river, Joe found a place to cross, and he led his men back over. Just as they emerged on the other side, a small group of mounted riders approached the bluff. Joe looked up and saw Tom Custer. He let out a whoop of joy.

"Tom! Tom, am I glad to see you! You don't know what we've been through, and you . . . how did you escape the—"

Joe suddenly gasped. It wasn't Custer; it was an Indian! He was wearing Custer's buckskin suit, complete with hat, insignia, gloves, and revolver. The Indian raised his pistol and fired. Joe pulled his own revolver and fired back. The Indian in Custer's uniform tumbled from the saddle. The others rode away, quickly.

"Let's go before they come back!" Joe called, and the soldiers followed him as he climbed up the bluff away from the river.

Joe and the others ran in a low crouch for several hundred yards until finally they heard voices speaking in English. Joe held up his hand to halt his troopers.

"Hey, that's Sergeant McVey's voice," one of the men said. "I recognize him. Hey, Mac, don't nobody shoot! They's some of us comin' in!"

"All right, come on," Sergeant McVey called back. Joe had never heard a song that sounded more beautiful than did McVey's voice at that moment.

When Joe reached Major Reno, he discovered that Captain Benteen's troops had linked up with him during the day, and they were now dug into fortified positions on the side of the hill. They couldn't attack the Indians, but their combined positions were strong enough that they would be able to defend themselves against any attack the Indians might make.

"Where is the general?" Joe asked, as he drank a cup of coffee Benteen offered him. The coffee was liberally laced with whiskey, Joe noticed.

"We haven't heard from him," Benteen answered. "I fear the worst. I think we should try to find him."

"Nonsense," Reno said. "He is the commander. It is his responsibility to find us. Why didn't he come to my aid as he promised me? And why doesn't he come now? Doesn't he realize we are trapped here?"

"He may not be able to come," Benteen said.

"Nevertheless, I am not going to send anyone out to look for him. We will just stay here until he contacts us."

"Major, there may be more stragglers trapped on the other side of the river," Joe suggested. "I'd like to take my company over to look for them."

"No," Reno said. "I'll not risk a company. Not a company, not even a platoon. If anyone is left over there, they shall simply have to return on their own."

"What if they're wounded?" Joe asked.

"It can't be helped."

Joe stood up. "Then I request permission to return on my own."

"What can you do?"

"If I find them, I'll show them the best way back."

"Don't be foolish. You'll get yourself killed."

"I did it once and got away with it," Joe said. "I can do it again."

"Very well, Captain, if you insist," Reno said. "It's your life, if you want to throw it away like that—"

"Hell, Marcus, leave him alone," Benteen said. "We may none of us get out of here alive, anyway. Go ahead, Joe." Benteen put his hand on Joe's shoulder. "It seems to me that in a day of killing and stupidity, yours has been the only sane voice I have heard. Good luck."

"Thanks," Joe said.

He made five more trips across the river, right into the heart of the Indian camp, and brought seventeen more soldiers back to safety, the last group after day-break.

By early afternoon it became apparent that the Indians were leaving. They were striking their village and pouring out of the valley, heading toward the Big Horn Mountains, moving in a large column that consisted of eight to ten thousand people.

"Major, the Indians are leaving. I think we should try and link up with Custer," Benteen said.

"No," Reno said. "Suppose they have him surrounded, just as they do us?"

"We aren't surrounded," Joe said. "We can leave anytime we wish. I think Colonel Benteen is right. We should try to find the general."

"No," Reno said again. "We will wait right here for General Terry."

Joe sighed. "Then do you care if I go look for him?"

"If you want to be so foolish, go ahead," Reno said.

"Major, for God's sake, the man is practically out on his feet now," Benteen said. "None of us rested the night before last, and last night Murchison was up all night leading the stragglers in. And now you expect him to find Custer for you?"

"I didn't suggest it," Reno said. "He did. I merely gave him permission. You may go or stay, Captain Murchison. It's all the same to me."

"Thank you, sir," Joe replied. Wearily, he mounted a borrowed horse and started back toward the last place he had seen Custer. As soon as he crossed Medicine Tail Coulee, he could see the buzzards circling ahead, and he prepared himself for what he would see on the other side of the ridge. Urging the horse into a canter, he rode to the top of the hill.

Even with preparation he was nearly overwhelmed by what he saw. There, in the valley below him, were the remains of Custer's command.

Every last man was dead.

Slowly, Joe rode down the gentle slope, into the valley of death. The bodies were white, so terribly white. At first he didn't understand why; then he realized it was because most of them were naked, stripped of the last trappings of their mortal life.

A few were still in uniform. Joe saw that the reporter, Mark Kellogg, was also clothed. Joe dismounted and, leading his horse, began walking through the grisly area. Already buzzards were feasting on the remains, and he turned away and retched when he saw one bird pull the brain out of the scalped cranium of one of the soldiers. The soldier was lying with his back to Joe, and Joe didn't want to look into his face because he didn't want to recognize him. The bodies were somewhat more spread out than he would have thought, as if there had been several defensive positions rather than one large consolidated position. But, given the fluidity of battle and the fact that there was no availability of cover, such as that found by the Reno and Benteen battalions, Joe assumed the soldiers had done the best they could do.

As he passed by the bodies, one after another, his presence would cause the nearest buzzards to take to the air with a dry, blood-chilling flap of wings. They would circle once, then return as soon as he was by. Then Joe caught his breath. He saw Seth Todd sitting up, leaning back against the carcass of a horse. Todd was wearing his trousers, but no boots and no shirt. His eyes were wide open, and there were no marks on his body.

"Todd!" Joe said excitedly, running toward him. "Todd am I glad to . . ." Joe stopped short. Todd's eyes were open, but they were flat and dull-looking.

"Oh, Todd!" Joe moaned. He knelt down on one knee beside him, putting his hand on Todd's shoulder. When he did, Todd tumbled forward, and Joe saw that the back of his head was shot away. He gasped loudly and jerked his hand away as if he had touched a hot stove.

He felt a constriction in his throat, then a burning in his eyes. Tears began to stream down his face. "I should have kept you with me, Todd," he said. "Damn you, Custer!" Joe suddenly shouted, his voice echoing back to him. "Damn your arrogance! So many men! Look what you have done!"

"The soldier chief was Long Hair? We did not know," a woman's voice suddenly said.

Startled, Joe leaped up and reached for his pistol.

He found himself confronting half a dozen Indians appearing as if from nowhere.

"We do not want to hurt you," the woman said, holding her hand out toward him. Seeing that at least three of the Indians were pointing their rifles at him, Joe left his pistol in his holster.

"I . . . I know you," Joe said. "You are Quiet Stream." He looked over at the men. "And you are Wind in His Hair," he said to the most regal-looking of them.

"Why did the soldiers come?" Quiet Stream asked. "We were not making war. We wanted only to hunt and to live in peace. Now many are dead. My people. Your people. Why did the soldiers come?"

"We had no choice, we had to come. We are soldiers," Joe said. "We follow orders, we don't make policy."

Wind in His Hair spoke, and Quiet Stream interpreted for him.

"You were with the soldiers on the hill?" She pointed to the south, where Reno and Benteen were.

"Yes," Joe answered.

Wind in His Hair spoke again, and again Quiet Stream interpreted.

"We could have killed all of you, as these soldiers were killed," Quiet Stream said. "But we did not. Go back to your people. Tell them we want no more war. We have beaten you. We have killed your soldier chief, Custer. Do not come here again. Let us live in peace."

Joe shook his head. "It is too late for that. There are many more soldiers coming," he said. "And they will not stop until all the Sioux have returned to the reservations."

"Then many more soldiers will die."

"And many more Indians. Why will you not return to your reservations? It is good for you there. You are given beef and clothing. You are given blankets, and rifles for hunting. You can live there in peace. And we can live in peace. And there will be no war."

After the translation, Quiet Stream spoke again.

"We are not like cattle, to be kept in pens. We are like buffalo, to go where we wish."

"I wish it could be like that for you," Joe said. "I really do."

The Indians turned to leave then, but Quiet Stream stopped and looked back. She pointed to Todd's body.

"He is Soldier without Shoes, the one who came with you when you had no clothes and no food," she said.

"Yes."

"He died bravely." Quiet Stream looked around. "All died bravely, for there were no cowards on this field. I am sorry your friend is dead. I saw your tears. You do not weep alone. Many of our people shed tears today, as well."

She turned to follow the others. Because of the lay of the land, they were quickly below the ridgeline. A moment later Joe heard horses; then as they rose up out of the valley, he saw them ford the river and ride across the area where the village had been, marked now only by the residue left behind . . . hundreds of lodge frames, a thousand or more old campfires, bits of cloth, canvas, and buffalo skins.

Joe found Custer then, lying on his back, stripped naked but otherwise left untouched by the Indians. There was one bullet hole in his chest, another in his head. Tom Custer was nearby, but as the Indians seemed to have singled out his body for their particular retribution, Joe was almost unable to recognize him. He wandered around for the next several minutes, locating Cooke, Reily, Crittenden, and Sturgis. He had particularly wanted to find Jim Calhoun, but by now the carrion birds had grown so bold as to be unconcerned by his presence, and the sight of them plucking out the eyes and tearing into the flesh of the dead, sometimes within three feet of him, became more than he could take. He remounted and started back to rejoin Reno's command.

Joe made no effort whatever to wipe away the tears that streamed down his face or to stifle the racking sobs that came from his throat.

★★★

Seventeen

UNITED STATES MILITARY ACADEMY
WEST POINT, NEW YORK
JUNE 1941

The West Point Glee Club concluded their program to generous applause, and as the cadets filed off the stage and back into the audience where they joined their classmates, the audience buzzed with conversation. General Murchison turned in his chair and began looking around until he located his wife. He would have preferred to be sitting with her, but the program committee had been very specific about the seating arrangements: All VIPs were to sit in designated areas.

He spotted Tamara across the crowded auditorium and saw that she was looking at him. He smiled and nodded and she nodded back. From the expression on her face, Joe knew that she, too, had been revisiting the past.

As his eyes continued to sweep across the part of the auditorium where sat the corps of cadets, he picked out of the sea of white faces three that were black. He knew that they were not the first Negroes to attend the academy, although they were still a very tiny minority. Joe wondered if these three cadets ever gave any thought to the Negro soldiers who had blazed the trail for them. He wondered if any of them had ever even heard of First Sergeant Deacon Travis, Corporal Sigmund Sylvester, or Trooper Dooley Webb.

FORT CANFIELD, ARIZONA TERRITORY
SUMMER 1886

The train, called the Pacific Parlor Express, was the best the Southern Pacific Railroad had to offer. It was the latest in luxury, boasting a library, a hair-dressing salon, two organs, and its own private newspaper. The parlor car was resplendent in plush upholstery, rich hangings, and hand-carved inlaid paneling. The seats were individual overstuffed chairs, fitted so they could rotate to allow the passengers to look out the windows, turn back toward the center of the car to allow conversation, or recline so the passengers could take a nap without having to return to the roomettes at the end of the car.

As the Pacific Parlor Express passed through New Mexico Territory, clicking off forty miles every hour, Tamara Murchison kept herself occupied by reading the latest *Harper's Weekly.* Her son, eight-year-old Todd Armstrong, was wandering around the car, exploring it thoroughly. Tamara's admonitions to him not to disturb the other passengers brought their assurances that he was a "sweet boy and no problem at all." To Todd's credit, he was well-mannered, spoke only when spoken to, and spent most of his time looking through first one window and then another, watching the great Southwest countryside pass by.

Joe's tunic was hanging on a hook in the roomette, and he was wearing only his shirt and trousers. The shirt was fitted with epaulets, however, so that even the most casual observer could see that he was a full colonel in the U.S. Cavalry. He was currently reading a description of Fort Canfield, which was to be his newly assigned post.

Established February 12, 1877, Fort Canfield is named for Lieutenant John S. Canfield who was killed in the Battle of Big Knife Creek, Dakota Territory. Fort Canfield is located at the mouth of Central Canyon toward the southwest end of the Dragoon Mountains. It is west of the San Pedro

River and fifteen miles north of the Mexican border, and currently the home of the Ninth Cavalry. The mission of the Ninth Cavalry is to protect settlers and travelers from the Apache Indians. There is ample wood, water, and grazing for animals.

The physical facilities of the post consist of more than 50 structures, providing quarters for 12 companies. There are 13 single-unit quarters available for married officers, plus 4 multiunit quarters for bachelor officers. The hospital, built in 1879, has just been enlarged to accommodate 24 patients.

Joe recalled Lieutenant Canfield, the man who had been his adjutant at Fort Berthold, so many years ago. He thought it ironic that he would now be commanding a post named for him, especially since Joe had also been a participant in that battle.

"Oh, my!" Tamara said, interrupting Joe's reverie.

He looked up from his file and took off his reading glasses. "What is it?"

"What an ingenious idea I have just read," she said, indicating the magazine. "Someone has proposed connecting Mr. Edison's phonograph machine with the telephone."

"To what purpose?" Joe asked.

"Well, suppose a telephone subscriber is away from home when someone places a call to him? The writer of this piece proposes that the telephone be connected to the phonograph, enabling it to answer the phone, play a prerecorded message explaining that the subscriber is away from home, then receive a message from the caller so that, when the subscriber returns, he need merely play the phonograph to see what was wanted of him."

"How will the machine answer the phone?" Joe asked.

"I don't know. The article didn't say. Though men of science can do so many wonderful things, I suppose they can devise some method."

Joe put his glasses back on and returned to his reading. "There can't be any future to such an idea. I can't imagine anyone leaving their message with a machine. I would think they would just call back when the subscriber is in."

The door to the parlor car opened, and a uniformed steward came in. He approached Joe.

"Good evening, Colonel Murchison, Mrs. Murchison," he greeted with a slight nod. He handed Joe and Tamara a menu. "There are seats available in the dining car at six-thirty, seven, and seven-thirty. Which seating would you prefer?"

The steward had a slight French accent, and Joe, remembering his own time in France, had inquired about it. He learned that the accent was actually more Creole than French, though the steward concentrated on making it sound French for the overall effect of elegance.

"I think we will take the six-thirty seating," Joe replied, opening the menu.

"Very good sir. And your order?"

Though Joe had ridden many trains that limited their meals to sack lunches or the very unappetizing fare served at stations along the way, the dining car of this train offered a veritable feast. The menu featured blue-winged teal, antelope steaks, roast beef, boiled ham and tongue, broiled chicken, corn on the cob, fresh fruit, hot rolls, and corn bread.

"I'll have roast beef," Joe said.

"And I'll have broiled chicken," Tamara said. "And boiled ham for our son."

"Very good," the steward replied. "Your table shall be reserved for you. I hope you enjoy your meal."

"I'm sure we will," Tamara said, smiling at him as she returned the menu.

After the steward left, Joe and Tamara stared through the large windows at the wide-open spaces outside.

"Are you nervous about your command?" she asked.

Joe smiled, then reached over to take her hand in his. They had been married for nearly ten years now, marrying shortly after Joe had returned to Fort Lincoln from the ill-fated summer expedition to the Little Big Horn. They had remained at Fort Lincoln for six months longer; then they went to Fort Riley for three years, followed by a five-year tour of duty at Jefferson Barracks. Their most recent assignment was two years with the War Department in Washington, D.C., where Joe was in charge of procurement of cavalry mounts for the entire army.

For the previous two years, the couple had been able to participate in the social life of the nation's capital, including many receptions that were also attended by the president. But it had not been an assignment to Joe's liking, and he found himself, as he had many years earlier, begging to be reassigned. Then, one month ago, concurrent with his promotion to full colonel, Joe was assigned to Fort Canfield, Arizona Territory, where he would become both the post and the regimental commander, commanding the Ninth U.S. Cavalry.

"I've had commands before," Joe said.

"Not like this," Tamara replied.

Joe brought his wife's hand up to his lips and kissed it, though as he continued to stare through the window it was almost as if kissing her hand was a secondary thought.

"No," he admitted. "Not like this."

He recalled a discussion he had with Colonel Gaithers, his most recent commanding officer.

"You are crazy if you take that assignment, Joe," Colonel Gaithers had told him. "The Ninth Cavalry is Colored. Don't you realize that?"

"Yes, I know that," Joe said.

"All the troopers, all the noncommissioned officers, even your first sergeants and sergeant major are Colored."

"Yes."

"Only the officers are white, and for the most part they are the very dregs of the earth, given that assignment because no other unit in the cavalry will take them."

Joe laughed. "Thanks," he said.

"Oh, hell, I don't mean you, Joe, you know that. You won the Medal of Honor for your action at the Little Big Horn. Nearly everyone agrees that you were practically the only one who acquitted himself well in that debacle."

"Not true," Joe said. "There were several brave men that day."

"I meant among the officers," Colonel Gaithers said. "Look at Reno, for example. He was tried for cowardice and has since left the army in disgrace."

"His leaving the army had nothing to do with his performance at the Little Big Horn," Joe insisted. "He was discharged for peering into the bedroom window at Colonel Sturgis's daughter. And I believe that charge to be as without foundation as was the charge of cowardice on the battlefield."

"Yes, I know that those of you who were there, Benteen and the others, take up for him. But Mrs. Custer still holds him responsible for her husband's death."

"Libbie has not yet come to terms with her loss," Joe replied.

"Well, that's neither here nor there," Colonel Gaithers said. "The point is, you have accepted the command of a Colored cavalry unit, and I fear it may well be the end of your career."

"I'm not concerned," Joe said.

"I beg your pardon?" Tamara asked.

Joe smiled sheepishly, realizing he had spoken aloud in response to his recalled conversation with Colonel Gaithers.

"I said I'm not concerned that the soldiers are all Colored. I have looked up their records. Do you realize they have the lowest desertion rate and the highest reenlistment rate of any regiment in the army?"

"No, I didn't know that."

"It's true," Joe said. "And when you consider the plight of the Colored man in most places in our society, it's easy to see how the army offers them more opportunity than they can get just about anywhere else. They are sure to be motivated, Tamara—and men who are motivated make fine soldiers."

"I suppose so."

"Tamara, you aren't concerned because they're Colored, are you? I mean, being from the South and—"

"Joseph!" Tamara gasped. "How can you ask such a question? Have you ever seen me be rude to anyone of color?"

"No."

"Then that is your answer."

"Papa, I'm hungry," Todd said coming up to them from the rearmost window, where he had been looking outside. Joe took out his pocket watch and examined it.

"Are you, now?" he said.

"Yes, sir. Very hungry."

"Well, that's good, because according to my watch it is time to eat right now."

Dinner was a leisurely and delicious affair. Retiring to their roomette afterward, the Murchisons slept well that night. They had grown accustomed to the motion of the train, and the sound of the wheels clacking on the tracks had as soothing an effect as a lullaby. Within a short time after young Todd's head hit the pillow he was asleep, and his parents weren't too far behind him.

"Tombstone!"

Joe was awakened by the conductor's crisp call. The train was slowing, and Joe pulled the curtain to one side to look out the window. Raising the window, he looked ahead to see a cluster of low-lying buildings gathered beneath the mountains that he knew from his map was the Dragoon Range. This was the northern end of the range. Fort Canfield lay thirty miles to the south.

"What is it, dear?" Tamara asked, just now waking.

"Tombstone," Joe said. "This is where we get off. It's as far as the train goes. From here to Fort Canfield, we go by stage."

"Tombstone," Tamara said, shivering. "What an awful name for a town. Well, I'd better wake Todd and get him ready."

Quickly, Joe dressed, then left the roomette and walked to the forward vestibule. He was standing there when the train ground to a stop in front of a low, wood-frame building from which hung a white sign with the word TOMBSTONE painted on it.

It was early in the morning, and only a few of the citizens of Tombstone had turned out to welcome the train. Joe saw a couple of old men sitting on a platform near the station house, a small group of people who were apparently meeting arriving passengers, and a young man and woman standing together sadly, obviously soon to be parted.

A few moments later Tamara and Todd joined him, then they stepped down onto the platform. An army sergeant, his black face shining in the early morning sun, strode up to them and saluted.

"Beggin' the colonel's pardon, sir, but would you be Colonel Murchison?"

"Yes," Joe said, returning the salute.

"I'm First Sergeant Deacon Travis, sir. I've got a coach and a detail here to see the colonel and his lady to Fort Canfield."

Sergeant Travis was obviously a veteran of many years' service, evidenced not only by his rank and service stripes but by his salt-and-pepper gray hair, and weather-lined face. Joe noticed also that, like himself, First Sergeant Travis was wearing the Medal of Honor.

"Very good, First Sergeant," Joe replied. "Would you have someone see to our luggage?"

"Yes, sir," Sergeant Travis replied. "Sir, if the colonel and his family would care to have breakfast now, I'd advise you to do so. We won't be raisin' the stagecoach relay station at the San Pedro crossing until around one."

"Where's a good place to eat in this town, First Sergeant?"

"Well, sir, now I can't rightly tell you that," First Sergeant Travis replied, "seein' as how Coloreds ain't welcome. But I'se seen lots of folks go into that place over there." He pointed to a restaurant with the unlikely name of City Pig.

"But where will you and the men eat?" Todd asked.

Travis smiled and bent down to the boy. "Well, we done eat, little sir," he said. "We had us some coffee 'n bacon while we was waitin' on the train."

Joe gave his son's shoulder an affectionate squeeze. "I guess that settles matters. Thank you, First Sergeant. We'll join you after our breakfast," he said.

Breakfast was disappointing. After having been spoiled by first-class train travel with omelets, pancakes, and other delicacies, tough steak and fried potatoes were quite a comedown.

When they left the restaurant a short while later, the sun had climbed higher in the sky and already was promising the heat of a long summer's day. As they approached the coach, Joe saw it was a Spring coach, built along the same lines as Concord stagecoaches though somewhat smaller and lighter. This particular coach was painted blue with yellow trim. A crest of crossed sabers was on the door, framing the number 9. Joe was surprised when he looked just under the window and saw that his name had already been painted there:

COLONEL JOSEPH T. MURCHISON
COMMANDING OFFICER
NINTH U.S. CAVALRY
FORT CANFIELD, AT

Joe had never seen a coach sparkle so brilliantly, and he commented on it.

"Yes, sir," Travis said. "The boys takes real good care of it. They don't want nothin' but the best for the commander of the Ninth."

With the luggage already loaded, there was nothing left to do but board the coach for the trip. The driver opened the door, then put a mounting step down for Tamara.

"Thank you," she said.

"What's your name?" Todd asked the driver.

The driver smiled. "Why, I'm Trooper Webb," he said.

Todd looked up at his father.

"Papa, can I ride up top with Trooper Webb?"

"I think you had better ask Trooper Webb that question," Joe replied.

"Trooper Webb?" Todd asked hopefully.

Again, Trooper Webb smiled. "I reckon you can if you wants to," he said.

With a shouted "Thanks!" Todd climbed up over the front wheel and onto the seat. A moment later the coach pulled out of town with two mounted cavalrymen in front and two following.

It was soon after one o'clock in the afternoon when the coach pulled into the way stop at San Pedro ford. The San Pedro ford relay station was directly on the line between Tombstone and Nogales, and there were two other coaches in the station, one of which was having its team changed. Joe heard Trooper Webb call to the horses, then the brake being applied as the coach came to a stop. Almost instantly, it seemed, Sergeant Travis had the door open and was standing at attention alongside.

"We'll be feedin' an' waterin' the horses here, Colonel," Travis said. "There will be time for you and the missus to take your lunch inside. I'm told they serve a fine meal."

Joe had read about San Pedro ford while he was researching his new assignment. Two years ago it had been attacked by Apaches, but a squad of Ninth Cavalry soldiers, on the Apaches' trail, had correctly guessed that the way station at San Pedro ford would be the Indians' target. Riding hard, the cavalrymen reached the way station before the Apache raiding party. When the attack came, six of the Apaches were killed, and the raid was broken up. Not one passenger or employee of the way station received so much as a scratch, though one of the cavalrymen was killed and two were wounded.

When Joe, Tamara, and Todd stepped inside, he saw

that the place was busy with its midday meal. Two of the three long tables were completely filled with passengers from the other two coaches. They were engaged in animated conversation and gave only a passing glance to the three who had just entered.

The proprietor came over to them, smiling and wiping his hands with a towel as he greeted them.

"Charley Baxter is the name, Captain," he said, extending his hand after he wiped it.

"My papa is a *colonel*," Todd corrected.

"Todd!" Tamara scolded.

Baxter laughed. "That's all right, miss," he said. "The boy's right in correctin' me. Never was in the army myself, so I never learned the ranks that good. Come on in, seat yourself, and let me bring you lunch. We're havin' a beef stew today."

"Thank you," Joe said.

As Baxter brought them their meal a few minutes later, one of the stable hands came inside.

"Mr. Baxter, them niggers is out there just big as you please, cookin' their food and makin' their coffee," the stable hand complained.

"Damn their hides," Baxter said. "I warned them about that."

"Wait a minute," Joe said. "If you aren't going to feed them in here, where do you expect them to eat?"

"I don't mind 'em fixin' their meals outside, 'long as they do it around back so no one can see 'em. It's bad for business when people sees a bunch of Coloreds hangin' around."

"How bad was it for business a couple of years ago when they stopped the Apaches from pillaging and burning this place?" Joe asked.

"Well, I'm man enough to admit that I was sure glad to see 'em that day. And don't get me wrong. They're good boys, the most of 'em. It's just that ever' now an' then you'll get a bad nigger, an' they sort of spoil it for ever'body."

When Baxter left, Todd leaned over to his mother and whispered. "Mama, he said 'nigger.' That's a bad word."

"Yes, it is, dear," Tamara replied. "And it's not a word we'll ever say, is it?"

"No, ma'am," Todd said resolutely.

When the coach arrived at Fort Canfield later that afternoon, Joe was surprised to see the entire regiment turned out in parade formation. They were in full dress uniform, including their black-felt helmets with yellow mohair tassels and shining brass shields. As Joe stepped down from the coach, the trumpeter played three flourishes, and the artillery fired an eleven-gun salute.

"Battalion commanders, bring the regiment to attention!" a white-haired major shouted as the smoke from the cannon discharges drifted across the parade ground.

The three battalion commanders, all captains, responded: "Battalion!"

Twelve company commanders gave the supplementary command: "Company!"

Thirty-six platoon leaders responded: "Platoon!"

After the supplementary commands were given, returning almost as a distant echo, there was a beat of silence. Then the three Battalion commanders said as one: "Attenhut!"

Guidons were raised and held steady as the banners snapped and popped in the late afternoon breeze. The white-haired major approached Joe, then saluted.

"Colonel, my name is Major Owen Ross. I am pleased to report that the regiment is formed for inspection. We have a mount for you, sir, if you would do us the honor of reviewing the troops."

"It would be my honor, Major Ross," Joe replied, returning the salute.

An orderly brought Joe a horse—a particularly good-looking animal. The saddle blanket was blue piped in gold, with the eagles of a full colonel in the corner. The orderly held the stirrup out for Joe, and he mounted, then rode by in front of the regiment, taking the salute from all the officers as he passed. As his eyes swept over the formation, he looked into the faces of several of the soldiers, picking them out at random to study their expressions. In every case the expression was one of pride. It was as fine a body of men as Joe had ever seen.

The next morning he stood at the parlor window of the commanding officer's quarters, drinking a cup of coffee and looking out over his new post. Actually it wasn't his post yet, and it wouldn't be his until he signed all the books to officially relieve Major Ross. Ross would then become his executive officer.

While Joe was still in Washington, just after he received his orders for Fort Canfield, he went into the personnel files to look up the man who was to be his second in command:

> Maj. Owen W. Ross entered the army in 1861, fought at Wilson's Creek in Missouri, at Fort Donnelson, and at Shiloh. At Antietam, though only a second lieutenant, he rallied an entire battalion when all the officers senior to him were killed or incapacitated. He was also at Gettysburg and the Wilderness. A captain at the war's end, he was assigned to the Ninth Cavalry and duty in the west, which assignment he has held until the present date.

Joe also read Ross's last Officer's Efficiency Report, filed by General Nelson Miles:

> Major Ross is a classic example of an officer whose brilliant potential has gone unfulfilled due to intemperance. Because of his alcoholism, his present position as commanding officer of the Ninth Cavalry is, and should be considered, temporary only. Though drink has rendered him unfit for further promotion or command, Major Ross does enjoy a rather unique relationship with the Colored soldiers of the Ninth Cavalry and should continue to provide valuable service as an executive officer.

At the moment Major Ross was standing in the shade of the sally port, which connected the commanding officer's quarters with the headquarters building at Fort Canfield. Shielded from the sun and constructed in such a way as to create a breeze, the sally port was cool and pleasant. In fact, despite the heat, it was not that unpleasant in any of the buildings, for they were all cooled by olla jars—large widemouthed clay pots filled with water and suspended from the ceiling. The evaporation of the water cooled the room, a trick the army had learned from the Mexicans, who had learned it from the Indians many years earlier.

Behind him, Joe could hear Tamara supervising the business of getting moved in. Their furniture was already here when they arrived last night, having been sent ahead as soon as they received their orders. Joe and his little family had been in transit for an entire month, spending some time with Tamara's folks in Virginia and some time with Joe's mother in Hillsboro, Illinois. Joe's father had died three years ago, though he did live long enough to see his grandson.

"Joe, do you want the clock in the foyer or in the parlor?" Tamara called.

"I want it wherever you want it," he answered. "You'll be spending more time with the furniture than I will."

"Put it in the foyer," Joe heard Tamara tell one of the soldiers.

"Yes, ma'am."

Joe put on his hat, then walked outside to see Major Ross.

Ross saluted as Joe approached. "I've had the regimental clerk prepare the books for you, if you are ready to assume the command now," Ross said.

"Yes, thank you," Joe replied. "But before I do that, I would like to take a look at one of the barracks, if you don't mind."

"I'll have the sergeant major select one for you," Ross suggested.

"Never mind, I'll pick it myself."

Ross smiled. "Trying to see if you can catch them off

guard, are you? Well, I tell you true, it won't make any difference which barracks you choose, it's going to be clean. Folks can say what they want about Colored people, Colonel Murchison, but I'm here to tell you that I've never served with finer soldiers."

"Let's look in this one," Joe suggested, pointing to one of the long, T-shaped buildings.

Because the soldiers were at drill, only the barracks orderly was in the building when Joe stepped through the door. The orderly was polishing a rifle rack, and when Joe and Ross entered, he walked up to them, stopped, and saluted sharply.

"Sir, Trooper Evandale reporting the barracks ready for inspection," he said.

"How did you know I was going to inspect?" Joe asked.

"I didn't know, sir," Evandale replied. "But the barracks is always ready for inspection."

Evandale wasn't lying. The barracks was immaculate. The white adobe walls were clean, the wooden floor was waxed, and the twelve double-stacked bunks on either side of the room were perfectly aligned, with the U.S.-embossed, blue-gray army blankets pulled so tightly over the thin cotton mattresses that Joe knew he could bounce a coin on them. The barracks was heated by two stoves sitting on brick pads, one at each end of the room. It being summer now, the stoves were cold, and spotlessly clean. The uniform issue was neatly folded on shelves above the beds.

"Carry on, Evandale; the barracks is in order," Joe said.

"Thank you, sir," Evandale replied, saluting.

"Now, Major Ross, I am ready to sign the property books," Joe said as they walked back across the post to the headquarters building.

Inside the headquarters building, the regimental clerk already had the books spread out. The regimental clerk was a young, thin black man with rimless glasses.

"What is your name, Corporal?" Joe asked as he began looking over the books.

"Sylvester, sir. Corporal Sigmund J. Sylvester."

Joe looked at the books. "Did you prepare these, Corporal?"

"I did, sir."

"Very impressive. Your penmanship is excellent."

"Thank you, sir."

"Corporal Sylvester has a Ph.D. from Columbia University," Ross pointed out.

Joe looked at Sylvester in surprise.

"You have a Ph.D. and you're a corporal in the army?"

"Yes, sir, well, there aren't a large number of positions for Negro doctorates. And I'm afraid the army isn't ready for Negro officers, as evidenced by the dismissal of Lieutenant Flipper."

"Henry Flipper. Yes, I've heard of him. He was the first Colored graduate of West Point—though he was discharged for embezzlement, I believe?"

"He was cleared of the embezzlement charges." Sylvester said. "Think about it, Colonel. He survived four years of the silent treatment at West Point to become the first Negro officer. Do you really think he would risk that to steal a few measly dollars from the mess fund? He was kicked out of the army for being Colored."

"Enough of that, Sylvester. He was kicked out for conduct unbecoming an officer and a gentleman," Ross said. The major looked at Joe. "He went horseback riding with a young white woman. I cautioned him against it, but he wouldn't listen. It's a shame, too, because he was one of the most brilliant young officers I had ever met."

"What is he doing now?" Joe asked.

"I believe he is a surveyor with an American land company down in Mexico," Ross said.

"I hope he does well," Joe said. He picked up a pen then and began signing the property books. First came the "station property," which meant all buildings, bedding, lockers, rifle racks, stoves, outhouses, and accoutrements of the post itself. Then he signed for the "Table of Organization and Equipment" property, meaning the weapons, tools, saddles, horses, wagons, and equipage used by the men. Finally, he signed the roster report, assuming command of 1,273 officers and men. Each time he signed, his signature was counter-signed by Major Ross, after which Corporal Sylvester took the book and put it away. When it was all done, Ross stood up and rubbed his hands together.

"Well, now," he said. "I would say this calls for a drink, wouldn't you?" He pulled a bottle of whiskey from a cubbyhole and poured himself a very generous portion. When he started to pour for Joe, Joe took the bottle and poured just a splash into his own cup.

"Come, you can do better than that," Ross said.

"It's a little early in the day for me," Joe said without actually condemning Ross.

"Yes, well, wait until you've been out here a while," Ross said. He raised the glass. "To absent comrades," he said.

"To absent comrades," Joe echoed.

That night a chorus gathered just outside Joe's house and began singing. Their voices blended beautifully, and Joe, Tamara, and Todd came out to sit on the front porch and listen. The chorus sang half a dozen songs, concluding with "The Battle Hymn of the Republic."

"Being a southern girl, I never thought I could get teary eyed over that song," Tamara admitted. "But I don't think I have ever heard anything sung so touchingly."

Two Weeks Later

"Raise the right side up a little, would you, Mrs. Kelly?" Elaine Holt directed. In honor of Joe's assumption of command, the officers and ladies of Fort Canfield were planning a dance. Mrs. Holt, the wife of the post surgeon, was in charge of the event, and she was directing the other officers' wives as they decorated the officers' mess. Charlene Kelly was the wife of one of the battalion commanders. "There, that looks nice, don't you think?"

"Yes, I think it is very lovely," Tamara replied.

"I realize it's nothing like the fine parties you no doubt attended while in Washington, but we do what we can out here."

"I'm sure it will be a wonderful party," Tamara said.

"Tell me, Mrs. Murchison," Mrs. Holt said as the ladies continued to work, "I have been dying to ask. What was Custer like? One hears so much about him, but it's difficult to separate the fact from the fancy."

"You would have to ask my husband that," Tamara replied.

"But I thought you met him."

"I did, though only for the briefest time. From that short period I would have to say that he struck me as a wonderfully charming man. I was a houseguest of the Custers when he left for that last, awful scout."

The other women gasped. "You mean you were with Mrs. Custer when she received the news of her husband's death?"

"Yes. Not only her husband, but three brothers-in-law and one nephew-in-law, as well."

"It must have been devastating to her."

"It was, but she scarcely had time to grieve, so busy was she in comforting the others who had lost loved ones." Tamara was silent for a moment. "One of those lost was my father," she added.

"Oh, dear me. I . . . I had no idea," Mrs. Holt said. "How terrible to bring up such a tragedy now. Please forgive me."

Tamara smiled. "There is nothing to forgive. Given the nature of the event, it is a subject that has been discussed in my presence many, many times."

"I'm sure it has," Mrs. Holt said. "No, no, don't put any bunting there," she suddenly called out to one of the other ladies, interrupting her conversation with Tamara. "I intend to fill that space with a picture of President Cleveland."

"What about the regimental colors?"

"Over there, in the corner," Mrs. Holt answered. Then, turning back to Tamara. "Now, you won't forget to ask the colonel to designate mess dress for the officers?"

"I won't forget," Tamara promised.

Mrs. Holt smiled. "I do believe this will be the most gala event we have ever had here."

At the very moment the ladies were decorating the mess, First Sergeant Deacon Travis was leading a detail of fourteen men on a routine patrol. For the last several minutes they had been following Prospect Creek. Travis held up his hand to bring the patrol to a halt. He was chewing tobacco, and he leaned over to expectorate, then wiped the back of his hand across his chin.

"Trooper Webb, why don't you hand me that fancy spyglass you got tucked away in your saddle boot?" he asked.

"Do you see somethin', First Soldier?"

"Not exactly," Travis answered. "But I been chasin' Injuns ever since I come here from the War of Freedom, and I know that you don't always see 'em. Sometimes you just feel 'em. And I been feelin' 'em now for the better part of an hour."

Webb pulled the telescope from his saddle boot and handed it to Travis. "Here it is, Sarge. Be careful an' don't break it. I got my name signed for—"

The singing *swoosh* of an arrow cut him off. It made a hollow *thock* as it hit Webb's saddle. The arrow stuck and the shaft quivered right in front of his leg. Webb, struck dumb for just an instant by the shock of the near miss, looked at it in surprise. His horse nervously jumped once, though it had not been hit.

"There they are!" one of the other troopers shouted. A band of Apaches came swooping over the crest of a hill, whooping and shouting at the top of their lungs. Travis didn't take time to count them, though he estimated there were about thirty in the band.

"Let's get out of here!" he shouted, slapping his heels against the flanks of his horse, urging it on. They raced along the bank of Prospect Creek, occasionally slipping down into the water itself and sending up sheets of spray.

Travis led the troopers out of the creek bed and onto
flat terrain to an area large enough to allow him to
swing his men around. At first it was unclear to the
others what he was doing; then they realized that their
sergeant had, by describing a large circle, turned the
rout into an attack. The Indians realized it at about the
same time. They wheeled about in confusion and
started to retreat themselves.

"Let's go get them!" Travis shouted. He charged after the confused, retreating Indians, urging his horse
on faster and faster. He rapidly drew closer to the Indians, though he was also pulling away from his own
men. Within a short time he was abreast with the rear
ranks of the Indians.

The Indians had abandoned all thought of attack
and were now fleeing for their lives. They turned their
rifles on Travis and fired, the bullets buzzing by his
head angrily. Travis pulled his pistol, took slow and deliberate aim, fired, then watched as his target tumbled
from the saddle. The Indians broke up, scattering in
every direction like a covey of quail. After that, it was
no longer possible to pursue them as a body, so Travis
broke off the charge, regrouped his men, and started
them back toward the fort.

"Whooeee, First Soldier! You are one kind of soldier
man!" Webb said admiringly, and the others echoed
the sentiment.

It was time for retreat, and the regiment had turned
out onto the parade ground for the ceremony. Joe received the reports from the battalion commanders,
then turned toward the flag. At the flagpole a sergeant
was standing tall and straight, staring at his pocket
watch with his hand up. A three-man gun crew stood
by the cannon, awaiting the sergeant's signal. At the
precise hour of five, the sergeant brought his hand
down sharply. The cannon fired with a flash and boom;
then, while the smoke was still drifting across the
parade ground, the trumpeter played retreat, and the
flag was lowered.

Out of the corner of his eye Joe could see Tamara

and Todd standing on the porch of their quarters with their hands across their hearts as the flag was lowered. Tamara had been a part of the military for almost ten years now, and Joe knew that the retreat ceremony was one she had come to love.

Shortly after the ceremony, as Joe was walking back to the headquarters building, he heard a call being passed from the front gate.

"Corporal of the guard! Patrol returning!"

Joe turned to watch as the riders came through. They rode to the center of the parade ground, then stopped. Sergeant Travis gave the orders dismissing the detail; then he dismounted and gave the reins of his horse to one of the other soldiers. Joe walked out to meet him.

"We engaged the Injuns this afternoon, Colonel," Travis reported. "We killed one, but the rest got away."

"Did you sustain any casualties?"

"None, sir."

"How many were there?"

"About thirty, I'd say."

Joe stroked his chin. "That's more than we've seen for a while, isn't it?"

"Yes, sir, it is. Looks like Keytano is gettin' a few more of the young bucks to follow him."

"Maybe we had better increase the number of patrols we're running," Joe suggested. "Also, starting immediately, we will provide escort details for the stage runs."

"Yes, sir," Travis replied, saluting.

All the ladies agreed, the officers' mess had never looked more festive than it did that night. Bunting in red, white, and blue was hanging from every wall, and streamers of the same colors flowed from the center of the ceiling to each corner. A long table, drawn to one side of the room, was covered with white linen and set with plates of sandwiches, dried fruits, cookies, and cakes. A large, cut-glass punch bowl, filled with a fruit-juice concoction that had been liberally spiked with several different types of blended whiskey, dominated the center of the table.

The regimental band sat on a raised dais, their instruments gleaming brightly in the reflected glow of candles affixed to their music stands. Additional illumination was provided by kerosene lamps so that the mess was ablaze with light. Several soldiers, acting as strikers, moved through the mess attending to the needs of the officers and their ladies. The officers were wearing their mess-dress uniforms, while the women were garbed in their finest ball gowns.

Joe was wearing the Medal of Honor, won for his performance of duty at the Little Big Horn. *"At great personal risk, Captain Murchison made repeated trips back into Indian territory to locate the wounded and disoriented and lead them to safety,"* the citation read.

In addition to the Medal of Honor, Joe also wore the Croix de Guerre, given to him by France during his time there. It had required special permission from the War Department to wear it, and Joe would have never requested such permission, but his duty in Washington caused him to have frequent contact with members of the French embassy, and it was they who had made the request on Joe's behalf.

As the dance went on into the night, it was obvious that everyone present was enjoying it. Major Ross was in a corner, nearly insensate from drink but with the excuse that this was a party. Tamara danced not only with her husband but also with the young, single officers, as did the other ladies of the post. The sharing of wives during such dances was not at all suspect, for it was expected of the wives to dance every dance to make the bachelor officers' plight on the frontier a bit easier.

Joe was standing on the side, watching the activities, when a civilian approached him.

"Colonel Murchison, I'm Avery Thorpe. Welcome to the Arizona Territory."

"Mr. Thorpe," Joe said. "I believe you are the Indian agent?"

"Yes. I'm sorry I haven't had the opportunity to

meet you before now, but I've been conducting some business in Tucson. What do you think of our country out here?"

"Very impressive," Joe replied.

There was a commotion in the corner at that moment, and Joe looked over to see that Major Ross, in attempting to stand up, had pulled off the tablecloth, upsetting the punch bowl.

"Sorry, ladies. My most humble apology," Ross said. He belched, then staggered out of the room.

"I don't mind telling you, Colonel, I'm glad we have been sent another officer to replace that drunken sot," Thorpe said.

Alcoholism was one of the major problems facing the army—particularly the Army of the West—and Joe disapproved heartily of anyone who was intemperate in that area. However, Major Ross was a fellow officer and Thorpe was a civilian, and even greater than Joe's distaste for intemperance was his dislike of an outsider criticizing one of his own. Joe looked at Thorpe with an expression that bespoke his feelings.

"If you will excuse me, Mr. Thorpe, I think I will see if Major Ross requires any assistance," he said coolly.

Joe walked away from the civilian, then stepped outside. The music and the lights were behind him as he walked out to the end of the porch to look for Major Ross.

"Good evenin', sir," a voice said. First Sergeant Deacon Travis seemed to materialize from the darkness. He was holding a salute and Joe returned it.

"Good evening, First Sergeant," he said. Joe studied the darkness, looking for Major Ross.

"Is the colonel having a good time?"

"Yes, yes, very good, thank you," Joe said, almost disinterestedly. Where could Ross have gotten to so quickly?

The unasked question was answered when he saw two troopers pulling a Gatling gun caisson. The gun had been removed, and Major Ross was lying on a board frame that was stretched across the caisson. Ross raised his head. "First Sergeant Travis?"

"Yes, sir, I'm right here."

"You have my appreciation, First Sergeant," he mumbled. He lay his head back again.

"I also appreciate your looking after him," Joe said. "And I would like to add my apology, as well. There is no excuse for an officer to appear in such a state before enlisted men."

"Beggin' your pardon, Colonel, but Major Ross don't need no one apologizin' for him," Travis said.

The remark was uncharacteristically challenging, and Joe looked at Travis in surprise.

"Don't mean to be disrespectful, sir," Travis said quickly. "It's just that I don't think the colonel understands. You see, sir, Major Ross just drinks to escape the devils chasin' after him, and I don't know no man who has greater cause."

"You were waiting out here for him, weren't you?" Joe asked, just now realizing the obvious. "This must be old hat for you. As a matter of fact, I believe you had the caisson modified for just this purpose."

"Yes, sir, that's the truth of it."

"Well, I find your loyalty commendable, First Sergeant, but I don't think retrieving an intoxicated officer is the correct utilization of men or equipment."

"No, sir, it may not be correct," Travis said. "But it be right. Colonel, you ever heard of a place called Stinking Pond?"

"I can't say that I have," Joe replied. "And from the sound of it, I'm not sure I'd want to."

"Well, I reckon that all depends on how thirsty you be. You see, out here in these parts, a man can get mighty thirsty. And if you happen on to a pond, even one that stinks of sulphur, you'll drink it an' be glad of it. And if water be scarce enough, it's a place a man will fight an' die for.

"Back ten years ago, a bunch of Apaches left the reservation and started spreadin' their mischief aroun', burnin' a ranch here, killin' a few miners an' prospectors there—the kind of thing they're good at doin'. Wasn't enough of 'em to justify sendin' out more'n a company, so Colonel Merrit—he was our regimental commander then—he sent out A Troop. I wasn't the First Sergeant back then, but I was in A Troop. The troop commander was Major Ross, only then he was a cap'n.

"The Apaches know'd we was out after 'em, and they also know'd we'd have to stop at Stinkin' Pond, bein' as that was the only water for fifty or sixty miles in any direction. So, they was waitin' for us. They hit us pretty good. We got three good men killed right off, and four more was wounded. We pulled back to some rocks, but we couldn't get our wounded out in time, so the Apaches took 'em. One they took was our first sergeant. The Apaches staked 'em out in front of us and they skint First Sergeant DuBois—alive. First Sergeant DuBois screamed somethin' terrible before he died, and we had to listen to 'im.

"Well, sir, it bothered all of us, but it didn't bother none of us more'n it did Cap'n Ross. Him bein' the commander and all, he figured he was responsible for his first sergeant gettin' kilt that way. So Cap'n Ross tied a white flag to the end of his saber and walked down to see couldn't he make a deal with the Injuns. He told 'em how he was our chief, and how killin' him would be bigger medicine than killin' the three soldiers they was holdin'. Do you understan' what I'm sayin', Colonel? Cap'n Ross traded himself for the three troopers the Injuns hadn't started killin' yet. A white officer, doin' that for three Colored privates."

"So what happened? The Indians didn't accept his offer?"

"Oh, yes, sir, they accepted all right. Trooper Webb, you know him, Colonel. He was one of the three privates they was holdin'."

"Then how is it that—"

"That the major ain't dead?" Travis finished the question for Joe.

"Yes."

"The only reason he ain't dead now is 'cause the Injuns wanted to kill him slow. So they tortured him all the rest of that day—cuttin' on 'im here, burnin' 'im there. And there was nothin' we could do about it.

Come night, though, we was able to sneak down on 'em." Travis smiled. "Us buffalo soldiers got a special knack for not bein' seen in the dark," he interjected. "And it helped that it wasn't a real Apache war party. It wasn't nothin' but a bunch of young bucks without a leader. They was outlaws, even to their own people. We was able to surprise 'em, and I don't mind tellin' you, Colonel, we wasn't in no prisoner-takin' mood, if you know what I mean. We killed 'em all, an' we cut Major Ross free."

"I can see how such an ordeal could be unsettling for the major," Joe said.

"Yes, sir, only you don't know the half of it yet, Colonel. You see, Cap'n Ross was engaged to be married. She was a general's daughter, as pretty as a spring flower. She'd already come out here for the big weddin' they was to have, an' ever'one was lookin' forward to the big event. Only . . ."

Travis fell silent.

"What?" Joe asked. "What happened? Did the girl change her mind?"

"No sir, Major Ross changed his mind. You see, Colonel, when the Apaches was torturin' the major, one of the things they done was to cut off the part of him that makes a man a man."

"You mean the Indians *castrated* Major Ross?"

"No, sir. They left his balls on. What they done was cut off his pecker."

"Good Lord!"

"After that, the major couldn't face the woman he was goin' to marry, so he sent her back to her papa. That's when he started drinkin'. Don't get me wrong, Colonel. I ain't sayin' the major was a teetotaler before. I'm just sayin' that the devil didn't have ahold of 'im then quite like he does now."

"I'm glad you told me the story, First Sergeant. I didn't know."

"He done that for us, Colonel. For three Colored troopers. Consequential, they ain't a man jack in the entire Ninth who wouldn't soak his drawers in kerosene and ride to hell to kick the devil in the ass for the Major. Now, by your leave, sir, I think I'll go check that he got put in bed all right."

"Yes, by all means. And good night, First Sergeant," Joe said.

"Good night, sir," Travis said, saluting again, then disappearing quickly into the darkness.

It was a week later when Tamara walked across the breezeway that separated the commandant's living quarters from the headquarters building, carrying a letter the mail clerk had delivered that morning. She went into Joe's office, smiling and holding it out for him to see.

"We got a letter from Sally today," she said. "She sent a picture of her son."

"Did she, now? Well, let me see it."

The picture showed a young boy, wearing a velvet suit, holding a wooden saber, and standing by the head of a small pony. On the back was written FRANKLIN DELANO ROOSEVELT, AGE 4.

Joe took out the letter.

My dear friends Tamara and Joe:

Please accept my apology for waiting so long before answering your last letter. My husband, James, has been so actively engaged in politics of late that I have been busy hosting receptions. Democratic politics. Can you imagine that, Joe, Republican that I once was? But, even poor Republican papa agrees that a wife's duty is to her husband. Tamara, you can understand that, I am sure. Are you not now facing the rigors of frontier life?

I must confess that though I admire your courageous spirit and envy you your adventure, I do not feel I would be able to accommodate myself to such rigorous living conditions as you must face. I much prefer the conveniences of indoor plumbing, streetcars, gaslights, and the telephone. I shall, however, continue to enjoy your experiences vicariously—and in comfort.

I wish I could see Todd. He must be quite the little man now. I have enclosed a picture of young Franklin. This week he announced that he wants to be a soldier, though last week it was the sailor's life that held his interest. Who knows what his future shall be? Whatever it is, his father and I intend to see that he has every advantage. We are taking him to Europe next year, for James says it is never too early for a person to learn of the world.

Joe, so many years have gone by since the rash young girl added her name to the dance card at the Cadet Graduation Ball. How upset you were with me then! But what friends we have become over the years. Now, of course, our letters are much fewer and farther between, but this is as it should be, as we have each found a loving mate with whom to share our lives. That these wonderful people accept our unique relationship—and understand the innocence of our many years of exchanged intimacies—speaks eloquently for their character, and makes us love them all the more.

                         Your friend,
                         Sally Delano Roosevelt

Eighteen

Tamara Murchison, Elaine Holt, and Charlene Kelly were in the small town of Mule Pass on a shopping excursion, having made the twenty-mile trip from Fort Canfield in the commanding officer's special coach, escorted by six troopers. They were looking at hats when a rather smallish man with a gray beard came into the shop to ask if they were from the fort.

"Yes," Tamara answered. "We are."

"The name is Riley, ma'am. Did them six niggers come in with you?"

"Our coach was escorted by six Colored troopers, if that's what you mean," Tamara replied coolly.

"Yes, ma'am. Well, the reason I ask was 'cause one of 'em's been hurt real bad."

"Hurt? What happened? Was there an accident?" Tamara asked.

"Weren't no accident. Fella by the name of Martin Clay shot him in the leg. Busted his kneecap up real bad."

"Where is he?" Tamara asked.

"He's down at Pike's Palace. It's a saloon at the end of the street."

Tamara started out the door.

"Ma'am, I wouldn't recommend you goin' there," Riley said, stepping in front of her. "It ain't a fit place for ladies."

"Mr. Riley, would you please get out of my way?" Tamara asked.

"Mrs. Murchison, you aren't actually going to go into that place, are you?" Charlene Kelly asked.

"If one of our troopers is in there, then, yes, I am going. You and Mrs. Holt don't have to go with me, but I would appreciate it if you would locate a doctor and the sheriff."

"Ain't no doctor any closer'n Tombstone, ma'am," Riley said. "And Sheriff Pike owns Pike's Palace. He's there now."

"Come along, Charlene. We can't let the wife of the commanding officer go in there alone," Elaine Holt said.

"All right," Charlene said weakly.

Tamara and the other two ladies swept down the boardwalk toward Pike's Palace, holding their skirts up as they crossed the two streets that bisected Main Street. Seeing officers' ladies walking with such determined steps—and toward the least respectable establishment in the entire town—aroused everyone's curiosity, so that by the time Tamara reached the batwing doors, she was leading not only the other two women but quite an entourage of townsfolk.

Inside, the saloon was already crowded, though strangely silent. Most of the men were standing around looking down at the black trooper, who was lying on the saloon floor in a fetal position, holding his bloody knee. His light-brown face was twisted in pain, but he was making no sound. The other five troopers were standing near the wall, in handcuffs.

Tamara went immediately to the soldier's side, kneeling down beside him without regard to the filthy floor.

"Yo' dress, ma'am," the soldier said in a strained voice. "You goin' to get all dirty."

"Never mind the dress," Tamara said. She reached out lightly to touch his knee and saw him wince, even at that slight touch.

"Now, ain't that tender?" a sibilant voice said. Tamara looked up to see a rather smallish civilian with a drooping mustache and cold, beady eyes.

"What happened here?" Tamara asked. She tore a

strip off the bottom of her petticoat, then began bandaging the young soldier's wound.

"The nigger was dancing for drinks," the man explained. "I poured him a drink, but he wouldn't dance —so I shot him."

"You . . . you shot a man because he wouldn't *dance* for you?" Tamara sputtered in barely repressed rage.

"You might call it a contract. I give 'im the drink he asked for, but he wouldn't dance."

"Ma'am," one of the soldiers said, "he spit a big old wad of tobacco in the glass before he give it to Trooper Whitehead."

"You boys keep quiet over there or I'll have you all in jail," another man said. He was a large man with silver hair and a pockmarked face. He was wearing a badge.

"Who are you?" Tamara asked, looking up at him.

"I'm Sheriff Pike, Mrs. Murchison," the man said, touching the brim of his hat. "At your service."

"You know who I am?" Tamara asked, surprised that Pike had called her by name.

"It's my business to know who comes into my town."

Tamara finished applying the bandage and stood up. "Sheriff Pike, would you tell me why these soldiers are in handcuffs while the man who shot Trooper Whitehead is free?"

"I figure what went on between Mr. Clay and the nigger was their own private disagreement," Pike said. "I don't meddle into private disagreements. Hell, if I did, that's all I'd be doin'." He laughed, and several of the other patrons laughed with him. "But then these boys started to butt in, an' I figured I'd better act quick, else things could turn into a riot."

"You have no right to hold them."

"That's where you're wrong, Mrs. Murchison. Your husband might be the high and mighty over at Fort Canfield, but I am in charge of this here town and of anyone who comes into it, includin' soldiers." Pike took out a handkerchief and blew his nose. "Howsomever, seein' as I'm feelin' real bad 'bout the trooper gettin' hurt an' all, I'm goin' to turn these boys loose into your custody. That is, provided you get 'em out of town real fast, before they get into any more trouble."

"Take the handcuffs off them now," Tamara said sternly. "You men, load Trooper Whitehead into the coach. We'll take him to the post hospital."

"No, ma'am," Whitehead said. "I couldn't be ridin' in the colonel's coach. It wouldn't be fittin'."

"Nonsense."

"No, ma'am," Whitehead insisted again. "I couldn't do that, ma'am."

"All right, if you won't ride inside, will you ride on top of the coach?"

"Yes, ma'am, I reckon I could do that, all right," Whitehead agreed.

By now the handcuffs had been removed from the other five soldiers, and they stood there rubbing their wrists. Tamara noticed that the restraints had not been applied very gently, for a couple of the men were bleeding at the wrists. She nodded at them.

"Please put Trooper Whitehead on top of the coach," she said. "And let's go home."

"Yes, ma'am," one of the others said. "Let's go home."

"What did you say the man's name was?" Joe asked. "The one who shot Trooper Whitehead?"

"Clay. Martin Clay."

"I've heard that name," Joe said.

"I don't doubt it," Major Ross put in. "Trooper Whitehead is lucky Clay only shot him in the leg. Martin Clay is one of the most notorious gunmen there is. Some say he's killed more men than Billy the Kid, and I wouldn't doubt the truth of that claim. He has certainly been around long enough. He started up in Dodge City, Kansas, back when the cattle had to be driven up there to the railhead."

"Kansas! Yes!" Joe said. "Troopers Eddie Quinn and Ben Daniels."

"Who are they?" Tamara asked.

"They were with the Seventh when we were at Fort

Hays," Joe explained. "They were killed by this man Clay. Over a bottle of whiskey, as I recall."

"Heavens, what kind of man would kill another man over a bottle of whiskey?"

"The same kind of man who would have no compunctions over crippling Trooper Whitehead for life."

"I'm sure Clay is the same man you're talking about," Major Ross agreed.

"But I don't understand. Someone with a record like that is bound to have paper out on him," Joe said. "Why doesn't Sheriff Pike arrest him?"

"Ha!" Major Ross replied. "Because Ross and Pike are business partners, that's why."

"Why would Pike ally himself with someone like Martin Clay?"

"Colonel, have you noticed something about Mule Pass . . . something that's different from all the other towns out here?"

"Nothing that leaps to mind," Joe admitted.

"Mule Pass has only one saloon. Can you imagine a cow town with only one saloon?"

"Now that you mention it, that does seem strange," Joe said.

"I assure you, Colonel, it is not because Mule Pass has a strong temperance union," Ross said. "It has only one saloon because Sheriff Pike, and his partner, Martin Clay, intimidate anyone else who might want to go into competition with them."

"I see. So, what about our soldiers? Have we had many incidents like the one with Whitehead?"

"With Pike? Quite a few," Ross said. "We had a civilian mule skinner killed there last year. The inquest held that it was self-defense. They claimed Hoskins had a pistol in his hand when Clay shot him. Only thing is, Hoskins never carried a pistol. He carried a Springfield rifle. And nobody who knew Hoskins had ever seen the pistol before."

"Why haven't you put the town off-limits?"

"Two years ago a band of Apaches left the reservation and started toward Mule Pass. We managed to get a troop of the Ninth Cavalry between the Indians and the town. The Apaches were stopped and the town was saved. There are still several people in town who remember that, and those people appreciate our soldiers, regardless of their color. They welcome our men and are decent to them. Besides, if the men didn't have the town to go to, they would be virtual prisoners out here."

"Then why haven't we put the *saloon* off-limits?"

"Colored troopers are no different from white troopers, Joe," Major Ross said, taking the liberty of his years to address a superior officer by his first name. "If they go into town, they'll want to go to a saloon, even if they are subject to the kind of mistreatment Whitehead suffered. If we put the saloon off-limits, some of the men will continue to go, and then we'll have succeeded in doing nothing but making violators out of our own men."

"Then we're going to close down the saloon," Joe said resolutely.

Major Ross shook his head. "I've tried that already," he said. "I've been to the United States marshal with no luck. And look, let me show you something on the map."

Responding, Joe walked over to the wall to look at the map.

"Do you see this dotted line here?" Major Ross pointed out. "That's the extreme northern border of the Canfield Reservation. As you can see, it cuts right through the south end of the town of Mule Pass. In fact, Pike's Palace is actually on our side of the line. I figured that would give us a reason to place the town under martial law, but when I went to General Miles, he turned me down. I'm afraid there is nothing we can do about it."

"I had no idea the Canfield range went that far north," Joe said. "It isn't that way on any of the maps in the War Department."

"No, sir, the War Department maps wouldn't show this. You'd have to check with the Department of Interior for that. You see, Canfield was laid out to be a reservation for the Chiricahua Apaches, but the Department of Indian Affairs decided to use San Carlos instead."

Tamara, who had been listening intently, now excused herself and returned to the house. Taking his own leave of Ross, Joe walked over to the post hospital to visit Trooper Whitehead.

"Tenhut!" someone shouted when Joe stepped into the ward. There were three troopers in the hospital in addition to Whitehead, and all of them tried to get up.

"As you were, as you were!" Joe said quickly, holding out his hand. Major Holt, the post surgeon, hurried over to report to Joe.

"How is Private Whitehead?" Joe asked.

"I got the bullet out, and it looks like I won't have to take off his leg," the surgeon said. "But the knee is going to lock solid. He's going to have a stiff leg for the rest of his life. His riding days are over."

Joe walked down to Whitehead's bed. He was surprised to see tears coming down Whitehead's face.

"Does it hurt?" Joe asked.

"Not much, sir," Whitehead replied.

Joe put his hand on Whitehead's shoulder. "Well, the surgeon tells me you won't be losing your leg. That's good news."

"Yes, sir," Whitehead said quietly. "That's good news."

Joe said a few words to the other patients, then left. The surgeon walked outside with him.

"I'll be giving him a medical discharge," Major Holt said. "But as his wound wasn't sustained in the line of duty, he won't be eligible for any kind of a pension."

"Who determines whether or not it was line of duty?" Joe asked.

"Why, we do. You and I," Major Holt answered.

"He was in Mule Pass as part of an escort detail, wasn't he?" Joe asked.

Major Holt smiled. "Yes, sir, I guess he was."

"Then he was there on duty, and his wound was sustained in the line of duty."

"Yes, sir, I'll concur with that."

As Joe returned to the headquarters building, he

looked out at the parade ground. The men of the Ninth were busy drilling, some on foot and some mounted. A couple of artillery crews were going through a dry-shooting exercise.

"Corporal Sylvester," Joe said when he stepped back into the office, "prepare a medical discharge for Trooper Whitehead. Line of duty."

"Yes, sir," Sylvester said glumly. He opened a drawer and pulled out some forms. "I suppose, all things considered, that's the best you can do for him."

Joe had started into his own office, but he stopped and looked back at Sylvester. "What do you mean? I'm stretching it to do this. What more would you have me do?"

"Colonel, I'm not certain you understand exactly what the Ninth Cavalry is to these men."

"I know they have an inordinate sense of esprit de corps," Joe said.

"It isn't just that, sir. To men like Trooper Whitehead, Trooper Webb, First Sergeant Travis . . ." Sylvester was quiet for a moment, then added, "and to me, the Ninth is more than just a military unit. It is our country, our home, our family—even our church. It is uniquely ours, and to have served, then be cast aside . . . It will mean the end of Whitehead, sir."

"Are you proposing that I keep him on active service?"

"You could do that, sir."

"Impossible. According to Major Holt, he will have only one serviceable leg. The other will be stiff."

"General Howard has only one arm, sir. The other one isn't stiff, it's gone. Of course, he is a white officer, whereas Trooper Whitehead is just a Negro enlisted man."

"That has nothing to do with it," Joe replied.

"Then why is General Howard still in active service with but one arm, sir? And, if we go back in history, General Benedict Arnold remained in active service with just one leg. And *he* was a traitor."

"Whitehead is an excellent mechanic, Colonel Murchison," Major Ross put in. "I'm sure we could find a use for him in the blacksmith shop."

Joe smiled. "All right," he said. "You win. White-head stays in the army."

"Thank you, sir," Sylvester said, grinning broadly as he put the forms away.

Joe laughed. "Sylvester, if I didn't know you better, I'd say you were just trying to get out of a little work."

"You've guessed my secret, sir."

Joe walked over to the window to look again at the drilling taking place on the quadrangle. Suddenly he turned to Ross.

"Owen, how often do we have actual firing exercises?"

"Beg your pardon, sir?"

Joe nodded toward the parade ground. "I was watching the gun crews out there going through the motions. That has to be boring after a while. How often do we actually let them fire the guns?"

"Generally no more than once or twice a year, sir. It's a matter of expending shot and powder."

"I want you to schedule a live-firing exercise."

"Yes, sir. When do you want it, sir?" Ross replied.

"Tonight."

"Tonight?"

"Yes, tonight," Joe said. "I want three guns and Troop . . . which is Whitehead's troop?"

"I don't know."

"Trooper Whitehead is in Troop G, sir," Sylvester answered.

"Prepare the orders, Sylvester," Ross ordered. "Troop G and three cannon will be engaged in firing exercises tonight."

"Yes, sir," Sylvester replied. "For the artillery, will that be half charges and flash shells?"

"Yes, of course," Ross answered.

"No," Joe said, quickly. "I want full charges and solid shot."

"Solid shot, sir?" Ross questioned. "With solid shot

at night, how will the men be able to see how they are shooting?"

"Don't worry. They'll be able to see clearly enough."

The live-firing detail was set to leave immediately after the retreat ceremony. There was always a lot of interest when there was going to be live firing, especially if the firing included artillery. Interest was even higher now because the exercise was going to take place at night. That was unusual, so after retreat those troopers who weren't actually involved in the upcoming detail were gathered on the parade ground to watch as G Troop led their horses out, then stood by. Even Trooper Whitehead, still in his bed, was brought out onto the parade grounds to watch the preparation and departure. By now word had spread all over the post that Colonel Murchison was not going to force Trooper Whitehead to leave the army, and the effect was electric. If possible, there was even more of a bounce in the steps and a gleam in the eyes of the men of the Ninth than there had been.

The three artillery pieces were brought out. These weren't the new Hotchkiss breechloaders, they were the old, smoothbore twelve-pounder Napoleons. They were, however, well-maintained, and they had proven their effectiveness throughout the Civil War.

"They're carryin' full charges and solid shot," someone said, noticing the ammo boxes.

"What? No flash shells? How they goin' to see where they hit?"

"Never mind that. They carryin' full charges. Why they doin' that?"

Questions and conjectures rippled through the ranks of the soldiers who had gathered to watch the detail depart. Wonder and excitement reached a fever pitch when they saw Colonel Murchison and Major Ross arrive—on horse and obviously ready to accompany the detail.

"What's the Colonel and the XO doin' out here?"

"Never seen no commandin' officer go out on a

night firin' detail before. Most especial the CO *and* the XO."

"Not only that, Cap'n Kelly, the battalion commander, is goin', too."

Captain Kelly reported to Joe.

"Sir, G Troop and the artillery detail are formed and ready."

"Very good, Captain Kelly. Lead them out."

"What is our destination, sir?"

"We're going north," Joe answered.

Some of the troopers gathered around watching were close enough to hear Colonel Murchison's orders. Surprised by the orders, they passed them on to the others. The firing range was south of the post, exactly opposite of the direction Joe gave. They asked each other what was going on.

By midnight the mystery of *where* they were going was solved when Joe brought the column to a halt about a quarter mile south of the hamlet of Mule Pass. But the mystery of *why* they were here remained.

A cloud passed over the moon, then moved away, bathing in silver the little town that rose up like a ghost before them. A couple of dozen buildings stretched out along the main north–south road, which trailed off into the desert on either end of town. The two crossroads in town each boasted two or three houses and no more. Clearly, the biggest and most impressive building of the town was Pike's Palace, a huge white building that stood at this end of town.

"Lieutenant Spooner!" Joe called.

"Yes, sir?" the artillery officer replied.

"Bring your guns on line, Mr. Spooner. Your target is that white building."

"I beg your pardon, sir?" Spooner asked, gulping.

"I didn't stutter, Lieutenant. I said your target is that white building. Bring the guns on line, load and aim them, but hold your fire until I give the word."

"Yes, sir."

"Captain Kelly?"

"Yes, sir."

"Do you know this town?"

"Yes, sir."

"What is the name of that first cross street, the one at this end of town?"

"That is South Street, sir."

"Very well, Captain. Take your troop into town. Enter the saloon and every building on this side of South Street. Enter by force, if need be. Get everyone out of the buildings and move them to the north side of that street. Then establish a skirmish line and allow no one to come south of it. When you have this end of the town cleared, get word back to me."

"Yes, sir."

"Lieutenant Spooner?"

"Yes, sir."

"Do you believe you can destroy just the white building, while limiting the damage to all other buildings in town?"

"Colonel, as we're using solid shot, we won't even break a window in the barbershop next door."

"I'll be holding you to that. Captain Kelly, move out."

"Yes, sir."

Kelly gave the orders to his troops, and, resolutely, they started down into the town.

"Colonel, are you ready for the repercussions of this?" Major Ross asked.

"You may enter your protest, Major Ross. I will duly note it."

"Protest? Hell no, I'm not entering a protest! As far as I'm concerned, we are utilizing Canfield property to conduct a legal firing exercise. The fact that we are firing at night might cause some inadvertent damage to a civilian building, but one would have to ask the question, What is a civilian building doing on military property in the first place?"

Joe watched through his binoculars as Captain Kelly, his two officers, and troop of cavalry, began moving the townspeople out of the buildings. As most of the residences were at the far end of town, there were not that many people involved. He saw four women leaving Pike's Palace. They were the whores who worked and lived there, and two of them were with all-night customers. The men were carrying their boots and trousers as they picked their way up the street prodded by the soldiers, their white longjohns shining brightly in the moonlight. The men were strangely quiet, but Joe could hear the complaints of the women, even from here.

A man and his wife and two kids came down the side stairs from the apartment over the barbershop. Two more men were moved out of the livery stable.

"Owen, do you know Pike or Clay on sight?" Joe asked.

"I know them," Ross replied. He was also studying the town through his binoculars. "But I don't see them."

A galloper came up from the town. He stopped in front of Joe.

"Captain Kelly's compliments, sir," he said. "This end of the town is evacuated."

"Very good. Return to Captain Kelly, have him pass the word that everyone is to keep their heads down. We will commence firing in three minutes."

"Yes, sir," the trooper said, pulling his horse around and galloping back into town.

"Lieutenant Spooner!" Joe called.

"Yes, sir?"

"Are your guns ready?"

"Loaded and ready, sir."

"At my command, commence firing, and continue to fire until the building is totally destroyed."

"Yes, sir!"

Joe watched the town through his binoculars. He saw that every trooper and those townsfolk who had been evacuated were safely out of the line of fire. He also checked very closely to make sure there was no one who had been missed. Seeing no one, he held his hand up.

For a long moment there was a vivid tableau: three twelve-pounder artillery pieces, each manned by a crew of four dark men silhouetted against a dark sky. Then Joe brought his hand down.

Before his hand even reached the bottom of its arc, the three guns roared as one, their booming report rolling out across the desert like thunder and, like thunder, returning from the hills in a roaring echo.

"Reload!" Spooner shouted, even as the three solid balls crashed into the side of Pike's Palace.

The heavy balls hit at approximately the same time. Their weight, plus the velocity, created an energy impact of several tons. The entire back side of the building caved in.

From the other end of town dogs began barking, and Joe heard a man's startled but indistinct shout. Here and there, lamps were lit.

"Fire!" Spooner ordered, and the second report was as coordinated as the first. This time the balls crashed into the roof, bringing it down and causing the side walls to fall inward.

"What the hell is going on here?" someone shouted. Even from this distance Joe could hear the anger and disbelief in the voice.

"There he is," Major Ross said, pointing to someone who was running up the street. "That's Pike! And that's Clay just behind him."

"Fire!" Spooner ordered again, and again the three cannons boomed as one. The last volley brought the front of the building crashing down as well, so that now there was nothing at all left of what had been Pike's Palace but a large pile of kindling. With the last volley, Pike and Clay were forced to dive for cover behind a watering trough.

Joe took a long look through his binoculars. As far as he could determine from up here, not one other building had suffered the slightest scratch.

"Cease fire," Joe ordered.

"Cease fire!" Spooner repeated.

"Let's ride down into town, Major Ross," Joe said. "I would like to meet Sheriff Pike and Mr. Clay."

The two officers mounted up, and when Joe and Ross reached the main street of town moments later, it was crowded with townspeople—men and women in their sleeping gowns and nightshirts, some with trousers pulled over long johns, some wearing boots and little else, and a few even treading through the horse manure piles in their bare feet. All had been awakened by the bombardment and were now out in the street to see what was going on. Pike and Clay were standing closest to Captain Kelly. Pike was screaming.

"What the hell is going on here? Do you know what you have done? You are going to hear from me about this! I'm not going to take this lying down! What is your name?" As Joe approached, Pike quit shouting, recognizing not the man, but the rank and realizing that he had been shouting at the wrong person.

"You must be Colonel Murchison," he said angrily.

"That's right," Joe replied as he dismounted. "And you must be Sheriff Pike."

"What are you going to do about this?" Pike shouted.

"I'm going to apologize. I'm really sorry we destroyed your building. It was an accident."

"An accident? *An accident?*" Pike sputtered, so enraged that he was nearly choking. "You come into a town and blow up a building with cannons, and you say it was *an accident*?"

"Yes," Joe replied easily. "We were conducting a night-firing exercise aimed at the extreme north end of our reservation. Of course, we had no idea a civilian building was there. We had no record of granting permission for such a structure."

"You're going to pay for this! I'm going to write to Washington, and you're going to pay for this!"

"I don't think so," Joe replied. "You see, I found a regulation today that allows me to set the rent for any property we lease to civilians. I have set the rent for the building you formerly occupied at ten thousand dollars per year. That means you owe the U.S. Government fifty thousand dollars in back rent. How soon can we expect payment?"

"*What?* You know I don't have that much money! Why, I'll bet there's not that much money in the whole Arizona Territory!"

"That's where you're wrong, Mr. Pike," Joe said.

"You see, there is that much money every payday at Fort Canfield. Money that could be spent in this town if the men were made welcome . . . and if they didn't have to put up with the likes of you and your hired gunman. But of course, if this town doesn't want the money of Colored troopers . . ."

"Keep your damn niggers and your niggers' money!" Pike shouted. "Just get the hell out of my town!"

"Hold on there, Pike!" one of the townspeople shouted. "The way I look at it, their money's the same color as anybody else's. If they want to come in, I say let 'em. Let 'em and be welcome."

"Pike, if there's any gettin' out of town to be done, I'd say it's you should be doin' the gettin'!"

"Yeah!" someone else yelled. "You been ridin' roughshod over too many folks for too long. Why don't you leave? We can get along fine with the buffalo soldiers if you ain't here."

Pike clenched and unclenched his fist several times in impotent rage. "All right," he finally said. "But I'm goin' to find another town. And if any of you folks who are supposed to be my friends and neighbors ever show up there, you'll have me to answer to."

"Kiss my royal arse, Pike!" someone shouted, and everyone laughed.

"Mr. Pike, the army regrets the damages to your building," Joe said. "And even though it sat on government property, and even though you are in arrears in rent, I want to be fair. I intend to see that you are adequately compensated for the damages. I should think two hundred dollars would cover it."

"Two hundred dollars?" Pike gasped. "Why, that wouldn't even buy the liquor that was lost!"

"Nevertheless, Mr. Pike, that is the offer. I have brought that sum with me. You may accept or decline."

"You brought it with you?" Pike shouted. He turned to the others. "Did you hear that? He brought the money with him! Now, why would he do that if he wasn't plannin' on this from the very beginning?"

"Oh, I didn't say I wasn't planning it, Mr. Pike," Joe

said easily. "Captain Kelly, have the trumpeter sound to horse. We are leaving."

"Yes, sir," Kelly replied.

Joe started toward his own horse when suddenly, and unexpectedly, he heard the bark of at least a dozen carbines. Spinning around quickly, he saw Martin Clay spread-eagled on his back, his arms thrown out to either side of him. Just out of his right hand, lying in a pile of recent manure, was his unfired pistol. He had been hit three times in the head and half a dozen or more times in the chest and stomach. His eyes were open and sightless.

"He had a bead on you, Colonel," one of the sergeants said. "We didn't have no choice. It was either him or you."

Joe looked down at Clay, noticing with some sense of ironic justification that his position was almost identical to that of the two troopers Clay had murdered back in Hays City so long ago.

"I'd say you did have a choice," Joe said as he mounted his horse. "And I'd say you made the right one."

★ ★ ★

Nineteen

"Pershing, sir. Second Lieutenant John J. Pershing. I have a letter from General Miles."

Joe took the proffered envelope from the lieutenant, then sat back in his chair to read. Noticing that the officer was still standing at attention, Joe said, "At ease, Lieutenant."

Pershing shifted his feet, then put his hands behind his back.

Commanding Officer
Fort Canfield, and Ninth Cavalry Reg't

Colonel Murchison:

May I have the honor of presenting to you, the bearer of this letter. He is Second Lieutenant John J. Pershing. Don't be deterred by the fact that he is only a second lieutenant. He is an officer of singular intelligence who possessed a degree even before he attended the academy. He was also cadet captain at the time of his graduation.

Lieutenant Pershing is an excellent linguist who speaks Apache. In addition, he is skilled in the use of the heliostat, by which messages can be sent across great distances through an arrangement of flashing mirrors.

As you know, the Apache chief Keytano is terrorizing all of southern Arizona. It is my intention

to put several troops of cavalry into the field, coordinating the movements and reports of Indians
by means of heliograph signals. I want you to put
at least three troops of the Ninth into the field as
soon as you can make them ready. Lieutenant
Pershing will be my liaison and your signal officer.

> Good luck,
> Nelson A. Miles
> Brig. Gen. Cmndg.

"What do you need from me, to accomplish your
mission, Lieutenant?" Joe asked.

"I have brought one man with me, sir," Pershing replied. "It would be better if I had another who could
read and send Morse code. I could teach such a person
to use the device, but I was told that, this being an all-
Colored unit, my chances of finding someone would be
small."

"Have you ever worked with Colored soldiers, Lieutenant?"

"Yes, sir," Pershing replied. "I also taught in an all-
Negro school in St. Louis, after I graduated from college and before I went to West Point. I'm sure I would
have no difficulty in teaching one of the Colored
soldiers to operate the device if he is otherwise qualified."

"Corporal Sylvester!" Joe called.

Sylvester came into Joe's office, then stood at attention.

"Corporal Sylvester, do you know anything about the
heliostat?"

"Yes, sir," Sylvester replied. "It is a means of sending messages, composed of alphanumeric characters set
in fixed signals, by the use of flashing mirrors."

Joe smiled. "Will he do, Pershing?"

"He'll do quite nicely, thank you," Pershing replied.

The next afternoon the entire regiment was turned out
in parade front to watch the three selected troops depart. Civilians, wives, children, and visitors to the fort
were also present.

Joe, who had decided to accompany the three troops, was on horseback under the flagpole, looking out over his command. It was a hot, dry afternoon, and for the moment there was absolute silence, save the snapping and popping of the garrison flag flying high overhead.

"Major Ross, post!" Joe called, and Major Ross rode to the front of the formation to take his position. "Major Ross, in my absence you have command of the garrison."

"Very good, sir!" Ross replied, saluting smartly.

Joe stood in his stirrups. "Troops B, D, and G. Column of fours. Right flank!"

"Right flank!" the troop commanders echoed. The guidons were raised. For a while troop guidons were swallowtail versions of the national flag, such as were carried by the Seventh Cavalry when they rode to the Little Bighorn. Recently, however, the national flag design had been replaced by the same type of pennant the cavalry had carried during the Civil War. Still swallowtailed, it was white on top and red on bottom, embossed with crossed sabers and the number of the regiment, and the letter of the troop.

"Ho!" Joe shouted.

The guidons were brought down smartly, and the troops moved out. The band began playing. At Joe's request, the first song played was "Garryowen," and though the Ninth Cavalry had no particular attachment to the song, the band played it as spiritedly as Joe had ever heard it played by the Seventh Cavalry band.

The three troops paraded smartly around the square and passed in review before the regiment, the band, and the assembled civilians. As Joe passed his quarters, he saw Tamara and Todd standing outside. Todd was in the uniform Tamara had made for him, and he was holding a salute. With a smile, Joe returned his son's salute. He saw Tamara smiling bravely at him, and he nodded at her. He knew she was recalling that day, ten years ago, when the Seventh had marched so smartly and self-confidently out of Fort Lincoln with Custer at its head. She must be feeling some apprehension about this scout. He wished there were some way he could relieve her anxiety, but there was not. He knew, however, that Tamara would handle it all right. That was part of being a soldier's wife.

Two days later they came upon the Quigatoa Mountains, a long, steep spine that ran north and south for a distance of thirty miles. This was known to be one of the Apache routes into Mexico. They would cross into Arizona, raid farms and small towns, then retreat across the Mexican border, where they enjoyed immunity from American reprisals. The only way to strike back was to catch the Apache on the American side of the border.

"If we go up the east side and they're on the west, they'll be able to cross over into Mexico and there won't be anything we can do about it," Captain Kelly said.

"Same thing if we go up the west side and they're on the east," Captain Colby replied.

"Colonel Murchison," Pershing spoke up, "if I may make a suggestion, sir?"

"I'm always open for suggestions, Mr. Pershing."

"If you would divide your troop into two elements, you could send one group up the west side and the other up the east side. We could put a signalman with each group and a third on top of the mountain ridge, moving in coordination with the two elements on the valley floor. If one element should encounter the Indians, they can signal the others."

"Lieutenant Pershing, that is a great idea," Joe agreed. "Captain Kelly, you take G Troop and half of D Troop and go up the east side. Captain Colby, you take the remaining troop up the west side. If either of you encounter the Indians, make an attempt to push them to the north end of the range, at which time we will have them trapped between us. Corporal Sylvester, First Sergeant Travis, you come with me. We're going to be the ones on top of the mountain."

* * *

It took them two hours to reach the top of the mountain. They had their horses, but the trail was so steep as to make it necessary for them to dismount so that the horses could make it. They got some relief from the constant climbing by being able to hold on to the tails of the animals. Finally they reached the top, then sat on a rock, winded from the exertion.

Sylvester, being the youngest of the three, recovered his wind first, and he walked over to look down at the eastern side of the mountain.

"Do you see them?" Joe asked.

"Yes, sir, they're moving up the valley now."

"Good." Joe walked over to look down at the western side to see the other half moving, as well.

"Send the signal that we are up here and monitoring both groups," Joe said.

Quickly, Sylvester set up the equipment, flashed a signal down to Captain Colby, and then to Captain Kelly. Joe stood alongside, watching the winking lights from below. Sylvester laughed.

"What is it?" Joe asked.

"I'd rather not say, sir."

"What did they say, Corporal?"

"Captain Kelly said he was surprised you could make it up here, old as you are."

"Oh, he did, did he? You tell him—" Joe abruptly stopped. "Never mind, I'll tell him myself when I see him again. Take up your equipment, Sylvester. Let's move out."

"Yes, sir."

With the setting of the sun four hours later, they were no longer able to exchange messages. In the last few messages they were able to exchange, Joe ordered both elements to halt in place and to post sentries. If they blundered into the Apaches in the dark, they would have no way of coordinating their attack.

Joe was up before sunrise the next morning. Remembering the trick Sergeant Todd had taught him long ago, he started searching the horizon. Then, on the east side of the range, about fifteen miles north of

Captain Kelly's column, he saw a little sun flare of dust.

"Corporal Sylvester?" he called.

"Yes, sir?"

"Signal Captain Kelly that the Indians are ten miles in front of him. Then signal Captain Colby to start moving up with all deliberate speed."

"Yes, sir," Sylvester said, preparing his instrument. Sergeant Travis walked up beside Joe.

"Colonel, I thought I had pretty good eyes, but you're better'n I am. I don't see a thing."

Joe chuckled, then explained Todd's theory of being able to catch a light flare from dust just at sunrise or sunset.

"Yes, sir! I do see 'em now!" Travis said when he located the flare.

"Colonel, Captain Kelly wants to know if we are going to join him now," Sylvester said.

"Tell him to start moving," Joe replied. "We'll join him at the north end of the range. I think we'd best stay up here where we can continue to be in contact with both sides."

"Yes, sir." Sylvester sent the signal, then struck his equipment.

Packing their horses, they started north along the spine of the mountain.

It was nearly noon. Twice, Joe had sent or relayed messages between the two elements down on the valley floor. When they reached a saddle between two peaks, they stopped for lunch. Joe was just reaching for a strip of beef jerky when there was a singing sound, followed by a sudden, excruciating pain in his right thigh. Looking down in surprise, he saw an arrow shaft sticking out of his leg. A rapidly spreading pool of blood began spilling down the leg of his blue kersey trousers.

Joe was about to shout a warning, but before he could even call out, a second arrow hit his horse in the neck. The horse went down, falling on Joe's injured leg and trapping him underneath.

Four Indians came over the peak from just ahead.

They were screaming and yelling as they charged toward him, firing wildly. Joe tried to get to one of his weapons, only to discover he couldn't reach either one. The pistol was in its holster on his right side, pinned to the ground. The rifle was in the saddle holster, pinned under the horse.

Joe heard two pistol shots and saw two of the Indians go down. Twisting around, he saw that Travis and Sylvester had managed to get their pistols out. Two more shots brought down a third Indian. The fourth turned and ran back over the rise in front of them.

"Colonel! Are you all right?" Travis shouted, kneeling beside him.

"Get me out from under this horse," Joe grunted.

Both Travis and Sylvester began working to get Joe clear from his horse. While they were thus engaged, four more Indians suddenly appeared from the same place as before. Travis and Sylvester used the carcass of Joe's dead horse for cover as they returned fire. Then, behind them, they heard the scratching sound of shod hooves on stone, and when they looked around they saw that an Indian was stealing Travis and Sylvester's horses.

"Where the hell are they comin' from?" Travis asked.

"Stop those horses!" Joe shouted. "Shoot them if you have to! We need that signaling device!"

Sylvester got up and started running toward the horses, firing as he did so.

"No, Sylvester, not that way!" Joe shouted.

"Sylvester, get down, you crazy fool!" Travis called.

Travis's shout was too late. Both he and Joe could hear the sound the bullet made as it hit Sylvester in the back of the head. They could also see the spray of blood, brain matter, and bone chips as Sylvester pitched forward.

Travis turned back around and saw that the Indian who had just shot Sylvester was taking a dead aim at Joe. Travis shot him, and the Indian went down.

After the last exchange, the sound of shooting came back in a series of echoes; then once again all was quiet, except for Joe and Travis's ragged breathing. Travis, his smoking pistol in his hand, knelt behind the carcass of Joe's horse and stared in the direction from which the Indians had come.

"You'd better get away from this exposed position," Joe warned. "If they've got a party just on the other side of that ridge, they can come after us anytime they want."

"Yes, sir," Travis said. "Soon's I get you free." Travis began pushing at the horse, and pulling on Joe's leg. The pain was excruciating, but Joe knew he had no choice. Finally they were able to get the leg free.

"See if you can get my carbine," Joe said. "Yours and Sylvester's are still with your horses."

Travis reached under the dead horse and managed to grab hold of the stock of Joe's carbine. Unlike the Springfields the cavalry had carried when Joe was with Custer, this was a Winchester .44–40, a repeating rifle with seven rounds in the tube. Travis was able to extract the Winchester, and then he and Joe moved over to a small cairnlike pile of rocks on the eastern edge of the ridge. The cairn made a natural fortress.

"Colonel, we need to get that arrow out," Travis said.

"I know," Joe said. He touched it, then jerked his hand back as the pain hit him. "I can't do it, First Sergeant. You're going to have to do it."

"Colonel, I—"

"Do it!"

"Yes, sir."

Joe put one arm over his eyes, then bit into the shirt-sleeve of his other arm. He felt a wave of pain-induced nausea wash over him as Travis grabbed hold of the arrow shaft. Then he passed out.

When Joe came to a short time later, the bloody arrow was on the ground beside him, and his leg was bandaged with yellow kerchiefs.

"I got Sylvester's kerchief to help make a bandage," he said. "I got his pistol and ammo belt, too."

"Good man," Joe said.

"Sorry we don't have nothin' to take away the pain."

"I'll be all right," Joe said. "It's subsiding a little." Laboriously, he moved into position to look out over the rocks. "Have you seen any more of them?"

"No, sir, but I know they're here."

"What has me puzzled is what they're doing up here," Joe said.

"Maybe they seen the flashin' signals an' they come up here to kill it," Travis suggested.

"Could be," Joe agreed.

Travis started looking around.

"What are you looking for?" Joe asked.

Travis pointed to a very narrow stricture in the rocks, a chimney of sorts, closed on three sides.

"Colonel, if I was to climb up that chimney there, I think I could get a look over the other side of the crest, maybe see what's goin' on."

"I don't know, Travis. That looks like it might be a pretty hard climb."

Travis smiled. "For you, maybe, not for me. My pappy was a mountain goat. That's why I can climb like one."

"You aren't a young man, First Sergeant."

"That just means I ain't goin' to make no young man's mistakes," Travis replied. He took off his pistol belt, boots, and socks. Then he emptied the cartridges from his belt and formed it into a loop.

Joe watched Travis start up the chimney, finding hand- and footholds where he could and using the belt as a climbing rope when it was helpful. Once the stricture got narrow enough, Travis was able to put his back on one side and his feet on the other and wedge himself up. It took about forty-five minutes to reach the top, but he finally made it. Once there, Travis went down the other side.

For fully fifteen minutes he was out of sight, and Joe didn't know if he was dead or alive. He found himself mouthing a constant prayer that Travis was all right, for he knew his own survival would probably depend upon Travis's survival.

Finally, after what seemed like an eternity, he saw a

pair of bare black feet easing down over the rocks, followed by the yellow-striped kersey trousers, then the rest of Travis. He descended the chimney, coming down much faster than he had gone up. He came back to the little rock fortress, then sat there for a moment, breathing hard.

"What did you see?" Joe asked.

"Colonel, you ain't goin' believe this," Travis said. "But just on the other side, there's a hidden canyon. And it's full of Apaches. I bet they's over three hundred of 'em in there."

"Three hundred?" Joe gasped.

Travis nodded. "At least that many," he said. "And they got women and children with 'em, too. The women's cookin' supper!"

Joe smiled. "Sergeant Travis, you know what you have just discovered?" he said. "You have found Keytano's mountain hideout. The army's been looking for this for ten years!"

"Yes, sir, I reckon that's just what we've discovered," Travis said, quickly sharing the credit. "Only thing is, I sure wish there was more'n the two of us up here."

"First Sergeant, you've got to get back down. Get word to Captain Kelly what you've found."

"Yes, sir," Travis said. "Soon as you feel up to it, we'll start down."

"No. You go now. Leave me here."

Travis shook his head. "No, sir, I can't do that."

"First Sergeant, I am ordering you to leave me."

"Colonel, I go down there without you an' you not dead, what you think that's goin' to look like? It's goin' to look like I showed the white feather," Travis said.

"First Sergeant, I've never known you to disobey an order nor even give me any backtalk," Joe said. "Now, for one of the most critical orders I've ever given you, you start talking back. I am very disappointed."

"Colonel, it ain't my intention to disappoint you."

"Then do as I say."

Travis looked at Joe for a long moment, and in his face Joe saw the most pained expression he had ever seen in any man. Finally, Travis sighed. He laid out his pistol, Sylvester's pistol, and the carbine.

"You keep these," he said. "I won't be needin' no gun."

"Don't be foolish, First Sergeant. You can't leave here unarmed."

Travis pulled out his knife. "I won't be unarmed, Colonel, I've got this," he said. "You ever seen any of my people use one of these?"

Joe shook his head. "Can't say as I have."

"Time was when no Colored folks was allowed a gun of any kind," he said. "Blades was all we had to fight with, and we got pretty good. Besides, I'll be able to travel better if I don't have a gun to keep up with."

"Whatever you say, First Sergeant," Joe said.

Travis climbed over the low wall of rocks, then started down the eastern slope of the mountain.

"Deacon," Joe called, using his first name.

Travis looked back at him.

"Tell my wife and son—"

But Travis held up his hand. "I ain't goin' be tellin' 'em nothin', Colonel, 'cause you goin' to tell 'em yourself. I'm comin' back for you. You can write that in a book. I'm comin' back for you."

It was over three hours since Travis started down the side of the mountain. Joe had fought the pain all afternoon until, mercifully, it began to dull. Now his right leg was numb, and he started worrying that he might be developing gangrene. If he got gangrene, he would more than likely lose his leg. And if he lost his leg, that would be the end of his career.

Joe thought about Trooper Whitehead, and he knew now how Whitehead felt. Except Joe had managed to keep Whitehead on active service and, even now, Whitehead was working in the wagon repair shop. Who would do for Joe what he had done for Whitehead?

Joe sensed more than heard a movement, and, cocking his pistol, he eased himself up to look over the lip of the rocks. Three Indians were on their stomachs, working their way toward him. He shot one of them, hitting him in the top of the head, scattering his blood all over the rocky surface. The other two got up and started running away. Joe managed to hit one of them high in the back, just to the right of his right shoulder blade. The Apache fell and the other leaned over to pick him up. Joe had a perfect bead on the third one, and could have killed him right there. But as· he touched the trigger, he thought of Travis helping him when he was in the same situation a few hours earlier and some sense of compassion made his finger move away from the trigger. He watched as the two Indians struggled back over the crest.

Now Joe began to worry. He was afraid that the two who got away would be able to tell the others that Joe was alone. Then he got an idea. He spread the pistols out so that he would have to move from one place to another to fire them. That might make the Indians think Travis was still with him. At the least, it would cause him to change positions so that he would be a less likely target than if he remained still.

Three more times during the afternoon one or two Indians appeared. Joe exchanged shots with them each time, though he didn't believe he hit any more of them. He was, however, able to put his plan into effect, moving from one position to another as he fired at them, in the hopes of convincing them that Travis was still here with him.

As the afternoon wore on, Joe became aware of a problem he had not previously considered. He had not had a drink of water since early morning. His canteen was on his horse, and his horse was one hundred yards away, lying in the open. He cursed himself for not thinking of his canteen when he had Travis get the Winchester. Now it was out there, mocking him with its nearness.

If not for his injured leg Joe would have made a try for it. But the wound made it difficult for him to move, and if the Indians caught him out there, he wouldn't be able to make it back.

Joe picked up a rock and put it in his mouth. He got no moisture from it, but somehow it seemed to help.

Night fell, and from the other side of the crest Joe could hear the Indians. They beat their drums and sang their songs, and Joe could see a flickering of reflected orange light from their fires.

Thirst continued to dog him, and he could not get out of his mind the fact that the canteen was out there, so close. Surely, now that it was dark, he could make it to his horse and back. Slowly—not only because he didn't want to give away his position but also because all movement, no matter how carefully undertaken, was excruciatingly painful to him—Joe eased himself over the rim of the rocks.

Once clear of the rocks he began crawling on his belly toward his horse.

Joe was halfway there when he sensed something ahead. He stopped and stared into the darkness. From the corner of his eye he thought he caught a movement . . . a shadow within a shadow. There, he saw it! An Indian was watching his horse. And another. And another!

The bastards! They knew he was without water, and they were using his canteen as bait, like using cheese to catch a mouse!

Frustrated and angry, Joe turned around and began working his way back to the cairn. There was, however, one benefit from his failed excursion. By the time he got back, his leg was throbbing so much that he could almost forget his thirst.

Sometime after midnight—Joe wasn't sure exactly what time it was—he heard a faint scraping sound. The sound startled him because he had been asleep.

"Travis, Sylvester, wake up! They're out there!" Joe shouted. He raised up and fired twice and, in the flame pattern of the gun blast, saw an Indian running back. Someone *had* been sneaking up on him.

Joe had yelled the names out loud, hoping the Indians would believe he wasn't alone and that someone was always awake and on watch. That meant he would have to stay awake for the rest of the night. No more drifting off to sleep, for if he did, he might not wake up again.

Joe discovered that the pain in his leg could be useful. Anytime he felt himself drifting off, he had only to press on the wound to bring about a sharp, eye-opening spasm of pain. This method of staying awake worked, for just before dawn, when he heard the sound of someone climbing, he was awake and ready. He cocked the pistol and waited.

"Colonel! Colonel, it's me, Sergeant Travis!" a voice hissed.

"Travis? Travis, you've come back!"

"Yes, sir, I told you I would."

Joe stared toward the sound of the voice and saw Travis materialize out of the darkness. The sergeant pulled himself over the ledge of rocks, then dropped down inside. He held something out to Joe.

"Thought you might need this," he said.

A canteen! Joe grabbed it, pulled off the top, and began drinking deeply. He drank until his stomach hurt.

"God, Sergeant, I would've given everything I've got for that water."

"I brought you a can of beans, too," Travis said.

Joe had a small pocket can opener, but his mess kit was still on his horse. He didn't need a spoon. He ate the beans right from the can, turning it up as if he were drinking from a cup.

"Did you tell Captain Kelly about the Apache hideout?" Joe asked.

"Yes, sir," Travis answered. "Colonel, you 'member the dust we saw yesterday mornin'?"

"Yes."

"Turns out that wasn't nothin' more'n a bunch of squaws and kids draggin' branches. They was making sign like the Apaches was way off, when the truth of it was they was doublin' back to their hideout here. Cap'n Kelly's done found the entrance to the canyon an' he's got it blocked off so's Keytano can't escape."

"What about Colby?"

"Cap'n Kelly's sent a rider around to Colby to tell him to block the other end of the canyon."

"That leaves only one way out for them," Joe said. "Right through us."

Travis smiled, broadly. "Yes, sir, I reckon it does," he said. "Only if they try, we goin' to have a little surprise for them."

"What sort of surprise?"

"I figure Corporal Dakota will be up here by the time it gets daylight. It's takin' him and his boys a little longer than it did me. They're havin' to move their guns up by hand."

"The Gatling guns!" Joe said. "My God, yes, Sergeant! If we can get them in place up here, we can keep Keytano's whole tribe bottled up!"

Half an hour later, huffing and puffing from the exertion, Corporal Dakota, Trooper Webb, and seven others arrived, laboriously dragging the three Gatling guns behind them. They had the guns in position by the time the sun came up.

Travis fired three shots into the air.

"It's not as good as the flashin' mirror," he said. "But it lets Cap'n Kelly know we're up here and in position."

Three shots were fired in answer.

"That means they're movin' into the canyon," Travis said. "I reckon we'd better get ready for them."

The gunners fitted the long magazines into the guns; then one man got on each wheel to traverse left or right, while the third stood behind to sight, elevate or depress, and turn the crank.

Suddenly about fifteen Apaches appeared over the ridge, screaming and firing as they charged toward the rocky cairn. Believing there were no more than one or two soldiers holed up, they thought to make quick work of them.

"Fire!" Joe shouted, and the three Gatling guns opened up.

Half a dozen Indians went down in the fusillade. The others ran back, screaming in shocked terror.

A few minutes later they heard several gunshots, and they knew Captain Kelly was engaged.

"Keep an eye open," Joe said. "They may try and come this way again."

"There they are!" Webb shouted, pointing. There were as many this time as before, but their tactics had changed. Instead of making a screaming charge as the earlier group had done, these warriors were trying to gain the advantage by using the rocks as cover, moving up by degrees.

"Corporal Dakota!" Joe said. "Aim at that shelf of rocks up there. Maybe we can get them by ricochet."

"You heard the colonel!" Dakota said. "Fire!"

Again the guns opened up, filling the mountaintop with sound. They fired for a full thirty seconds before they stopped, and the bullets whizzed and whined as they struck the rocks and bounced crazily, some of them even rebounding all the way back to the rocky cairn itself.

The Apaches who survived the last burst of firing withdrew to the relative safety of the other side of the crest.

"First Sergeant, we need to advance to that crest," Joe said. "If we can keep them bottled up down in there, Kelly can make quick work of them."

"You need some help movin', sir?"

"You just make sure the guns get into position," Joe said. "I'll get myself over there."

Bending low, Travis rushed across the open area until he reached the crest. Then he went down on his stomach and inched his way up for a look. After a moment he turned and waved at the others.

"Come on!" he called.

The three guns were moved, followed by Joe, who, though limping badly, still managed to get into place. He moved up to the crest to have a peek over to the other side.

There was a sharp drop of some twenty feet or so before the wall angled out enough to allow someone to negotiate it. That was why the attacks against him yesterday afternoon, last night, and again today had been so sporadic. As it turned out, the mass attack Joe had feared could never have taken place, for only the most skilled climbers would have been able to negotiate the sheer wall.

The Indians down inside the canyon were in well-fortified positions, waiting for Captain Kelly's troops to work their way up.

"Look at that, Colonel," Travis said. "The Apaches got Cap'n Kelly's men outnumbered three to one. And they got the advantage of position. Our boys come up here, they goin' to get slaughtered."

"Except we've got the guns behind them," Joe said.

"Colonel, we only got about fifty rounds apiece left for these things," Dakota said. "That's only about ten or fifteen seconds of firin'."

"Yeah, well, the Indians don't know that, do they?" Joe said. "Have two of your guns open fire. Keep the third one in reserve."

"Yes, sir," Dakota said. "Guns one and two, fire!"

Again the Gatling guns opened up, this time pouring a deadly fire down onto the Indians' backs. Startled and frightened by the terrible effect of the guns, the Indians began screaming and running. Many left their own rifles behind as they dived for cover wherever they could find it. Then, amazingly, Joe saw one of the Indians waving a white flag.

"Cease fire, cease fire!" he shouted, and the guns fell silent. One by one the Indians began to stand, holding their hands over their heads. They were still standing that way ten minutes later when Captain Kelly's men arrived.

★★★

Twenty

"But, General Murchison, you have spent your entire military career in the cavalry. I cannot believe you're declaring it obsolete!"

The speaker was a major, a student in the army's command and staff school, attending a class in military tactics. The class was being given by the commandant of the school, Brigadier General Joseph T. Murchison.

"I didn't say the cavalry was obsolete, Major. I said the classic concept of the cavalry is obsolete. By traditional definition, the cavalry is to be held in reserve behind the infantry when a battle starts. Then, when the infantry has the enemy on the run, the cavalry is supposed to flank and complete the rout with flashing sabers. The saber has been so much the cavalry's principle weapon that we once counted our numbers in 'sabers present,' such as: 'Present are three officers and one hundred men of A Troop, one hundred three sabers in all.' That is the definition you learned in West Point, is it not?"

The thirty students, ranging in rank from senior captains to junior lieutenant colonels, nodded in the affirmative.

"In actual fact, gentlemen, I have been unable to confirm so much as one saber-inflicted casualty in the last one hundred years. Not during the War of 1812, nor the War with Mexico, nor the Civil War, nor the Indian campaigns. In short, the cavalryman now does what an infantryman does, only instead of walking or being drawn up by wagon, he rides his horse to battle, and when he dismounts to fight, he does so with a carbine instead of a rifle."

"General Murchison, you were a part of General Custer's debacle at the Little Big Horn, as well as the successful campaign against the Apache. To what do you attribute the failure of one campaign and the success of the other?" a lieutenant colonel asked.

Joe smiled. "Colonel, I'm sure that question will be debated by military scholars and historians for the next hundred years or so. But when you come right down to it, there is still only one dictum for success on the battlefield, and it was articulated in poor grammar, but brilliant logic, by Confederate General Nathan Bedford Forrest during the Civil War. 'Get there fustest with the mostest.'"

The class laughed appreciatively, and Joe looked at the clock on the wall.

"Gentlemen, I see that this period is over. Tomorrow we will discuss Karl von Clausewitz's assertion that war is only a 'continuation of policy by other means, an act of force to compel an adversary to do one's will.'"

As the class filed out, Brigadier General Joseph T. Murchison put his papers and books back into his briefcase, erased the blackboard, then turned off the electric lights. It was just after five on a cold, gray December day, and without illumination the room darkened quickly.

Corporal Billy Bates, Joe's striker, had been sitting in the hallway just outside the classroom reading a magazine. He stood up and came to attention as Joe approached.

"Hello, Billy," Joe said. "Is the coach here?"

"Yes, sir, I brought it around a few minutes ago, General," Corporal Bates answered.

Joe took his overcoat from the rack and put it on. "What do you say we go home?"

It was ten days before Christmas, and seasonal decorations were in abundance, not only in the classroom building where Joe had given his class but outside as well. Greenery hung from corner street lamps and on the fronts of official buildings and private quarters. Outside the post headquarters, a huge tree was decorated with one of the new strings of colored electric lights. A wreath hung, rather incongruously, around the barrel of the signal cannon.

As a brigadier general, Joe had a large two-story, white-frame house. Compared to the quarters they had occupied at Fort Canfield, this house was enormous. Only the post commander had a larger house, and the difference between the two was so small as to be negligible.

Joe had thought the big house a waste of space, but Tamara insisted that with the birth of Sarah Louise, they needed more room. Whether it was the increased space required by their daughter or the old principle of expanding into the space one had, Joe didn't know. What he did know was that the house was now so fully used that he often wondered how they had ever gotten along with a smaller place.

When the carriage stopped in front of Joe's house, it was met by fourteen-year-old Todd.

"Hi, Pop."

"Hello, Todd," Joe said as he stepped out of his carriage. "What are you doing out here? Shouldn't you be doing your homework?"

"No, sir."

"What do you mean, no? You know you have to keep your grades up if you are going to go to West Point."

Todd smiled. "Today was the last day of school before the Christmas vacation," he said. "They don't give homework over the Christmas vacation."

"They don't? Well, they did when I was your age," Joe insisted. "I guess I'll just have to go speak to the school board."

"Oh, Pop!" Todd said, sounding frightened that his father might actually do it.

"How's your mother doing?"

"Fine. And we have company."

"Company?"

"Not company, really," Todd explained. "He's a reporter from a newspaper."

"What does he want?"

"He wants to talk to you," Todd said.

Joe put his arm around his son's shoulders. "All right," he said. "Let's go see what the gentleman of the press wants."

Corporal Bates moved the coach around back to the carriage house. Here the general's horses were stabled and the carriage and a smaller trap were kept. There was also an apartment above the carriage house for the maid and her husband, the groundskeeper. Corporal Bates actually lived in the barracks, reporting for duty just after reveille each morning and returning to the barracks after retreat each evening.

The living room of Joe's house was furnished in the style prevalent among his socioeconomic peers, which followed the theory that "too much is not enough." There were bric-a-brac, vases, lamps, bowls, trays, doilies, and pillows on every table, chair and sofaback. On the floor there were carpets upon carpets, and the wallpaper—covered with a pattern of huge, flower-filled baskets—was liberally decorated with photographs of every size and description, hanging at different heights, suspended by long wires from the picture rail that encircled the room at the top of the wall.

A man wearing a brown suit with vest and tie stood as Joe entered. He was holding a cup in one hand and a saucer in the other. The maid took Joe's coat and hat as Tamara came over to greet him.

"Dear, this is Mr. Gillman. He is a reporter for the *Kansas City Star.*"

"How do you do, Mr. Gillman?"

Gillman started to reach out, saw that he was holding a cup, set it down, then walked over to shake Joe's hand.

"What's this about, Mr. Gillman? What interest has the press in me?"

"More accurately, General, we are interested in your opinion."

"I never give my opinion," Joe said.

"Ha!" Todd barked.

At first Gillman was surprised by Joe's answer; then, seeing the exchange of smiles between the general and his son, he realized Joe was making a joke.

"I assure you, General," Gillman said, "I would be interested in your opinion. As would all of our readers."

"And on what subject would you like my opinion?" Joe asked.

"The trouble that's going on with the Indians up in Dakota right now, General. What exactly is ghost dancing?"

The maid brought Joe a cup of coffee and he thanked her, then took a swallow of his coffee before he answered Gillman.

"It is the delusion of a dying race," Joe finally said.

"There are many who don't think so," Gillman said. "I'm sure you've heard the Indians claim that they were going to rise up and sweep all the white men back into the sea?"

"Mr. Gillman, what is the population of the United States?" Joe asked.

"Sixty-seven million," Gillman said proudly. "We are now more populous than England or France or Germany or any other European nation with the exception of Russia. And Russia is nearly as Asiatic as it is European."

"Sixty-seven million," Joe echoed. "Do you know how many Indians there are?"

"No, not exactly."

"I don't suppose anyone knows exactly," Joe replied. "But a good estimate would be one-third of a million. Now, Mr. Gillman, do you honestly think one-third of a million Indians—and that's all tribes, from Navaho to Sioux and Apache to Iroquois—do you really think they could throw us into the sea?"

Gillman chuckled. "No," he said. "No, I don't guess they could. Still, there are a lot of people disturbed by this ghost dance business. And I thought if I could get a handle on it, if I could write about it, I might put a few people at ease. I understand you've researched it."

"Yes," Joe said. "It seems to have started with a Paiute named Tavibo. Tavibo had a vision that if he wore a shirt decorated in a special way, and if he would do a special dance while he was wearing that shirt, the old ways would return. The buffalo would come back, the white men would leave, and the Indians would own the land again.

"If it had stopped there, no one else would have ever heard of it. But before Tavibo died, he told his son of his vision. Now, his son was totally civilized. He had taken the name Jack Wilson, and he was Christian. Wilson was a fruit picker and a farm worker who became dissatisfied with his lot, so he started thinking about his father's vision and decided there might be something in it for him. He sort of changed the vision around a bit, putting some Christian doctrine into it; then, like a tent preacher, he started spreading the gospel.

"It turns out that Wilson, who took back his Indian name of Wovoka, was a good preacher. And the Indian is, by nature, a spiritual being. Wovoka's message came at the right time for the Indians. They had nothing else to hang on to. They had lost war after war to the army, they were no longer able to roam free on the range, and they had been pushed onto reservations that were no different from being put on little islands in the vast sea of the plains."

"Reservations are like islands in the sea of the plains," Gillman said, making notes. "I like that."

"The Indians had nothing left but blind faith," Joe continued. "Ghost dancing, which should more properly be called ghost-shirt dancing, is the manifestation of that faith. Now the idea has spread throughout the rest of the Indians. They are looking for the disappearance of the white man and the return of the buffalo. As soon as they see that more white men than ever are moving West, and that the buffalo are not coming back, their faith in the ghost-shirt dance will be shattered,

and they will give it up . . . dispirited and broken people."

"You sound almost as if you're sorry," Gillman said.

"Have you ever heard the idea 'the death of one man diminishes us all'?"

"Yes, of course."

"If the death of one man can diminish us all, how much more, then, can we be diminished by the death of an entire people?"

"Yes, I guess I see what you mean," Gillman said.

"You asked for my opinion, Mr. Gillman. It may not have been what you wanted to hear, but it is my opinion."

"Thank you, General. I'm sure our readers will be most interested in the words of a genuine hero of the Indian wars." Gillman pulled out his pocket watch and looked at it. "I must be going if I am not to miss the train into the city. Again, I thank you for your hospitality."

"Todd, tell Billy to take our guest to the depot," Joe said.

"That won't be necessary, General, I can walk."

"It's no problem," Joe said as Todd hurried to find Corporal Bates.

A few minutes later Joe stood in the window watching as Corporal Bates drove the reporter toward the depot. Tamara came up to stand beside him.

"Dinner will be ready shortly," she said.

"Smells good. What is it?"

"Roast beef, potatoes, and butter beans."

"Horseradish?"

Tamara laughed. "Have I ever had roast beef without horseradish? I know how much you like it."

PINE RIDGE INDIAN RESERVATION

"I want some meat," Yellow Bird said.

"I am sorry, my husband. We have no meat," Quiet Stream answered.

"Did you not go to the agency today?"

"Yes."

"Then where is the beef ration?"

"They had no beef. They had only potatoes and corn."

Irate, Yellow Bird stood up and kicked the tin plate Quiet Stream had put before him. It bounced across the tepee, spilling its contents. Five-year-old Running Fox ran over to the spilled potatoes and began picking them up, eating with his fingers.

"Leave it alone!" Yellow Bird shouted angrily to his son. "You are not a dog to eat scraps! You are Yankton!" Yellow Bird cuffed Running Fox on the side of the head, and the little boy began to cry.

Quiet Stream rushed to her son and picked him up, soothing him with shushing sounds.

"He is just a child," she said. "And he is hungry."

"We are *all* hungry!" Yellow Bird stormed. "And we will always be hungry until the white man is destroyed." He rolled back a blanket, then pulled out a shirt. It was white, with a blue collar and a crescent moon beneath the collar. Blue-tipped feathers decorated the shoulders and cuffs of the shirt, and a yellow cross was over each breast.

"With this shirt we will drive the white man back into the sea," Yellow Bird said. "But all the Dakota must believe. *All* the Dakota," he stressed, using their word for Sioux. "You must believe, Wind in His Hair must believe, Capture Heart Woman must believe, and Sitting Bull must believe."

"Wind in His Hair and Sitting Bull have no need of shirts for medicine," Quiet Stream defended. "They have made their own medicine."

"And what has their medicine done for the Dakota?" Yellow Bird asked. "Our children cry because they have no milk. Our women cry because they have no meat. And our men are like women because they have no strength." He held the shirt up. "I go now to be with the other dancers."

Yellow Bird pushed through the flap of the tepee and went out into the snow. Already tonight there was dancing, as there had been on nearly every other night

since the little band of Yankton who were still with
Wind in His Hair arrived at Pine Ridge. The dancing
would go far into the night, until the dancers fell into a
trance. Many would then awaken to tell the others of
their visits with the spirits of the ones who had already
died. And always they would tell the same story: Wearing the shirts would make them invincible against the
bullets of the soldiers.

"We need not fear the soldiers," the people were
told. "If the soldiers come for us, their horses will be
swallowed by the earth. And if the riders jump from
the horses, they, too, will be swallowed by the earth."

Quiet Stream picked up the potatoes her husband
had spilled in his anger and gave some to Running Fox.
The rest she took herself. From outside the tepee she
could hear the throbbing of the drums and the wailing
chant of the dancers.

The tent flap opened again, and she looked up,
thinking it would be Yellow Bird. Instead it was her
brother, his hair gray and his face lined with wrinkles.

"Where is Yellow Bird?" he asked.

"He dances."

"They all dance," Wind in His Hair said.

"My brother, do you believe in the shirts?"

"I do not believe."

"But so many do believe," Quiet Stream said. "Is
there not medicine in the belief of many?"

"I do not know," Wind in His Hair admitted. "If
Sitting Bull believed, then I, too, would believe."

"Perhaps Sitting Bull believes now," Quiet Stream
suggested.

"I do not think he believes."

"He is in his cabin on Grand River," Quiet Stream
said. "Could we not go to him and see what he says
about this new religion?"

"Yes, it would be a good thing to go and ask him,"
Wind in His Hair replied. "We will do this. You may
leave your child with Capture Heart Woman."

"No," Quiet Stream said. "I want my child to see
Sitting Bull so that when he is an old man, he will re-

member he once saw the shaman who foretold Custer's defeat."

"It is cold," Wind in His Hair said. "Wrap the child warmly. I will prepare the horses."

It was late under a frigid overcast sky when Quiet Stream and her brother reached the cabin of Sitting Bull. Wind in His Hair dismounted, but Quiet Stream remained on her horse, holding Running Fox close to her while her brother knocked on the cabin door. After a moment a dim light appeared inside the cabin; then the door opened. Sitting Bull stood wrapped in a buffalo robe, holding a candle and peering out into the night.

"We have come to visit," Wind in His Hair said.

Sitting Bull looked at him, then at Quiet Stream. He nodded and stepped back to let them in.

The cabin was very sparsely furnished. There was a low table, a fireplace, some iron cooking utensils, and several blankets, rugs, and buffalo robes. But there were no chairs and no beds since Sitting Bull and his wife sat and slept on the floor.

"We have come to speak of the ghost shirts," Wind in His Hair said.

Sitting Bull filled his pipe, then offered some tobacco to Wind in His Hair, who filled his own. Quiet Stream and Running Fox sat quietly against the wall beside Sitting Bull's wife, while the two shamans smoked and talked.

"Yes, the ghost shirts," Sitting Bull finally said. "Do you wish now to convert me to the belief in the medicine of the ghost shirts?"

"Do you believe?" Wind in His Hair asked.

"I have gone to the sweat lodge many times, and I have asked the Great Spirit to send me wisdom about this thing. But the wisdom has not come."

"I, too, have gone to the sweat lodge to seek the answer," Wind in His Hair said.

"And did you find the answer?"

"No. Only more questions."

"In your youth, did you do the *Okipa*?" Sitting Bull asked.

Wind in His Hair removed his coat and shirt to show Sitting Bull his bare chest. Above each breast were large, irregular scars. Sitting Bull touched each scar, then closed his eyes and chanted a short prayer.

Quiet Stream shivered with fear, for she could remember when her brother went through the ordeal of the Sun Dance, and she knew that her child would one day face the same torture.

The Sun Dance was four days of elaborate ceremony that took place in the hottest part of summer. The ceremony allowed the soul to be liberated from the body, to join, for a short time, with the Great Spirit Watakan. Only the bravest of warriors would undertake the Okipa for it pushed pain and courage to the edge of human endurance.

The volunteers would be bound, mocked, and tortured by having wooden dowels skewered through the muscles of their chest. They could not show the slightest reaction to the pain. In fact, they were required to laugh at those who were inflicting the torture. Leather thongs were then tied to the bloody dowels, and thrown over a crosstree, high atop the Sun Pole. Then the warrior would be drawn up into the air so that all his weight hung suspended by the dowels that stuck through his flesh. He would have to hang there in excruciating pain, unflinching and unblinking as he stared into the sun while the drums beat and others sang and danced around him. Only after several minutes of such agony could he free himself—and doing so was, perhaps, the most agonizing ritual of all. The Sun Dance warrior could only free himself by calling upon his friends to pull him down until the flesh would no longer support his weight and he would tear free, leaving the dowels, covered with bloody chunks of his muscle tissue, hanging from the pole.

It was no disgrace not to undergo the Okipa, though it was a great disgrace to start it and not finish. Those who did undergo it were inducted into the Buffalo Society. That was a very honorable estate, and anyone who was a member was regarded with great respect for the remainder of his life.

"How can putting on a shirt and dancing compare with the medicine of the Okipa?" Sitting Bull asked.

"It cannot," Wind in His Hair replied.

"Then that is our answer. Let lesser men wear their shirts and dance their dance," Sitting Bull said. "It will do no good, but it can do no harm."

"Yes, I agree," Wind in His Hair answered. "And I will share your counsel with others."

"It is late and cold, and I think more snow will come tonight," Sitting Bull said. "You and your sister and her child may stay here with my wife and me, and return tomorrow."

"For making your home our home, I thank you," Wind in His Hair said.

The snow fell heavily, in large, white flakes that drifted down from the black sky and added inches to what was already on the ground. It fell silently, and its presence deadened all sound, so that the movement of horses went unheard. The door to Sitting Bull's small log cabin was tightly shut, and wisps of blue smoke curled up from the chimney, providing a scene of peaceful tranquility to the setting.

Two hundred yards away from the cabin lay the lower reaches of a great pine forest, and from the darkness of those trees came a long line of riders. The horses moved silently, as if treading on air, and only their movement and the blue vapor of their breath gave any indication of real life and not mere ghostly vision.

A small clinking sound of metal on metal came from the party, a sound unnatural to the drift of snow and the soft whisper of trees. Quiet Stream heard it while in the deepest recesses of her sleep, and her eyes came open as she lay beside her child and wondered what could have caused the sound. But the buffalo robes were too warm, and the feel of her child beside her too sweet, and she believed she must have dreamed the unusual sound. She pulled her child closer to her and went back to sleep.

Outside, the silent horses and the quiet men approached.

A sudden loud pounding on the door awakened everyone within the cabin. Sitting Bull sat up and looked around. It was not yet dawn, though the snow had stopped and the sky had cleared, so that a bright silver moon shone through the three cabin windows.

"Who is there?" Sitting Bull called.

Without answering, the door suddenly burst open, and several men rushed inside. They were wearing uniforms and Quiet Stream pulled her child to her, frightened that these were soldiers. When one of them lit a candle, however, she saw that they weren't soldiers, they were Indian police.

"I am Lieutenant Bull Head," the one in charge of the party said.

"What do you want here?" Sitting Bull asked.

"You are my prisoner," Bull Head replied. "You must go with me to the agency."

"Why?" Quiet Stream asked.

Lieutenant Bull Head pointed to Quiet Stream. "This does not concern you," he said.

Sitting Bull yawned. "All right," he said. "Let me put some clothes on, and I will go with you. Please get my horse ready. I will ride the white horse, the one given to me by my friend Buffalo Bill."

"Sergeant Red Tomahawk, get his horse," Bull Head ordered one of those standing close to him.

"Am I to go, as well?" Wind in His Hair asked.

"My orders are only to bring in Sitting Bull."

A few minutes later Red Tomahawk stuck his head just inside. "Sitting Bull's horse is ready."

"Come now," Bull Head said.

When they emerged from the cabin, Quiet Stream found that well over one hundred Indians were now gathered outside, despite it being so early in the morning. Most were ghost-shirt dancers, which she could tell by their shirts, and yet they were here. She thought it a good indication of the power of Sitting Bull's medicine that they would be drawn to him now, even though he had not accepted their beliefs.

One of the dancers, a man Quiet Stream recognized as Catch the Bear moved toward Lieutenant Bull Head. "You think you are going to take him!" Catch the Bear shouted. "You are not!"

"Come along quietly," Bull Head said to Sitting Bull. "Don't listen to these people."

At first, Sitting Bull cooperated with Bull Head. Then, suddenly, he decided to hold back, making it necessary for Bull Head and Red Tomahawk to force him to his horse.

"You will not take him!" Catch the Bear shouted. He threw aside his blanket, showing a rifle. He fired at Bull Head, hitting the Indian policeman in the side. As Bull Head fell, he tried to return fire, but his bullet struck Sitting Bull instead.

Red Tomahawk fired at almost the same moment, hitting Sitting Bull in the head and killing him instantly.

As the gunshots echoed up and down the stream the show horse given to Sitting Bull by Buffalo Bill began to go through his show routine. The great white horse, shining against the black, predawn sky, raised one hoof and started dancing.

"Look! Look!" Quiet Stream shouted, pointing to the horse. "The spirit of Sitting Bull has moved into his horse!"

"The horse dances the dance of the ghosts!" another said.

"Kill them!" one of the ghost-shirt dancers shouted. "Kill the ones who came to kill Sitting Bull!"

A quick, blazing gun battle broke out between the Indian police and those who had gathered around Sitting Bull's cabin. Almost immediately a troop of cavalry, which had been waiting just inside the trees, arrived. They quickly brought the fighting to a close, but not before six of the policemen and eight of Sitting Bull's followers had been killed. One of those killed was five-year-old Running Fox.

* * *

When Wind in His Hair was arrested for his actions on the morning Sitting Bull was killed, Quiet Stream went to James McLaughlin, the Indian Agent at Pine Ridge.

McLaughlin was eating his lunch, a large steak that spilled over the sides of the plate. Making no effort to stop eating, nor offering her anything, he waved Quiet Stream over to the table.

"What do you want?" he asked as he cut off a big chunk of meat.

Quiet Stream's heart was heavy with sorrow over the loss of her child and the arrest of her brother, but the sight and aroma of meat practically made her forget everything else. She stared at it as if mesmerized.

"Well?" McLauglin asked, looking up at her. Juice ran down his chin, and he dabbed at it with a napkin. "Come, come, woman, I don't have all day! I'm a busy man!"

"When the police came to arrest Sitting Bull, they killed my son," Quiet Stream said.

McLaughlin tore off a piece of bread and dragged it through the juices. He stuck it in his mouth.

"Yeah, I heard that," he said. "I'm real sorry, but there's nothing I can do. Remember, it was the Indian police who killed your son, not white men." He started carving another piece of meat.

"The police, and the soldiers, arrested my brother, Wind in His Hair," Quiet Stream said.

McLaughlin stuck another piece of meat in his mouth and began chewing. "Yeah," he said. "Well, Wind in His Hair had no business being there. You either, for that matter. If you had both stayed home, your son would be alive today, and Wind in His Hair would be free."

"But my brother did nothing. We had gone to visit Sitting Bull the night before, and because it was late, he asked us to stay with him. We were there when the police came the next morning, that is all. My brother did not resist the police. He did not even have a gun."

"Well, you don't have to worry about it," McLaughlin said, with a wave of his hand.

"Why do you say that?"

"Because General Miles is going to release your brother as a goodwill gesture. I don't agree with him, but it is his decision. Now, is there anything else you want?"

"When will we get our beef ration?"

"We've had a shortage," McLaughlin explained. "You've gotten all the meat you're going to get until after the end of the year. You people are just going to have to wait it out like the rest of us." He cut off another piece of meat. "But it's only another week or so until the new year. You won't starve between now and then. Mason?" he suddenly called.

McLaughlin's assistant stuck his head in. "Yes, sir?"

"Show this woman out." McLaughlin took another bite of his steak.

"Now will you believe in the power of the ghost shirts?" Yellow Bird asked when Quiet Stream returned to her tepee.

"My brother wants to leave here," Quiet Stream said. "And so do I."

"Leave here? Why do you want to leave here?"

"The medicine is bad here. Our son was killed, and nothing good can happen here."

"Where does your brother want to go?"

"To the Miniconjou. Big Foot is the brother of our mother. He will take us in."

"Very well. If you want to go, we will go," Yellow Bird said. He smiled. "I will teach the dance of the ghost shirt to the Miniconjou."

FORT LEAVENWORTH, KANSAS
CHRISTMAS DAY 1890

Joe settled down in an overstuffed chair in the living room, then held his feet up to examine the new slippers he had received for Christmas.

"Are they comfortable?" Tamara asked.

"Very."

"Todd was so concerned about them. He didn't know if you would like them or not."

"What is there not to like? They are warm and comfortable. And as fine a looking pair of house slippers as I have ever seen."

Tamara laughed. "Well, there is certainly no doubt that Todd is enjoying *his* Christmas gift. He hasn't been off that horse since early this morning. He's going to wear the poor creature out."

"Well, a future cavalry officer certainly needs his own horse. I should have gotten him one long before this," Joe said. "And what about you? Do you like your bonnet?"

"I love it," Tamara said. "But all the way from Paris? Don't you think that is a bit extravagant?"

"If you can't be extravagant every once in a while, what good is it to be a general?" Joe quipped.

The telephone rang.

"That infernal machine," he grumbled. "I confess I don't know if it's a blessing or a curse."

"General Murchison's quarters, the maid speaking," Joe heard Mrs. O'Toole say from the hallway. "Just a moment, sir, I will get him."

"Who would call you on Christmas Day?" Tamara asked as Joe got up from his easy chair.

"Probably someone just wishing me a Merry Christmas," he replied. He took the earpiece from the maid, then leaned toward the mouthpiece on the wall-mounted box. "General Murchison," he said. There was a moment's pause before he responded. "Yes, of course, General. I'll come over right away." He put the earpiece back in the hook, then returned to the living room. "Mrs. O'Toole, would you get my coat and boots, please? And since my striker is off for Christmas Day, perhaps you would be so kind as to have your husband saddle my horse."

Joe took off his slippers and reached for his boots.

"What is it, dear?" Tamara asked.

"That was the post commander," Joe said. "He has received a telegraph message from General Miles.

General Miles wants me to go up to the Pine Ridge Indian Reservation right away. I'm to leave tonight."

"What in heaven's name for?"

"The ghost dancing seems to be getting more frenzied since Sitting Bull was killed. General Miles thinks that if I go up there, my very presence might have an ameliorating effect on the Indians."

"Joe, you aren't going to have to go into the field?" Tamara asked.

"No, nothing like that," Joe said. He chuckled. "Though two of my old regiments are there. The Seventh and the Ninth."

"But, Joe, on Christmas? Do you really have to leave on Christmas?"

"I'm a soldier, darling," Joe replied. "I go where I'm told and when I'm told. You know that."

"I'm sorry," Tamara said. "Of course you have to. And I'm a soldier's wife who should know better than to ever complain—or question orders. So I'll just pack your bags, kiss you good-bye, and plead with you to be careful."

"I don't think this ghost dancing business is anything to worry about," he said. "General Miles wants me to go up to calm the Indians, but if truth were known, I imagine it's the Indian agent and a few of the army officers who need to be calmed. I expect it will all blow over pretty quickly, and I can come right back home. I'll be here in time to receive on New Year's Day."

PINE RIDGE RESERVATION
DECEMBER 28, 1890

"Here's the situation, Joe," General Nelson A. Miles was explaining as he pointed to a map on the wall. "I've got Colonel Sumner and the Eighth, Colonel Forsyth and the Seventh, as well as elements from the Ninth and the Sixth Cavalry, all in the field. In addition, I have an infantry battalion and an artillery battery. That is a total of about two thousand effectives."

"How many Indians?" Joe asked.

"We estimate that there are at least six thousand armed warriors among the ghost dancers."

"Why are you so nervous, Nelson? Have the Indians done anything besides dance?"

"As a matter of fact, they have." General Miles pointed to the map. "They attacked a band of settlers here, at Spring Creek, killing several of them. Then they attacked an army supply train here. Seven soldiers were killed, and the hostiles took a wagonload of guns and ammunition."

"They've been busier than I thought," Joe said. He stepped away from the map. "What do you want me to do?"

"I've been told you have a rather special relationship with Wind in His Hair."

"I don't know that you would call it a relationship, as such," Joe replied. "I know him, and I've known him for a long time. Our paths have crossed at some rather critical junctures."

"I would like for you to speak with him," the general said. "See if you can convince him to talk to his people and calm this ghost dance business down. You know, McLaughlin had him arrested when Sitting Bull was killed, but I let him go, hoping he might be able to help us. I think they would listen to him. He's one of the last of the old chiefs. Also, he's a member of the Buffalo Society, and that carries a lot of weight with the Indians."

"Where is he now?"

"He and his group are with Big Foot and the Miniconjou. And that's the problem. Big Foot has agreed—at least three times—to come in. But every time we start in with him, he changes his mind and runs off. And when he runs off, all his people run off with him. That's about six hundred or so . . . and they are all armed."

"General Miles, sir," a lieutenant said, sticking his head into the room. "We just got word that Big Foot and his band have been brought into camp at Wounded Knee."

"Good, now maybe we're getting somewhere. Who have we got in position there?"

"Colonel Forsyth and the Seventh, sir," the lieutenant answered.

"Well," General Miles said, smiling. "There's a bit of irony for you, Joe. The Seventh and the Sioux. That'll make people like Myles Moylan happy."

"Is Moylan still with the Seventh?" Joe asked.

"Still with the Seventh, still a captain," General Miles replied. "I tell you what. We can ride out there tomorrow. You can talk to Wind in His Hair, see if he will help us. And you can renew a few acquaintances with the officers and men who are still with the Seventh."

"Okay," Joe said. "Have you got a tent for me?"

"We've got one put up with a floor and a stove, all ready for you. Right next to mine. I hope my snoring doesn't keep you awake."

"General, after that long train ride, I don't think anything would keep me awake tonight," Joe replied.

WOUNDED KNEE
THE NEXT MORNING

"More soldiers are coming," Yellow Bird said.

"Do nothing to anger them," Quiet Stream cautioned.

"They should be careful that they do not anger me."

"These soldiers are from the Seventh Cavalry," Quiet Stream said. "I am fearful they will want revenge because we killed Custer. I do not understand why you have no fear of them."

"You do not understand because you do not believe. I am not afraid of the soldiers because my ghost shirt will protect me from their bullets."

"I do not think your shirt will protect you from the soldier's bullets."

"Soon I will prove it to you."

"I fear you will get yourself killed."

"Food!" someone started calling from within the circle of tepees. "The soldiers are giving out food!"

Yellow Bird started toward the tent flap.

"Are you going for food?" Quiet Stream asked. "Good, we will go together."

"It is not food. It is tasteless cracker that even the soldiers will not eat. They call it hardtack."

"For one week we have eaten nothing but the meat of our ponies," Quiet Stream said. "If the soldiers give us hardtack, then I will eat hardtack. Will you not go with me to get it?"

"You go alone. I am going to see Big Foot and the others," Yellow Bird said. "If all the people would listen to me, we could defeat the soldiers." He left the tepee.

Disgusted with her husband's insistence upon clinging to the foolishness of ghost dancing, Quiet Stream put on her buffalo robe to go get the food herself. It was bitterly cold as she walked through the camp toward the food distribution point, and she pulled the robe more tightly around her.

The camp was surrounded by soldiers, some on horseback, some standing. In addition, she saw several big guns, all of which were trained on the village.

Quiet Stream walked by Big Foot's tent, over which flew a large white flag. Several braves were inside his tepee, and as she passed by, she could hear them talking. The loudest voice was that of Yellow Bird. He was urging the others to put on their ghost shirts, then dare the soldiers to fire at them. "The shirts will turn aside the bullets," he promised.

"What do you say, Big Foot? Shall we do as Yellow Bird says?"

Big Foot was suffering from pneumonia. He coughed, then answered in a voice so weak that Quiet Stream could barely hear it.

"I will put my faith in the white flag that flies overhead," he said. "The soldiers will not fire on a white flag."

Quiet Stream was thankful that someone like Big Foot was still listened to.

She got two pieces of hardtack by telling the soldiers that her husband was too weak to come for his own. At first the soldier hesitated, but then he relented and handed another piece to her. She would try to get Yellow Bird to eat it, but if he didn't want it, she would save it for another time, for she was sure there would be many more times ahead of her when she would be without food.

She was just starting back to her own tepee when several soldiers came into the camp, accompanied by an interpreter. Through the interpreter, the soldiers ordered the Indians to begin surrendering their guns.

"No!" one of the Indians replied. "We bought these guns with our own money. We need them. Without our guns, how will we hunt the elk, the deer?"

The soldiers were insistent, reminding the Indians that the entire camp was surrounded, and there was nothing they could do but comply. The soldiers ordered the warriors to be broken down into groups of twenty, each group to surrender its weapons in turn.

The first twenty men surrendered two very old muzzle-loaders, telling the soldiers that was all they had. When the soldiers sent word back, the soldier–chief, Colonel Forsyth, came down into the camp. He spoke through the interpreter, though as Quiet Stream could speak English, she listened to Forsyth directly.

"I do not believe for one minute that twenty warriors have among them only two old guns," he said. "I thought we could do this as honorable men, and as honorable men I asked you to surrender your weapons. Since you did not do so, I will now send my soldiers among your tents to find and bring to me whatever weapons they may discover."

At first the soldiers had very little luck. Frustrated at not being able to find guns, they began hauling out crowbars, firewood axes, cooking and skinning knives, and finally, twelve old firearms that were barely serviceable.

"Do not fear the soldiers!" Yellow Bird shouted. "Come, dance with me! Dance, and we can turn aside the bullets!"

He started dancing, but no one would dance with him. Once or twice he reached down to pick up a handful of dirt, which he threw at the soldiers. It was only a gesture; none of the dirt got on them.

"Sit down now!" Colonel Forsyth ordered angrily.

Yellow Bird continued to dance, and when Forsyth started toward him, one of the Indians held up his hand.

"Let him be, soldier–chief," the Indian said calmly. "He must finish the circle; then he will sit down."

When Yellow Bird finished his dance, he glared at Colonel Forsyth, then walked away.

"Husband, I have food for you," Quiet Stream called.

"I do not want it!" Yellow Bird called back, waving her off with his hand. Quiet Stream started after him, but one of the soldiers put out his hand to stop her.

"Do you have a gun?" the soldier asked.

"No."

"I don't believe you. I am going to search."

Quiet Stream stood still as the soldier ran his hands over her body. "You have so many clothes on that you could be hiding a rifle underneath your dress and I would never know," the soldier said. He stuck his hand down inside the top of her dress and she could feel his coarse fingers on her skin, then on her breast. He squeezed her breasts, first one, then the other, and she stared into his eyes, keeping her own as flat and emotionless as if they were dead. His eyes reminded her of the eyes of a rat—beady and evil.

"I reckon you don't have any weapons up here," the soldier said, pulling his hand out from the top of her dress. "What about down here?"

Before he could reach his hand under her dress, Quiet Stream pulled her skirt up, exposing herself from the waist down. The soldier started to reach for her.

"McMurtry!" a sergeant called. "Leave that woman alone!"

Quiet Stream let her dress drop, making her mind a blank so that she felt no shame from the exposure.

Several more rifles were turned in; then, out of the

corner of her eye, Quiet Stream saw Yellow Bird re
turning. He was carrying a Winchester. At first Quie
Stream thought he was turning it in, and she breathed
a sigh of relief that he had come to his senses. The
she saw him raise the rifle to his shoulder, and she
knew that he had no intention of turning it in.

"Yellow Bird, no!" she shouted in her own language

Yellow Bird fired and a soldier fell. Ironically it wa
McMurtry, the one who had been putting his hands or
her a moment earlier. She knew Yellow Bird had no
shot him for that reason. He just happened to be the
first soldier Yellow Bird saw.

The soldiers reacted immediately to Yellow Bird's
shot. They shot back, killing Big Foot instantly.

The braves who had not yet surrendered their rifle
began returning fire. Women screamed, and from the
throats of warrior and soldier alike came shouts o
challenge.

Soldiers and Indians ran to get out of the line of fire
Quiet Stream was hit in the leg, and she went down
Bullets whistled over her head, and she could hear
them as they slapped through the buffalo-hide tepee
or slammed into flesh. She saw Capture Heart Womar
running by a tepee, then a bullet hit her in the head
splattering her blood and brains on the side of the tepee. Several other women and children went down, a
well.

Then Quiet Stream heard a sound that was much
louder than the previous sounds, and she realized that
the big Hotchkiss cannons had opened up. Unlike the
cannon of old, these guns could fire one round every
second. The shells made terrible, rushing sounds as
they passed over her, then exploded in the middle or
the camp, sending out killing pieces of shrapnel in every direction.

Quiet Stream saw Yellow Bird run into their tepee
Then one of the Hotchkiss shells hit the tepee and exploded. Yellow Bird staggered back out, his ghost shir
red with blood from half a dozen wounds.

The firing continued for several minutes. It stopped
as suddenly as it had begun. For a long moment a gro-

tesque silence fell across the village; then the silence was filled with the groans and cries of the wounded.

PINE RIDGE

It was after dark and a snowstorm had started when the first wagonloads of wounded Sioux began to reach the agency. Joe had not gone out to Wounded Knee because word of the fighting reached him before he and General Miles could leave. Now he stood in shocked silence, watching as the wounded were brought in. There were four warriors and forty-seven women and children lying on the straw-covered floor of the Episcopal mission. It was four days after Christmas, and a creche decorated the sanctuary. Above the creche was a sign:

BEHOLD, I BRING YOU TIDINGS OF JOY. THE PRINCE HAS COME.
PEACE ON EARTH, GOODWILL TO MEN.

***

Twenty-one

WASHINGTON, D.C.
JULY 19, 1900

When the carriage stopped in front of the Capitol Building, half a dozen reporters and photographers rushed forward to meet the occupants. A tall, handsome young man in the uniform of an army first lieutenant stepped out of the carriage. He stood at attention while the principal occupant, a major general, exited.

"General Murchison! General Murchison, is it true that Buffalo Bill talked you into making an appearance here today?" one of the reporters asked.

"Mr. Cody asked me to make an appearance. Once I learned what it was about, I didn't have to be talked into it. I am here of my own accord."

"What are you going to say to the Senate committee, General?"

"Now, gentlemen, I'm sure you will be in the committee room, listening to everything that goes on," Joe replied. "Surely you wouldn't want me to use up all my thunder before we even get started."

"But we have a deadline, General," one of the reporters said.

"You can be a little patient," Joe said. "After all, Wind in His Hair has been patient for ten years." Joe turned to the lieutenant who was with him. "May I introduce my aide-de-camp, who also happens to be my son, Lieutenant Todd Armstrong Murchison?"

"Todd Murchison? Yes, I remember you," one of the

reporters said. "You won one of the new Silver Stars at the Battle of San Juan Hill, I believe."

"That he did," Joe said proudly.

"You were with the Rough Riders?"

"No, sir," Todd answered. "I was with the Tenth Cavalry."

"The Tenth Cavalry? But isn't that a Colored regiment?"

"It is," Todd replied.

"How did that happen? You're the son of a well-known general. One would think you could have any assignment you might want."

"I *did* have the assignment I wanted," Todd replied. "Now, gentlemen, if you will excuse us? As the general's aide, it is my responsibility to get him to all his appointments on time, and we must be on our way."

Gently pushing the reporters aside, Todd opened the way for his father, and the two men strode quickly and purposefully up the wide concrete steps to the Capitol entrance.

"I thought you handled that quite well, Lieutenant," Joe said as they left the reporters behind.

"Thank you, General," Todd replied. Stepping in front of his father, he opened the door for him. "Pop, do you think your testimony will do any good?" he asked.

"I don't know, Todd. But I have to try."

The two officers hurried down the hall toward the committee room where the hearing was to be held. The hall was crowded with people going about the business of the United States government, and a general in their midst caused very little stir. No one seemed to notice him until just before they reached the door to the committee room, when a woman, who was standing near the wall, suddenly stepped out in front of them.

"General Murchison?" she said.

The woman was well-dressed in something Joe knew that Tamara would call a "summer calling toilette." She was wearing a white hat trimmed with violet feathers, and her hair, which was more gray than black, hung in long braids across each shoulder. The braids were tied

at the bottom with red ribbons, and it wasn't until then
that Joe realized she was Indian.

"Yes?" Joe replied.

"I want to thank you for what you are doing for my
brother."

"Your brother?" Joe gasped. Suddenly he realized
who this was, and as he looked at her, he saw not the
middle-aged woman standing before him, but the
young, svelte beauty who, to protect him, had bared
herself in the river so many years ago. "You are Quiet
Stream, aren't you?"

"Yes."

Joe took her hand in his and, spontaneously, put his
arms around her. He pulled her to him in an embrace
while Todd looked on in total shock.

"I will do what I can for Wind in His Hair," Joe
promised.

"Thank you," Quiet Stream replied.

"Oh, General, there you are," a civilian said, coming
up to them at that moment. "My name is John Hunter.
I represent Buffalo Bill Cody. He has asked me to
make myself available to you, should you need my services."

"Are you an attorney?" Joe asked.

"Yes, but not practicing. I am merely someone who
is familiar with the workings of these committee hear-
ings, in case you wanted to ask a few questions."

"Well, it's good to have you along, Mr. Hunter."

"Would you come with me, General? There are only
a few minutes before you're scheduled to appear."

"All right," Joe said. He and Todd followed Hunter
down the hallway. As they walked away, Todd looked
back at Quiet Stream and saw how intently she was
watching them.

"Pop," Todd said, "tell me about that woman."

"She's Wind in His Hair's sister."

"I know. But there's more to it, isn't there?"

"Is there?"

"I mean the way you were . . ." Todd let the sentence hang because he didn't know how to finish it.

"Son, everybody needs a few secrets in their past," Joe said easily. "Why don't you let me keep that one?"

"All right," Todd said, though it was clear from the tone of his voice that he was dying of curiosity about her.

"Okay, General, we can wait in here," Hunter said, opening a door. "It's a small anteroom just off the hearing room. When they call the hearing to order, someone will notify us."

"Very good," Joe said. There was a conference table in the room, surrounded by several chairs. A window was open, while overhead a paddle fan turned, stirring the breeze.

"Damn, it's hot in here," Hunter said, pulling at the collar of his shirt.

"I see a carafe and an ice bucket, sir," Todd said, looking over at a sideboard. "Would you like a glass of ice water?"

"Yes, thank you, that would be nice," Hunter replied.

"Pop?"

"Yes, thank you," Joe said.

Todd clinked ice into the glasses and added water, then brought them over to the table.

"Buffalo Bill Cody seems to think a lot of this Indian," Hunter said.

"Mr. Cody is loyal to his old friends and comrades," Joe replied.

"Yes, well, he seemed to think you might be able to do this Indian some good. The only question I have is, Why would you want to? I mean, didn't you spend most of your life fighting Indians?"

"Yes."

"Then why would you go to all the trouble to come to Washington to speak out on behalf of one of the worst of the lot?"

"I'm not sure I can make you understand," Joe said.

"Yeah, well, if you can't make me understand, General, how do you expect to make the senators understand?"

"All I have to make them understand is that this is the right thing for them to do," Joe said.

The door opened and a young man stuck his head inside.

"General, the hearing is about to be called to order."

Joe took another sip of water, put his glass on the table, then walked through the door into the hearing room. Once inside he would be on his own. Cody's personal advisor, Mr. Hunter, and Joe's own son and aide-de-camp, First Lieutenant Todd A. Murchison, would be sitting back in the gallery. Joe would be up front, at the witness table, all alone.

The hearing room was fairly large, longer than it was wide, with a long desk sitting up on a dais and stretching all the way across the front of the room. The desk was large enough for all nine members of the Senate Committee of Indian Affairs. Just in front of the long desk, at floor level so that the senators could look down upon the witnesses, was the witness table. To the left of the witness table was another table occupied by a civilian attorney and by Wind in His Hair. Wind in His Hair was wearing pants and a shirt of white doe-skin, beautifully decorated with red and blue porcupine quills. His hair was in two long braids plaited with blue ribbon, while around his neck was a necklace of bears' teeth. He fixed Joe with a defiant stare as Joe came in, and, for a moment, Joe recalled the Battle of Big Knife Creek when he had put a carbine ball through Wind in His Hair's feathered headdress.

Senator William Pettibone, Republican of Ohio and the committee chairman, banged his gavel on the table.

"This hearing will come to order," he said. He picked up a paper. "We are meeting to decide upon whether or not to bring to the floor Senate Resolution zero-one-five-zero, which reads as follows: 'Whereas, the Sioux Indian Chief Wind in His Hair was sentenced to fifteen years in prison for his part in the disturbance that led to the Battle of Wounded Knee; and, whereas he has served ten years of that sentence, said time constituting two-thirds of the sentence; therefore be it resolved that the United States Senate, in session, does hereby recommend to the president of the United States that Wind in His Hair be granted amnesty.'

"Any amendments or adjustments to the proposition as read?" Senator Pettibone asked, looking up and down the dais. Finding no dissenters, he banged the gavel. "Very well, let us begin this hearing. Who comes now to address the committee?"

"Mr. Chairman?"

"The chair recognizes Mr. Walter Bowen, counsel for Wind in His Hair."

"Thank you, Mr. Chairman," Bowen said. "We would like to call as our first witness General Joseph Thomas Murchison. General Murchison is a graduate of West Point, graduating first in his class in 1866. He has a long and distinguished military career, having participated in the Indian campaigns from the Battle of Big Knife Creek to the Battle of Wounded Knee. He was with Custer during the Battle of Washita, and with Reno's battalion during the ill-fated Custer campaign at Little Big Horn. For the battle at Little Big Horn he was awarded the Medal of Honor. He was also with General Crook in the pacification of the Apache Indians. Most recently he was chief of logistics and planning for the Spanish–American War, for which he was given a citation of meritorious performance by a joint session of Congress. He is currently the deputy chief of staff for the United States Army."

"The chair recognizes the distinguished General Murchison," Senator Pettibone said. "And, General, let me extend my own personal congratulations to you on a lifetime of honorable service to your country."

"Thank you, Senator," Joe said.

"General, do you know the prisoner, Wind in His Hair?"

"I know him."

"How long have you known him?"

"I met him thirty-four years ago," Joe said. "He saved my life."

There was an audible reaction among the spectators to the hearing.

"I beg your pardon, General? He saved your life?"

"Yes," Joe said. He told how Wind in His Hair had found him and another soldier, nearly dead of starvation. He told how the Indian had fed them, then led them to safety.

"Mr. Chairman, if I may ask a question?" one of the other senators said.

"Chair recognizes Mr. Sells of Georgia."

"Thank you, Mr. Chairman. General, my staff prepared some information about you for me, and as I read through it, I find that Wind in His Hair was the leader of the Indians in the Battle of Big Knife Creek. Is that correct?"

"Yes, Senator."

"And in that battle you lost your commander, plus several of your men. Is that also correct?"

"Yes, Senator."

"And this battle, correct me if I'm wrong, took place *after* the incident you just told us about?"

"It did, Senator."

"Then I don't understand. I mean, on the one hand the Indian saves your life, on the other he tried to kill you—and was successful in killing one officer and several soldiers. What happened between the two of you? How did you go from being friends to being enemies within such a short time?"

"We never were friends," Joe replied.

"But didn't you just tell us a touching story of how this Indian saved your life?"

"Yes."

"If you weren't friends, why did he save your life?"

"For my medicine," Joe said.

"For your medicine? You mean potions? Nostrums? That sort of thing?"

"No, Senator," Joe said. "To the Indian, medicine is magic . . . power . . . spirit. *That* sort of thing," he added, mimicking Senator Sells's phrase.

"And you gave him some of this magic for saving your life?"

"No. If I had given it to him, it would have been worthless. He had to take it."

"He had to take it?"

"Yes, sir."

Senator Sells shook his head. "I don't understand."

"If you understood it, then it wouldn't be," Joe said.

"It wouldn't be what?"

"Medicine."

"I . . . I . . ." Senator Sells threw up his hand and shook his head. "I have no more questions, Mr. Chairman."

The gallery laughed, and Senator Pettibone banged his gavel until they were quiet.

"Now, General, you say you weren't friends when Wind in His Hair saved your life. At what point would you say that you did become friends?"

"We never became friends," Joe said. "Not to this day."

"But you are here testifying on his behalf."

"Yes."

"If not as a friend, then what?"

"As an enemy," Joe said. He held up his finger. "But as an enemy of honor."

"An enemy of honor?"

"Many years ago Wind in His Hair and I took an oath of enmity," Joe explained. "But we tempered that enmity with honor. And down through the years we have maintained the honor between us—though I have always felt that Wind in His Hair believed I may have violated that honor when I allowed him to be arrested and imprisoned shortly after Wounded Knee." Joe turned in his chair and looked over at Wind in His Hair. The old Indian chief was staring straight ahead. "I say to him now, before this committee, that I protested, in the most vigorous way I could, his arrest. I tried to stop it, but I could not."

"Why would it be a violation of honor to put one of the perpetrators of that battle in prison?" Senator Pettibone asked. "He was a leader and a war chief, was he not? And, as such, shouldn't he expect to pay the price?"

"Senator, one of the biggest myths the white man has ever had about Indians is that they have an absolute government. White men think that because someone is a chief, he has merely to speak and all others will obey. Well, it doesn't work that way."

"Are you telling me that Wind in His Hair is *not* a chief? That he is just another Indian?"

"Yes and no," Joe replied. "He *is* a chief, but he is a chief because he earned that position by winning the respect and the admiration of the others in his tribe. Men who make suggestions persuasively, and who have been proven to be right in their suggestions, are chiefs, and they will be followed—so long as the others want to follow them. But never, at any time, can an Indian demand something of another."

"Do you mean to say that the Indians have no command structure in battle?"

"That's exactly what I mean. Ten soldiers make up a squad. Ten Indians make up ten Indians, each one fighting his own battle. Let me give you an example of the independence of the Indian warrior. We were successful in the Battle of Washita because we had the element of surprise. We had the element of surprise because there were no Indian sentries to see us coming. And there were no Indian sentries to see us coming because it was very cold that night and no one wanted to stay out in the cold to stand guard. And no one, from Black Kettle on down, had the authority to order someone else to stand out in the cold if they didn't want to. Can you imagine a private in the U.S. Army refusing to stand guard?"

Again the gallery laughed.

"I did not know that about Indians," Senator Pettibone said. "But as you are a proven expert in this area, I will defer to you on this matter. However, you just said that Wind in His Hair had earned the right to be called chief by the fact that he had the respect and admiration of his people. And, you said, they would listen to his suggestions if they believed them to be right. Does it not then follow that he led them into the Battle at Wounded Knee?"

"No, Senator. Quite the opposite. I happen to know for a fact that Wind in His Hair never did accept the doctrine of ghost dancing. He thought, as I did, that it was the delusion of a desperate society. He was with Sitting Bull when Sitting Bull was killed because he had gone there to solicit Sitting Bull's help in turning back the ghost dancers before things got out of hand. And at Wounded Knee he was Big Foot's ally in trying to bring the Indians in peacefully."

"How do you know this to be fact?" Senator Pettibone asked. "Is that what Wind in His Hair told you?"

"It is what he told me," Joe said. "And if I had only his word to go on, I would accept it, for I accept Wind in His Hair as a man of honor. But I have been told this by other Indians, as well. That is why when Buffalo Bill asked me if I would speak on behalf of my old enemy, I readily agreed. Senator, not only do I believe that Wind in His Hair should be paroled now, I don't believe he should have ever been in prison in the first place."

"Thank you, General. I have no further questions," Senator Pettibone said. He looked up and down the dais, and when he saw that there were no other questions, he turned back to Joe. "You may stand down, General. Mr. Bowen, you have another witness?"

"I do, Mr. Chairman. I would like to call before the committee Mrs. Leslie Standhope. Mrs. Standhope is the wife of the Honorable Judge Leslie Standhope of the Third Circuit Court of the state of South Dakota."

"I don't understand the purpose for this witness, Mr. Bowen. Why would the wife of a judge be testifying in this matter?"

"She is full-blooded Yankton Sioux, Mr. Chairman. Her Indian name is Quiet Stream, and she is the sister of Wind in His Hair."

There was a prolonged buzz of interest as Quiet Stream came to the front and took her seat at the witness table.

"Mr. Chairman, as Mrs. Standhope's command of the English language is quite excellent, I would like for her to begin her testimony by reading a statement drafted by her brother."

"Without objection," Senator Pettibone replied, and when none were voiced, he nodded at Quiet Stream.

She took a piece of paper from her purse, then put on glasses and began to read her brother's statement:

"Before the white men came to this place, we were already here. We were given the land by the Great Spirit. At one time I believed the Great Spirit was for the Indian only, but I am now a Christian, like the white man, and I know that the Great Spirit of the Indian is the same being as the God of the white man.

"God gave the Indian the land, because there was no one for the Indian to buy it from. And if the land was ever ours, it remains ours, for God did not take the land from us and we did not sell it. Now there are white men in our sacred Black Hills. How did they come by the Black Hills? We did not sell the Black Hills to them. In the treaty signed with President Johnson in 1868, the Black Hills were given to us. Where is the treaty that took the Black Hills from us?

"There are farms and ranches and towns in this place that the white men now call South Dakota. South Dakota is a state, you say, and because it is already a state, it belongs to the government. Even our name, Dakota, has been stolen from us. We did not sell our land to the government in Washington, and we did not sell our name to the government in Washington, but the government in Washington has both our land and our name.

"For ten years I have been a prisoner because of what happened at Wounded Knee. More than three hundred of my people were killed at Wounded Knee. My wife, Capture Heart Woman, and my two sons were both killed at Wounded Knee. The son and husband of my sister were killed at Wounded Knee. The soldiers came with their big guns and they surrounded the camp and they shot everyone. Twenty-nine soldiers were killed, but most of these were killed by the soldiers' own guns.

"I went to Wounded Knee to try to stop the

ghost dances. I was not yet a Christian, but I knew even then that the ghost dance was a false religion. I knew that it would not make the buffalo come back, and it would not make the white men go away, and it would not stop the soldiers' bullets. I knew this and I told my people this, but they were hungry, and they longed for the old days, and they were ready to believe.

"When the shooting started and I saw my people dying, I wanted to die also, so I walked upright through the middle of the village, chanting my death song, praying that I would be killed. It is a strange thing, I think, that many who were wearing the ghost shirts to turn away the bullets were killed, while I, who was not wearing a ghost shirt, was not killed.

"I have been in many battles with the white men. I was in the battle the white men call Big Knife Creek. It was a battle fought with honor on both sides. I was in the battle of Greasy Grass, called by the white man 'Custer's Last Stand.' This, too, was a battle fought with honor on both sides. But the killing at Wounded Knee was not a battle, and it was without honor. On that day the medicine of the hoop was broken, and since that day the Dakota's place in the sacred circle of the universe is no more."

It was now late afternoon, and the Senate Committee on Indian Affairs had heard, in addition to Joe and Quiet Stream, an Indian agent who testified against recommending amnesty. Both agents claimed that the more than ten years of peace that had been enjoyed in South Dakota would be disrupted if one of the old war chiefs should now be returned.

"Chief Joseph, Geronimo, Keytano—all are being held in federal prisons," Indian Agent Crabtree said. "Their crimes are no greater nor no less than the crimes of Wind in His Hair."

"Mr. Crabtree, are you then proposing that Chief

Joseph, Geronimo and Keytano be included in this Senate resolution?" Senator Pettibone asked.

"No, sir, I most certainly am not!" Crabtree replied quickly.

"Then I don't understand the relevance of your remark," Senator Pettibone said. "We are discussing Wind in His Hair. Now, do you have any compelling reason, other than your own prejudice, why we should not recommend that Wind in His Hair be released to return to the reservation?"

"None, other than those reasons I have already stated," Crabtree said.

"Thank you, Mr. Crabtree. The witness is dismissed."

"Mr. Chairman, I move that we call the question," Senator Sells said.

"Second."

"Very well. All in favor of bringing to the floor a favorable recommendation for the resolution granting amnesty to Wind in His Hair, signify by saying *aye*."

There were eight *ayes* and one *nay*.

Senator Pettibone brought his gavel down sharply. "The resolution is remanded to the floor with the recommendation that it be passed."

Quiet Stream let out a little squeal of excitement, then hurried over to her brother. Smiling, Senator Pettibone came down from the dais as well, just as Joe walked over to join them.

"You understand, Mrs. Standhope," Senator Pettibone said, "that this is only a recommendation that the Senate pass the resolution. And the resolution is only a recommendation that amnesty be granted."

"I understand," Quiet Stream said.

"Senator," Joe said, "I know that you are particularly good at what you do. And I know that you would never even consider such a resolution unless you had broad-based support in the Senate, as well as an assurance from the president that he will accept the resolution."

Senator Pettibone laughed out loud. "Maybe that's why you're such a good general. Yes, I do have such assurances. I think I can say, without fear of contradiction, that Wind in His Hair will be back among his people within two weeks."

"Thank you, Senator," Quiet Stream said. "From the bottom of my heart, I thank you."

"Well, I must say that you were most persuasive, Mrs. Standhope. The statement you made on behalf of your brother was brilliant. Never have more moving words been uttered before a Senate committee."

"They were my brother's words, Senator. I only supplied the English translation."

"Is that a fact?" Pettibone looked at Wind in His Hair who had remained stoic for the entire conversation. "If he can speak like that, no wonder he has gained the respect of his people." Pettibone smiled. "I'm just glad he can't run for the Senate against me."

"Senator, there is a roll call," someone announced, and Pettibone turned to leave. As he reached the door leading out into the hall, he turned and looked back at Wind in His Hair.

"Congratulations, Chief," he called. "I wish you a long life."

Wind in His Hair grunted. "Would that my life be ten years longer to replace what I have lost," he said.

"You know English!" Joe said, surprised to hear Wind in His Hair speak.

"I learned in prison," Wind in His Hair replied. "But I do not speak so good as my sister."

"I thought the chief's words would have more impact coming from her," Bowen suggested.

"I can't argue with you there," Joe replied. "Quiet Stream made a very powerful presentation."

"I thank you, Chief without Shoes," Wind in His Hair said.

"I beg your pardon?" Joe replied.

Quiet Stream laughed. "It is the name my people gave you many years ago when you and the other soldier came into our camp without shoes," she said. "We did not know your white man's name then, but we knew that you were the chief of the two. You were

Chief without Shoes and the other was Soldier without Shoes."

"Soldier without Shoes," Joe said. "On the battlefield at Little Big Horn, that's what you called Sergeant Todd."

"Yes."

"Chief without Shoes," Wind in His Hair said again, "once you offered to shake my hand and be my friend. I would not do so then. If you will forgive me for refusing in the past, I would like to shake hands now. And I would like to call you friend."

Joe smiled. "You aren't afraid I will take the medicine back?"

"The medicine has been good," Wind in His Hair said. "But it belongs to you, and I return it now."

The two men shook hands. There was a flash, and Joe looked around to see that an enterprising reporter had remained behind long enough to get the picture he wanted.

"Chief, we have to return to your cell," Bowen said. "You belong to the federal marshals for a few days longer; then it will all be over."

Wind in His Hair nodded, and with a final squeeze of Joe's hand, he, Quiet Stream, and Mr. Bowen left.

"Good-bye, my friend," Joe called. Wind in His Hair nodded back.

"I'm glad for him, Pop," Todd said after they were gone. He and Hunter had come up to stand as quiet observers during the previous dialogue.

"I want you to remember well this moment, son," Joe said. "It is the last act of a noble century."

UNITED STATES MILITARY ACADEMY
WEST POINT, NEW YORK
JUNE 1941

A burst of applause brought Joe's wandering thoughts back to the present, and he looked up to see that Secretary of War Stimson was at the podium. The time had come for Stimson to introduce the featured speaker of the program: Major General Joseph T. Murchison, United States Army Retired, Class of '66. Joe had spoken on many occasions to many different groups, but in all the years since he had graduated from West Point, this would be the first time he had ever spoken to the corps of cadets. He had to confess that, despite his preparation for the talk, he was a little nervous about it.

Cadet Throckmorton appeared at the end of the row of seats. Smiling at Joe, Throckmorton offered his arm for support. Slowly, they walked to the front of the room, then Joe climbed the steps and walked over to the podium, knowing that all eyes were on him. What they were seeing was an old man, shuffling laboriously across the stage.

How did that happen? Joe wondered. How did the ramrod-straight young cadet, the eager second lieutenant, the curious captain, and the vigorous colonel, become this tired old man? In his mind, and in his heart, he could still leap into the saddle to follow the guidon.

The master of ceremonies, the commandant of cadets, William Donovan, and Secretary Stimson, all of whom were on the stage, stood as Joe approached. He nodded at them, then reached the podium. Gripping both sides, he looked out over the audience.

A few of the very senior officers he recognized as having been students of his during his tenure, first at the Command and Staff College at Fort Leavenworth, and later with the Army–Navy War College at Carlisle, Pennsylvania. He looked over at President Roosevelt, then at Sally, the president's mother. The smile and the look of pride on Sara Roosevelt's face was mirrored in Tamara's face as well, for the two women were sitting together. General Murchison's son, Retired Colonel Todd Armstrong Murchison, holder of the Silver Star from the Spanish American War and the Medal of Honor from World War I, was sitting next to his mother. Also present in the audience was General Murchison's grandson, Lee Arlington Grant. Lee, who was Sarah Louise's son, was a captain in the armored cavalry and a devotee of the tank. Joe had visited his grandson at Fort Knox the summer before, and over drinks in the Fort Knox Officers' Club, Lee and his friend George Patton had talked to Joe far into the night, trying to convince him of the wonderful potential of the tank as the ultimate battlefield weapon.

Still another member of Joe's family was present today, Joe's great-grandson, John J. Murchison, was a member of the Corps of Cadets, the fourth generation of Joe's family to attend the Academy.

Joe continued to stand silently at the podium. He was silent and motionless for so long that some in the audience began to get nervous, thinking perhaps the old man wasn't up to the ordeal. They didn't realize that Joe was just putting all his memories to rest, stepping out of the continuum so that he could be here in this time and place, and with these people. Finally his busy mind stilled, and the calendar stopped tumbling. He could hear an airliner droning by high overhead. From outside somewhere, an auto horn honked. A gentle breeze of artificially cooled air refreshed him. He was back in 1941, and he was ready to speak.

"We have gathered here to help launch the careers of a new class of officers," General Murchison began. "And, by virtue of the fact that I am now the oldest graduate of this august establishment, I have been selected to pass on the torch. I am honored by that selection, for while the minds of these young graduates are —as they should be—on the future, my mind, my heart, and my very soul are with a thousand comrades around a hundred campfires in a time long ago. It is a time that, to many of you, may seem never to have been.

"I am the last of my class and the last member of Custer's own to answer roll call. I answer it, not for myself alone, but for every soldier who served this country so gallantly in the second half of the century previous: cavalry troopers and infantry men, buffalo soldiers and engineers, officers who rode to glory, and men who served in noble obscurity. And in answering this call I am introducing a new generation of Americans . . . a generation that visualizes the movie actor

Errol Flynn when they think of George Custer . . . a generation that accepts the airplane, the automobile, the radio and the motion picture as commonplace, to the last vestige of a generation that knew none of these things, but which did know the value of loyalty, honor, faith, and courage.

"Perhaps in this joining of our two generations there will be a melding of the spirit—the values of the old strengthened by the vigor of the new—in a reaffirmation of the motto of West Point. For they are words that are as valid today as they were when the motto was conceived: Duty, Honor, Country.

"To my comrades who answered yesterday's reveille, and to the generations of Americans as yet unborn who will hear the bugles call in our glorious future, I salute you, and I say, 'All present and accounted for, sir!'"

THE TRAIL DRIVE SERIES
by Ralph Compton

From St. Martin's Paperbacks

The only riches Texas had left after the Civil War were five million maverick longhorns and the brains, brawn and boldness to drive them north to where the money was. Now, Ralph Compton brings this violent and magnificent time to life in an extraordinary epic series based on the history-blazing trail drives.

THE GOODNIGHT TRAIL (BOOK 1)
_____ 92815-7 $5.50 U.S./$6.50 Can.

THE WESTERN TRAIL (BOOK 2)
_____ 92901-3 $5.50 U.S./$6.50 Can.

THE CHISOLM TRAIL (BOOK 3)
_____ 92953-6 $5.50 U.S./$6.50 Can.

THE BANDERA TRAIL (BOOK 4)
_____ 95143-4 $4.99 U.S./$5.99 Can.

THE CALIFORNIA TRAIL (BOOK 5)
_____ 95169-8 $4.99 U.S./$5.99 Can.

THE SHAWNEE TRAIL (BOOK 6)
_____ 95241-4 $4.99 U.S./$5.99 Can.

THE VIRGINIA CITY TRAIL (BOOK 7)
_____ 95306-2 $5.50 U.S./$6.50 Can.

THE DODGE CITY TRAIL (BOOK 8)
_____ 95380-1 $5.50 U.S./$6.50 Can.

THE OREGON TRAIL
_____ 95547-2 $4.99 U.S./$5.99 Can.

BEFORE THE LEGEND, THERE WAS THE MAN...

AND A POWERFUL DESTINY TO FULFILL.

On October 26, 1881, three outlaws lay dead in a dusty vacant lot in Tombstone, Arizona. Standing over them—Colts smoking—were Wyatt Earp, his two brothers Morgan and Virgil, and a gun-slinging gambler named Doc Holliday. The shootout at the O.K. Corral was over—but for Earp, the fight had just begun...

WYATT EARP

MATT BRAUN

WYATT EARP
Matt Braun
_____ 95325-9 $4.99 U.S./$5.99 CAN.